Wilde Thing

JANELLE DENISON

Wilde Thing

BRAVA

KENSINGTON PUBLISHING CORP.
http://www.kensingtonbooks.com

BRAVA BOOKS are published by

Kensington Publishing Corp.
850 Third Avenue
New York, NY 10022

ISBN 0-7582-0359-4

First Kensington Trade Paperback Printing: July 2003
10 9 8 7 6 5 4 3 2 1

Printed in the United States of America

To Karen Drogin, a.k.a. Carly Phillips. Chance brought us together, but fate made us the best of friends. I'm so incredibly blessed to have you in my life. Thank you for being the person who makes my stories stronger and helps me bring my ideas to life. Thank you for being the one to boost my confidence on those days when I have none, and for giving my stories your love and attention and discipline, as if they were your own. Your friendship is a beautiful, priceless gift I'll always treasure.

To my daughters, Danielle and Kellie, for your patience and understanding when Mom is on a deadline, which seems to be all the time. I love you both very much.

And to my husband, Don, for living with me through the ups and downs of this crazy business. Thank you for your faith in me, your unending love, and your unconditional support. You are my best friend, my inspiration, my life. I love you!

Dear Reader,

First you met Eric Wilde in SOMETHING WILDE, a story in the "I Brake for Bad Boys" Brava anthology out in November 2002, which introduced you to my sexy, gorgeous "Wilde" brothers, who are just as untamable as their last name implies! Now, get ready for a fun, red-hot read about Steve Wilde and his brazen pursuit to seduce the woman who has tempted him for too long. It doesn't get any hotter than this!

WILDE THING. The title of this book conjures up all kinds of shameless, erotic possibilities, doesn't it? How about an irresistible bad boy who rides a Harley, enjoys everything about women, and has his sights set on sensual Liz Adams? Throw in a bit of steamy, erotic phone sex between the two of them, along with a provocative, anything-goes affair filled with a wealth of sexual indulgence, and get ready to be swept into a world of decadent desires that will leave you restless and breathless.

I hope you enjoy Steve and Liz's sexy, sizzling story, and keep a look out for Adrian Wilde's story in THE WILDE ONE, which will be part of the BAD BOYS TO GO Brava anthology, out in November 2003. Be sure to check my website at www.janelledenison.com for updated information on all my books, Brava releases, and more Wilde stories! I love to hear from my readers, and you can write to me at P.O. Box 1102, Rialto, CA 92377 (Send SASE for goodies!), or at janelle@janelledenison.com.

Happy reading,

Janelle Denison

Chapter

1

He had *bad boy* written all over him, and Liz Adams wanted him in the worst possible way. From his rumpled sable hair and striking, seductive blue eyes to that lean, honed body she'd imagined naked and aroused, he exuded raw sex appeal and brought her feminine instincts to keen awareness like no other man had in a very long time.

Simply put, she was completely and totally in lust with her gorgeous, head-turning customer who'd recently started frequenting her café, The Daily Grind. Over the past month, he'd become a pleasant visual distraction from other responsibilities and worries that had been weighing heavily on her mind.

He lifted his head from the latest best-seller he was reading, and from across the room their eyes met briefly and she caught a glimpse of the to-die-for grin that raised the corner of his sensual mouth. An undeniable warmth and excitement stirred within her, and she had to resist the urge to close the distance between them, rip his black T-shirt and tight jeans off his long, muscled body, and have her wicked way with him. On the countertop, on one of the couches in the sitting area, or even the floor. She wasn't picky about the *where* part of her fantasy.

Picking up a damp towel, she wiped down the stainless steel espresso machine and let out a wistful sigh that conveyed three long years of suppressed desires. She'd recently turned thirty-one, and she swore she was hitting her sexual prime, because for the past few weeks she'd been craving sex—ever since *he'd* strolled into her coffeehouse and jump-started her libido, fueling her nightly dreams with carnal, sinful fantasies.

Undoubtedly, it had been too long since she'd felt the exquisite caress of a man's mouth sliding across her sensitized flesh. Too long since she'd experienced the delicious heat of a hard, strong body covering hers, the silken texture and erotic friction of a man sliding deep in a slow, grinding rhythm. Those realistic sensations were something no artificially enhanced sex toy could duplicate, and she missed that kind of physical connection with a flesh-and-blood man.

But as much as her fantasy man over in the corner tempted her, everything from that black leather jacket he wore, to his come-hither eyes and self-confidence, screamed *rebel*. And she'd vowed after her marriage to Travis that she'd never get involved with another man who was wild and impulsive and had the ability to leave her devastated in the process.

Unfortunately, despite being burned by one bad boy who'd turned out to be bad in the extreme, she couldn't prevent her attraction to the kind of man who possessed a bit of an edge. A take-charge kind of man who was decisive and straightforward yet unpredictable, with a sense of reckless adventure. That Harley-Davidson motorcycle her customer rode told her a lot about the man—that he was secure in his masculinity, didn't like to be constrained by rules, and was untamable, intrepid, and daring as well.

Even knowing he was most likely all wrong for her, that those qualities could only lead to trouble and heartache, she still wanted him. Badly.

"Mind if I make myself a chilled mocha before you finish cleaning up?"

The sound of Mona Owen's voice snapped Liz out of her private thoughts and jolted her back to reality and the cleanup still awaiting her attention. She glanced at her good friend and owner of The Last Word, a new-and-used bookstore that directly connected to her coffeehouse café, and caught Mona eyeing the last of the drink mix in the blender.

Liz grinned, having grown used to Mona's tendency to mooch leftovers near closing time. "Sure. Help yourself."

Mona tossed ice into the concoction, switched the blender on for a few seconds, then poured the frothy drink into a plastic cup and added a straw. "I've been meaning to ask you if you've heard from your cousin Valerie yet."

The reminder of Valerie's vanishing act brought Liz out of her fantasy and back to the helpless feeling that had grown with each passing day. "I haven't heard a word from her since she left me that vague note Friday night." And all the message had said was that she was going to a weekend work party with a new boyfriend, Rob, a wealthy client she'd met through The Ultimate Fantasy, the phone sex place where she worked.

Admittedly, it wasn't out of the ordinary for Valerie to do something as frivolous as to take off with a boyfriend for a short getaway. Her twenty-four-year-old cousin had always possessed an impetuous streak and often did outrageous things to get attention, but the weekend had come and gone and here it was, Tuesday evening, and Liz had yet to hear from her.

She knew Valerie enjoyed her unconventional occupation, but there had been other aspects of her job that her cousin had mentioned that had troubled Liz—like those fantasy parties that dealt in other services and sexual escapades. She couldn't help but worry that Valerie had gotten herself in over her head with this man she'd taken off with. A guy Liz had never met, and the only connection she had to Val's disappearance was The Ultimate Fantasy.

"Are you thinking about contacting the police?" Mona asked.

"I already tried that." Grabbing the steaming pitcher, she

dunked it into the hot, soapy water in the sink and took out her frustration in scrubbing the stainless steel pot. "I called and spoke with an officer, but once I told him about the note Valerie left, stating she was off on her own free will, he said at this point there wasn't any evidence of foul play to warrant an investigation, and all I could do was file a missing-persons report on her behalf."

And with every day that passed without a word from her cousin, Liz's concern grew. So far, she'd been able to keep Valerie's vanishing act from Val's parents, Liz's aunt and uncle, who'd moved from Chicago to Southern California almost a year ago. Ben and Sally Clark were wonderful, kindhearted relatives who'd raised Liz from the age of twelve after her own parents had died. The two of them had always treated her like a second daughter, which Valerie, as an only child, had resented at times. Thus her cousin's penchant for being excessive and irresponsible, and much too self-centered.

If Liz hadn't promised her aunt and uncle she'd watch out for Valerie as well as keep her out of trouble, she'd probably write this scenario off as one of her cousin's eccentric antics. But she had agreed to look after Valerie, even going so far as to share her apartment with her cousin. Liz had taken on the request as an opportunity to prove that she was reliable and responsible after her disappointing fiasco with Travis. She'd desperately wanted to please her aunt and uncle and earn back their respect.

Guilt and frustration drove her, and this situation with Valerie certainly wasn't going to earn Liz any extra brownie points. Especially since she'd had to lie to her Aunt Sally, who'd called on Monday evening to talk to her daughter. While Liz had told her that Valerie was out of town for a few days with a "friend," it was only a matter of time before her aunt phoned again. Liz hated covering for Valerie, yet she had no choice for now.

"So what are you going to do?" Mona asked as she stirred her straw through her thick, icy drink.

Not wanting to shell-shock her aunt and uncle with the news that Valerie indulged in phone sex for a living unless she absolutely had to, Liz had opted to pursue her cousin's absence herself, in the only way she knew how. She bit her lower lip and gathered the fortitude to spill her secret to Mona.

"I applied at the same phone sex company where Valerie was working," Liz said. "I have an appointment for an interview at The Ultimate Fantasy tomorrow morning at eleven."

Concern creased Mona's dark brows. "Do you think that's safe or smart?"

Liz didn't want to respond directly to that question, because she knew the answer would be a resounding *no,* and she wasn't about to give up on the idea. "It's the only way I can think of to get inside information on Valerie or where she might be. Someone there has to know something, even if they just saw her at the party."

Mona shook her head, her expression adamant. "I don't think this is something you should do on your own."

Liz dragged her fingers through her hair and sighed. "The police aren't willing to get involved, so I don't have much of a choice."

Her friend was quiet for a few moments while she considered Liz's idea, her gaze focused on something out in the lounge area. Then a bright smile spread across her face. "Why don't you hire Steve Wilde?"

Liz frowned in confusion as she filled a basket with scones and another tray with gourmet cookies. "Who?"

Mona pitched her empty plastic cup into the trash and hooked her thumb toward Liz's fantasy man. "Steve Wilde. The guy you've been lusting after for the past month. And don't bother denying it. I've been watching the two of you, and when you're not ogling him, his eyes are following you. And from my astute observations, that lingering gaze of his is hungry for more than just your pastries." She gave Liz a playful but encouraging wink.

Wilde. God, even his last name insinuated trouble of the most sensual variety. Her gaze strayed back to the lounge just as he unfolded his big, lean body from his chair and shrugged into his well-worn leather jacket, causing the muscles in his arms and across his chest to shift temptingly as he moved. Her pulse quickened with female appreciation. He was so compelling, his magnetism so potent, she couldn't help but respond to his stunning good looks.

He picked up his book and keys from the coffee table and glanced up, his disarming gaze locking with hers—as bold, direct, and unapologetically sexual as the man himself. He tipped his head in acknowledgment, causing a lock of unruly sable hair to fall across his brow, accentuating his rakish appearance. The private, sinful grin he graced her with literally stole her breath and sent her hormones into an overwhelming frenzy of sexual longing. Her breasts swelled and tightened, her nipples tingled, and a surge of liquid desire settled in intimate places.

Oh, yeah, he was most definitely trouble personified.

He exited the café, leaving her with more than enough new, stimulating material to fuel another night of erotic mind candy. She returned her attention to Mona. "So, tell me, how do you know his name?"

Her friend snagged a biscotti from the glass jar on the counter and munched into the baked treat. "He's come into The Last Word to purchase a few books, and we've talked a time or two."

Which essentially meant that Mona knew not only his name but his age, marital status, and occupation as well.

Finishing off her cookie, Mona licked the crumbs from her fingers. "And knowing the attraction between the two of you is mutual, I'm thinking it's time you took off that gold band you wear on your finger that makes men think you're taken, and take a walk on the *Wilde* side."

"Ha-ha. Very funny," she said, though the idea was one she'd already considered . . . in her fantasies.

"I'm being completely serious." Mona's tone reflected just how resolute she was. "At least about taking that ring off your finger and putting yourself back on the market. There's a time and place to shed everything—your ring, your clothes, your inhibitions . . ." she added meaningfully.

The lights overhead glimmered off the gold band she'd worn since Travis's death, mocking her solitary, abstinent lifestyle—of her own choosing, she reminded herself. She was still struggling to dig herself out of the financial mess her late husband had left her in when he'd died three years ago, and she didn't want or need the complication of a binding relationship. Not when her focus was on her café and seeing her savings account back in the black again.

Feeling useless resentments clawing their way to the surface, she redirected their conversation back to their original topic. "You mentioned hiring Steve Wilde. What for?"

"Because while he might have all the markings of a bad boy, he's definitely one of the good guys. He's a private detective with his own agency, and I'm betting he can help you out with Valerie." Excitement infused Mona's voice. "At the very least, he can offer advice or follow up on your cousin's disappearance without you putting yourself at risk."

So, he was a good guy with a bad-boy demeanor, a combination Liz found much too intriguing. "It's not like I have a lot of extra money to pay a private investigator. You know that." She'd spent the past three years on a tight budget while Travis's debts had drained a huge portion of her savings. "I could barely afford to have the alternator on my car fixed, let alone a PI's professional services."

"Maybe Mr. Wilde would be willing to work out a payment plan of some sort," Mona offered with a sly smile, leaving no doubt in Liz's mind what her friend meant. "I have his business card back in my shop if you're interested."

On a purely business level, Liz supposed an initial consultation with Mr. Wilde couldn't hurt, and any free advice he

might impart could only help her in her search to find her wayward cousin.

"I'm definitely interested in Steve Wilde," she said to
Mona, and realizing how those simple words could be miscon-
strued, she followed that up with a quick, "I mean, in his business card."

"Of course." Amusement and satisfaction flashed in Mona's
eyes. "I'll be right back."

Liz watched her friend trek across the short distance to her
bookstore, anticipation making her heart pound hard in her
chest. She swore that contacting Steve Wilde—the object of
her fondest, most carnal dreams—had nothing to do with her
attraction to him, and that her interest was strictly professional.

Her mind accepted the lecture. Unfortunately, her neglected
body wasn't completely convinced.

Steve Wilde wasn't a man easily shocked. Yet he couldn't
have been more stunned when his secretary, Beverly, announced that Liz Adams was there to see him. Seconds later,
the woman who'd occupied too much of his thoughts lately
appeared in his office, her vivid green gaze meeting his from
across the room.

She looked incredibly sexy. He'd only seen her in her work
uniform of jeans, T-shirt, and a bib apron that tied around her
neck and waist. Nothing overtly suggestive or clingy, but he'd
seen enough of her coming and going to know that she had
the kind of full, luscious figure he liked on a woman. And the
thigh-length form-fitting cocoa-colored skirt and matching
blouse she was currently wearing confirmed a knock-out,
head-turning shape he couldn't help but admire and appreciate.

Unlike his brother Eric, who was drawn to a woman's ass,
and Adrian, who went for long, shapely legs, Steve was first
and foremost a breast man; he liked them full and firm and

preferred more than a dainty handful to fondle and play with. The V neckline of Liz's blouse dipped low, giving him a glimpse of an ample amount of cleavage that made his mouth water and his fingers itch to touch. He assumed she was wearing a bra with no padding, because he could see the faint outline of her nipples pressing against the silky fabric of her top. He imagined the velvet texture of those stiff crests in his mouth, against his tongue, and felt a rush of pulsing heat spiral straight to his groin.

With a barely perceptible nod from him, his secretary, Beverly, quietly closed the door as Liz continued to walk into his office. The skirt she wore accentuated the indentation of her waist and the provocative sway of her shapely hips. From there, he took the liberty of continuing the sensual journey, taking in the curvaceous outline of her thighs and long, lightly tanned legs designed to wrap around a man's hips and clench him tight in the throes of passion.

God, he just wanted to eat her up, inch by delectable inch— from her soft, glossy lips all the way down to those pink-painted toenails peeking from the opening of her heeled sandals, and everywhere in between.

Much to his delight, there was nothing dainty, delicate, or petite about her. No, she was a well-built woman with a voluptuous body made for hot, hard, lusty sex. Which was just the way he liked his physical encounters, though it had been too long since he'd been with a woman who matched his sexual appetite and could fulfill his needs and demands in the bedroom.

Shaking off his surprise at Liz's impromptu visit, along with the thrum of arousal taking up residence within him, he stood and casually rounded his desk to greet her. "You're Liz, from The Daily Grind." He held out his hand and waited for her to acknowledge the gesture.

"That's correct." With a slow, sensual smile that made him feel sucker-punched, she slipped her palm against his, allowing his long fingers to envelop her hand in the superior strength of his grip.

Her flesh was warm and soft, but her handshake was firm and confident. As for the instantaneous chemistry that leaped between them at first touch, well, that was nothing short of a simmering heat just waiting for the right flame to ignite their attraction into a blazing inferno.

She didn't try to tug her hand away when he lingered and brazenly brushed his thumb along her skin. Rather, she maintained eye contact and waited until he chose to release her, confirming his first impression of her at the coffeehouse: that she was a strong, independent woman who was secure in her femininity and had no problem giving as good as she got when it came to the battle of the sexes.

He liked those unique qualities about her and knew she was a woman with enough tenacity and daring to keep him stimulated physically as well as intellectually. A rare feat and challenge he'd more than welcome, if it weren't for the ring encircling her left-hand finger, which told him she belonged to someone else.

As soon as he let go of her hand, she said, "I hope you don't mind, but Mona gave me your card."

Ahh, Mona, the chatty albeit friendly woman from The Last Word who enjoyed prying information from her customers. "I'll have to thank her for the business." Though he'd always thought of Liz in terms of pure, unadulterated pleasure. The kind that made him wake up sweating in the dark of night, his muscles rigid and his cock granite-hard from erotic images of Liz beneath him, her body soft and inviting and just as tight as his own fist stroking his erection.

Before his libido reacted to the nightly, obsessive dreams that plagued him, he leaned his backside against his desk and crossed his arms over his chest. "What can I do for you, Mrs. Adams?"

"Actually, it's *Ms.* Adams," she clarified.

He glanced at the ring she was absently twisting around her finger. Since she'd come to him and was in his territory, he figured he had every right to ask frank, personal questions. "So, you're not married?"

She shook her head, causing her silky, shoulder-length blond hair to brush along her jawline. "No, I'm single."

She didn't give an explanation for the band she wore that indicated otherwise, but he'd just learned all he needed to know to give him the incentive to pursue her on a more intimate level. With less than two feet of space separating them, there was no denying the awareness between them, and their attraction was something he had no qualms about using to get what he wanted.

And what he desired was *her.*

But first, he was curious to know her reasons for seeking him out. He inclined his head and prompted, "And you're here because . . . ?"

She inhaled a deep breath, causing her breasts to rise and fall in a very beguiling way. "I'd like to inquire about your services."

Her tone was very businesslike, but he couldn't stop the slow, shameless grin her double-edged words evoked. "By all means, have a seat and let's discuss what services of mine you're interested in," he drawled, and indicated one of the tweed chairs behind her while he rounded his desk to his own leather seat.

Her cheeks flushed a becoming shade of pink at his subtle innuendo as she settled herself in the chair facing his desk and crossed one leg over the other. "Since you're a private investigator, I'm hoping you can help me out. My cousin, Valerie Clark, is missing."

Her statement took him momentarily off guard. While he'd been surprised that she'd shown up at his agency without an appointment, the last thing he'd expected was her soliciting his help on a professional level. Years of training, first as a beat cop, then as a PI, told him she was being completely straightforward and serious with her request, and the distress he detected in the depths of her eyes was real.

Interest of a different kind took hold, and he set aside the file he'd been reviewing and reached for his pen and pad of paper, his mind already in an investigative mode. "Why don't you tell me what you know about your cousin's disappearance, from the beginning, and we'll go from there."

He jotted down notes as she proceeded to brief him on Valerie Clark's situation, from her involvement in The Ultimate Fantasy, a phone sex business, to the new boyfriend Valerie had started seeing recently, who'd been a client. With thought-provoking questions, he drew more information from Liz and discovered her concern that The Ultimate Fantasy offered more "behind the scenes" services, which were an extension of the phone sex business, and her belief that her cousin was involved in those extracurricular activities with the man she'd been seeing on the side.

Leaning back in his chair, he rolled his pen between his fingers as his gaze took in her hopeful expression—hope that he'd agree to help find her missing cousin. "Quite honestly, I wouldn't be surprised if The Ultimate Fantasy did offer their clients more than basic lip service. These places are notorious for inviting certain clients who spend a lot of money on phone sex to private parties that offer drugs and stimulants, prostitution, and other sexual services. Sex is a big moneymaker, and a place like The Ultimate Fantasy has the employees and clients to capitalize on such a lucrative side business."

She nodded in agreement, obviously having come to the same conclusion on her own. "As much as I hate the thought of Valerie being involved in such a shady organization—and believe me, I discouraged her as much as possible about taking on the job—I know she's attended those work parties with other coworkers and with this guy she recently started seeing."

"Do you know this man's name?" he asked.

"Rob. Valerie never mentioned a last name." Seemingly feeling restless, she stood and paced to the windows overlooking the building's parking lot from two stories up. "Valerie and I live together. Over the past month, there have been times when she's been gone a day or two with Rob, but she's never been away longer than a weekend," she said, her voice tinged with what sounded to him like a heavy weight of guilt. "Since I haven't heard from her and it's already three days into the week, I can't help but worry that she's gotten herself in over her head with this guy she's seeing. And the only link I have to her right now is through The Ultimate Fantasy."

As his gaze lingered on her profile, he listened as she went on to explain her conversation with the police, and heard the frustration in her tone when she told him that they refused to do anything more than file a missing-persons report until they had something more substantial to investigate. As a former police officer, he was familiar with the department drill. He also knew how important it was to start a trace on a missing person ASAP, when there was still a warm trail to follow and before potential leads dried up.

He needed something substantial to give him a solid lead. Something more tangible to trace.

Steve thought about the scenario Liz had laid out for him, his gut instinct agreeing with her suspicion that her cousin's disappearance was somehow connected to her date and The Ultimate Fantasy party she'd attended. Which made his normal, straightforward investigative procedures a bit more difficult to follow. Because in a case like this, he needed inside connections to pursue eyewitness accounts of Valerie actually being at the party, when she'd left, and whether any of those people knew who her date was, or even his last name. At this point, any small kernel of information would help him to trace Valerie.

He wished the proceedings could be as simple as flashing

his badge to an employee or office manager and asking questions about Valerie and The Ultimate Fantasy parties, but he was certain any mention of an investigation on his end wouldn't go over well with the owners. He'd probably immediately get tossed out on his ass with a warning not to return.

He wasn't looking to bust anyone, but he needed to unearth related and helpful facts, which meant going undercover to dig up details on Valerie Clark's whereabouts.

"If you decide you want me to take on the case, I'll need to find a way to get an invitation to attend one of the fantasy parties, which might take a little time since I'll have to establish a calling pattern with one of the operators and work my way in from there."

She turned around quickly, her green eyes bright with enthusiasm. "Maybe I can help you with that."

He frowned, unable to guess what she was getting at. "How so?"

She cast a glance at the watch on her wrist, then back at him. "I have an interview at The Ultimate Fantasy in about an hour for part-time evening work as a phone operator. My cousin told me it was pretty easy to get hired on, and I thought if I could get inside the company, I could ask around about Valerie and find out where she was last seen, and with whom."

He raised a dark brow at her daring. "That was—"

"Stupid?" she interjected before he could finish, her spine straightening defensively.

A slow burn of arousal ignited in his blood. God, even that determined spark and fire of hers turned him on, because he knew she'd be just as zealous and hot in his bed. "I was thinking more along the lines of *gutsy.*"

"Oh." She relaxed and offered him a contrite smile he found too damned sexy. "Thanks."

"You're welcome." He meant the compliment. Not many women would have the nerve and fortitude to embroil themselves in the business world of sex and sin, all for the sake of finding a cousin. It made him wonder if Liz would be willing to indulge in fantasies and erotic games for the pure pleasure of it. With him, of course.

Having established that she was single, he intended to find out.

But for the moment, he tapped his pen against his notepad and considered her willingness to help find her cousin. While he didn't usually allow his clients to get directly involved in the cases he chose to investigate, he couldn't deny that having Liz working the inside track of The Ultimate Fantasy would give him easier and faster entry to the private parties they held. Which in turn would, hopefully, provide the access and information to Valerie's whereabouts they needed, especially with Liz, an employee of the business, on his arm. And since he had a strong hunch she'd pursue the phone sex business with or without his agreement, he figured she'd be better off with him on her side, making sure she remained safe.

"I'll take the case," he said, knowing he was offering his services for more reasons than just to find her cousin.

Being with Liz added a huge incentive as well, but Steve had a sixteen-year-old daughter of his own, and Steffie was never far from his mind when he came across cases that involved young girls or women in perilous situations. The "What if it were Steffie?" question always seemed to prey on his conscience and prompted him to accept the case in hopes of securing a happy ending for all and peace of mind for himself. Based on what Liz had told him about Valerie's personality, his gut told him she wasn't in mortal danger, but he'd never play Russian roulette with another person's life.

"I'll need as much information as you can give me on Valerie." He withdrew an application from a side drawer for her to fill out. "Any bank account numbers you know of, statements, credit cards, social security number, driver's license. And I'll need a recent photograph of her, too. Give me anything you think would be helpful in tracing her."

"I'll go through her mail." She was quiet for a moment, then said, "There is one thing that I found in a pile of papers on her desk at home that seemed odd. I found a receipt for a passport."

"Great. That's exactly the kind of stuff I need to know." He made a note of the passport receipt on the form. "Did she ever mention that she was planning on leaving the country?"

Liz shook her head. "No. Surprisingly, that's one thing Valerie hasn't done yet. But I suppose there's a first time for everything."

"It's definitely something to consider, along with the possibility that she left the country with this Rob guy. We just need more crucial pieces to the puzzle, like Rob's last name, to figure out where the hell she is." He made another notation on the application before setting his pen aside.

"By the way, I normally charge one-fifty an hour, plus expenses," he went on, laying out his fee and terms. "But on a case like this that might take hours of prep work, I can offer a flat rate of five grand for up to a month's time, which will include my services, twenty-four-hour access to my pager, as well as my protection and professional advice in terms of you working for The Ultimate Fantasy."

She visibly winced at the amount he quoted. "Five grand? Wow, that's more than I expected."

A shrug lifted his shoulders. "I may not be the cheapest PI in town, but I'm definitely one of the best."

She laughed, but the sound was tinged with disappointment. "While I don't doubt your abilities and professional expertise, that's about four times more than I can afford."

The defeat in her tone, along with the despair he saw glimmering in her eyes as she met his gaze, hit him hard and low.

Despite that, a semblance of a smile touched her lips. "I guess I should thank you for your time and advice and be on my way."

An odd sense of panic clenched his belly, one he couldn't

fully define, but before she could clear the front of his desk, he blurted, "Wait."

She stopped and turned back to face him, her expression both startled and curious. "Yes?"

He scrubbed a hand along his tense jaw and knew there was no stopping what he was about to offer. "Tell you what, I'll take on the case for a thousand bucks." Though he hated even taking that much from her, since she was obviously financially strapped despite the success of her coffee shop—a fact he found unusual and interesting.

She lifted her chin and squared her shoulders, and damned if he didn't detect a hint of vulnerability beneath all that bravado. "Why would you do that for me?" she asked, her tone cautious and wondering.

Why, indeed. A variety of reasons popped into his head, mainly that he wasn't about to let her traipse into The Ultimate Fantasy on her own without any outside connections to keep tabs on her. If something happened to her, he'd never forgive himself, especially since he knew the details of the case. She needed guidance and more advice, and he wanted to be the guy to dole out both.

He spread his hands out in front of him, striving for a casualness he didn't completely feel. "Let's just say I have some extra time on my hands these days."

A bald-faced lie that she obviously didn't believe, either, judging by the skepticism that etched her classical features. But she didn't argue with him—that was how strong her desperation was to find her cousin.

"All right, if you're sure about that, consider it a deal." She exhaled a relieved breath and headed over to her purse and withdrew her checkbook. "And I'll sign my paychecks from The Ultimate Fantasy over to you, as well. That should help compensate some of your expenses."

"Don't worry about my expenses." He'd eat the rest himself, every last cent over a grand. "A thousand flat fee is fine."

Her lips thinned into a determined line. "I don't want to take advantage of you or your services, and I don't like being indebted to anyone. Signing my paychecks over to you is part of our deal."

He handed her the application to take, fill out, and return to him, impressed with her tenacity. "If it makes you feel better, then fine."

"It does, and I insist." She took the paper, then continued writing out the check. When she was done, she handed him the payment voucher.

He took their agreed-upon fee, folded it in half, and put it into his top drawer, to hand over to Beverly to deposit later. He glanced back at Liz and watched as her tongue darted out and dampened her bottom lip in a gesture that made him think of that sweet mouth and soft tongue of hers stroking elsewhere . . . lapping at his taut, heated skin, sliding along male erogenous zones, and swirling along the length of his rigid cock.

Oh, yeah, especially that.

The sexual tension between them was strong and undeniable, triggering a hunger in him that settled in his lap in the form of a killer hard-on.

If they were going to be working side by side, she deserved to know exactly how he felt about her, and just how much she tempted him. "I have to warn you, I don't know how the hell I'm going to keep my hands off you," he said.

Liz's chest tightened at Steve's unabashed statement, and an internal kind of heat rippled through her. Her pulse kicked into high gear, and she managed, just barely, to remain outwardly composed.

But she couldn't deny that his blatant interest aroused her. As did the casual way he sat in his chair and held her gaze, so confident and one hundred percent male. A dark-haired, blue-eyed rogue who had no qualms about hesitating to go after what he wanted.

At the moment, she was the object of his desires.

And he'd been hers for weeks.

She knew a challenge when she heard one, and she displayed an ample amount of daring to match his. "Who says I want you to keep your hands off me?"

A dark brow rose over one of those disarming, see-everything eyes of his. He looked both taken off guard at her brazen response and pleased at her temerity. "Nice to know the sentiment is reciprocated, especially since I've wanted you since the first time I walked into The Daily Grind for a drink and you asked me what my pleasure was," he said, stunning her with his confession. "It's that ring on your finger that's kept me from pursuing you sooner, but now that I know you're single and our interest in one another is mutual, maybe it's time we found out what my pleasures really are."

She pressed a hand to the fluttering in her stomach. She couldn't believe where this conversation was heading. Couldn't believe what he was suggesting. Letting this irresistible fantasy man of hers become reality in the purest sense awakened her baser feminine needs and beckoned to the wanton woman within her, who was drawn to that intoxicating blend of bad-boy eroticism and adventure he exuded.

When she remained quiet, he went on. "As much as I want you, I suppose it's only fair to let you know that I've been married before and I'm not looking for anything long-term or complicated—just in case that matters."

She offered him a wry smile, appreciating his honesty, even while her mind absorbed the enormity of what he was proposing. "Well, we definitely have *that* in common."

He tipped his head and regarded her speculatively. "You're divorced?"

"Widowed, actually, though the marriage should have ended in divorce," she said, revealing more than she'd intended. She highly doubted that sharing details of their private lives was part of any deal between them.

"Yet you're still wearing your wedding ring?" His curious gaze dropped to the ring on her left hand, silently asking for an explanation.

She twirled the gold band around her finger, for the first time ever feeling self-conscious for wearing it for the sole purpose of avoiding men's advances. "The ring isn't mine. It was my mother's, and my aunt saved it for me after my parents died, then gave it to me on my eighteenth birthday. I wear it because I'm not looking for anything complicated right now, either."

He rocked back in his chair and rubbed his thumb along his jaw in an absent caress, studying her from across the expanse of space separating them. Then, abruptly he asked, "Are you afraid of me?"

Odd question, she thought. "Should I be?"

"Depends on the situation and circumstances," he said, giving her the distinct impression that he was testing her, though she had no idea why. "Yes or no?"

Her heart beat hard in her chest, the thrill of the forbidden heightening her anticipation. "No, I'm not afraid of you."

Sliding back his chair from his desk, he crooked his finger at her, his striking blue eyes smoldering with a heady, come-hither invitation that made her insides turn to jelly. "Then come here, sit on my lap, and prove it."

Chapter

2

Liz was coming to realize that Steve Wilde was a take-no-prisoners kind of guy, especially when it came to seducing women. Her, to be exact.

He sat casually in his office chair, so utterly male, so intensely sexual without trying to be, while waiting for her to obey his command. The arrogance in his gaze was entirely unapologetic, as if he had every right to be confident. As if he knew she found his calm self-assurance not only a challenge but a huge turn-on as well.

He was right.

She could only imagine what he had in mind for her, but she was ready for anything. Anticipation swirled low in her belly, and unable to resist his allure, she moved across the space separating them and settled herself across his lap. His thighs were firm and muscular beneath her bottom, and the denim material of his jeans scratched the backs of her bare legs in an arousing way.

Even though she wasn't used to playing such impulsive sexual games with a man, she was determined to be as bold and confident as he was. After all, if she intended to become a phone sex operator, didn't she need to become a brazen, fearless vixen?

Slipping one arm around his neck, she splayed her other hand on the soft cotton T-shirt covering his wide chest and met his gaze. This close, she could see flecks of gold in his hot blue eyes, could smell the heady warmth of his own arousal, could feel his deep, even breaths beneath her palm.

He countered her advance by placing his big hand just below where the hem of her skirt ended. The heat of his long fingers branded her flesh while his callused thumb swept slowly, tantalizingly across the smooth, sensitive skin of her inner thigh.

"Kiss me," he said simply, and left the next move up to her.

She'd instinctively known he wasn't a man who'd let her go on her way with a politically correct, chaste handshake. Not after they'd brought their attraction out in the open and she'd all but told him she wanted his hands on her. It appeared Steve was a man who enjoyed the chase, as well as issuing outrageous dares. And right now, he apparently expected her to put her money where her mouth was and give him physical proof of her desire for him.

Surprisingly, she didn't feel as though she was compromising her virtue—or anything else, for that matter—because she wanted him, too. After three years of being sensible, practical, and celibate, she was beyond ready to indulge in a little excitement and adventure—a sexy, temporary fling that would end as soon as they tracked her wayward cousin.

Lowering her head, she touched her lips to his warm, firm mouth—soft, slow, and sweet. He didn't seem inclined to deepen the kiss, and confusion and uncertainty made her draw back to assess his expression.

He appeared unimpressed by her initial attempt to seduce him. "Is that the best you can do?" A lofty smile quirked the corner of his mouth.

She should have been insulted, but she saw his taunting

comment as the direct provocation he meant it to be. He was testing her to see how far she'd go with him, how willing she'd be to satisfy his every whim. She'd craved him for so long, she was eager to experience whatever he had to offer. And she intended to demonstrate that she was game for anything and everything he tossed her way, and that she wasn't about to be a passive partner to his more assertive nature.

Threading her fingers through the thick, silky hair at the nape of his neck, she curved her other hand along his strong jawline and pushed his chin down with her thumb so that his lips parted for her. This time when her mouth met his, she bypassed all slow, coaxing preliminaries and went straight for hot and devouring. Her tongue swept into his mouth and tangled with his, and she tasted the pure, unadulterated sensuality that was so much a part of him. She shivered, unable to stop the slow, sultry ache spreading through her belly, or the slick moisture settling between her thighs.

Certain she'd given him more than enough proof of her enthusiasm, she started to pull back, only to have him thwart her attempt. He cupped the back of her head in his palm to hold her in place, and with a low growl she felt rumble up from his chest, he slanted his mouth across hers and took control of the embrace.

Presumptuous and dominant, he kissed her with potent male heat. Branded her with the strength and depth of his passion. Excited her with the heated stroke of his hand on her bare thigh, and the promise of forbidden, illicit pleasures to come.

His unmistakable erection pressed against her hip—long, hard, and thick, fueling her imagination of what it would feel like to have that impressive, solid length filling her. Stretching her. Pumping deep inside her in a grinding, full-bodied rhythm.

She shuddered at the thought and groaned. Oh, God, it had been so, so long . . .

Her breasts swelled within the confines of her bra, and she

shifted restlessly on his lap, wanton and needy as his lips and tongue continued their lush, hungry assault on her mouth and senses. Knowing their relationship was nothing more than a temporary diversion and purely for the sake of mutual pleasure gave her the freedom to let go of inhibitions. To give generously and take greedily. To grasp and enjoy one last provocative fling with an untamable bad boy before she turned her sights on a man more straitlaced and ordinary. A steadfast man who'd make her aunt and uncle proud of her choice and make up for the huge disappointment Travis had turned out to be.

With that thought filling her mind, and her body desperate for a more physical contact, she released three of the buttons on her blouse, then reached for the masculine hand still on her thigh. Lifting his long, warm fingers to her neck, she flattened his hand against the erratic pulse in her throat and brazenly skimmed his palm down to the slope of her breast, silently telling him what she wanted. What she needed.

He effortlessly took over from there, slipping his fingers into her stretch-lace bra and molding them to her feminine curves. A delightful sigh escaped her as he cupped and kneaded her soft flesh in a firm, sensuous caress.

The hand at the back of her head pulled her closer, and he continued to kiss her, damp lips melding and silky tongues mating intimately. He plucked at her sensitive nipple, rolled the stiff crest between his fingers, and she moaned into his mouth and shamelessly arched into his touch, begging for more.

Abruptly he ended their seductive interlude and buried his face against her throat, his breathing coming as fast and ragged as her own. "Christ," he muttered in awe, the one word summing up just how fiery and intense their attraction was.

She laughed huskily, understanding just how dazed he felt. "I need to go," she said, trying to hang on to a semblance of rational thinking.

He lifted his head from the crook of her neck, his lashes half-mast and a sinful grin in place. "Yeah, you do, before you end up sprawled on my desk with your skirt up around your waist and me between your thighs." He gave her breast a possessive squeeze.

Her cheeks warmed at his blatantly sexual statement, and while temptation beckoned, other more immediate responsibilities demanded her attention—the kind of duty and obligation that took precedence over her desire for Steve.

"I don't want to be late for my interview at The Ultimate Fantasy," she reminded him.

"You're right. We'll have plenty of time to finish this later." Slowly he withdrew his hand from her breast, buttoned up her blouse, and lifted his gaze to hers. "And just for the record, your second attempt was much better than the first, sweetheart. I like a woman who isn't shy or modest about taking what she needs—or giving me what I want. You do both quite well."

The compliment boosted her confidence in a way nothing had in a long time, and she couldn't resist flashing him a quick grin. "Thank you." She slid from his lap and straightened her skirt, doing her best to smooth out her appearance and regain her composure.

He stood, too, and grimaced as he adjusted the noticeable bulge straining against the fly of his jeans. Then he grabbed the keys on the corner of his desk and started for the door. "Come on, let's go."

Confused, she caught his arm as he passed her, forcing him to stop. "What do you mean, 'Let's go'?"

"Since I'm officially on this case, I'm driving you to the interview," he replied simply.

She frowned. "Steve, I don't need a chauffeur. I'm more than capable of driving myself."

In a split second, his demeanor turned commanding, his expression reflecting a compelling amount of authority that made it clear who was in charge. "Look, in order for this partnership between us to work, when it comes to your involvement with

The Ultimate Fantasy, you need to trust my judgment and reasons without questioning them. I need to stick close to your side whenever possible, especially where this case is concerned. I also need to know where the offices for The Ultimate Fantasy are located, and while you're in your interview I can get a gut feeling for the establishment and decide whether or not I need to put the place under surveillance."

Unable to argue his valid point, she nodded and reached for her purse. "You're the boss." She turned back around, startled to find that he'd moved directly in front of her.

He clasped her upper arms in his big hands, his eyes direct and darkly sensual. "And I'll advise you not to forget who's in charge," he said gruffly. Pulling her to his muscular frame, he kissed her—a hot, deep act of possession that left her weak-kneed and light-headed.

Once he released her, she skimmed her tongue along her lower lip, growing used to the arousing taste of him and his aggressive nature. Both thrilled her. "What was that for?"

"Because I wanted to," he said, most definitely staking a claim on her and letting her know he was a man who took what he wanted—sometimes without asking. "And since you're mine for the time being, you might as well get used to enjoying a bit of spontaneity."

Anytime, anywhere. She read the tantalizing message in his eyes and accepted his challenge. Spontaneity and impulsive acts, she could handle. It was what she *craved*, to add some spice and excitement in the current sensible, straitlaced life she'd led for the past three years.

And she was depending on Steve Wilde to deliver on both accounts.

From behind the dark lenses of his Oakley sunglasses, Steve casually surveyed the five-story brick building that Liz had disappeared into for her interview—which looked like every other building in the general vicinity of downtown Chicago.

According to the directions the receptionist at The Ultimate Fantasy had given to Liz, the business occupied the entire third floor. He counted up three stories, but the tinted, reflective film on the windows protected the company's privacy and hid their secrets well.

Over the course of the next twenty minutes he kept a low profile in his black SUV, situated in the back section of the parking lot. He watched people come and go from the building—some dressed in business suits and carrying briefcases, and others in casual wear. There was nothing out of the ordinary that caught his attention, or anything to indicate that an illicit sex operation dominated the third floor of the building.

Setting up surveillance was unnecessary, he concluded. If The Ultimate Fantasy hosted swinging, wild erotic sex parties, he was positive they didn't take place here, in an openly public district. No, most likely there was another private, secluded haven in which their elite clients explored sexual fantasies and other illegal dealings. And it was up to Liz to gain them access to that exclusive world of sin and iniquity in order to find out more information on Valerie's whereabouts and on the boyfriend who'd accompanied her to a previous party.

But first, Liz had to get hired on as a phone sex operator, and he had no doubt she'd be successful in obtaining the position. She had determination and sass aplenty, along with an innate sensuality about her that would no doubt appeal to her employer—just as she'd stirred his baser male instincts from the first time he'd laid eyes on her.

As the minutes dragged on, he kept his gaze locked on the front entrance of the building, but his mind wandered to Liz's enthusiastic participation in the kiss they'd shared earlier. They'd all but caught fire from that sizzling embrace, confirming that everything about their agreed-upon affair would be an equal give-and-take of untold pleasures. Hot, satisfying sex—lots of it, and any way either of them wanted it.

Despite the sampling he'd taken in his office, he was still

hot and hard for her. Arousal buzzed through his veins, making him too damned restless and reminding him just how long he'd been without a woman.

Oh, he'd had plenty of offers, but there was no one else he'd wanted in his bed other than Liz. For the past month she'd played a starring role in the nightly erotic dreams that taunted him. Now those wicked fantasies were going to become reality. Soon he'd have Liz stripped naked beneath him, her voluptuous breasts and nipples all his to lick, suck, and feast on. Soon he'd be able to inhale the feminine scent that clung to her skin and taste all her hottest, sweetest places. Soon he'd finally get to bury his cock deep inside her and feel the tight clasp of her body around his sex as they drove each other to completion.

His groin throbbed in anticipation, and he shifted in his leather seat with a harsh exhale, which did nothing to ease the fierce erection making itself known. *Soon.* He needed to be patient and bide his time. First and foremost, their main priority was to locate her missing cousin and ensure her safety. Their affair and mutual attraction was merely a bonus they'd indulge in after hours, when there was nothing to concentrate on but each other.

Giving himself a firm mental shake back to his present situation, he resumed his watch for Liz. Five minutes later, he released a grateful stream of breath when she emerged from the double glass doors, giving him something other than his unruly, sorely neglected libido to focus on.

She wasn't alone. A petite brunette accompanied Liz out of the building, with the two of them carrying on a conversation until they reached the other woman's car. They talked for another minute or so, then went their separate ways, with Liz heading toward his vehicle, hips swaying and a light bounce in her step that captivated him—as did everything about her.

She slid into the passenger seat, shut the door, and flashed him a bright smile. "I got the job," she announced, looking extremely pleased with herself.

Her exuberance made him grin, too. "I had no doubt that you would," he said, and turned the key in the ignition. He drove out of the parking lot and headed back toward his office. "Tell me how the interview went."

"It certainly wasn't your typical kind of interview," she said, her tone wry. He'd left the windows rolled down, and as he turned onto the freeway and picked up speed, the wind ruffled her silky blond hair around her head and plastered her blouse against her breasts. "Once I checked in with the receptionist, she led me to a large private office, where a man named Antonio Cardenias introduced himself as one of the company's partners. He briefly glanced over my application, but he didn't seem interested in my references or past employment record, which excluded any mention of The Daily Grind."

Steve's grip tightened on the steering wheel as he imagined the kind of credentials Antonio might require in potential female employees whose main talent would be based in sexual experience. "What *was* he interested in?"

"The sound of my voice, since that would attract and keep a client on the phone." She smoothed her hair away from her face and shrugged. "He said I had a soft, sexy voice that would turn men on."

"You do," he said gruffly, knowing how that husky voice of hers could turn a man inside out with wanting. Rolling up the windows, he turned on the air-conditioning, needing a blast of cool air on his heated skin.

"What else?" he prompted.

"He wanted to know if I had any fantasies or fetishes that I refused to discuss with a caller, or any sexual situations I considered off limits."

"Do you?" he asked, curious to know what her personal boundaries were when it came to sex.

"I told him I wouldn't take calls requesting anything to do with pain and torture, bestiality, rape, or incest." She visibly shuddered at the same time he winced in reciprocal disgust. "Antonio said that was fine, that they had other operators who handled those kinds of requests—enjoyed them, even."

"Well, I'm right there with you, sweetheart." Stretching his arm across the back of her seat, he curved his fingers along the nape of her neck. "I don't get off on any of those perverse fixations, either."

"That's good to know." She smiled indulgently. "Other than those lewd fetishes, I think I can handle just about anything, or fake my way through it."

He glanced from the road to narrow his gaze at her, then realized she couldn't see his expression hidden behind his sunglasses. "Don't expect to fake *anything* with me."

She rolled her eyes, somehow containing the laughter he saw glimmering in the green depths. "That's such a man statement."

He traced the soft skin of her throat with his thumb and felt her shiver, watched as her nipples puckered tight against her blouse. "What do you expect," he drawled good-naturedly. "I *am* a man."

She arched a blond brow his way, seemingly trying to maintain her composure even while her body's arousing response to his touch gave her away. "A very arrogant one, at that."

"Yeah, I'm confident when it comes to pleasuring my partner," he admitted unabashedly, wanting her to know exactly what she was in for.

"I like everything about sex," he went on, "especially foreplay and the hot, frenzied buildup to an explosive orgasm. And the best part of being with a woman—being with *you*—is going to be making sure you're having a good time, too. Turning you on turns me on. And when it's the right time, I'm going to enjoy making you come, feeling you come, against my fingers, my tongue, and around my cock. Those inner con-tractions and the way your body clenches in the throes of climax is something no woman can fabricate."

She squirmed in her seat and cleared her throat, which didn't quite camouflage her whimper of longing his words evoked. "I don't think faking it is going to be an issue between us."

"Didn't think so." Now he sounded arrogant, and like he didn't give a damn.

"Umm, back to my interview," she managed, her voice still breathless with the sexual tension he'd instigated between them. "Antonio also talked about promotions and opportunities to advance within the company if I 'performed well' and established a steady, repeat client base. There are monetary bonuses given for keeping a caller on the line for more than fifteen minutes."

He nodded but remained quiet as she continued.

"He also mentioned private, by-invitation-only parties that were available to their most requested operators and their regular clients, but didn't elaborate on what those parties consisted of. He said we'd discuss those extracurricular activities more later, when I've built more than a casual rapport with a caller and I'm ready to advance to that next level."

"Which I'll make sure happens, with *me*."

She looked relieved and grateful. "You're the only one I'll attend those parties with, so let's include that in your services, too."

"That goes without saying, sweetheart." Now that she was his, there was no way he'd allow another man to accompany her to one of the fantasy parties. "When do you start?"

"Tonight, believe it or not, which is fine with me. The sooner I get in there and get acquainted with the other operators, the sooner I'll be able to get some information on Valerie." Her fingers absently traced the hem of her short skirt, drawing his gaze to her tanned thighs while she talked. "I told Antonio that I worked another job and I was only looking for something part-time, so he gave me a nine-to-midnight shift. But this does mean I'll have to reschedule my employees at The Daily Grind to close up the shop."

He glanced back at the road and made a turn onto the side street where his offices were located. "Is that going to be a problem?"

"No. I'm certain my two main employees will welcome the full-time work and extra hours, since I've had to cut them back in order to keep costs down."

Once again he was intrigued. Her comment coincided with her not being able to afford much when it came to his fee, despite running what appeared to be a very successful café.

"If there's something that my employees can't handle, I've got Mona at the bookstore to help out," she went on. "But I trust the people who work for me. Most have been there for over a year, and right now I'll do whatever it takes to find my cousin." Her tone was adamant.

He maneuvered his SUV into his parking space, killed the engine, and turned toward her. "By the way, who was that woman you walked out of the building with?"

Liz gathered up her purse. "Her name is Roxanne, and she goes by the call name of Roxie. She was very friendly and seemed willing to talk about the ins and outs of the business with a 'virgin,' as she called me, since this is my first foray into the world of phone sex. Oh, and before I forget to tell you, Antonio signed me up under the call name of Sindee, spelled *S-I-N-D-E-E*, which I have to use for anything business-related as a precaution to attracting any wackos who know my real name. And here's the phone number you need to call."

"Sindee it is." He grinned, accepting the business card she handed him, with THE ULTIMATE FANTASY emblazoned in bright red, and a prefixed number followed by the appropriate call word *Ultimate*. "As for Roxanne, she seems like someone you can easily befriend. When the time is right and you feel you have an opening, you can mention that you're a friend of Valerie's and she's the reason you applied for the job. You can ask about Valerie, maybe mention Rob's name and that you haven't heard from her in a while, to see what Roxanne says. But keep your questions about your cousin casual, to a minimum, and discreet. Let Roxanne do the talking so she doesn't feel like you're interrogating her."

She nodded and sighed, the soulful, weary sound affecting him on a basic emotional level. She had a load of concern weighing on her conscience, and he'd even seen flashes of guilt in her eyes today that he didn't fully comprehend. Steve hated that Liz's irresponsible cousin had her so upset. He hoped Valerie knew how damned lucky she was to have such a caring family member who was willing to go to such lengths to find her, to ensure her safety.

He wished he could make Liz promises to ease her worries, wished he had the right to tell her everything was going to be okay, but he wasn't one to offer false hopes. And no way was he going to bank on his gut instincts with Valerie's frivolous behavior until he had more evidence to back up his theory.

Startled by the sudden urge he experienced to reach out and comfort her, he opened the driver's-side door to dispel the sensation. "Come on, I'll walk you to your car," he said, and exited the vehicle.

She followed, and side by side they silently made their way to her silver Celica that was at least ten years old and in need of body work and a paint job. Obviously not a priority for her. Once they were there, she turned to face him, and he caught a barely perceptible flicker of nervousness in her eyes before she blinked it away. "I guess I'm all set for tonight, then."

Sensing she was overwhelmed by the true realization of what she was getting herself involved in, he gave in to that impulse to reach out and skim his knuckles down her cheek in a reassuring caress. "I'm sorry that you have to go through all this crap."

She visibly relaxed, and a small smile turned up her too-tempting lips. "I would have done it without your help, but I have to admit that I'm grateful that we were able to work something out. It's nice to know I'm not going into this situation alone."

"No, you're not." Withdrawing a business card from his wallet and asking her for a pen, he jotted down his home phone beneath his cell and pager numbers. "If you need me for anything, day or night, I'm only a phone call away."

Accepting the card, she tucked it into her purse, then adjusted the strap over her shoulder. "Thank you."

"No thanks necessary. It's all part of my services." He wasn't about to tell her that he'd never given his home phone number to a client before. "And I'm sure you'll do just fine tonight."

"Thanks for the vote of confidence." A good amount of her initial worries seemed to have faded away, though some concerns still lingered. "I'm not used to talking about down-and-dirty sex to just anyone, and I have to do better than fine if I want to stay hired on long enough to ask around about Valerie."

"Just take it one step at a time and do whatever feels right." Taking off his sunglasses, he tucked them into the collar of his shirt. "And when it comes to fraternizing with your coworkers, act open to anything. Also, it's important that you dress and look the part of someone willing to play around."

"I guess I'll be raiding Valerie's closet, because my wardrobe is a bit outdated when it comes to looking like a sophisticated party girl." She touched her hair, as if considering how to transform her sleek, conservative look into something wilder as well. "So, where do you come in on all this?"

"I'll call in at about eleven-fifteen, and the best part is, you get to talk dirty to me." He bobbed his eyebrows teasingly, doing his best to keep things light, to keep her anxiety about her new job at bay.

She laughed and shook her head, amusement dancing in her vibrant green eyes. "Oh, I can't wait."

"Neither can I," he said, and meant it. While her lip service was for the sole purpose of finding her cousin, there was no reason why he couldn't use their phone sex conversations to his advantage by sharing their own personal fantasies.

Seconds passed, filling the air between them with subtle expectations and deeper desires. He stared at her, enthralled by the way the sun behind her highlighted her shoulder-length blond hair with gold streaks and kissed her smooth skin with a glowing warmth that he wanted to skim with his mouth and taste with his tongue. If he hadn't had a few cases he needed to follow up on, he would have persuaded her back to his place for a lazy afternoon of hot, satisfying sex.

Instead, he decided he'd have to settle for a kiss to get him through the long hours until they were together again—and alone, so they could indulge in something far more intimate and satisfying.

Slowly stepping toward her, he backed her up against the driver's-side door and braced his palms on the edge of the low roof on either side of her shoulders, securing her between the heated metal of the car and the hard, muscled length of his body.

She didn't seem to mind being trapped. With her gaze locked brazenly with his, she countered his move with one of her own. Hooking her fingers into the belt loops on his jeans, she pulled him closer until their bellies, hips, and thighs were intimately aligned and his thickening shaft found a home at the welcoming notch between her legs.

A blissful sigh escaped her, and she whispered silkily, "I like the way you feel against me. We fit perfectly together."

"Damn," he murmured, singed to the core by her honest admission and inflamed by a reciprocating need he couldn't hold back. He rubbed himself against her mound, which made him even more painfully erect, with no relief in sight. "Imagine how good it'll feel when we're both naked."

"I already have," she divulged, her candid words and soft, dreamy expression sending his libido straight into orbit. "You've been a fantasy of mine for the past month."

Upon that shocking revelation, her lashes fell to half-mast, and a pale pink color swept over her cheeks, as if she wasn't used to being so sexually outspoken with men but liked the power and control that came with being forthright in what she wanted.

Sliding her hands from his waist to his lower back, she splayed her palms against the muscled slope of his spine, the heat of her touch seeping through his shirt. Her chin lifted in an amusing— and arousing—display of daring. "You know that hot, frenzied buildup you mentioned earlier today?"

He groaned, realizing that she somehow intended to use his own seductive words against him, which was nothing less than he deserved. "Yeah, I remember," he managed around the knot that seemed to have tightened his vocal chords.

Her lips skimmed his jawline, teasing his senses. "Well, just so you know, a month is a very long time to lust after one particular person, and my anticipation level is already near to bursting."

His breath left his lungs in a tight exhale. Scorching heat curled inside him at the thought of her body primed and ready for his. The notion threatened his restraint, making him *burn* to give all that confined excitement within her a proper and very provocative kind of release.

God, she was so damned sexy, she made his insides ache and his palms sweat—a feat no other woman had ever accomplished. She was a beguiling witch, a temptress who would undoubtedly hold her own when it came to fulfilling his sensual and erotic demands in the bedroom.

Lifting one of his hands to her face, he cupped her cheek in his callused palm, dragged his thumb along the curve of her jaw, and addressed that anticipation problem of hers. "I guess we'll just have to make sure we do something about all that pent-up desire of yours," he drawled.

Unable to hold back the rampant male instinct firing his blood or to resist the hot female invitation in her eyes, he lowered his head, and she eagerly met him halfway. Her lips parted beneath the coaxing pressure of his, and his tongue swept inside, slow and teasing, then gradually taking possession of her mouth in a deep, wet, ravenous kiss that was unmistakable in its carnality and sexual intent.

The distinctive, familiar rumbling sound of a sports car pulling into the parking lot penetrated the mind-numbing pleasure of the moment. Reluctantly he pulled back, preparing himself to deal with the consequences of putting his relationship with Liz on public display.

"Shit," he muttered, and at her startled, wide-eyed stare he explained, "It's my partner, Cameron. And I apologize ahead of time for putting you in the middle of an embarrassing situation."

Her cheeks were flushed with color, but she didn't seem the least bit ashamed or uncomfortable at their predicament. "You mean getting caught making out?"

The humor threading her husky voice relieved him and made him smile. "Yeah."

"Well, let's get something perfectly straight," she said, her gaze holding his as she boldly ran a hand from his shoulder to his chest. "I *let* you kiss me, of my own free will, and I wanted it as much as you did. So I can handle the consequences of getting caught if you can."

This woman never ceased to amaze him, and he liked having proof of just how adventurous she could be. He gave her a nod of agreement, stepped back, then turned to face his partner and best friend since college, who'd just unfolded his big body from his new metallic-blue Porsche Boxster. Cameron headed their way, his curiosity undisguised as he looked Liz over and obviously liked what he saw.

Steve's stomach churned with an uncharacteristic bout of male rivalry. He'd never been a jealous man, and he'd certainly never felt any competition from his love-'em-and-leave-'em partner, yet he couldn't deny the protective, possessive impulses making themselves known where Liz was concerned.

Cameron neared, and knowing an introduction was inescapable, Steve decided to do the deed and get it over with. "Liz, this is my partner, Cameron Sinclair. Cam, Liz Adams."

Liz politely held out her slender hand in greeting. "It's nice to meet you."

Cam shook her hand. "The pleasure is all mine," he said as an unmistakably charming grin slid into place.

Unaffected by his blond good looks and flirtatious attempt, Liz merely smiled and glanced back at Steve. "I really need to get going."

He agreed. The sooner she was on her way, the sooner Steve could set Cam straight about a few things, namely, that Liz was taken, and second, that she was a client as well.

Opening the driver's-side door for Liz, he waited for her to get settled in the seat and buckle herself in, knowing damn well that his partner was ogling her smooth, tanned thighs where the hem of her skirt had ridden up.

Steve stepped more fully in front of Cam, blocking the other man's view of Liz's assets. "I'll talk to you tonight," he said, and enclosed her in the small car.

As soon as Liz turned onto the main street, Cam asked without compunction, "So, who's the hot number?"

Steve knew what his friend wanted to know: beyond Liz's name, what was her connection to him, and what was the *real* scoop between the two of them? "She's a client, and someone I'm seeing, so I'd advise you to keep your eyes, hands, and thoughts to yourself."

Cameron's brows rose in surprise, and he held said hands out to his sides in supplication. "Whoa, what's with the territorial attitude?"

Feeling irritable and provoked, when he was normally so

calm and collected, Steve scowled at Cam. "I'm just letting you know up front that she's taken."

"By you, obviously . . . judging by that kiss I interrupted and that boner you're sporting."

"Go to hell, Sinclair," he growled.

Cameron chuckled and slapped Steve on the back, unfazed by his foul mood. "I've been telling you for months now that you ought to get laid. I'm just glad to see you've taken the advice to heart with one hell of a sexy woman." Cam's affable disposition ebbed into a more serious expression. "But I do have to say, this is the first time I've ever seen you mix business and pleasure. What's up with that?"

Steve shrugged. "Extenuating circumstances." Along with the need to get one certain woman out of his system.

Cameron narrowed his gaze, obviously guessing that there was much more at stake. "Must be some case."

"It is." Steve rubbed his fingers against the throb beginning in his temple. The heat of the sun beating down on his head, along with Cam's line of questioning, was giving him a headache.

Knowing there was no avoiding the inevitable conversation to come—the discussion where he gave his business partner a rundown of the situation so that Cam was familiar with the dynamics of the case should he need to get involved, which was standard practice between the two of them—Steve headed back toward the office building.

"Come on, I'll explain everything inside."

Chapter

3

The tension vibrating through Steve was due to a culmina-tion of sexual anticipation and a keen restlessness he couldn't shake—a hindering impatience that had grown with each hour that passed since Liz had left his office building that afternoon.

Exhaling a harsh stream of breath, Steve continued his agi-tated pacing across his living room floor. Normally, he was a patient, relaxed kind of guy when it came to delays and lengthy downtime on a case. So many aspects of his job had trained him to endure long waits and even longer hours of dull and monotonous surveillance. It was boring, tedious work at times—no unruly hormones or other unwanted emotions in-volved—and tonight's prolonged wait should have been no different.

Unfortunately, the mind was a powerful stimulant and had the ability to conjure up all kinds of provocative scenarios that could drive a man crazy. Unlike a straight surveillance job, there was nothing to watch or observe in terms of Liz's case. Not yet, at least.

At the moment, and until the clock struck 11:15 P.M., all he could do was imagine her somewhere on the third floor of that building, titillating callers with frank sexual talk and using her feminine wiles to bring men's explicit requests to life over the phone lines. Servicing other men verbally and getting them off on the dark, carnal fantasies she wove for their pleasure. And what about the callers who deigned it their duty to talk dirty to her in return?

"Christ," he muttered, unable to fend off the surge of frustration adding to the other unexplainable feelings that had consumed his thoughts for the past hour and a half. He shoved his fingers through his thick hair, annoyed with his possessive behavior and the unexpected realization that this one certain woman could get to him on such a gut-deep level—and so damn quickly. He was a man used to being in control of every aspect of his life, his sex life and the women he chose to date included, and he didn't like the fact that he couldn't subdue his uncharacteristic reaction to Liz's temporary job.

Rolling his taut shoulders, he soothed his irritable mood by reminding himself that very soon it would be his turn to increase the heat and level of excitement between them, to share some of his most forbidden desires with Liz and find out what she craved, as well.

And then, later tonight, they'd unleash those fantasies and fulfill them.

Over the arousal settling like molten heat in his belly, his stomach managed a hungry growl—a surprising bid for *food* in the midst of his turbulent thoughts. Although he'd eaten dinner hours ago, apparently all his keyed-up energy and the circuit training he'd put himself through in his home gym earlier had quickly burned off his meal. Figuring he had time for a late-evening snack before he called Liz, and welcoming the distraction, he headed into the kitchen, rummaged through the refrigerator, and cringed at the lack of sustenance that greeted him. He hated grocery shopping and hated cooking more—those were two aspects of being a bachelor that sucked.

Grabbing the last cold bottle of beer and finding an open

bag of chips in the cupboard, he headed upstairs to a secondary bedroom he'd converted into a fully equipped home office. Sitting down at his desk, he booted up his computer. While he waited for the unit to warm up, his mind wandered to the conversation he'd had with Cameron after Liz's departure that afternoon. They'd discussed the nature of Liz's case, The Ultimate Fantasy, and her cousin's disappearance, so that Cam was at least briefed on the case.

Steve didn't bring up his personal relationship with Liz— what happened between them beyond the case was nobody's business but their own. As a good friend and understanding partner, Cam had respected his privacy and hadn't pushed for details.

He tossed a few potato chips into his mouth, took a long drink of his beer, and checked his personal E-mail account. He chuckled through the series of raunchy, ribald jokes that his brother Adrian enjoyed sending to him and Eric, but it was the E-mail from Steffie Wilde that made him smile and his chest expand with affection.

He loved hearing from his sixteen-year-old daughter, especially since she'd moved to Texas with her mother, Janet, and stepfather, Hugh, nearly three years ago. Steve missed Steffie— E-mails, talking on the phone, and seeing her only a handful of weeks out of the year didn't seem like nearly enough time with her during these crucial teenage years.

But he'd take whatever he could get, including the E-mails and digital pictures she sent through the Internet, which kept him updated on her life. Opening the letter, he read the contents, imagining in his mind how her expressive blue eyes would sparkle as she regaled him with her latest tales of school, her involvement in the drama club, and the boy who'd taken her to one of the high school formal dances.

He clicked on the attached files and looked through the collage of photos she'd taken with the digital camera he'd bought for her this past Christmas. There were pictures of Janet and

Hugh, happily married and enjoying their life in Texas, along with shots of Steffie posing for the camera with her beloved golden retriever, Buffy.

And then there was his little girl in a long formal gown, looking absolutely stunning and too sophisticated for her tender young age, standing with a sandy-haired boy who had his arms around her waist and held her much too close for Steve's liking. Her hands rested on his chest, their heads were touching, and the look of adoration glimmering in Steffie's eyes made Steve's heart constrict with a startling sense of déjà vu.

Steve took another gulp of beer as a jarring realization crashed over him. His daughter, age sixteen, was not only allowed to date, but she was the same age that he and Janet were when they'd started going steady. They'd become high school sweethearts, and after two years of dating exclusively and just a month after graduation, Janet discovered that she was pregnant.

Eight months later, Steve was a married nineteen-year-old, and a daddy to a sweet baby girl who'd wrapped him around her little finger the moment she was born. He'd worked two back-to-back jobs to support his new and unexpected family, until he'd graduated from the police academy and landed a decent-paying job with Chicago's finest.

For ten years, he'd devoted himself to raising Steffie, done his best to keep his marriage together despite the growing tension between him and Janet, and taken his job as a police officer seriously—until he'd taken a bullet to his upper right arm, which had affected some nerve endings in his hand. The injury hadn't caused any paralysis, thank God. The only time he felt any discomfort was when he did a lot of heavy lifting or worked out with his weights too much. But there had been enough damage for the doctors to worry about his reflexes when it came to shooting his weapon. They'd made the recommendation to Steve's lieutenant that he be reduced to modified work duty, which in essence meant sitting behind a desk pushing paperwork, or writing tickets for expired meters. That hadn't been an option for him, since he wasn't one who could handle a desk job, thus his change in careers to a private investigator.

The shooting, and the stress of his job, had brought a lot of things to a head in his marriage that he and Janet had ignored for far too long. When she asked him for a divorce, he didn't protest. He'd known for years that they were only going through the motions of being husband and wife, more for Steffie's sake than anything else. Their split had been amicable, and they were both much happier as a result of going their separate ways.

And now here he was, six years divorced and a confirmed bachelor who enjoyed his lifestyle and career. He just wished that Steffie didn't live so damn far away.

He sent an E-mail back to his daughter and checked a few other messages. Finally, the time arrived for him to call Liz, to establish himself as a regular caller and client. To do his best to unearth some of her secrets and fantasies, and share a few of his own.

Anxious to hear her voice and be the recipient of her attempt at verbal seduction, he finished off his beer, shut down his computer, and headed to his bedroom down the hall. He striped off his clothes and donned a pair of boxer shorts for the sake of comfort, grabbed the cordless phone from the nightstand, and sat down on his king-size bed, which suddenly seemed much too big and empty when all he could think about was having Liz filling the vacant spot next to him.

Punching in the phone number he'd memorized the moment he'd seen it on the business card Liz had given him, he settled himself against the pillows pushed against the headboard, more than prepared to seduce and be seduced.

The phone on the small table jangled, and Liz's gaze automatically shot to the watch on her wrist, to gauge the time, as she'd done with each call since the beginning of her shift over two hours ago. It was 11:15, her designated meeting time with Steve, but that didn't mean another call couldn't slip past the switchboard operator before Steve's and keep her on the line for another ten or twenty minutes of sex talk.

Please, please, please let it be Steve, she silently prayed as another shrill ring echoed in the small confines of the room. She wore a headset, which left her hands free, and all it took to connect the call was a press of a button on the phone unit on the table. She reached out, touched the flashing button with her index finger, and hesitated, her heart drumming hard and fast in her chest—in an odd combination of anticipation and dread, because she had no clue who was on the other end of the line.

God, she didn't think she could handle another anonymous caller desperate for sexual attention, and a down-and-dirty verbal exchange to get him off. She shuddered in disgust, knowing the previous men she'd talked to this evening had climaxed from the requested fantasies she'd fulfilled—or had pretended exceptionally well, just as she'd fabricated loud and robust orgasms on her end just to end the call as quickly as possible. So far, her act had been convincing enough to earn her praise and compliments from her male patrons.

She couldn't even begin to imagine what her cousin found so enticing about being a phone sex operator. Liz was far from being a prude, but she found the job downright creepy in terms of engaging in intimate and very explicit conversation with so many faceless strangers. It had taken monumental effort for her to separate her real personality from the sex kitten the caller expected her to be, and that meant pretending to be a woman who was sophisticated and experienced when it came to lewd, outlandish, and kinky sex acts.

All for the sake of finding her wayward cousin and saving Liz from having to involve her aunt and uncle in another one of Valerie's impossible escapades.

A third loud ring jarred her back to the present, demanding

she pick up the line before someone peeked in on her to find out why she wasn't answering. Forcing herself back into the role she'd been playing, she inhaled a calming breath and connected the call.

"Hi, baby," she greeted huskily, using the opening line another operator had suggested she use to immediately break the ice and make the customer feel like he was special.

"Hello yourself," a familiar male voice drawled, the low, sexy timbre making her heart beat even faster.

Steve. Thank God. Relief flooded through her, so strong, she felt light-headed.

"Is this Sindee?" he asked, playing the game like the dedicated nightly caller he would become.

"In the flesh," she replied automatically, her flirtatious comment coming easily with him, and without any pretense.

"Mmm, I like the way that sounds." There was a smile in his tone, one she knew would be all male and pure seduction in person.

Letting the night's tension drain from her limbs, she leaned back in her chair, closed her eyes, and conjured his image in her mind. Thick, silky black hair that was undoubtedly tousled around his head. Sinful blue eyes filled with heat and hunger. And a lean, muscled, aggressive body she couldn't wait to see and feel in action. There was only one thing left she needed to know to complete the picture.

"Where are you?" she asked curiously, and readjusted the earpiece to her headset to make it fit more comfortably.

"In my bedroom, in my bed," he said softly, seductively. "Wearing very little."

Oh, he was very, very bad. Unbidden, more mental images appeared, of Steve stretched out on his mattress in a classic *Playgirl* centerfold pose—hands behind his head, a come-hither look in his eyes, and a whole lot of sleek, naked skin showing around the silk sheet draped strategically over one thigh and the bulge between his legs. The delicious, arousing fantasy caused her breasts to swell and her nipples to tingle and pucker tight, her first physical response to a man tonight. One she welcomed, because it was Steve.

It was hot and stuffy in the small room, and she was certain he'd just raised her internal temperature into the triple digits. Reaching for her bottle of water, she took a quick drink to quench her suddenly parched throat before responding. "I didn't think eleven-fifteen would ever get here. I can't tell you how glad I am to hear your voice."

"Likewise. I guess it's been a long night, for both of us." He paused, letting the subtle insinuation in his words—that he'd been equally anxious to talk to her—settle between them before he asked, "What's it like there?"

"Claustrophobic," she said, and laughed as her gaze swept the six-by-six area she'd been assigned for the evening. The walls were a dingy beige color, with no extras to bring a little brightness or cheer to the room. "My so-called office is about the size of a janitor's closet. And it's so warm in here, it's almost stifling. But at least it's private." And thank goodness for that, considering all the moaning, groaning, and heavy breathing she'd had to feign.

"Have you been able to talk to any of the other operators?"

"Only briefly before I started my shift and during my ten-minute break." Kicking off her sandals, she propped her feet up on the table and wiggled her toes in front of the small handheld fan she'd set on the table to stir up the air in the room. Another thirty-five minutes of idle chitchat with Steve, and her shift was over, she thought gratefully. "Roxanne wasn't here tonight, but I introduced myself to a few other girls."

"That's a good start." Approval resonated in his tone. "Any mention of Valerie yet?"

"No, and there hasn't been an opportune time to bring her up, either." She sighed, hoping it wouldn't take more than a few evenings for her coworkers to warm up enough to give her the answers she sought, or for her employer to extend an invitation to The Ultimate Fantasy private parties.

"Don't be so hard on yourself. It's only your first night," he said, as if reading her mind. "So, how has it been with the callers?" His question was direct and undeniably curious.

She bit her lower lip, undecided whether or not she wanted to share the sordid details with a man who was the epitome of sexuality. A gorgeous, virile man who was her personal fantasy in every way. "You want the truth?"

"Sweetheart," he drawled smoothly, "I always want the truth."

And no faking anything. He'd made that abundantly clear, too. The man was a stickler for honesty and took a person's integrity very seriously. They were qualities she herself appreciated in return.

Still, she fudged with her response, which wasn't a lie at all. "Well, let me put it this way, being a phone sex operator is definitely not my cuppa tea."

"Maybe it all depends on getting the right caller on the phone," he suggested, a mischievous note lacing his low, mellow baritone.

A caller like me, his voice implied. She silently admitted that he had a very valid point.

"What have your clients requested tonight?" he persisted.

Obviously, he saw through her attempt to evade the issue with her simple and pat comment, and he wasn't about to let her off so easily. The rogue. "You don't want to know the nitty-gritty details."

"Sure I do," he murmured huskily, and she shivered at his assertive and very insistent behavior.

The man was ruthless and shameless, and she was smart enough to know he wouldn't let the subject die until he got whatever he wanted from her. And in this case, he wanted her to spill all the provocative details of her new job.

"You promise to still respect me after I tell you the kind of fantasies I fulfilled for other men?"

He chuckled, low and deep, though the sound was oddly strained. "Of course I will."

Exhaling a slow breath, she recalled the fairly tame and normal fantasies she'd performed, because the others were too crude, perverted, and bizarre for her to repeat out loud. "I had a few straightforward calls from men who were just interested in a quick verbal exchange simulating a common sex act. A few requested blow jobs, and one caller asked me to pretend I was a virgin, which was . . . *different*, since it's been a long while since I've been one," she said wryly, and shook her head. "Some callers were downright lewd, and I used words, descriptions, and phrases that would make my parents roll over in their graves."

"I'm sure they forgive you," he said, a definite hint of humor in his voice.

She smiled, and relaxed enough to enjoy their amusing conversation. "Another caller told me that he wanted me to wear something sexy, then do a striptease for him over the phone."

"And what did you wear for him?"

"A slinky, barely-there black dress and high heels. And beneath it, black lace stockings, garters, a skimpy bra, and no panties. Isn't that every man's fantasy?"

"Personally, I prefer red on a woman, but I'm sure you made your caller very happy."

She couldn't stop the silly grin that curved her lips. "Judging by his moans and groans, I think he got his money's worth."

"Undoubtedly." His chuckle warmed her deep inside, as did their fun, playful repartee. "Did any of tonight's calls turn you on?"

His abrupt switch to a more intimate discussion startled her, but she replied without hesitation. "No," she said, and could have sworn she heard him exhale a relieved stream of breath. "I didn't know any of those men, and the exchange was mechanical, detached, and, well, very impersonal." This job and the men she talked to were a means to an end for her, a way of locating information on her cousin, nothing more.

"Then let's see if I can change that and be the one to turn you on tonight."

She suddenly felt hot and anxious with a delicious, undeniable kind of need. Oh, she knew he could accomplish the task of turning her on, far too easily. His silky bedroom voice had already aroused her, making her crave the taste and feel of his mouth on hers, and his slow, knowing hands stroking her bare skin . . . making her body burn and come alive for him with just a touch.

She crossed her ankles and squeezed her thighs together to try and quell the sweet ache of anticipation gathering below. What Steve was proposing didn't include any of that sensual physical contact, just words. Erotic, provocative words and naughty suggestions designed to stimulate and thrill. A fun, illicit mind game that would tantalize and tease both of them. A game she wanted to play with him, because he was ultimately the man she desired and fantasized about.

And unlike her previous callers, the idea of indulging in mental foreplay with Steve excited her.

"Tell me . . . what are you *really* wearing tonight?" he asked.

In reality, she was dressed casually, in nothing quite so daring or indecent as what she'd described to her earlier caller to fulfill his request. She debated whether to come up with another risqué outfit, something red and racy to rev up Steve's libido, but decided she'd forgo any frills when it came to their first foray into phone sex. Their chemistry and attraction was potent enough without adding any extra props.

She touched her fingers to the base of her throat, where her skin was slick with a light sheen of perspiration and her pulse beat erratically. "I'm wearing a light cotton blouse and a miniskirt. I told you it was hot in here, and I've clipped up my hair so it's off my neck, but it's not helping much to keep me cool," she said, giving him a good dose of visual imagery. "The receptionist is selling small handheld water-misting fans to the employees, and she's making a damn good profit at it, too," she grumbled good-naturedly.

His lazy laughter drifted through the phone lines, the sexy vibrations of that masculine sound touching tender, secret places within her.

"I take it you bought one of those fans?" he asked.

"Yeah." Said battery powered minifan was currently sitting on the table, doing its best to create a breeze her way, albeit a warm, recycled one. "Every so often I'll spritz my face, just to keep my skin cool."

"We'll have to think of a way to put that fan to even better use." His voice was positively wicked, impenitently so, and husky with promise. "Open your blouse for me so that I can see your breasts. For real."

His bold command gave her a jolt of momentary confusion, but there was no mistaking what he was asking. He didn't want her to pretend the action, didn't want her to use just verbal description to create a mental picture for him.

He wanted the real thing.

Her heart beat an unsteady rhythm against her chest. While she had absolutely no qualms about getting into his request, actually stripping off her clothes and openly enacting his fantasy was another thing altogether. Besides, he wouldn't even be there to see and enjoy the show.

She moved her legs off the table to the floor, needing the stability of solid ground beneath her feet. "Steve—"

He cut her off before she could issue a protest, obviously hearing the uncertainty in her voice. "Has anyone come in to check on you tonight?"

"No." She glanced at the door, which had remained firmly shut during her shift. No one had so much as poked his or her head inside to see if she was still alive in the small, hot room they'd assigned her to. "They can monitor everything out on the switchboards," she told him.

"Then they aren't about to disturb you, since they can see you're busy with a caller. A very *demanding* caller, and one you don't want to displease." His voice was rough around the edges, just like the man himself. "And since I'm paying for this call, I damn well want to get my money's worth. Now, do as I say and unbutton your blouse."

Under normal circumstances, she would have bristled at such a forceful and dominating command, but she knew his suddenly aggressive nature was all part of the fantasy. Feeling self-conscious, she scanned the bare room for anything in the ceiling or walls that might look suspicious—like a spy camera. Finding nothing, she turned her chair so that she faced the wall opposite the door, then worked to unfasten the first five or six buttons on her blouse. As she exposed the taut swells of her breasts, her midriff, and her abdomen, the thrill of the forbidden kicked up her adrenaline a few notches. Despite her initial reservations about performing such a scandalous act in a place where she could get caught at any moment, she couldn't deny that a small, rebellious part of her welcomed Steve's dare and *liked* the risk she was taking—with him.

She also delighted in the way her flesh quivered where her fingers brushed against her skin as she made her way to the final button. "It's done," she said, hearing the breathless, eager quality of her own voice.

"Pull the front of your bra down so I can see your breasts."

Licking her dry lips, she did as she was told. Peeling the stretchy material down over her voluptuous curves, she released her taut, heavy breasts from the confines of her bra. Her puckered nipples immediately thrust forward, begging to be stroked and fondled. She was tempted to do just that and describe every illicit caress to Steve to enhance the fantasy, but he seemingly had his own sexual agenda in mind.

"Now pull up your skirt so I can see your panties." Once again, his voice demanded obedience.

Standing on unsteady legs, she shimmied her skirt up until the material bunched around her thighs, and her pale pink underwear was in plain sight. She sat back down, grateful that he hadn't asked her to take her panties off, though she felt just as exposed. Unable to resist the lure of Steve's fantasy and the part she was playing, she glanced down at herself, and her face heated at the brazen, wanton display of flesh that greeted her.

He'd turned her into a shameless hussy. And she loved the naughty, uninhibited woman he'd coaxed out of her.

"Are you ready for more?" he asked.

"Yes." Her voice cracked with the truth, and she swallowed in an attempt to clear her throat. *"Yes."*

"Take the fan you bought and spray water on your breasts, belly, and thighs," he murmured. "Then position the fan so the breeze drifts over your wet skin."

Obeying, she shivered as the first fine droplets of water beaded on her hot, naked skin, both refreshing and arousing her to higher level of need, which she was sure was Steve's intent. She continued to mist her way down her body, then set the fan on the table so that an exhilarating draft of air kissed her bared, moist flesh.

Letting her head fall back, she closed her eyes, saturating her mind with the highly electrifying sensations awakening long-dormant desires. "Oh, God, this feels absolutely decadent."

"I wish I were there to see you," he said, his breathing a bit deeper than before. "But since I'm not, I want you to touch yourself and imagine it's my fingers, mouth, and tongue on your skin. Tell me what you feel and how you like to be touched and caressed. Make me a part of your pleasure."

Ignoring the little voice in her head reminding her that she could get caught, she lifted her hand and lightly drifted her fingers along her collarbone and down to the slope of her plump breast, leaving goose bumps in the wake of her slow, insidious touch. "My skin is so hot," she whispered, deliberately using sexually engaging words designed to pull him into the carnal image she was weaving. "Hot and wet and slippery. Can you feel how slick my flesh is?"

"Yeah," he said, his tone low and guttural.

She let her lashes flutter closed again, imagining he was sitting right beside her, his voice in her ear, and his hands on her body instead of her own. "Your long, warm fingers are on my breasts, massaging and squeezing them, and your thumbs are flicking across my rigid nipples, back and forth—"

"My mouth is open and hot on your breasts," he cut in abruptly, reversing their roles and taking over. "My teeth are teasing your nipples, tugging on them, and now my lips are parting, taking you deep, suckling you hard and strong..."

She whimpered, overwhelmed by the heat sizzling through her veins, building higher and hotter and more intense with every erotic word he spoke. She felt the game careening out of her control... and right into *his*.

"Your thighs are so smooth. I'm licking the moisture from your skin and using my tongue to taste my way all the way up to your sex. I can smell your heady scent, your arousal. You want to come, don't you?"

Her thighs trembled. Hunger unfurled inside her like a sweet, insistent ache. Pulsing. Throbbing. Demanding to be appeased. It was nearly too much to withstand. "Steve..."

"Press your fingers to your panties, Liz," he said, his tone allowing no refusal from her. He made her wait long, agonizing seconds before asking, "Are they damp?"

Beneath the panel of cotton, her sex was swollen and she was positively drenched with desire and need, and she told him so. "They're soaked."

"For me?"

"Yes, for you." *No one else.*

"God, you make me rock-hard." His voice was low and

thick, devastatingly aroused and aggressively unrestrained. "Feel how much I want you."

She put herself *there*, with him, and worked up the nerve to be just as bold as he'd been. "I've got your cock in my hand," she told him huskily, "and I'm stroking the rigid length in a firm, steady grip."

"Oh, yeah," he encouraged.

"You feel so hard, so hot and throbbing . . ."

"Yeah, I am. Take me in your mouth," he ordered in a rough, thrilling whisper.

In their private fantasy world, she did, filling his mind with vivid, provocative details of how silky-wet her mouth was as she sucked him . . . faster, stronger, deeper. She could hear his breathing grow ragged, and her own quickened, too.

"Oh, shit . . . *I'm coming.*" His gruff oath rolled into a deep grunt and a harsh, hissing exhale of breath. Then, a long, low groan of satisfaction.

Liz had been so wrapped up in the fantasy, it took her a few extra seconds to resurface from their virtual tryst. The sensual haze clouding her mind dissipated bit by bit as her surroundings came back into focus, reminding her that she wasn't in an intimate setting with Steve but in a small, warm, dingy room—half dressed and excruciatingly aroused.

She found herself both fascinated and miffed that he'd actually climaxed. Or had he? "Did you really . . . ?"

"Yeah, I really did," he muttered. "And I can't begin to tell you how badly I needed that, since I've been walking around with an erection ever since you left my office this afternoon."

She knew exactly how he felt, because her body was still in that tense state of discontent, burning as though she were in the throes of a growing fever.

"By the way, your shift is over."

"Oh." She glanced at her watch and realized it was three minutes after midnight. Surely he wasn't going to leave her so . . . unsatisfied?

"I'll talk to you soon, okay?"

Guess so. She blinked, feeling entirely disappointed and disillusioned by his abrupt farewell after what had just happened between them. "Sure."

Disconnecting the call, she took off her headset and straightened her clothes, unable to believe the rogue had slaked his own lust and left her unsatisfied and completely and totally worked up!

Damn him, anyway, she thought irritably. She tingled all over, every part of her quivering with intemperate need. Blowing out an upward stream of breath that ruffled her bangs, she wondered how she was going to be able to make it all the way home without giving her own body the release it was clamoring for.

She had no choice but to wait, she knew, because she had a feeling it would take more than just one quick self-induced orgasm to satiate the fire smoldering inside her.

Forcing a semblance of calm and double-checking her blouse and skirt to make sure everything was back in order, Liz grabbed her spritz fan and purse and stepped outside her office. The outer hallway was filled with echoing sounds of other operators still servicing customers behind their own closed doors as she made her way back toward the front of the establishment, where Doreen, the night manager, told her to check in after her shift was over.

The front reception area was plush and well furnished, with nicely upholstered chairs, and recognizable artwork hanging on the cream-colored walls. No one who strolled inside the office and took a casual glance around would ever guess what really went on down the hall and behind all those closed doors.

Doreen, a pretty forty-something woman with short brunette hair and a slender figure dressed in designer clothes, sat at the main workstation. A large computer system and a flickering screen gathering caller and employee information seemed to be her primary source of tracking the evening's business.

Behind Doreen, in another partitioned corner of the spacious room, four switchboard operators worked steadily and efficiently to connect calls as they came in, and passed on detailed information and reports to the main network system. Judging by the equipment and latest technology they were using, it was easy to surmise that The Ultimate Fantasy was no rinky-dink company operating on a shoestring budget. No, Antonio and his other partners, whoever they were, took their business very seriously.

Liz came up to the counter, the jingling sound of the keys in her hand catching the other woman's attention. "I'm done for the night."

"Give me a sec to sign you out," Doreen said, and executed a few quick keystrokes on the computer, which prompted another piece of equipment to print out sheets of paper. She gathered the copies and scanned the numerous pages as the machine continued to produce more documents. "For a first-timer, you sure did catch on quick. Nice job on that last call. You had him on the line for over forty minutes."

Liz felt compelled to offer an explanation for that excessively long call. "He was very lonely and just needed someone to talk to."

Doreen laughed and rolled her eyes, her expression one of pure cynicism. "Yeah, every once in a while one of those bleeding-heart types gets suckered in, which helps you make those extra bonuses."

Liz continued to play along and act like an enthusiastic employee. "He promised to call back, so if I'm lucky, I can count on him to fatten my paycheck."

"That you can." Doreen slid one of the papers onto the counter and handed her a pen. "Sign this report and you can be on your way."

Glancing at the document, Liz tried to decipher the various columns, numbers, and information on the statement—one she wasn't about to approve with her signature until she knew exactly what the printout meant. "What's this for?"

"It's a log of your hours, time spent on the phone with a customer, and the last four digits of the client's phone number. Just basic tracking information on our end." She opened a file folder with Liz's name and employee number on the tab. "Once you sign the report, it goes into your personnel file, which then goes to Antonio when he gets in tomorrow morning. He reviews all the statements and transcripts of employee calls before approving payment."

"Transcripts?" A chill slithered down Liz's spine when she thought about her conversation with Steve being copied, which had included mention of Valerie, and way too much familiarity between the two of them before they'd gotten to all the sexy stuff.

Doreen nodded. "All calls are monitored and recorded."

That's illegal, Liz wanted to say, but bit back the response, certain that Doreen wouldn't appreciate her being a stickler for constitutional rights and legalities when the company obviously wasn't. "So, all my calls tonight were recorded?"

"Every one of them."

Liz felt her legs go weak. Why hadn't Steve warned her of such a possibility?

The older woman gathered up the last of the pages that had printed out, and absently glanced through them. "I know it seems a bit unnerving at first, but Antonio insists on reading the transcripts. Don't worry; you'll get used to it, and after a while, you won't even think about big brother listening in."

Dread tightened Liz's chest, and with a sickening feeling in the pit of her stomach, she signed her name to the report and left the building, grateful for the night watchman standing guard outside the building, keeping an eye on the parking lot and watching to make sure she made it to her vehicle without incident.

No sooner had she gotten into her car when her cell phone rang. Frowning, she dug the unit out of her purse, and though she didn't recognize the number on the display, she connected the call, wondering for a hopeful moment if it was Valerie.

"Hello?" she answered anxiously.

"It's me." Steve's deep voice rumbled through the line, infusing her with a combination of disappointment and relief. "I just wanted to make sure you made it to your car safely."

"I'm here now." Sitting in the darkened interior of the vehicle, she stared up to the third floor of the building. The tinting on the windows muted the lighting and gave her brief glimpses of shadowed movements behind the plate glass. "I'm glad you called, because there's something I need to tell you."

"Is everything okay?"

The obvious concern in his tone curled through her and once again made her grateful that she wasn't in on this alone. "I don't know. When my shift was over, Doreen, the night manager, made me sign a statement logging my hours, time spent on the phone with each individual client, and part of their phone number. They also print out transcripts of customer calls, which go to Antonio for him to read and review before approving payment."

"That must be his way of choosing the clients he wants to invite to The Ultimate Fantasy parties."

"I'm sure it is." How could he seem so calm when she felt so frantic? And how could he not understand the implications of their intimate chat tonight? "Steve . . . we talked about Valerie, and our phone call was recorded." Her voice was threaded with both frustration and fear.

"No, it wasn't," he replied matter-of-factly. "I wasn't sure how this business operated, so I took precautions and put a scrambler on my phone."

She exhaled hard. At least *he'd* been thinking on his feet, which was all part of his job, but they could no longer use the protection of a scrambler. "You have to take it off. Especially if the time we spend on the phone and the length and content of our conversations is what determines who Antonio extends invitations to."

"I'll take care of it," he assured her.

As relieved as she was, she couldn't help but ask, "Why didn't you tell me that the calls could be recorded?"

"Because I wanted you to be calm and get some real practice the first night on the job, without censoring yourself. By the way, you were great tonight. Amazing, actually."

The switch in topic reminded her that she was still ticked off at him for being so selfish with her pleasure, the cad. "I'm glad *you* had a good time."

"You didn't?" He sounded genuinely surprised.

Yes, she'd enjoyed their tantalizing conversation, but her body was still buzzing with unquenched need. "Let me put it this way: you came; I didn't."

His low, sexy chuckle only added to her agitation. "Poor baby."

Unable to take any more of his teasing, she decided it was time to end the call. "Good night, Steve," she said sweetly, and not waiting for a reply, she disconnected the line and started her engine.

She drove home with all the windows rolled down, letting the evening breeze tangle through her unclasped hair and help to ease the lust thrumming through her body. Unfortunately, the cool wind on her skin and caressing her bare thighs reminded her too much of her escapade with Steve and the fan he'd turned into an erotic form of foreplay.

She shifted restlessly in her seat, which only served to add an enticing friction to the liquid heat settling between her thighs. Her fingers flexed around the steering wheel—it was apparent she'd have to give herself the orgasms her body craved if she had any intention of getting a good night's sleep tonight.

She turned down her street, and her pulse leaped when she spotted a familiar black Harley-Davidson parked outside her apartment complex. Then she shook her head. No, it couldn't be Steve—she hadn't yet returned the filled-out application with her home address on it.

Yet as she walked toward the apartment she shared with her cousin, she wasn't all that stunned to find a tall, dark, and gorgeous man dressed in black jeans and a leather jacket, leaning impudently by her door, waiting for her. Despite the surge of temptation and, yes, damn him, *excitement* flowing through her, she approached him slowly, tentatively, refusing to rush eagerly into his arms.

His pose was all arrogant, self-assured male, like he had every right to be there. His thick, midnight hair was mussed from his ride over, dark stubble lined his jaw, and his blue eyes were bright and seductive against all that sinful black he wore. His thumbs were hooked into the belt loops on his jeans, and a booted foot was propped against the wall behind him, giving the impression that he didn't have a care in the world.

She knew better than to underestimate that casual stance of his, or his reasons for being there. He was, after all, a dauntless, overly confident bad boy who took what he wanted, when he wanted it.

Just as he had tonight, on the phone.

As she neared, she could sense the latent power he exuded, could feel the raw eroticism of his hot stare as he watched her close the distance between them. Could feel her own body soften and respond instinctively to that intense awareness sizzling between them. By the time she stood next to him, she was breathless and battling the urge to rip off his clothes and have her way with him.

Summoning a bit a defiance to keep from giving in to that favorite fantasy of hers, she lifted her chin and pinned him with a direct look. "How did you know where I live?"

"Where there's a will, there's most definitely a way." Taunting amusement flickered across his features.

And he was a PI, trained in tracking people and digging up secrets. "What are you doing here?"

A lazy, seductive grin curved his lips. "Sweetheart, I don't think this is a conversation you want to have out here, where your neighbors might overhear."

She ignored the warning note threading his voice, unwilling to make any of this easy on him. "And you're not getting inside until you tell me why you're here."

"I think we both know the answer to that question," he said, and leaned in so close, his warm breath fanned her neck and his lips brushed the lobe of her ear. His damp tongue added to the shivery sensations, and he added in a rough, wicked whisper, "But just in case you have any doubts in that pretty head of yours, I'm here to fuck you."

Chapter

4

Steve heard Liz suck in a quick breath, and watched her eyes widen at his blatant and earthy declaration of what he wanted to do to her. He wouldn't apologize for his outrageous behavior, nor did he intend to back down from the statement he'd just issued.

He deliberately meant to startle Liz, shock her even, and he expected her reaction to go one of two ways. If he'd offended her, she'd probably slap him or turn him down flat, and he'd know he'd stepped beyond her comfort zone. If she was daring enough to join him in a more erotic, forbidden world of pleasure that included unrefined, primitive sex, then she'd welcome him inside her place and they'd indulge those carnal fantasies, and more, together.

Now that the time had come to take that next step, he needed to know she was game for everything uninhibited and unadulterated. He wanted to be assured that she was a match for his sexual appetite and a willing partner to his aggressive, more dominant nature when it came to sex. He liked his encounters hot and vigorous, and what he had in mind beyond that closed door was not gentle, polite, or altogether civilized by most women's standards.

Her answer would be the determinating factor of whether he kept their affair tame and within the confines of conventional sex or she granted him permission to allow his inner wild man loose with her.

Few women had.

He lifted a dark brow. "Well?" he prompted.

Her expression gave none of what she was thinking or feeling away. "Let me put it this way. If you weren't here to fuck me, I'd be pretty pissed after the way you left me hanging tonight."

Oh, yeah, the woman definitely had spunk, and that turned him on even more. "Touché."

He plucked her apartment key from her lifeless fingers, and when she didn't object to his take-charge attitude, he opened her door and swept a courteous hand inside the darkened entryway. "After you."

Once they were both in her apartment and Steve had the door shut and locked behind them, that was where his gentlemanly manners ended. Taking advantage of the first hard surface they came into contact with, he maneuvered her up against the living room wall and pinned her in place with his big body, wanting complete control of tonight's seduction— and Liz's surrender. He dropped her keys to the floor, along with her purse and that small fan she'd told him about over the phone, which intrigued him with all the possibilities inherent in that little toy.

With one arm braced on the wall next to her head, and a dim light from the kitchen illuminating them, he held her gaze and slowly, gradually freed the buttons on her blouse with his other hand. "Did you think I was going to leave you on edge all night long?"

Mild accusation glimmered in her gaze. "That's what you wanted me to think, wasn't it?"

He dipped his head and nuzzled her neck, mostly to hide a smile at her accurate guess, though he wasn't about to admit that she was right. No, it was more fun sparring with her, and he liked her fearless, rebellious attitude, which would make her acquiescence all the sweeter.

"Only a cad would be so insensitive," he replied playfully. Done opening her blouse, he pushed a sleeve and bra strap over one shoulder, tenderly kissed the flesh he bared, and felt her shiver in response.

Her hands fluttered between them, finding her way into his leather jacket and tugging the hem of his shirt from his jeans. "Funny, that's exactly what I thought of you after we hung up."

He laughed, low and deep. "I guess I'll just have to do my best to redeem myself after being so greedy and leaving you so hungry."

"You're going to have to work hard for my forgiveness," she said brazenly, though there was no mistaking the provocation in her tone.

"Oh, I plan to." He brushed his fingers over the swells of her breasts and watched them quiver from his touch. "The thing is, if I hadn't come earlier, I wouldn't have been able to go this slow with you now. Think of it this way. Our earlier phone sex was merely an appetizer for me, and you need to catch up before we get to the main course."

A blond brow arched humorously. "That's quite an analogy."

He shrugged. "I needed that release so I can concentrate on giving you what you need now." Leisurely he drifted his fingers to the hard points of her nipples, straining against her sheer bra, and pinched the engorged tips gently, just enough to give her a taste of what was to come. "And what I plan to do to you is much more effective and pleasurable in person. And I can take my time doing it, too."

As much as he'd enjoyed sharing fantasies earlier, their phone sex hadn't been enough for him, despite what he'd gained from the encounter. He was a man who ultimately needed a physical connection when it came to sex. He needed to feel Liz's soft curves against him, taste her skin, hear her moans, and feel her hands on his body, too. *Eventually.*

Her eyes shone bright with hot anticipation and female invitation. "Who says I want slow?" she asked, all sultry, seductive temptress.

He recognized her taunting for what it was, but wasn't about to let her take charge this early in the game, if at all. "I'm not giving you a choice, sweetheart. Not this time, because I've thought about this moment since the first time I laid eyes on you at the café. Of stripping you naked, seeing your breasts bared, and watching you come, again and again."

She looked up at him through lashes that had fallen to half-mast. "Considering how you left me earlier, I don't think *coming* is going to be a problem."

He groaned at the thought of all that pent-up passion just waiting to be unleashed. "Once I'm done with you, I think you'll forgive me for being so selfish earlier."

"We'll see," she taunted once again.

She reached out, and the muscles in his stomach flexed and rippled as her cool, slender fingers caressed the heated skin of his belly. Knowing he'd never last as long as he intended to with her hands all over him, he dragged the other sleeve and bra strap down her arm, just past her elbows. The stretchy lace material covering her breasts lowered, too, and his mouth watered at the bountiful flesh he'd exposed—ripe, full breasts that begged for the touch of his fingers, the wet rasp of his tongue, the slow, heated suction of his mouth . . .

Summoning patience, he quickly and efficiently used Liz's bra straps as makeshift ties by wrapping the corded material and the loose ends of her blouse around her wrists. Before she realized what he was doing, he had her hands tethered and fastened, and the excess fabric of her top secured into a knot just below her breasts, which effectively pinned her arms to her sides and restricted her reach.

She tugged on the bindings, her expression reflecting bemusement that he'd so easily managed to restrain her with her own clothes—leaving her physically vulnerable and sexually defenseless. "My . . . aren't you clever," she murmured.

"I'm a very resourceful kind of guy. I said *slow*, and I meant it, and tying you up assures me that I've got your full cooperation and I can do as I please with you." He took a small step back, giving himself just enough room to reach down, slip his hands beneath her skirt, and shove the hem up around her waist. Unable to help himself, he skimmed his palms around to her backside and squeezed her buttocks, liking how soft and giving her body was—*everywhere.*

She gasped, the sound filled with surprise—and excitement, too. "Now what are you doing?"

"Feeling you up," he said with a grin, then took in his handiwork, pleased with the effect he'd created. Half dressed and trussed up in the bondage he'd devised, she looked deliciously sensual with her breasts swelling, nipples stiff and dark, and her honey-blond hair tousled around her pale shoulders and beautiful face.

Her legs were long, her thighs gently curved—the kind that could cradle a man's hips in infinite softness as he thrust hard and deep. He'd left her panties on—mainly to save his own sanity, but those would be gone just as soon as he took care of other matters first.

Shrugging out of his jacket, he tossed it onto a nearby chair that was part of a dinette set, then unbuckled the shoulder holster he wore. He carefully laid his weapon on the table, then stripped out of his black T-shirt and added it to the pile.

"This is *so* not fair," she complained huskily, her eyes glazing with desire as she watched him undress. "I want to touch, too."

It was nice to know that she liked what she saw. "I never said I play fair." He strolled back to where she was still leaning up against the wall. His cock pulsed, already hard and aching for her. Again. "But maybe, if you're a good girl, I'll let you play later."

Her appreciative gaze traveled over his well-defined chest; then she eyed the tattoo encircling his right biceps, with undisguised interest. "I like your tattoo. Any special meaning to it?"

Not one he wanted to discuss at the moment. He'd gotten the tattoo right after his divorce years ago, as a symbol of his newfound freedom and bachelor lifestyle, and to cover up the scar the bullet had left on his arm. Yet despite the rebellious act, he'd been compelled to weave a name within the intricate design, of the one and only female who would ever be permanently linked to his heart. And he didn't want to discuss that with Liz, either.

He smiled lazily. "It's just a plain ol' tribal band."

Her fingers flexed at her sides, as if she wanted to reach out and touch the etched design. "It makes you look tough and dangerous."

"I *am* tough and dangerous." His attempt at being serious was lost in the light laughter vibrating in his tone.

"Of course you are," she agreed generously, though it was obvious to him that she wasn't intimidated by him at all. At least not in a malicious sort of way. Sexually, however, he was feeling very aggressive and intense.

She licked her lips, leaving them damp and shiny, beckoning for him to nibble and taste. "All that toughness and danger turns me on, and that tattoo makes me hot."

She was deliberately provoking him, he knew. "We can't have you burning up on me, now, can we?" Inspired by their earlier fantasy on the phone, he picked up the spritz fan and switched the small unit on, sending a cool gust of air across her skin.

Her nipples automatically puckered and darkened to a deep raspberry hue, and her luminous eyes widened in astonishment . . . and realization. "Steve . . ."

Dismissing the mild protest he heard in her voice, he pulled the trigger and sprayed a fine mist of water on her throat and breasts, then did the same to her bare belly and naked thighs.

Her entire body trembled, and her breathing deepened as he stared at her wet skin and lush body, fascinated at the way the dewy moisture gathered in places and slowly trickled downward like a soft, drizzling rain.

God, he'd never seen anything so sexy, so mouthwateringly tempting as the delectable feast she presented. Then again, she was the first woman to allow him complete trust with her body and so much control over her pleasure. And that in itself was a huge turn-on for him. Undoubtedly, Liz was a pure, reckless addiction to his senses, and like a junkie, he intended to get his fill of her.

Aching to caress all that slick, glistening flesh while she remained helplessly bound, he set the fan aside and flattened his palm around the curve of her throat and followed the slick path down to an enticing amount of cleavage. His hands captured her breasts, encircling them with long, possessive fingers and gliding his thumbs across her rigid nipples before he continued on with his lazy journey . . . skimming his palms across her quivering belly and down to her smooth, sleek thighs. Thighs he couldn't wait to feel wrapped tight around his waist.

Liz moaned, giving herself over to the delightful feel of Steve's hot, questing hands sliding along her deprived body, bringing feminine nerve endings to vibrant life and arousing her to the point of dizzying torment. His fingers gradually trailed their way back up her sides, tracing the dip and swell of her hips and waist, stroking the outline of her pale breasts; then finally his hands came to rest on the wall behind her, surrounding her with the male scent of him, the virile power and heat he emanated.

She whimpered at the momentary loss of contact, but he didn't make her suffer long. By slow, agonizing degrees, he closed the scant distance separating their bodies until the hard, masculine contours of his broad chest crushed against her sensitive breasts. Their bare bellies touched, skin searing skin, as he pinned her hips and thighs to the wall, leaving her no escape.

Their eyes met in the shadowed darkness, and there was no mistaking the hard, solid length of his erection jutting against her mound. He rolled his hips, letting her feel the full effect of that massive ridge, and she reacted with a low, purring sound she was helpless to hold back.

"You like that?" he murmured.

She widened her stance and arched toward him, silently seeking more. "Oh, yes," she whispered anxiously, frustrated at his slow, mindless seduction and her inability to use her hands to take what she wanted.

"Then I think you'll like this, too." Lowering his head, he brushed his mouth across hers, his breath warm and scented with mint. When he slid his silky tongue against her lower lip, she opened her mouth and eagerly let him inside. He deepened the kiss, voracious and hungry, and she answered, sliding her body sensually against his in a rhythm that matched the thrust of his tongue.

One of his hands grasped her gyrating hip while the other slipped over her panty-clad bottom, past her thigh, and hooked his long fingers behind her knee. He lifted her leg up to his waist, wedged his thigh tight between hers, and pressed his groin to her sex, urging her to feel him, all of him.

Every single hard inch.

The overwhelming pressure of his stiff male shaft rubbing against her intimate flesh, along with the friction of coarse denim stroking wet cotton, all combined to give her body the climax it had been craving for hours. Days. Weeks.

Sensations as exquisite as they were intense rippled through her in undulating waves of passion, beckoning her to let go. Curling her fingers into tight fists at her sides, she continued to move sinuously on his muscular thigh until her entire body began to shake. Tearing her mouth from his, she finally took her pleasure with a soft, keening cry of release.

If Steve hadn't had her pinned to the wall with his powerful body, she would have sunk to the ground in a boneless heap.

He nuzzled his way along her neck with soft, damp kisses until his mouth reached her ear. "Do you want more?"

"Yes," she said breathlessly, uncaring that she sounded greedy. It had been so long, and the orgasm had felt so good, but she knew once wasn't going to be nearly enough. Not if he was offering more. "But not like this. Untie me."

"Not yet."

Their bodies separated only long enough for Steve to unzip the skirt still twisted around her hips and yank that article of clothing and her panties ruthlessly down her legs and off, leaving only her blouse and bra knotted around her waist, which provided no covering at all. His eyes flickered appreciatively down the length of her bared body, still damp in places from the water he'd spritzed onto her skin, making her unbearably aware of her wanton appearance.

"This is one of *my* fantasies," he murmured, his burning gaze coming to a halt at the crux of her thighs. "Having you at my complete mercy."

And she was. He could do absolutely anything he wanted to her . . . and she knew she'd let him.

Lifting a hand, he glided one long finger through the thatch of blond hair covering her mons and traced the line between her delicate nether lips—a soft butterfly stroke that made her tremble all over again. She moaned and jutted her hips eagerly toward him, and he rewarded her with another brush of his fingertip, just enough to tease but not appease the renewed hunger building within her.

Her sex felt swollen, slick with her own desire, and his illicit caress was driving her mad. She rolled her head back against the wall, willing to beg for what she yearned for. "Steve . . . *please.*"

He rested his forearm next to her head, bringing her face to face with his bold, masculine features even as he lazily continued exploring the silken textures of her female flesh. She could see the restrained arousal blazing in his bright blue eyes, could feel his chest graze her aching breasts with each deep breath he drew.

He inclined his head impudently, giving her the impression that he could go on touching her just like this for hours. "Please, *what?*"

She licked her dry lips. "You promised me more."

His smile was full of sinful intent. "Umm. So I did."

He didn't give her what she expected—another quick, blinding orgasm. No, instead he lowered his gaze to the bountiful display of flesh he'd yet to pleasure. Her breasts grew tight in anticipation, her nipples puckering so hard they were almost painful.

Dipping his head, he rubbed his cheek against that pillowy softness, his dark, midnight stubble rasping deliciously across the tender tips. When his lips brushed across one of those beaded knots of flesh, she nearly wept with relief. His tongue lapped and swirled until he finally drew a nipple into his hot, wet mouth and suckled her. At the same time he pushed a finger deep inside her, and she gasped at the unexpected invasion. Before she could recover from that sensual assault, his teeth gently tugged at her nipple and he added a second finger, stretching her to accommodate him, making her whimper at the dual sensations he'd inflicted upon her.

Her mind slid into a long, slow spin, yet her entire body tensed when she felt him work the tip of a third finger into her. "Stop," she panted. "No more."

He immediately heeded her request but didn't remove the first two fingers still embedded deep within her. "You're so damn tight," he groaned against her breast.

She managed a burst of hoarse laughter. "I think it's a combination of it being a long time for me, and you having very big hands and long, thick fingers."

"Yeah, I do." He nipped at the underside of her jaw and laved his tongue down her throat. "And if you feel this snug with two fingers, then my cock is in for a real tight fit."

The image brought another rush of moisture spiraling down to her core, along with a tingling warmth right where he'd delved the pad of his thumb against the hood of her sex. The steady pressure was agonizing, and she knew she'd have to ask for what she wanted, what she *needed*. "Steve . . . make me *come.*"

He obliged her, stroking her with a knowing touch. That easily, he sent her over the edge again, her insides clenching in a deep, wrenching throb of pleasure. Before she fully recovered from that climax, before she had a chance to catch her breath and regain her equilibrium, Steve was on his knees in front of her, his dark hair an erotic contrast to her lightly tanned skin.

The tribal band encircling his upper arm flexed as he splayed his hands on her quivering thighs and pushed them farther apart, giving her no choice but to obey his command. His palms slid upward, and he used his thumbs to open her wide, to expose the tender nub of flesh hidden between her legs.

He groaned like a dying man and leaned in closer, inhaling deeply. His unshaven cheek chafed her thigh, and his breath gusted over her sex just before he tasted her with a long, slow lick. The air in her lungs felt trapped, and when he used his lush tongue to push delicately inside her, all she could manage was a whimper of sound. He leisurely slipped in and out of her feminine folds, leaving wet, burning trails in the wake of his languorous and very intimate French kiss.

He found her pulsing clit, and his tongue circled it with wet flicks and slow, suctioning swirls, accelerating her heart rate off the charts. Then his lips closed over her, and he took her eagerly, hotly, greedily, sending her over the razor-sharp edge of another orgasm.

She braced herself for another wild ride, and this time she came with a white-hot burst of passion that made her hips buck and her back arch away from the wall. Unable to stand being constrained by her blouse any longer, she tugged, hard, and loosened the tie around her waist. Another fierce yank, and the material completely unraveled, making her realize that she could have freed herself at any time.

Threading her fingers through Steve's hair, she grasped the strands in her fist and pulled his mouth away. "Oh, God, no more," she uttered on a long, shuddering breath. *"Please."*

He laughed huskily and leaned forward to nip at her soft belly. "We'll see," he said, mocking her with the same words she'd spoken earlier.

She pulled his head back before he could distract her again, forcing him to look up at *her,* instead of her naked body, though his gaze did stray to her breasts. His eyes were dark and fevered with desire, his lips damp with her essence, and in his subservient kneeling position, he looked like a slave worshiping his mistress.

A tiny thrill shot through her. Standing above him, and currently the one in control, she realized she sort of liked being on the dominant end of things.

"Are you threatening me with another orgasm?" Her tone was playfully imperious.

"Baby," he rasped, a shameless, bad-boy grin making an appearance, "I'd say it's more of a promise. I'm not done with you yet."

In one fluid, agile movement, he stood, his muscles shifting as he straightened. In another flash, he hefted her over his shoulder and had her dangling upside down with her bottom in the air and his strong arms wrapped around her thighs— proving to her who was really the master in this scenario.

"Where's your bedroom?" he demanded as he headed through the small living room and toward the darkened hallway.

"The first room on the left," she said, and seconds later he unceremoniously flipped her onto her back in the middle of her double-size mattress.

The room was dark with shadows, and the sound of him releasing the leather strap from his belt buckle sent a frisson of excitement unfurling in her belly. Wanting to see that magnificent body of his completely naked, she reached over to the side of the bed and snapped on the small lamp on the nightstand, illuminating the room in an incandescent glow.

She'd been running late this morning and hadn't made her bed, and the rumpled sheets felt wonderfully cool and crisp against her backside as she reclined against the pillows. She watched Steve remove a few foil packets from his pocket and toss them on the bed before ripping open the front of his jeans. He skinned the denim and his briefs down his legs and kicked them off, then straightened, giving her the first full-frontal view of him.

Completely, unabashedly nude and all hot and aroused for her, he stole her breath in a way no man ever had.

Her fantasies of this particular bad boy didn't compare to the real thing. She knew he had broad shoulders, but they appeared so much wider in comparison to his lean waist and narrow hips. And then there was that tattoo on his biceps that she found so fascinating, a mark of a rebel who seemed to live by his own rules and did whatever he pleased. The man *was* tough and virile, from the dark stubble of his beard to the intense look in his eyes, to the hard, square set of his jaw. Everything about Steve Wilde was powerfully, incredibly male.

She took in the light dusting of hair on his chest, followed the narrowing path down to his rippled belly, and lower, to the most prominent, impressive part of him. She swallowed hard. His thoroughly erect cock was parallel to his stomach, pointing straight up to his navel, impossibly long and hard and thick.

"Spread your legs for me," he ordered gruffly.

As she parted her thighs to make room for him, he grabbed one of the condoms, tore open the package with his teeth, and rolled the latex down his shaft. Sheer, primal lust shimmered off him in waves; she could detect his need in his quick, efficient movements and witnessed the hunger in his eyes as he swept a heated look up the length of her.

A muscle in his cheek clenched in barely controlled restraint, and his nostrils flared like an animal scenting his mate. "You do realize that this first time isn't going to be slow and gentle, don't you?"

There was a subtle warning in his tone, and while she appreciated the chance he was giving her to say no, he'd already given her *slow*. What she needed now was something just as untamed and uninhibited as he was suggesting. "I know."

From the foot of the bed, he crawled up onto the mattress and knelt between her legs. Hooking his fingers beneath her knees, he dragged her toward him until her widened thighs were draped over his and her pelvis was tipped up in offering. He eased over her, using his thighs to push hers up higher on his waist, which also effectively trapped her beneath the weight of his body. His forearms came to rest next to her face, and he shifted his hips, lodging the thick head of his penis against her very core.

Staring into her eyes, he pushed into her an inch, letting her feel the size of him, teasing her with the promise of more. "Once I'm inside you, it's gonna be hot, hard, and fast." His voice deepened into a rough growl.

She touched her fingers to the stubble along his jaw, the prickling sensation heightening her arousal. "I'm ready for that," she said huskily. "I'm ready for *you*."

"Then take me. *All* of me." He plunged into her, strong and deep, impaling her to the hilt with that first unbridled thrust.

Despite being primed for him, she sucked in a startled breath as her inner muscles clamped tight around his shaft.

His eyes flared wide in response, giving her a brief glimpse of passion, heat, and something else warring in their hot blue depths. Before she could analyze that last emotion, before she could dwell on the initial discomfort of being thoroughly consumed by him, he began to move, his body undulating and grinding against hers as he increased his rhythmic pace.

A low, throaty, on-the-edge moan escaped him, and he crushed his mouth to hers, kissing her with a desperate, fierce passion that caught her off guard. His tongue swept into her mouth, matching the rapid, pistoning stroke of his hips and the slick, penetrating slide of his flesh in hers.

Tremors radiated through her from the sensitive spot where they were joined so intimately. She felt thoroughly possessed by him, body and soul, in a way that defied their impersonal bargain and the simplicity of an affair. In a way that aroused feelings that had no business being a part of this temporary relationship.

Pushing those thoughts from her mind, she concentrated on the pleasure he gave her, and how alive he made her body feel. Running her hands down the slope of his spine, she curved her fingers over his taut buttocks and locked her legs around his waist to pull him closer, deeper, and abandoned herself to yet another stunning orgasm.

This time, he was right there with her when she reached the peak of her climax. Groaning, he broke their kiss and tossed his head back, his hips driving hard, his body tightening, straining against hers.

"*Liz.*" Her name hissed out between his clenched teeth as his body convulsed with the force of his release.

When the shudders subsided, Steve lowered himself on top of her and buried his face against her throat. His ragged breathing was hot and moist against her skin, his heart racing just as unsteadily as her own.

A smile drifted across her lips as she trailed her fingers back up his spine, all the way to the damp, silky tendrils of hair at the nape of his neck, savoring the delightful feel of him inside her, draped over her. She'd never felt so utterly satisfied, so sexually, physically content.

Undoubtedly, Steve Wilde was a fantasy worth waiting for, in every way. One she planned to take advantage of until their time together was over.

Chapter

5

Steve slipped back into Liz's bed after a quick trip to the bathroom, ignoring the little voice in his head that told him he ought to get dressed and go. It was late, and he didn't make it a habit of spending the night with the women he dated. Too many expectations were assumed from that particular intimacy, and actually *sleeping* with a woman meant taking the relationship to a whole new level. One that included lazy morning sex, shared showers, and breakfast together. It was a set of emotional complications he'd avoided since his divorce, and he'd never had any desire to break those personal rules of his.

Tonight he was sorely tempted. Liz was the first woman he'd been with in all those years who made him wonder what it would be like to wake up spooning himself against her soft, giving body, to start the morning with slow, leisurely lovemaking. To eat breakfast in bed with her and join her in a fun, playful shower before heading off to work—with his mind and body rejuvenated and a big smile on his face.

The notion beckoned to him, strong and undeniable. Damn. He *would* leave . . . in just a few minutes.

With a soft, replete sigh, she turned her head his way, her eyes dreamy as they met his. A mellow smile lifted her lips, which were pink and puffy from his aggressive kisses, and he responded with a lazy, knowing grin of his own.

She'd pulled the sheet up to her chest in the few minutes he'd been gone, in an attempt at modesty, which he found extremely amusing after everything they'd done and how brazen she'd been. But he could still see the outline of her breasts and nipples and the enticing swell of her hip against the thin covering. Her skin was flushed with warmth and ravishment, and her blond hair was tousled around her head and against her pillow in a soft cloud of silk.

She looked beautiful, besotted, and blissfully sated. Like a woman well and thoroughly *fucked*.

His cock twitched and tightened in renewed heat and awareness. He wanted her again, which was unbelievable since, just minutes ago, he'd felt wrung dry. Then again, just remembering how hungry and insatiable she'd been—so needy—was enough to energize any red-blooded guy for another go-around with someone so sexy and uninhibited. Fortunately, she was all his, as was all that wild, tempestuous passion of hers. She'd showed him tonight that he could do anything he wanted to her, that she was eager and willing to explore dark desires and forbidden fantasies.

Which was a good thing, since he had plenty in mind.

Not bothering to cover up his own nudity, he stretched out on his side, propped his head in his hand, and asked the one question that had him very curious: "How long has it been for you?"

She groaned and winced, and glanced up at the ceiling in an attempt to hide her embarrassment. "God, was I that obvious?"

He chuckled, finding her chagrin too endearing in the aftermath of such wild, hot sex. "Maybe just a little," he teased, and gently touched a finger to her chin to make her look at him again. "You were very enthusiastic—not that I'm complaining, since I reaped the benefits of all that pent-up desire."

She grinned wryly. "Sexual frustration will do that to a person."

"Trust me; I know. I've been feeling that same way myself since I first laid eyes on you," he said meaningfully—a month in which he'd lusted after her, and no other woman would do. Despite all those restless, erotic dreams that had left him hot and bothered and moody at times, Liz had been well worth the wait. "Now, fess up."

Her fingers absently bunched and pleated the sheet between her breasts. "You really don't want to know," she murmured.

"Sweetheart, if I didn't want to know, I wouldn't ask." He meant that sincerely. "So what are we talking here? One year? Two years?" he guessed.

"Almost three years," she admitted with a slight grimace. "Since my husband died."

That revelation raised his brows. "Wow," he said, stunned that she'd denied herself that long. Stunned that no other man had persuaded her into bed sooner.

Picking up her left hand, he ran his thumb over the gold band she wore. A treasure that had once belonged to her mother. "Then I guess this ring did its job."

She laughed, her eyes sparkling with agreement. "Until now, anyway." Then she shrugged and grew a bit more serious. "I suppose it was just a matter of waiting for the right guy to come along to sway me into an affair—that, along with the right set of circumstances."

And their circumstances had been ideal. "All I can say is, lucky me." He rubbed her soft, cool fingers along the light beard growth on his cheek and watched her nipples blossom and bead against the sheet. "But three years is a hell of a long time to be off the market. I understand grieving after your husband died, but why would you want men to think you're taken for so many years?"

He expected her to tell him that her husband had been her one true love, that she hadn't been able to bring herself to date after his death, because she'd been too devastated and it had taken her time to get past her feelings for him. It was the most logical explanation.

"Dating and men just haven't been a priority for me, not when I have The Daily Grind, which has demanded a whole lot of my time over the past three years." She gently pulled her hand out of his grasp, and though he felt her physically withdrawing from him and the conversation, he let her go.

Her answer surprised him. Her reply was convenient, too pat and evasive for a woman who'd gone to such lengths to give the impression that she was taken. He instinctively knew there was more to her reasons for remaining single. He'd heard the feigned nonchalance in her tone, which contradicted the sudden defensive tilt to her chin that told him he was traversing on deeply personal issues.

And because he was a man who liked puzzles and unraveling mysteries, he persisted. "Women run businesses of their own and date all the time. Some are even married with families."

"I'm sure those women weren't left in debt up to their eyeballs by a man they thought they knew and trusted."

He didn't miss the underlying bite to her tone, which did nothing to deter him. "Your husband?"

"Yes." She shook her head and blew an upward stream of breath that ruffled her bangs across her brow. "I can't believe we're having this conversation."

Neither could he, since he wasn't one to indulge in cozy, intimate chitchat and personal revelations after sex. But now that it was out in the open, he was intent on discovering the real story behind that ring encircling her finger, and a past that had obviously kept her celibate for an amazingly long time.

Slipping his leg beneath the covers, he found her calf and casually caressed her smooth skin with his toes. "What happened?"

She rolled to her side, facing him less than a foot away, and exhaled a slow, unraveling breath. "I was naive and fell for a reckless, untamable charmer who knew how to say all the right things to sweep a woman off her feet, and he did exactly that."

He tucked a strand of hair behind her ear that had fallen across her cheek, accepting the excuse to touch her for what it was. "You certainly don't strike me as naive." Not when it came to life *or* men.

"Okay, then I was a blind fool." Self-recriminations laced her voice. "Travis's impulsive, frivolous ways were so invigorating compared to my sensible, practical life, and he gave me something to look forward to at the end of all the hours I was working at the café. He was daring and adventurous, and that made me feel a sense of freedom that was new and exciting and addicting. So when he asked me to marry him after three months of dating, I said yes and we did the deed in a quickie civil ceremony that my aunt and uncle found out about after the fact." A noticeable wince creased her features.

He resisted the urge to smooth out those disturbing wrinkles with his thumb, a comforting gesture that took him off guard. "I take it they weren't happy about not being invited to the wedding?"

"They weren't happy about the marriage, period. Or Travis as a husband. They'd never really liked him." She yawned as the late hour, her long day, and physical exhaustion began taking its toll. "I had a huge argument with my aunt and uncle, my first ever yelling, screaming match with them, as I defended Travis and my right to marry who I wanted."

Her voice dropped in volume, the regret she harbored unmistakable. "In hindsight, they had good reason not to trust my judgement when it came to Travis, because they saw deeper than just the surface of a good-looking face and flirtatious smile. They saw his charming personality for what it was—a way to get what he wanted."

"And he wanted you?"

She nodded. "It seemed so, maybe because I was so eager to please, and yes, even naive when it came to men who were so good at deceiving women. He definitely conned me."

"How?" Another nudge to get her to spill more.

"Within the first six months of our marriage, after the honeymoon stage wore off, I started to see a different side to him, too. A selfish, self-centered, arrogant side he didn't bother to hide. During our two-year marriage, he couldn't hold down a job. I pretty much supported both of us while trying to get The Daily Grind to the point where it was solvent and making a profit. I'd started the business with a loan from my aunt and uncle, and a small-business loan from the bank, so there was a good chunk of money going out in repayment. And since I spent a lot of time at the café—over twelve hours a day—it gave Travis a whole lot of time to play."

Steve experienced a surge of anger on her behalf. "Sounds like he should have at least been at the café helping you out."

"Oh, he always had an excuse why he couldn't be there," she said with a bitter laugh. "His best one was that he had job interviews lined up, but none of them ever seemed to pan out. If I questioned him, we'd get in a big fight. Sometimes he'd storm out after accusing me of not trusting him and leave for a few days. And when he returned, he wouldn't tell me where he'd been, just that he needed time to cool off. After a while, I just couldn't take it anymore."

It wasn't difficult to figure out where the marriage had been heading. "You filed for divorce?"

"I never had the chance," she rasped, a flicker of pain passing through her gaze. "The night I intended to ask for a divorce and tell him to pack his bags and find another place to live, he wrapped his sports car around a telephone pole, going over eighty miles per hour, and was instantly killed because he wasn't wearing a seat belt. He was with a woman that also died on impact, who I later discovered he'd been having an affair with."

His chest squeezed tight. What in the world did he say to the terrible betrayal she'd endured? He felt out of his element, and shocked as hell at what she'd been through.

"See what I mean by *naive?*" She didn't wait for him to answer or refute her claim, obviously believing it was true. "And if that mess wasn't humiliating enough, within a month of his death, I started receiving all these credit card bills in the mail that he'd applied for under both of our names but had kept from me. He'd bought jewelry and meals at fancy restaurants I'd never eaten with him, and he stayed in some pretty fine hotels the nights he didn't sleep at home. He paid the minimum payment on the credit cards while purchasing tons of stuff for his girlfriend, from furniture to clothes to a five-thousand-dollar stereo system he'd obviously enjoyed while he stayed at her place. To my horror, I realized that *I* was now tens of thousands of dollars in debt because everything was in my name, too."

She lifted her left hand and wiggled her fingers, letting the lamplight glimmer off the shiny band. "Which brings us back to this ring I wear, and three years without sex," she said humorously, as if she hadn't just given him a very private glimpse into her past, and possibly even a part of her soul. "In a nutshell, I've been working my butt off to pay off all those creditors and make sure I don't lose my business in the process. And then there's the money my aunt and uncle loaned me as part of my investment that I haven't paid in full yet, either, since I had to cut back on their monthly payments in order to meet my obligations with those credit cards that I'm still trying to pay off."

Now he understood her desperation in accepting his cut-rate fee in exchange for his help in finding her cousin, as well as her insistence on signing her paycheck over to him so he wouldn't be one of those debts hanging over her head. Their deal was temporary the whole way around, yet he'd never expected to be so intrigued by Liz beyond anything sexual.

While she'd been an unabashed vixen an hour ago, this strong yet vulnerable facet to her appealed to him, too. She was so determined not to depend on anyone to get her out of the mess she'd gotten herself into with her deceased husband, and now she was taking on the responsibility of finding Valerie, too.

"Dating and men are a distraction I haven't been able to afford the past three years," she said, bringing his mind and attention back to her.

"And I am?"

"You, Mr. Wilde, are a very exciting fling that came around at an opportune time." Smiling drowsily, she brushed her fingers along the tribal band on his arm. "I know exactly where we stand with one another. Neither of us wants anything long-term or complicated, so our arrangement is perfect."

She was offering him the kind of reassurances and rules he would have demanded from any other woman, yet his jaw clenched in denial, his reaction knee-jerk and unexpected. But Liz was right about them, and he'd do well to remember the boundaries of their temporary relationship. Which meant ending their night together and leaving—now.

"I'd better get going," he said abruptly. "You're about to fall asleep on me, and I've got an early day at the office tomorrow. I plan to talk to a few people I know with some connections and see if I can get anything on the inside track of The Ultimate Fantasy." Moving off the bed, he pulled on his briefs and jeans. The rest of his clothes were still in the living room.

"I'll walk you to the door so I can lock up after you." Sliding off her side of the mattress, she grabbed the worn and faded cotton robe tossed on a nearby dresser. "I also have that application filled out with Valerie's personal information, or as much of it as I could find when I went digging through her bills. There's some bank and credit card numbers I pulled from statements, along with her social security number and mother's maiden name, just in case you need any of that to check her accounts."

"That's great. Every little bit will help." He caught one last quick glimpse of her sweet curves before she slipped into the thigh-length cover-up and tied the sash around her waist. "It's amazing how one little detail can lead to something substantial."

She headed out of the bedroom. He followed her back to the entryway, his eyes drawn to the gentle sway of her hips as she walked, his senses filling with the scent of soft, sexy woman.

She waited quietly while he yanked his T-shirt over his head, secured his weapon and holster back in place, and shrugged into his leather jacket. She watched him avidly, with sensual green eyes that seemed to eat him up. When he finished getting dressed, she handed him the application, which he glanced at briefly before folding the paper and tucking it into his pocket.

She started past him to open the door, but before she could execute the move, he gave in to the urge to catch her in his arms and lowered his mouth to hers, open and seeking. Like a woman in sync with her lover's demands, she wrapped her hands around his neck and responded enthusiastically, without hesitation. Her luscious body melted into his embrace, and she returned the sensual kiss with abandon, telling him without words that she wouldn't mind if he stayed.

He was unable to suppress a deep groan. Everything male about him acknowledged that she was naked beneath that flimsy robe she wore, that it was just a matter of unzipping his fly, pressing her up against the nearest wall, and sinking right back into her tight, lush body and losing himself once again in her dampness and heat.

God, if he didn't get the hell out of there, neither one of

them would get any sleep tonight, and he'd end up in a morning-after situation he didn't want or need.

Or so he had to keep reminding himself.

He ended the passionate kiss he'd instigated, and saw the questions in her slumberous eyes, an eager hope that he'd change his mind about staying. He took a much needed step away from her.

"I'm going," he said, his tone gruff.

She licked her lower lip, and gracefully accepting his decision, she opened the door for him. "Good night, then."

Their gazes met and held, and he paused, much too long for his own peace of mind. " 'Night," he finally said, then left while he still had the willpower to do so.

The early-morning rush of customers at The Daily Grind kept Liz's mind occupied and her hands busy making a steady stream of cappuccinos, lattes, and mochas. It was a diversion she welcomed, considering she'd spent too much time thinking after Steve had left her apartment last night—thinking about the incredible foreplay and sex they'd shared and how good it had felt to let go sexually in a way she'd never done before. She'd held nothing back with Steve, mainly because he hadn't allowed her to retreat. He'd been bold and dominant, yet so generous with her pleasure, and she'd been greedy and utterly shameless. Not that Steve seemed to mind at all.

Despite how tired she'd been after their time together, she'd tossed and turned in her bed, her mind replaying the conversation she'd had with Steve about her marriage—an intimate conversation she'd never intended to have with him. Their relationship was short-term and purely physical and, out of self-preservation, shouldn't have crossed over into anything emotional or personal.

Yes, he'd been persistent, but she could have refused to talk if she'd really wanted to. Instead, she'd allowed herself to be swayed by his questions, willingly so. With that deep, mesmerizing voice of his, his soothing touch, and the genuine interest she'd seen in his eyes, it had been so easy to open up to him, to reveal details of her relationship with Travis that should have remained private. It had been too long since a man had made her the sole focus of his attention and treated her as if he really cared about what she had to say, and she'd taken advantage of his listening ear. After revealing so much about herself, she was now doubly curious about his own marriage—and especially the female name she'd seen etched on the tribal band around his arm.

Despite sharing part of her personal history with Steve, there were a few emotional issues and deeper secrets she'd managed to keep to herself. While he'd been so understanding about her turbulent marriage, and even a bit riled over Travis's thoughtless actions, she didn't deserve Steve's vindication on her behalf, because she was hardly faultless.

What she hadn't revealed was the crushing sense of regret she'd lived with since Travis's death, for disappointing her aunt and uncle by marrying Travis when she'd known how much they disapproved of him. She'd gone against their wishes, seeking instead the kind of excitement and adventure he'd brought into her life, not realizing that his wild ways would come close to destroying everything she'd worked so hard to attain.

Now she was living with the consequences of her actions and trying to make amends for a past mistake that had not only cost her financially, but she'd also hurt her aunt and uncle with her own rash actions. She was working hard to gain their respect back, to make up for the disappointment she'd caused by letting someone so reckless sweep her off her feet and take advantage of her in the process.

At least with Steve, she knew where they stood with each other right up front. He wouldn't be sweeping her off her feet, and she instinctively knew he wasn't a man to take advantage of anyone. Least of all her. Not when she was giving him what he wanted of her own free will.

At ten after ten, when a lull in business finally presented itself and Liz was certain her morning employee, Gloria, had things under control, she heated up a café mocha for Mona and strolled over to The Last Word with her offering. The new-and-used bookstore that connected directly to The Daily Grind already had customers strolling the aisles for a good read, some with one of Liz's specialty drinks in hand. While her and Mona's businesses were their own, there was no denying that their patrons enjoyed the services they offered and loved being able to buy a best-selling novel and specialty coffee drink all in one convenient stop.

"Good morning," Liz greeted, and headed behind the front counter, where Mona was sorting through a box of used books, her movements slow and sluggish. "I brought you an eye-opener."

Mona's expression turned grateful, and she eagerly reached for the hot drink. "With a double shot of espresso?" she asked hopefully.

"Of course." Liz grinned.

Mona closed her eyes, took a long whiff of the fragrant vapors curling upward, and moaned in appreciation. "You are so good to me." She took a tentative drink of the steaming liquid and sighed. "How did you know I needed a good kick of caffeine this morning?"

"You know your mood is a dead giveaway." Liz leaned against the counter and slipped her hands into the front pockets of her apron, having learned long ago how to judge her friend's disposition in the morning. "When you don't cheerfully breeze through the café and yack with all my customers before opening shop, it's a sure sign that you're either tired, grumpy, or have something on your mind."

"Tired," she murmured, and eyed Liz above the rim of the

Styrofoam cup. "And if I wasn't so out of it, I'd take offense to that 'yacking' comment you just made."

Liz raised a brow, completely unfazed by her friend's cranky threat. "Late night for you, too?"

"Ummm. My current beau, Brad, took me out dancing until the wee hours of the morning, though I'm guessing my evening wasn't as interesting as yours." Mona tipped her head Liz's way, suddenly seeming very alert and awake. "How was your first night as a phone sex operator?"

Liz wrinkled her nose. "It's not a career I'd choose to pursue. I think I'll stick to what I do best, making coffee drinks."

"Did you find out anything on your cousin?"

"No, not yet. There's a few girls I'm trying to be friendly with, and hopefully they'll eventually open up and give me some information on Valerie, if they even know anything at all." She cast a quick glance back at the café, making sure that Gloria wasn't swamped with orders, which she wasn't. "I'm trying not to get discouraged. Steve did warn me that it could take time."

Mona nodded in understanding, but her gaze held a deeper curiosity she didn't hesitate to express. "So, did you at least have a good time talking about sex?"

"Not at first," she replied wryly. "Some of the callers were downright perverted and lewd."

Mona laughed. Obviously, the caffeine was kicking in and perking up her spirits. "That's only because they were strangers." She took another fortifying drink. "How did your call with Steve go?"

Liz had told Mona about her plan with Steve, to use him to get invited to one of The Ultimate Fantasy parties. "It was okay," she said, deliberately vague.

Mona's gaze narrowed skeptically. "Just okay?"

"All right, it was *good*." Her face flushed in remembrance, and she modified her rating. "Better than good."

A wide grin spread across Mona's face. "Now we're getting to the good stuff." A customer walked up to the counter with an armful of books, and Mona held up a stern finger at Liz. "Hold that thought."

As if Mona would let her drop the subject now that she'd managed to make Liz fess up. Liz waited while she rang up her customer and bagged the books for the older woman, and then she was back, anxious and eager to hear more.

"Spill all the juicy details," Mona said.

Liz gave her friend a very brief, clean-cut version of her phone conversation with Steve last night, not wanting to share just how sizzling and erotic the episode had been. She avoided specifics, giving Mona just enough information to draw her own conclusions, without really confirming anything at all.

Mona nodded. "So, things are working out between you and Steve, then, yes?"

"With business and finding Valerie, yes," Liz replied, deliberately misconstruing Mona's meaning.

"Your *business* with him happens to include hot and steamy phone sex," she said, and continued sorting the used paperbacks from the box on the counter. "So I'm assuming that your two-way banter was mutually satisfying?"

She absently turned the pencil in her pocket between her fingers. "Umm, you could say that." While Steve might have been the only one who'd climaxed from their phone conversation, he'd made up for that in spades later, as he'd promised.

Mona must have caught the dreamy smile that curved her lips, because she pounced on it like the curious feline she was. "It appears to me that the two of you have more than business going on." She gave Liz a quick once-over, then grinned slyly. "You slept with him last night, didn't you?"

Although an instinctive denial rose to her throat, Mona was her best friend, and Liz couldn't bring herself to lie to her—not when she trusted Mona unconditionally with something as private as her relationship with Steve. "Yeah, I did."

"Well I'll be damned." Mona stared at her in awed delight. "I knew you had it in you, and it's about time."

Liz shrugged, playing it off. "It's nothing serious."

"Nobody said it had to be," Mona said pragmatically but with genuine caring. "Just enjoy yourself, and Mr. Wilde, for as long as it lasts."

Now, that was something she could easily agree with. "I intend to."

"Tell me one thing I'm dying to know." Mona leaned toward her and lowered her voice secretively, obviously trying to keep her question just between them and out of earshot of any customers. "Was he as good in the sack as he looks?"

Memories of just how good he was filtered through Liz's mind, and her heart picked up its beat, making her feel like a teenager with a crush on the school bad boy. That was how he made her feel—young and vibrantly alive. And anxious to see him again.

"He was . . . incredible, in every way." It was the only adjective she could find to describe Steve Wilde and do him justice. "The best I've ever had, actually." And he had the wonderful ability to bring out the bad girl in her and let that naughty side have free rein with him. She'd never let loose like that with Travis, who believed sex was all about *him* achieving pleasure.

"After the past three years of flying solo, you deserve to treat yourself to a hot, guilt-free affair."

Liz laughed, because she knew Mona expected her to. Her affair with Steve was no doubt a guilty pleasure, but she wasn't about to admit to the deeper blame she was struggling to keep at bay for stringing her aunt and uncle along about Valerie, and for not being able to handle the simple request of watching out for their daughter.

She glanced back at the café and caught sight of Henry, the older guy who delivered her dairy products. Welcoming the interruption from her more troubling thoughts, she grasped the opportunity to refocus on business.

"I'd better go help Gloria get that dairy order put away," she told Mona just as another customer came up to the register with her choice of reading material.

"Okay, we'll talk more later." Mona flashed her a smile. "By the way, thanks for the kick of caffeine."

"Anytime." Liz headed around the counter and gave her friend a lighthearted poke in the side as she passed. "Since it seems to put you in a good mood, who am I to argue?"

"No, hearing about your evening with the incredible Steve is what perked me up," she countered sassily. "I should be so lucky, so I'll just have to live vicariously through you."

Liz just shook her head and continued back into the café. Back to real life and the responsibilities awaiting her.

Chapter

6

A few minutes before seven that evening, the familiar rumble of a motorcycle pulling up in front of the café caught Liz's attention and caused an immediate current of anticipation to ripple through her. Since all her customers were taken care of and her two second-shift employees had the tables covered, she started making the drink Steve always ordered—a caramel frappuccino, extra caramel.

As she blended the concoction, she watched him through the plate-glass window as he took off his helmet and combed his thick, tousled hair with his fingers. He slid off his bike in one smooth motion and retrieved what appeared to be a leather portfolio from the back compartment. Breathtakingly gorgeous and sinfully sexy, he strolled into the establishment, made eye contact with her, and winked. The private greeting started a slow melting sensation in the pit of her belly.

He made his way to the vacant couch in the corner, and she experienced a twinge of insecurity when she realized a group of flirtatious, model-thin women were doing their best to get his attention. There had always been a part of her that believed she hadn't been good enough to please Travis, that her body wasn't perfect enough, thus causing him to stray from their marriage. And those old self-doubts were obviously rearing their ugly heads with Steve, who could have any woman of his choosing.

She firmly reminded herself that he'd chosen her, and for the time being he seemed completely satisfied and dedicated. To his credit, he didn't seem to notice the other women who were staring at him, waiting for a smile or some other token acknowledgment as he passed their tables. A few of the interested females appeared miffed by his indifference, and Liz was admittedly amused by his subtle rejection.

Back off, girls, she thought with a bit of triumph. *He's all mine.*

Katie, a young college student who worked part-time in the evenings while going to school during the day, rounded the counter. "Do you want me to go take his order?" she asked.

"No, I've got it." Liz poured the drink into a plastic cup. "I'm going to take a break, but I'll be right over there if you need me for anything." She indicated Steve.

With a nod, the young girl picked up a damp rag and went to wipe down tables.

Liz topped the drink off with a small mountain of real whipped cream and drizzled a generous amount of caramel sauce on top of that, having learned that there was no such thing as too much caramel for that macho bad boy of hers.

Minutes later, she was delivering the drink to him in the private, semisecluded corner he'd picked, away from other patrons. "Hey, there," she said softly, her whole being fairly zinging with instantaneous awareness as she sat down beside him on the couch.

He graced her with a bone-melting smile that kicked up her pulse yet another notch. "Hey, yourself," he murmured, his tone as warm and intimate as the genuine affection glimmering in his eyes. He reached for his drink and poked a straw into the thick mixture. "I'm not going to get in trouble for fraternizing with the help during working hours, am I?"

Hearing the teasing note in his voice, she leaned back against the sofa cushion and relaxed, intending to enjoy her time with him in a casual environment. Their knees touched, and the slight physical connection between them seemed as natural as breathing. "Since I'm the boss, the only person you have to answer to is me."

"That doesn't sound like such a bad deal." He waggled his brows at her as he took a drink; then a long, low, appreciative moan escaped him. "God, you give good caramel frappuccinos."

The man was so outrageous, she couldn't help but laugh. And it felt so good to do so when her life had been much too serious lately. "What's this sweet tooth you've got for caramel?"

"It goes way back, to when I was a little kid," he said easily. "Whenever I'd go to my grandmother's as a boy, she'd always have caramel squares tucked into her apron pocket, and she'd share them with me. It was as if that pocket never ran empty, and sneaking and eating those caramels became a special treat for me since my mother didn't have them at home."

A fond smile softened his masculine features, giving her a rare glimpse of an endearing side to Steve that stirred a reciprocating tenderness within her. She turned more fully toward him and stretched her arm along the back of the sofa, her fingers inches away from touching his broad shoulder. She could feel the heat of his body, could smell his clean, masculine scent, and wished they were alone.

"I always thought it was our little secret, until my brothers told me that they got those same caramel squares from Grandma's apron pocket," he said with a feigned grumble. "I remember being so crushed when I found out about that, and ticked at my brothers for horning in on what I thought of as *my* treats. We actually got into a fight over it."

She chuckled, loving his story and imagining what mischievous rascals he and his siblings must have been. "You have brothers?"

"Two of them. Eric and Adrian. I'm the oldest, and they always were a pain in my ass when we were growing up." His gruff tone was underscored with a begrudging affection for his siblings.

As much as she wished he'd elaborate on his brothers and family beyond that tidbit, he didn't, and she didn't feel it was her right to pry for more. She was more afraid that if she learned too much about him, she'd grow to like him more than was prudent. "Obviously you weren't traumatized too badly by the incident, since your love for caramel hasn't diminished."

"Not in the least. As a kid, I loved the sweet, buttery flavor. Now, as an adult, I think of caramel as rich, creamy . . . and highly seductive." He dipped and swirled his index finger into the sauce covering the mound of whipped cream, then brought that caramel-coated digit less than an inch away from her mouth. "Taste it and tell me what you think."

Her pulse leaped at the provocative game he was instigating in a very open public place. The wicked look in his eyes dared her to play, and she knew she had two options—to revert to the sensible, practical woman she'd been for three years and push his hand away, or to embrace her newly emerging sensual side and indulge in his brazen challenge.

She quickly assessed the situation and their position. They were in a corner of the lounge area, his wide shoulders turned toward her and angled in a way that shielded her from prying eyes and gave them a cloak of seclusion. And that was all the reassurance she needed to match his shameless actions.

He grew impatient, touching her lips with the sticky-sweet confection, boldly pressing them apart. She held his gaze and obeyed his silent command, opening for him, letting him slide his finger into the warm, wet recesses of her mouth.

She knew what caramel tasted like. She was one of those rare females who preferred the buttery, rich candy over chocolate, but she never knew how arousing it could be when mixed with the flavor of hot, salty male flesh. Never knew how turned on she could get by lapping the treat off a man's finger. And judging by the tense set of Steve's jaw, the quickening rise and fall of his chest as he breathed, he was equally transfixed by the sexual connotation inherent in her stimulating performance.

He started to pull his hand back, but she encircled his wrist and stopped him before he could withdraw. He might have been the one to start this scandalous stunt, but she intended to finish it. She swirled her soft tongue around his long finger, grazed the length with her teeth, and nibbled the tip before taking him deep into her mouth again and sucking the last of the sweetness from his skin.

His breath hissed out between his teeth, and his pupils dilated—dark, hot, and glittering with a fierce hunger that gave Liz a sense of feminine power. The erection bulging against the fly of his jeans thrilled her, and knowing she was pushing Steve to the edge of his restraint, she finally released his finger.

"Definitely rich, creamy, and seductive," she murmured, and slowly dragged her tongue along her lower lip. "I think I just discovered a new aphrodisiac."

"Caramel?" he asked, his voice tight.

A beguiling smile tipped the corners of her mouth. "When it's drizzled over the right dessert."

His nostrils flared as her meaning sank in, and a slash of color highlighted his cheekbones. "If we weren't in a room full of your customers and employees, you'd be flat on your back right now and I'd be the one licking that caramel sauce off your body. Every single delicious inch of it."

The image of that erotic fantasy caused her nipples to pucker so tight they hurt. Her sex felt wet, swollen, and she managed—just barely—to maintain her composure and strove for a reckless, fearless reply. "You think so?"

He growled, the primitive sound sending delightful shivers down her spine. "Don't tempt me, sweetheart."

His tone was playfully intimidating, and while she didn't think he'd really follow through on his sexy threat and take her right there on the sofa, she wouldn't put it past him to haul her off to the storage room or women's restroom to have his way with her.

He released a harsh exhale and shifted in his seat. Setting his drink on the secondhand oak table in front of the couch, he grabbed the leather binder he'd walked in with.

"Let's talk business," he muttered, and unzipped the portfolio, revealing an all-in-one management system. He flipped to a tabbed section marked *Liz*, which contained pages of notes in his masculine handwriting. "Going on the passport tip you gave me about Valerie, I checked to see if an international or domestic flight had been bought under her name."

Forgetting their fun, sexy exchange in favor of information on her cousin, Liz focused on Steve and what he'd discovered. "And what did you find out?" she asked anxiously.

"Nothing on that, unfortunately." He thumbed through a few pages and skimmed over more written information. "I also managed to check the charges on her credit cards to see if she'd purchased a ticket from some other source, and again, no luck."

Hope kicked up the beat of Liz's heart. "So then, you think she's still here in Chicago?"

"No, not necessarily. Rob could have purchased an airline ticket for her," he said pragmatically. "As for your cousin, she made a bunch of other charges on her credit card, mainly clothing and lingerie purchases."

That detail didn't surprise Liz. "That's nothing unusual. Valerie has always been a clotheshorse." And very frivolous in her spending habits.

"It was a big expense, nearly a grand in all, which seems excessive, especially since the purchases were made all in one day. I went to the place the charges were made, talked to a few salespeople, and showed them the picture of your cousin that you gave me, but didn't get more than a confirmation that she'd been there."

His dark brows drew together in further speculation. "And there was also a four-hundred-and-fifty-dollar charge to a luggage store, which seemed pretty steep for an overnight bag. So, I followed up on the charge and found out it was for a full set of luggage, including a garment bag."

Liz's eyes widened. "I had no idea."

He studied her for a long moment. "You and your cousin aren't that close, are you?"

"We were raised together," she said, and heard the defensive note creep into her tone. "We're as close as sisters are."

"But you don't share a whole lot of stuff like sisters who live together would," he said, making his point in a gentle but direct way.

"No." The words felt thick in her throat. "Despite being raised together, we both have very distinctly different personalities, and that has contributed to a lot of strain between us over the years."

There was more, such as the old resentments her cousin harbored, and Valerie's craving for attention, that had shaped her into the impetuous, reckless woman she'd become. But Liz felt partially accountable for that drastic change in her cousin, because she'd come into Valerie's life unexpectedly, forcing her to adjust from being an only child, whom her parents absolutely doted upon, to having another girl— a rival in her eyes—steal away half of everything that was hers.

"I love Valerie," she said quietly, "and I'll obviously do anything for her, but no, I wouldn't call us best friends."

The admission hurt, more than she realized. Ever since the day she'd moved in with her aunt and uncle at the tender young age of twelve, Liz had always yearned for Valerie's friendship, and yes, on some level, her approval. She'd always wanted a sister, and she'd done her best to create that special bond between her and Val until she realized that her cousin had no desire to share anything with her beyond what was necessary. Still, Liz had always held out the foolish hope that Valerie would come around and change her mind about their being friends.

Steve stared at her with those intelligent eyes of his that seemed to reach deep into her soul and tug on emotions she'd spent years keeping under wraps, just as he had last night when he'd coaxed her to talk about Travis.

She grew uncomfortable beneath his penetrating gaze and wondered if he could sense her internal guilt—her sense of obligation both to Valerie and to her aunt and uncle for everything they'd sacrificed for her by taking her in when her parents died.

She looked away and inhaled a deep, calming breath. "What else did you find out?"

Much to her relief, he didn't pursue the emotional issue and smoothly veered back into their business discussion. "According to some bank information I was able to trace, Valerie made a five-hundred-dollar cash withdrawal from her savings account on Friday." He closed his portfolio and laid it back on the coffee table. "All those purchases and that cash advance happened last week, which leads me to believe that she was preparing for a trip."

His believable theory eased Liz's worry, but she wasn't willing to stake her cousin's life on an assumption, and she doubted Steve would, either. She needed to locate Valerie, hear her voice, and be reassured that she was safe and off somewhere of her own free will—before her Aunt Sally called again and put Liz into the position of lying to her or revealing the truth and admitting that Valerie had taken off with a man she knew nothing about, doing Lord knew what.

"What do we do from here?" she asked, trusting him to guide her through the next phase of his investigation.

He placed his palm on her jean-clad thigh and squeezed

gently. "We follow through on our original plan with The Ultimate Fantasy."

She found his touch not only reassuring but sensual as well, since he didn't remove his hand after branding her with that warm and comforting gesture. The heat of his fingers seeped through her jeans, singeing her skin and senses. Her pulse fluttered in her throat as she vividly remembered the exquisite feel of those fingers stroking over her body, petting her. The way they'd slipped deep inside her sex and set her on fire.

"Nothing's changed if you want more in-depth information about your cousin's whereabouts," he went on, oblivious to her aroused thoughts. "Other than what I've told you, I'm at a dead end with Valerie, which means the rest of this case, and finding your cousin, hinges on the man she's supposedly with. And all we have to go on is The Ultimate Fantasy and getting invited to one of those parties so we can at least find out a last name for Rob, so I can investigate who he is and put a trace on him, which will, hopefully, lead to your cousin."

She nodded, knowing he was right.

"Ohmigosh, is that you, Steve?" A light, feminine voice drifted toward them, her tone full of bubbly surprise. "I'll be damned; it *is* you."

The sudden appearance of a regular Daily Grind customer coming to a stop beside Steve jolted through Liz, making her excruciatingly aware of the intimacy of their position, and the familiarity evident in those possessive fingers of his curling around her thigh. She attempted to shift casually away, to give him the opportunity to remove his hand just as nonchalantly, but the pressure he exerted with his palm forced her to remain just where she was.

"Hello, Jill," Steve said with an affable smile as he glanced up at the other woman. "Fancy meeting you here."

Since Jill was a frequent patron, Liz knew her first name,

too, and had grown to like the other woman who was always so friendly when she came into the café. She wondered what Jill's connection to Steve was, since they appeared to know each other quite well.

"I should say the same for you." Jill lifted an inquiring brow at Steve, her green eyes sparkling with amusement. "I didn't think froufrou drinks were your style. What are you doing here?"

He took no offense to her teasing his manhood. "I'm enjoying the drinks and the atmosphere," he drawled, his words easily infused with double meaning, depending on how the recipient chose to analyze the situation.

Jill glanced from his drink on the table to Liz and grinned. "Hmm, so I see," she said, obviously drawing her own conclusions about what the atmosphere had to offer.

Steve's thumb absently stroked back and forth along Liz's thigh, but his gaze remained on Jill. "And what are you doing here?"

Jill adjusted the thin strap of her designer purse over her shoulder. "Eric and I went out for dinner to celebrate a big advertising account I finished that's kept me tied up for the past month, and we both thought coffee sounded good before we headed home."

Liz took that as her cue to make a smooth getaway. "I guess I should get those drinks for you."

"Stay put." Jill held out a manicured hand to stop Liz before she could stand up, her expression firm. "You look like you're enjoying your break, and that's what you have extra employees here for, isn't it?" Without waiting for a reply, she motioned Katie over with a smile.

"She's a take-charge kind of woman," Steve said out of the corner of his mouth, though he didn't bother to keep his comment from Jill's listening ears.

"Only when I need to be." Jill tossed back her sleek auburn

hair and winked conspiratorially at Liz. "I've learned with these Wilde men that I have to take charge when the opportunity presents itself."

Boy, could Liz ever relate to that with Steve, who seemed to hold tight to the reins of control when it came to the two of them. Obviously, the dominating trait ran in the family.

While Jill placed her order with Katie, Steve stood up and dragged two nearby chairs over to their corner spot, as if he was resigned to the fact that their guest would remain, invited or not. Once Jill was seated and Steve slid back into his spot next to Liz, he glanced from Liz to the woman sitting across from them.

"I take it the two of you already know one another?" he guessed.

"We're on a first-name basis," Liz said, and rubbed the tingly spot on her thigh now that Steve's hand was no longer there. "She's a fairly frequent customer in the mornings, though I had no idea that the two of you knew one another." A shameless throwaway comment that begged for more information, which Jill was only too happy to supply.

"I'm dating his brother, Eric."

One of the brothers Liz had been so curious about earlier. What a small world it was. She recalled seeing Jill with a dark-haired, good-looking guy a time or two, and had always assumed it was her boyfriend by the way the other man had doted on her, their affection for one another tangible.

Katie arrived with two chilled lattes, and when Jill went to pull her wallet from her purse to pay for her order, Liz waved away her attempt. "Your drinks are on the house tonight."

Appreciation brightened Jill's eyes. "How kind. Thank you."

Steve stretched his arm across the back of the sofa, his fingers grazing the back of Liz's neck and causing a smattering of goose bumps to rise on her skin. Was he deliberately throwing her off balance? If so, he was doing a darn good job of keeping her very aware of him, and not bothering to hide his attraction to her.

"So, where is my brother?" he asked Jill.

"He dropped me off out front, and since all the parking spaces were taken, he had to drive around back and find one there. He should be here any second." Jill glanced toward the front of the café, and her expression lit up when a tall, well-built man strolled in. Unlike Steve, who seemed to live in jeans, his brother wore a neatly pressed shirt, khakis, and loafers.

Searching blue eyes, just as striking as Steve's, swept over the customers in the establishment, and Jill waved to get his attention. Just as Steve had walked through the café with single-minded purpose earlier and hadn't seemed to notice the other women ogling him, Eric did the same, his gaze locked on his girlfriend as he approached—until he caught sight of Steve sitting on the couch across from Jill.

"Well, what do we have here?" Eric assessed his brother with interest and a flash of humor as he sat in the chair next to Jill's. "I didn't know they allowed riffraff in this place."

"If they allow you in, they'll obviously allow anyone in," Steve countered smoothly, though it was obvious their ribbing was based in mutual masculine comradery.

Jill rolled her eyes and shook her head. "Knock it off, you two," she chastised lightly, then laid a hand on Eric's arm and launched into introductions. "Eric, you remember Liz, the owner of the café."

"Sure do." He grinned, his gorgeous features reflecting those superior, sexy Wilde genes that apparently ran in the family. And just like his older brother, Eric oozed charm and plenty of sex appeal. "It's nice to see you off your feet for a change, instead of always working so hard."

His comment was sincere, and it earned him a smile from her in return. "Steve and I were discussing business," she said in an attempt to keep everyone's speculation about them to a minimum.

Except by their skeptical expressions, neither Jill nor Eric appeared to believe her, and Steve didn't bother to back up her claim.

Jill stirred her straw through her blended latte and addressed Steve. "Eric was just mentioning at dinner tonight that the two of you and Adrian need to go and buy that set of Callaway golf clubs your father wants for his sixtieth birthday, before the big party on Saturday."

Steve reopened his binder and skimmed through the calendar section. "How about tomorrow afternoon, about one?" he suggested to his brother.

"Only if lunch is on you," Eric replied.

"Cheapskate," Steve muttered.

Eric shrugged unapologetically. "Meals are a write-off for you, so why not take advantage?"

"Fine." Steve jotted down the date in the appointment book. "Lunch at McDonald's it is."

Eric chuckled. "Now who's the cheapskate?"

Listening to everyone's lighthearted banter, Liz suddenly felt awkward and out of place sitting there in her work uniform, being a part of this cozy social gathering when she'd never intended to let her brief affair with Steve extend to getting to know his family.

And then there was Steve himself, who was throwing her off kilter with his own behavior and the mixed signals she couldn't fully decipher. He'd openly stated that he'd been married before and wasn't looking for anything complicated or committed, but he obviously had no qualms about his brother meeting the woman he was seeing on a short-term basis. She wasn't sure how she felt about that. Wasn't sure she liked everyone knowing that their relationship was nothing more than a casual fling, because that was Steve's standard method of operation when it came to women.

Refusing to analyze her conflicting emotions when they had no business being a part of her relationship with Steve, she decided it was time for her to get back to work and not let Jill waylay her this time.

"If you'll excuse me, I have some things I need to get done before I leave for the evening." She stood, straightened her apron, and smiled at the couple sitting across from her. "It was nice talking to both of you."

"Likewise," Jill said, and tipped her head thoughtfully. "Maybe we can all do this again another time, but when you don't have to rush back to work."

"Unfortunately, if I'm here, I'm bound to work," Liz said, infusing her tone with a believable amount of regret. Not giving Jill the chance to make a different suggestion—like the four of them going on a double date somewhere away from the café—Liz turned toward Steve. "I'll talk to you later?"

His dark blue eyes were unreadable, giving none of his own thoughts away, which only added to her confusion. He gave her a nod, telling her with that quick, simple gesture that he understood the underlying meaning behind her question. "You can count on it."

Yes, she could count on him, she knew. To be the man who offered her his protection and advice while they searched for her cousin, and to give her the kind of pleasure and passion she'd only dreamed of.

Nothing more.

As she walked away, she heard Jill tell Steve that he ought to invite her to his father's birthday party on Saturday, that everyone would enjoy meeting her. Luckily, Liz didn't hear his response. She didn't want to hear him say no, didn't think she could bear to hear what kind of handy excuse he'd come up with as to why she might not be able to go with him. Not that she could blame him. She didn't belong at a celebratory gathering with his friends and relatives, no matter how much she ached to be a part of the kind of fun-loving closeness and acceptance Steve shared with his family.

Bypassing the coffee bar, she headed to the storage room in the back part of the café, which doubled as her office. Halfway there, she pressed a hand to her stomach to calm the unexpected rush of upheaval in her belly that told a tale of its own. She was getting in too deep with Steve, in over her head in a way she'd never anticipated. Involved more than they'd agreed upon.

And if she wasn't careful to keep pleasure and her emotions separated, this particular bad boy was going to steal his way into her heart. If he hadn't already.

Liz desperately needed a reprieve from the hot and heavy phone conversations she'd been fielding for the past hour and a half. Taking off her headset, she headed out of the small, stifling room at The Ultimate Fantasy and signed out for a ten-minute break. Instead of hanging out in the employee lounge that smelled of stale cigarette smoke and sharing war stories with other operators who seemed to perceive other women in the company as their direct competition, Liz opted for a breath of crisp, fresh evening air to clear her mind and lungs.

With her bottled water in hand, and the bag of sugar cookies she'd pilfered from her stock at the café to munch on, she rode the elevator down to the lobby. She pushed through the double glass doors to the well-lit sitting area just outside the building and was surprised to find Roxanne already sitting at one of the round tables, taking a break of her own.

She'd briefly seen the younger woman in passing when Liz had started her shift at nine, but they'd only had time for a quick hello before they'd both enclosed themselves in their assigned rooms and started taking calls. Liz knew she'd take advantage of the current opportunity that had presented itself, hopeful they could strike up a conversation now.

The night watchman was out strolling through the parking lot, giving them a semblance of safety, yet allowing them privacy, too. A full moon hung in the clear night sky, but it was the splash of flourescent light from a nearby overhead light that threaded through Roxanne's brunette hair and lent her an ethereal, peaceful appearance that contradicted what she did for a living.

The illusion of tranquility shattered when the younger woman glanced up at her, her gaze troubled and shadowed with a sadness that Liz automatically responded to on an emotional level. The day of Liz's interview, Roxanne had been the only woman to befriend her, even going so far as to offer her, a "virgin" of the business, a few tips about phone sex.

It occurred to Liz that she might be intruding, when Roxanne possibly wanted to be left alone. "Mind if I join you out here?"

"I'd love your company." The honest smile that appeared on Roxanne's lips validated her reply.

Liz sat down across from Roxanne. In the two days since first meeting the other woman, Liz had come to the conclusion that her kind was rare in this business, as was the friendship she'd extended. Unlike most of the women in the building, who came across as jaded, cutthroat, and blatantly sexual in dress, mannerism, and speech, Roxanne seemed the polar opposite—quiet, unpretentious, and pretty much keeping to herself. She came to work, put in her hours, and didn't seem to fraternize with anyone beyond that. And she was one of the few women who didn't look at Liz with suspicion and didn't eye her as if she were a threat of some sort.

Roxanne glanced up at the stars glimmering in the night sky, and a soft sigh unraveled out of her. "It's so nice and relaxing out here, I'd hate to deny anyone else the pleasure of enjoying ten minutes of this wonderful peace and solitude."

Liz was in wholehearted agreement. "That's what brought

me down here, too, instead of spending my break in the lounge."

"I only like to spend as much time as I absolutely have to up there in those offices," Roxanne said, crossing her arms in front of her on the table. "Sometimes I go home after work and I hear ringing phones in my sleep."

Liz laughed lightly, though the distaste in the other woman's tone gave her the distinct impression that Roxanne had taken on employment at The Ultimate Fantasy not because she enjoyed phone sex and titillating callers, like some of the other operators there, but out of pure necessity. And Liz understood and commiserated with that kind of desperation, because she was in the same predicament. But at least she knew this job was temporary for her, whereas she had no idea what Roxanne's situation was like, or how long she'd have to rely on phone sex for a living.

Opening the snack she'd brought with her, Liz held out the bag of treats to her new friend. "Sugar cookie? I've got plenty to share." And Roxanne looked like she could use some extra calories on her thin, petite frame.

Roxanne hesitated, as if she wasn't used to such kindness, then accepted the offer with a murmur of thanks.

Liz retrieved a cookie for herself. "Do you mind me asking how long you've been working here?" She kept her tone curious, remembering Steve's advice not to interrogate.

"It's been about four months now." Roxanne ducked her head, as if experiencing a bout of embarrassment—another anomaly for someone who made her living fulfilling verbal sex acts. "I know, you're probably wondering what I find so exciting about the phone sex business that's kept me employed here for so long."

"We all have our reasons," she said, suspecting Roxanne's were more extreme than most. "And like me, I don't think you find it exciting at all."

"No, I don't," she confirmed, and took a small bite from her cookie. "I have two young kids to support, and this is the best money I can make without any real work skills or a college degree."

Liz looked for a wedding ring but didn't see one. "You're not married?"

"I'm in the process of getting a divorce. My husband walked out on us six months ago and left me with the kids to raise and a mortgage to pay. He said he felt stifled, and off he went to find himself."

Liz inwardly cringed, knowing too well how badly a husband's rejection could lower a woman's self-esteem. She and Roxanne had a lot in common, it seemed.

Finished with her cookie, Roxanne brushed the crumbs from her fingers. "I haven't worked since my first child was born, five years ago, so finding an employer who'd hire someone as inexperienced as I am hasn't been easy. One look at my application with no previous jobs or references tends to turn off potential employers."

Liz pushed the cookies toward Roxanne, encouraging her to take another, which she did. "I'd like to think someone would give you a fair chance, despite your lack of experience." Liz was of the mind that everyone deserved the opportunity to prove themselves, and over the years she'd hired on a few people at the café without prior experience and had never regretted her decision. It was hard for her to believe that other employers could be so narrow-minded.

"A friend who used to work here told me how easy it was to get hired on and how much money I could make in a week's time. After so many other job interviews that didn't work out, I was getting to the point where I was feeling desperate enough to apply." Roxanne shrugged a slender shoulder. "Antonio hired me on the spot, so he gave me the fairest chance of anyone, I suppose."

"A friend told me about The Ultimate Fantasy, too," Liz

said, subtly shifting the direction of their conversation to her purpose for seeking out Roxanne in the first place. "Maybe you might even know her. Does the name Valerie Clark sound familiar to you?"

Roxanne thought for a moment. "Yes, it does. Does she have dark hair and green eyes?"

"Yes." Hope sprang within Liz, but she didn't let her anticipation show. "I haven't been able to get a hold of her lately, and I haven't run into her during my shifts. Have you seen her around, by chance?"

"I can't say I have. Not this week, at least."

With Roxanne answering her so candidly, Liz pressed her advantage. "She was dating some guy named Rob, a client of hers. Do you know anything about him, by chance?"

"I have no idea who she was seeing." Roxanne tucked long strands of brunette hair behind her ear. "Then again, I didn't really hang out with her."

Liz was certain that was Roxanne's polite way of saying Valerie hadn't been the type of person she'd pick for a friend. "If you happen to see her or hear anyone mention her name, will you let me know? I sure would like to get in touch with her."

"Sure, but you'd probably have better luck talking to some of the other operators." Roxanne's paused, then added, "If I remember correctly, your friend Valerie spent a lot of time with a woman who goes by the name of Trixie Lane, though I don't believe that's her real name. But she might know where Valerie has been."

Yes, finally a substantial lead, and one Liz jumped on. "Is she here tonight?"

Roxanne shook her head. "Unfortunately, Trixie doesn't work the phone end of the business anymore."

"She doesn't?" Confusion and disappointment mingled in her tone.

"Trixie is strictly one of the party girls, as they're known."

Roxanne filched another cookie, obviously feeling comfortable enough with Liz to help herself to another sweet treat. "I'm sure Antonio mentioned The Ultimate Fantasy parties to you, right?"

At Liz's affirmative nod, she continued.

"Most of the women want that promotion, because the party girls make three times as much money at one party, depending on how many clients they invite, than an operator makes in an entire week of calls," Roxanne explained. "Once you become a party girl, it's your choice whether you want to continue with the phone sex bit to keep the extra cash coming in."

Liz's eyes widened; she was stunned and amazed, and certain that Valerie had been one of those party girls. Now she had yet another reason to get invited to one of those parties—Trixie was now her best bet for more in-depth information on her cousin, and possibly on Rob.

Liz glanced at her watch, noting the time. They only had a few more minutes before their break was over, and she still had a few more casual questions to ask. "Do you go to the parties?"

"No." The one word was firm and adamant. "I've been invited, but I'm not interested. From what I've heard, those parties get pretty wild, outrageous, and sexual, and that's not my thing. Neither is phone sex," she clarified quickly, her chin jutting out with pride. "But right now it's paying the bills. Once I get my finances straightened out, I'm going back to school in the mornings to get a degree in nursing."

Understanding filled Liz, and she reached across the table to give Roxanne's arm a compassionate squeeze, feeling an undeniable kinship with this young, strong woman. "With a great attitude like that, you're going to be fine."

"Thanks." She smiled shyly. "That means a lot."

"You're welcome." Pleased with the details she'd gleaned

from Roxanne, Liz stood and gathered up the empty cookie bag to toss into the trash. "I think we need to head back up to our offices before we get docked for taking too long of a break."

Most important, Liz didn't want to miss Steve's call.

Chapter

7

"You called again." Liz's voice was breathless. Excited. And infused with a believable degree of coyness that added to her sexy act and effortlessly fired Steve's blood. "I wasn't sure you would."

Grinning lazily, Steve settled back against the pillows he'd shoved up against the headboard of his bed. Tonight there was no idle chitchat between them, no mention of anything work-related. Just a straightforward intro into phone sex, all for the benefit of the transcripts Antonio would read.

Playing along with the charade on his end was no hardship. He'd been contemplating their provocative conversation for the past two hours: what they'd talk about and where it would all lead. And just like last night, he was prepared to mix business with the kind of adventurous fun inherent in a titillating verbal exchange with Liz. All for the sake of establishing his interest in *Sindee*, which, hopefully, would in turn get them invited to one of the fantasy parties as a couple.

"I can't stay away," he murmured, low and deep, his groin already stirring in anticipation of the playful, naughty banter that would ensue between them. "I'm addicted to you, and there's no one else I want." All unerringly true statements that worked exceptionally well into their verbal performance. To anyone listening, he was definitely staking a personal claim on her. One that felt all too real and went beyond the benefit of persuading her boss that he was a client worthy of an invitation to the salacious side of The Ultimate Fantasy.

"Mmm, I like the sound of that—and you," she purred huskily, the sensual sound as intimate as a physical stroke across his abdomen and thighs. "I was sitting here, thinking about what we did last night and getting very hot and bothered."

Vivid and arousing images jumped into his mind, and he swallowed a groan. "Are you using your fan?"

"Of course I am. It's the only thing that's keeping me from burning up," she teased flirtatiously. "I was secretly hoping you'd call again, because I can't get you out of my mind, either. Not after last night. I can't stop thinking about the way your hands felt caressing my body, the wet warmth of your mouth on my breasts, and that wicked tongue of yours that brought me such incredible pleasure. Do you remember what you did to me last night?"

She could have been referring to the sexual act they'd performed during their phone call, but he instinctively knew she was talking about the hot, wild tryst that had followed at her apartment afterward. While he enjoyed how assertive she was with him now, how explicit and frank, he wasn't about to let her control all of tonight's seduction.

"I remember everything." Their encounter last night, and her uninhibited response to him, were indelibly etched in his mind. "The way you taste, how soft your skin is, and how feminine you smell—all over. You were so hot and wet for me that your cream drenched my fingers the moment I touched you. I especially remember the needy sounds you made in the back of your throat when I finally pushed deep inside you, and how tight and lush your body felt clenching around my cock."

A ragged breath rushed out of her, the only sign that he

might have shocked her just a little bit. But if he had startled her with his unabashed recollection of their time together, she recovered quickly.

"You were very good last night," she said, a sultry smile in her voice. "I've never been so thoroughly satisfied before."

The stroke to his male ego felt exceptionally good. But masculine pride aside, it was easy to believe her statement, because he'd felt her climaxes and those internal muscles contracting around his fingers, then cushioning his shaft in silky, binding heat as she milked him to his own release. And afterward, he'd witnessed the replete look of a woman completely satiated.

"I aim to please," he drawled in reply, and only with her would he be so blatantly arrogant, so sure of himself.

"You do," she assured him. "Tell me, what would you like tonight?"

"Are you on the menu?" he asked boldly. At the moment, he was feeling incredibly hungry, ravenous—for her.

"I'm always on the menu," she said, her laughter soft and oh, so bewitching. "Why don't you tell me a fantasy of yours, and we'll go from there?"

He glanced across the room and caught his reflection in the sliding mirrored closet doors opposite his bed. He'd never invited a woman into his bedroom, had never really given those decorative mirrors a whole lot of thought. Until now. With Liz. He found himself fantasizing, contemplating that length of mirror that spanned half his bedroom, and being able to watch his and Liz's naked images, her expression and his own as he moved over her, within her, their bodies entwined in the throes of heated passion.

Definitely a scenario he'd enjoy pursing with her.

He considered her question, and while he had no problem coming up with a dozen lusty male fantasies, he found himself very undecided. "I'm a guy, sweetheart. I have many fantasies." And lately they'd all featured her in the starring role.

"Pick a favorite, any one that excites you the most," she cajoled seductively. "And then we'll see what we can do about making it a reality for you."

God, she was good at this phone sex stuff, he admitted begrudgingly. The hard-on tenting his boxers was ample proof of her ability to entice and arouse his mind and libido with her velvet-lined voice and engaging words. Then again, she'd given him a very unforgettable demonstration of her ability to stimulate his senses that afternoon at the café, when he'd dared her to lick the caramel off his finger and she'd sucked on him in a very shameless, mind-blowing way.

Awareness licked through him, and a sinful grin lifted the corners of his mouth. He knew exactly what fantasy he wanted to share with her.

"How about you, covered in warm caramel sauce?" he suggested wickedly, playing on the risqué game he'd instigated at the café. *"Everywhere."*

"You're a *very* bad boy," she murmured, the knowing tone of her voice insinuating that she realized exactly what had inspired his fantasy.

"Someone once told me that they found caramel to be an aphrodisiac—when drizzled on the right dessert, of course," he said meaningfully. "I think I have to agree, and I want you to be my dessert."

"I'll be anything you want me to be."

He heard the tempting promise in her voice and felt the vibrations of the hot chemistry between them curl through his belly.

"Tell me what you want to do with the caramel," she prompted, obviously willing to indulge his private, whimsical request.

He stretched out into a more comfortable position on the bed and gave himself over to the fun, frivolous fantasy, so unlike anything he'd ever indulged in before with a woman—over the phone or in real life. "I want to pour it all over your body, starting at the hollow of your throat and continuing over your breasts and down your long legs. I want to watch the way the thick, golden syrup spills across your smooth skin, pools on your stomach, dribbles over your mound, and trickles between your thighs. And then I'd crown your nipples with the warmed caramel until they turn into taut peaks. . . . Are yours hard and stiff yet?"

"Yes," she exhaled into his ear, a soft, anxious sigh that quickened his pulse.

"I'm going to make them even harder when I lick the sticky sweet caramel from your breasts, suck your nipples into my mouth, and use my tongue and teeth to clean you up." His voice was pure gravel, and his own body heat rose a few notches. "I want more; do you?"

A breathy moan of acquiescence escaped her. "Yes, more."

The same sexual frustration that threaded her voice also strained against the front of his boxers, and he pressed his hand against the insistent, thick ache throbbing along the length of his erection. "I'm smearing the caramel over your belly with my hands. I'm coating your thighs with it and pushing them apart so I can rub the slick substance across the lips of your sex with my sticky fingers and let it mingle with your own sweet essence."

"Yes." The one word was hushed, almost a whisper, but the ragged need in her tone was undeniable.

Closing his eyes, he visualized what she'd look like with all those tempting curves and tender crevices glistening with caramel and her own desire. Absolutely, positively delectable. His mouth watered, and his heart pounded like a jackhammer in his chest.

"Now I get to feast on you," he rasped, and licked his lips in anticipation. "I'm nibbling on your breasts, and when I'm done with them I'm going to take a soft bite from your belly and dip my tongue into your navel." The images in his head were too much, and the sound that rolled up from his throat was a growl of pure male hunger. Raw and untamed. "You taste so damn good, and I can't get enough. I just want to eat you up."

Her breathing deepened, fast and shallow, as if she were on the verge of an orgasm. The thought had him stroking his cock, from the base of his shaft all the way up to the engorged tip, and wishing it were her hands on him instead. He imagined her skin flushed warm and pink, her expression reflecting erotic pleasure, and her soft green eyes feverish with the desperate need to release the tension he'd built within her.

"I want you to come," he said in a deep, rough timbre.

She paused, then, "No, not here."

She sounded slightly panicked, and he refused to push her for something she wasn't comfortable giving him. He understood and respected her hesitation, considering where she was. And as much as he wanted to hear the sensual catch of her voice and long, low moans as she brought herself to a climax, he'd much rather witness all that, and more, in person.

"Later?" The simple question held a wealth of underlying meaning he had no doubt she'd pick up on.

"Yes. It'll be worth waiting for."

He grinned at her huskily spoken promise and knew their night together had only just begun. "Then don't keep me waiting long." Another subtle but unmistakable message: he'd be at her apartment when she got home.

Liz disconnected the call with Steve—her last one of the night, thank goodness. Her skin was damp with perspiration, her heart beat erratically, and she felt hot and light-headed—not from the stifling air in the room, but from being so aroused.

She squeezed her thighs together and desperately tried to ignore how excruciatingly sensitive her breasts were, how pebble-hard her nipples felt, and the way the aching tips tingled as they rasped against the cotton lining of her bra.

Yes, she'd been so very close to coming and could have easily given Steve what he'd asked for, but something had stopped her from following through on his provocative request. After experiencing the real thing with him, the wild heat and excitement of his mouth, hands, and body pleasuring her, she didn't want to resort to a cold, impersonal orgasm in this small room when she knew how much more satisfying it would be to let go so completely when they were together.

She pulled in a deep breath, doing her best to calm her hormones and gather her composure before she exited the room. The man was so compelling, his magnetism so potent, even over the phone. He had an unerring way of mesmerizing her and pushing all her most sensually charged buttons. He was an expert at drawing her into his fantasies and making her an integral part of them, and what a doozy tonight's fantasy had been. Caramel, of all things, she thought with a grin, and had to give him points for being so inventive. Her sex life had never been so much fun, so playful and thrilling.

Taking off her headset, she stood and gathered up her personal things. She had no doubt that Steve would be at her apartment waiting for her. He'd insinuated as much at the end of their conversation, and she couldn't wait to see him.

She wanted him badly. Shamelessly. He'd turned her inside out with wanting earlier at the café, then had added to her restlessness with their seductive verbal exchange. And now her entire body vibrated with need and excitement, because she knew they were going to make love.

No, *have sex*, she amended, frowning at herself for making such a stupid mistake. Love wasn't something that was a part of their relationship, and she'd do well to keep her emotions out of the equation.

But they'd definitely agreed on enjoying erotic pleasures and each other, and that was something she'd decided to take advantage of with a virile, physical man like Steve. And with that in mind, she wanted to make Steve as acutely aroused as he'd made her with that irresistible fantasy of his. After the way she'd surrendered to him so thoroughly last night, she wanted to be the one in control of tonight's tryst; she was intent on driving him out of his mind with lust and satisfaction.

She knew exactly what she was going to do to extract her bit of sensual revenge, but first she had to make a quick stop at The Daily Grind on her way home, to pick up a few props.

As soon as Steve had Liz inside her apartment, he took charge with a hot, openmouthed kiss that she ended much too quickly despite the currents of awareness and sexual need sizzling between them. He had one hand under her T-shirt, palming her breast, another cupping her ass through the capri pants molding to her curves, and she deftly eluded both of his advances.

Gasping for breath, she placed a hand on his chest to hold him at bay, her eyes sparkling bright with laughter and desire. "Hold your horses, Mr. Wilde. I have something special in mind for you tonight, and at the rate you're going, I'm not going to be able to spoil you with the delicious, scrumptious treat I brought home for you."

"Spoil me, huh?" He grinned, unable to remember the last time anyone had gone out of their way to indulge him with something thoughtful. "I can't imagine anything more scrumptious than you, but you definitely have me intrigued."

"Oh, I think you'll find this surprise very mouthwateringly good," she teased, her expression a little on the sly side. From her fingertips, she dangled a white-handled paper sack with her café's logo, *The Daily Grind,* imprinted on the side. "And it's right here, in this bag."

So, it was from her café, which meant it was most likely something from her bakery shelves. "You brought me cookies," he said, and reached for the bag, certain he'd guessed correctly.

She danced out of his reach and shook her head. "Nope."

"A cream cheese pastry? You know how much I love your pastries." He lowered his gaze to her perfectly rounded breasts beneath the snug cotton T-shirt she wore, and waggled his brows lasciviously.

She laughed, the sound light and fun and infectious. "You're a very naughty boy tonight, you know that?"

Since he wasn't going anywhere anytime soon, except to Liz's bedroom, he took off his leather jacket and tossed it onto a nearby barstool and added his weapon and holster. "Would you have me any other way?"

"Absolutely not." She licked her lips, leaving them wet and shiny. "I want you bad. And I want to be bad, too."

"Sweetheart, you can be as bad as you want to be with me." Judging by her frisky, flirtatious behavior, he knew their encounter tonight wasn't going to be as intense as it had been last night, and he welcomed the playful change of pace.

Hands casually on his hips, he eyed the surprise she was still tempting him with, unable to contain his growing curiosity. "I really want to know what's in that bag you're holding."

"Hmm. I think I'm going to make you wait and wonder what's in here." She sashayed away and set it on the counter that separated the small living room from the kitchen area. Then she turned to face him again, too much space separating them for Steve's liking. "Before you find out what your surprise is, I have to ask, do you trust me to do whatever I want to you tonight?"

Her question was asked seriously, and for whatever reason, he realized his permission meant a lot to her. He spread his hands in front of him in a show of assent. "Baby, I'm all yours."

"I want to be the one in control." There was the tiniest defiant tilt to her chin, and her assertive and daring demeanor turned Steve on in a major way. "Is that going to be a problem for you?"

It was killing him, wondering what the hell was inside that bag and what wicked ideas she had in mind for him that she needed to secure his agreement to be the one in charge. While he enjoyed being the dominant one when it came to sex, he had no qualms letting her be the aggressor. He found her confidence extremely sexy, and what man in his right mind would balk at being at this woman's mercy?

Certainly not he.

Unable to resist her allure, he gave himself over to her safe-keeping. "Consider me your obedient servant tonight."

A soft, secretive smile curved her lips. "Then come with me."

"Oh, I plan to," he promised.

She lifted a chastising brow at the sexual connotation lacing his reply and held out her hand for him to take, making her meaning very clear. She wanted him to follow her.

He stepped toward her, placed his palm against hers, and was amazed by the surge of warmth and tenderness that engulfed him when she entwined their fingers.

He let her lead the way to her bedroom, and he glanced back at the white bag they were leaving behind. "Aren't we forgetting something?"

"Be patient." She tugged him along. "We'll get to your surprise soon enough."

Once they were inside her room, she released their hands and said, "Take your shoes and socks off for me."

He watched in avid interest as Liz went to the old oak dresser against the opposite wall while he unlaced his boots, toed them off, then removed his socks. She rummaged through the drawers and, seconds later, turned toward him, running a pair of sheer black pantyhose through her fingers—and damned if the thought of what she might do with those stockings didn't send a rush of insidious heat settling in his groin.

He didn't bother asking what the long length of black nylon was for, because he highly doubted she'd tell him, and he was certain he'd find out very soon anyway.

Tossing the intimate apparel onto the lavender comforter on the mattress, she came to him again, her posture deter-

mined and an air of sensuality surrounding her. Without preamble, she tugged his shirt from the waistband of his jeans,
and he helped her work the material up and over his head and
off. Holding his gaze, and with her teeth tugging on her lower
lip, she flattened her hand in the center of his chest and
skimmed her cool palm downward, her fingers dragging over
his ribs and taut abdomen. She didn't stop there, and he gave
a raw moan of pleasure as her fingers curled along the thick
length of his erection confined behind denim.

His body jerked in response when she stroked him, and it
was all he could do not to rip her clothes off and take her right
there, on the floor.

"Where are the extra condoms from last night?" he rasped,
trying to remember the important things before she totally
blew his mind—and other body parts exploded, as well.

"You don't need . . ." She cut herself off abruptly and shook
her head. "Never mind. I put them in the nightstand drawer."

She glanced away but not before he glimpsed what looked
suspiciously like hesitancy in her gaze, which contradicted the
unabashed woman she'd been thus far. With a finger beneath
her chin, he turned her face back to his. "What were you going
to say?" His tone was firm—demanding, even.

She sighed. "That you don't need them. I'm still on the
Pill." She shrugged, the gesture self-conscious. "It keeps me
regular, and I just thought . . ."

He put his fingers over her soft, damp lips, stopping her before she could say more. "I appreciate the offer, but I don't
have sex without a condom. Ever. I guarantee I'm safe in
every way, and I trust you are, too, but I have a daughter from
my first marriage, and I learned the hard way that there is
never such a thing as too much protection."

Her eyes widened at the personal information that had
slipped out before he could censure his words. But instead of
asking the questions he saw glimmering in her gaze, she obviously decided that his previous marriage wasn't a good source

of conversation to bring up when they were on the verge of being intimate.

So instead, she wrapped her arms around his neck and brought his mouth down to hers to finish the kiss he'd started in the entryway. Except this time he let her dictate everything about the embrace and followed along willingly as the pressure of her mouth parted his lips and her tongue slipped inside to tangle with his. Her fingers threaded through the hair at the nape of his neck, her breasts crushed against his chest, and the carnal mating of their mouths generated enough heat to make them both spontaneously combust.

Needing more direct contact, he slid his hands down her sides and over her hips, but before he could grasp her bottom and lift her into his erection, she pulled her mouth away and grabbed his wrists, halting his attempt to take over the reins of her seduction—something he hadn't even realized he was doing until she'd stopped him.

She pushed him back until the mattress hit the crease of his knees and he had no choice but to sit.

And watch as she stripped for him.

Just out of grabbing distance, she kicked off her sexy heeled sandals, then pulled her shirt over her head and dropped it to the floor. Next, she reached behind her back to unhook her bra, and as soon as the catch came undone, her breasts spilled free, lush and voluptuous, the tight points of her nipples jutting toward him as if begging for his touch.

Resisting the urge, he curled his hands into fists on his jean-clad thighs. He got the distinct impression she was testing his control, and he refused to let his restraint snap when she'd made it clear this was her show tonight.

She unzipped her capri pants and shimmied them over her hips, down her thighs, and off her long, slender legs, leaving her wearing nothing more than a pair of bikini panties and a come-hither smile that nearly unraveled his resolve. He waited for her to remove that last scrap of fabric so he could look his fill of her, but she had something else in mind.

"Lie back on the bed," she told him, and made another quick trip to the dresser to clip up her hair while he positioned himself in the center of the mattress.

She returned to the foot of the bed, and he stared at the fascinating sway of her breasts as she crawled up and over his prone form. His lips parted as he anticipated the taste of those nipples in his mouth, until she straightened and straddled his torso. The moist heat of her sex scorched him, even through the cotton barrier separating their bare flesh. This time, impulse won over, and he trailed the tips of his fingers up the inside of her thighs, until she gave him a stern look he decided to heed.

An impish grin made an appearance. "You can't straddle my stomach like this and not expect me to touch."

"No?" She picked up the stockings and brushed the silky nylon over his chest and across his nipples. "Put your hands above your head and grab on to the brass rungs of my headboard."

Oh, boy. He exhaled hard, did as he was told, and endured the torment of her leaning over him, her breasts inches away from his face but just out of reach of his mouth, as she wrapped the nylon around his wrists and secured him to one of the rungs with a very impressive knot.

He remembered restraining her for his pleasure last night, and he wasn't sure he liked being on the receiving end of bondage when he was a man who enjoyed touching and participating on every physical level. "Do you really need to tie me up?"

"You already proved that you can't keep your hands to yourself." She scooted down the length of him until her knees bracketed his thighs, and went to work unbuckling his belt, unfastening the snap of his jeans, and carefully lowering the zipper over his burgeoning shaft.

Grasping the waistband of his jeans and briefs, she pulled both downward, and he lifted his hips to accommodate her. When the last of his clothes were off, she added them to the pile on the floor and returned her attention to his stiff erection, which reminded him of a rocket ready for takeoff. At least, that's how he was feeling at the moment.

Seemingly fascinated with that part of his male anatomy, she brushed the pads of her fingers over the sensitive, plum-shaped head of his penis, and it twitched in response.

"Awww, isn't he cute," she murmured.

Incredulous laughter rumbled up from Steve's chest. *"Cute?"* Certainly there were better, more masculine adjectives to describe the most fundamental part of his manhood.

"Yeah, cute," she decided with a playful nod of her head. She kissed two of her fingers and transferred that affectionate gesture to the swollen tip of his cock. "Don't worry, *big guy*, you'll get your share of attention tonight."

He groaned, unable to believe she was talking to his penis. And when she moved off him and started back out the door, he couldn't believe that she was going to leave him alone, all trussed up to her bed—in the buff. "Hey, where are you going?"

"I'll be right back with your surprise," she said over her shoulder.

Her pert, panty-clad backside disappeared out the door, leaving him in a surreal state of bemusement and curiosity. When she returned minutes later, she was carrying a plastic squeeze bottle filled with a golden-hued substance.

He eyed the unidentifiable stuff as she set the container on the nightstand. "What is that?" he asked tentatively.

She shimmied out of her panties. Without an ounce of modesty, she straddled his middle again, and his voracious and admiring gaze took in all her naked glory—from her high, full breasts, along her waist and hips, to her spread thighs and the view of the thatch of dark-blond hair covering her sex.

"You wanted caramel, and you're gonna get it." She reached for the squeeze bottle and squiggled a line of sticky syrup from his breastbone to each of his nipples. "*Lots* of it. Rich and sweet and seductive."

The caramel was warm and silky against his skin, and the heady exhilaration of what she was about to do to him made him burn from the inside out. "Hey, I thought this was my fantasy, remember?" He'd been the one to bring up caramel earlier on the phone. "You should be the one who's tied to the bed, not me."

"Too late for that, don't you think?" She raised her eyes to his, a suggestive smile on her lips as she finger-painted the slick-textured caramel over his chest, across his rigid nipples, and down the line of his abdomen. "Besides, this is still your fantasy, but with a bit of a twist that lets me be the one in control. I'm going to eat *you* up."

The fragrant scent of buttery caramel filled his senses, and he groaned, certain he'd died and gone to heaven. She scooted a bit lower to continue a drizzling path of syrup down to his navel, and his erection slid along the crease of her buttocks. For a brief moment he wished his hands were free, so he could lift her hips and pull her down the last few inches and thrust inside her, and make her ride him hard and fast.

But he couldn't do anything but surrender to her slow, arousing ministrations, and that heightened his excitement, too.

Once she was finished painting him with the decadent treat, she leaned forward, ran her lips over a taut pectoral muscle, then took a soft, ravenous bite from his flesh. She groaned at the sweet taste filling her mouth, and a hot, wild tremor rippled through him in response.

Her sensual gaze lifted to his, and the smile that etched her expression was a combination of exhilaration and pure bliss, as if she were under the influence of a very potent aphrodisiac. As he watched, her pink tongue dipped down, swirling once again through the sweet mess she'd made on his chest, and lower. She found his rigid nipple and nipped at the sensitive disk, and that stab of erotic sensation spiraled all the way down to his groin.

She continued to lap at him and unhurriedly kissed her way down his torso to his belly, and kept nibbling her way lower with soft, delicious bites and the scrape of her teeth along his caramel-coated skin, eating him up like he was one big seductive dessert for her to feast on and enjoy. He was so lost in the fantasy she'd created that when she finally sat up again, he realized she was sitting astride his thighs like a pagan, her hungry gaze taking in his jutting, aching sex.

Licking her lips, she reached for the bottle of caramel and poured a generous amount in her hand, then rubbed her palms together, the enthusiastic light in her eyes making her intentions oh, so clear. She took him in her hands, her grasp slick and slippery as she measured the length of his cock in long, heated strokes that had him gritting his teeth in a painful kind of pleasure. Her thumbs grazed the lubricated head of his penis with every pass, drawing a fierce climax closer to the surface.

"Liz," he said, his voice a deep, husky growl.

She ignored the warning in his tone; she obviously wasn't done tormenting him. Lowering her head, she curled her tongue over the broad head of his sex, then licked and nibbled her way up and down his shaft, giving his cock the attention she'd promised earlier. Slowly, leisurely, she lapped off the caramel, savoring the taste of him with small, appreciative sighs and moans that made him writhe beneath her. Just when he was certain he was on the verge of going insane, she finally parted her lips and enveloped him in the wet heat of her mouth.

His nostrils flared, and savage lust reared within him as she took him deep, working his thick, solid member with her lips and tongue and the slick fingers wrapped tight around the base. She brought him to the brink of an orgasm, then eased back to let the wave of sexual tension ebb before starting in on him again.

His entire body shuddered with a fierce, roaring urgency, stunning in its intensity. He couldn't ever remember being the lucky recipient of such intense, all-consuming need. He'd had his share of blow jobs before, certainly, but no woman had ever enjoyed the act as much as Liz. She took her time, delighting in the act, luxuriating in his scent, his texture and responsiveness. She skillfully drew out his moment of fulfillment, as if his pleasure was directly linked to her own.

Her tongue swirled one last enthusiastic time; then she *sucked*, at first gently, then harder, stronger, devouring him all the way to the back of her throat in long, rhythmic strokes of her mouth. He exhaled a hiss of breath, and his arms flexed in an instinctive reaction to reach down and thread his fingers through her hair. The abrupt movement only served to tighten the stockings around his wrists and reminded him that she was the one calling all the shots.

He was under her complete power and command.

His stomach muscles clenched, and he dug his heels into the mattress, panting to keep his climax at bay. He wasn't going to last much longer. "If you don't quit *now*, I'm gonna come," he managed hoarsely.

She didn't stop, and he couldn't either. The last thin thread of his control shattered. His hips surged upward as she drew him to completion with her hands and mouth, sending him soaring on the wings of an awesome, shuddering orgasm that left him weak and wasted.

He finally came back down to earth to the wonderful feel of Liz making her way back up to his chest with more languorous licks and insatiable nibbles and kisses. Her knees straddled his ribs again, and her bottom rested lightly on his stomach.

Her breathing was ragged, and she looked down at him with eyes dark with passion and a hunger as raw as the one she'd just satisfied in him.

"Untie me so I can touch you," he said, wanting to give her what she needed, too.

She shook her head, a few wisps of hair that had escaped her clip brushing against her flushed face. She looked thoroughly aroused and incredibly sexy. "I'm not finished with your fantasy yet."

He couldn't imagine it getting any better, but he wasn't about to argue, not when he was certain that watching her would restore his stamina for a second round.

Picking up the plastic bottle of caramel, she drizzled a ribbon of the golden syrup over the tops of her breasts, and he stared, mesmerized, as the liquid trickled down to her quivering nipples, then beaded into tiny droplets that he ached to catch with his tongue. Holding his gaze with her own, she cupped her breasts in her hands and massaged them with the smooth, glistening caramel. She circled her nipples with her slick fingers, plucked at them, and gasped and shivered as the tips puckered tight.

Steve's blood sizzled in his veins, and he increased the stakes of their fantasy the only way he could—verbally. "Lift your breast to your mouth and lick off the caramel," he said huskily, and when a rare bout of uncertainty made her hesitate, he pushed the issue. "Do it."

This time, she fulfilled his request with more confidence. Sliding her hands beneath her full breasts, she raised her nipples to her parted lips and tentatively flicked her tongue across one of the crests, then the other. Her eyelids half closed, and she licked at the caramel again, her tongue gliding slowly, sensuously across her sweetened skin and lapping at the engorged tips.

"Suck them," he ordered gruffly, his cock stirring back to

life as she played out a very erotic male fantasy: watching a woman pleasure herself.

She caught a nipple between her lips, grazed it lightly with her teeth, and suckled the swollen peak into the depths of her mouth. Her eyes fluttered closed, and she grew bold and wanton, her lips and tongue and fingers playing across her breasts until that stimulant no longer seemed like enough, and a whimper rolled up from her throat.

His mouth watered, and he cursed his inability to use his arms to pull her down to him. "I want to taste, too."

Bracing her hands on his shoulders, she leaned down, arching her back so that her nipples brushed across his lips. He caught one in his mouth and suckled the delicious caramel from her skin and laved her with his tongue. She moaned fretfully, squeezed her thighs against his sides, and abruptly sat up again, seemingly caught up in her own sensual gratification.

Her head fell back, and her hands moved over her body of their own accord, skimming down her torso, smearing the caramel sauce over her belly and along her inner thighs. Her sticky fingers traced the pouty lips of her sex, then slid through her damp curls and into her wet heat.

With a soft moan, she stroked herself, and Steve gave a low growl of frustration because he wanted to be the one pleasuring her. The rumbling sound made her glance back down at him again, and a soft, sinful smile curved her lips as she removed her hand from between her thighs and touched her damp fingers to his mouth. Eagerly he parted his lips and accepted her offering, licking the flavor of caramel and her essence off her fingers and using his tongue and teeth to arouse them both all over again.

He continued to suck her fingers, and she moved on him restlessly, her taut, creamy breasts rising and falling as she breathed rapidly. Her hips gyrated and rocked against his torso in an attempt to increase the pressure and friction against the neediest part of her.

He wanted her so badly, to taste *her* and be the one to make her come. And with his arms still secured above his head, there was only one way to get what he desired and to give her body the release it was clamoring for.

He released her fingers from his lips for more carnal pleasures. "Come up here, baby, and ride my mouth," he rasped.

Her hot, dazed eyes registered his erotic request—a little bit shocked and a whole lot turned on. His mind spun as she eased her body upward, spread her legs wide, and knelt astride his head, giving him uninhibited access to her lush sex. She wrapped her hands around the brass bedposts to steady herself, and he slid his wrists up, entwined their fingers, and bound her hands to his so she couldn't escape or move very far.

For the moment, she was his, and he reveled in the capture and her submission as he had his wicked way with her.

She shivered as he nuzzled and kissed the inside of her thigh, whimpered when his breath gusted over her wet, delicate flesh, moaned when he finally tasted her with a slow, deliberate lick, and cried out as he swirled his tongue around her clit and gave her body what it ultimately craved.

Her fingers tightened around his, holding on while he took her greedily with his mouth and drank in the scent and taste of caramel and feminine desire. Both were incredibly sweet. His tongue was hot and aggressive, ruthless and demanding, unfurling deep and stroking and suckling with insatiable, rapacious hunger. Another thrust of his tongue, and a lusty moan ripped from her as the force of her orgasm shoved her over the edge and she climaxed in wild, exquisite abandon.

He didn't let her go right away. He lapped at her more slowly now, dragging out her pleasure, forcing her to endure, to ride out her release until the last small spasms jerked through her spent body and she was left gasping for breath. He released her hands, and she slid back down to his side, their skin sticking together from the drying caramel.

She reached up and unknotted the nylon from his wrists, setting him free, then looked down into his eyes, a contented smile on her lips. "That was incredible."

He brought his arms back down, and the cramped muscles along his shoulders relaxed. "Ummm, mind-blowing," he agreed, though after that outstanding performance of hers, he was hard and raring to go again.

She dropped a soft kiss on the corner of his mouth, her gaze dancing with gentle laughter. "Amazing," she countered playfully.

He grinned at her delightful, engaging mood and searched for a word to top hers. "Fun."

She skimmed her fingers down his chest and came away with a dollop of caramel, which she promptly sucked off in a very provocative way. "Tasty, and very messy."

"That was the best part." He loved her blissful enthusiasm and that she wasn't afraid to be daring and messy when it came to sex and exploring fantasies. Adored the way she enjoyed her body so much and reveled in his as well.

She lifted her splayed hand from his belly and winced at the gooey syrup adhering to both of them like glue. "Fun and all that aside, I think we both need a shower."

He chuckled. "You don't have to ask me twice," he said, and grabbed a condom from the nightstand on their way to the bathroom.

He wasn't done with her yet. They might have just eaten dessert, but the main course still awaited.

Chapter

8

Liz stood with her back beneath the hot shower spray and sighed as Steve soaped up the front of her body and washed away the remnants of caramel with luxurious sweeps of his big hands across her wet skin. He'd insisted on being the one to bathe her, and she'd let him do the deed for the most part, because after three years of devoting herself to her business it felt so good to be pampered for a change.

Through the steamy vapors swirling in the shower stall, his slumberous eyes latched on to hers, his dark, freshly washed hair finger-combed away from his handsome face. "Feel good?" he asked as his palms kneaded the slopes of her breasts and his thumbs lazily circled her ultrasensitive nipples.

"Oh, yes," she breathed, and because she couldn't stop herself from touching, too, she trailed her fingers up his muscular arms, deliberately taking the time to trace the tribal band around his biceps before continuing along his broad shoulders and down his muscled chest. He felt deliciously warm and sleek, exceptionally hard in all the right places, and she savored his virile strength even as he brushed his hands along her pliant body so gently, so eloquently.

While the sex they'd just indulged in had been hedonistic

in many ways and undoubtedly erotically charged, this was foreplay at its finest, she decided. He'd washed her hair as soon as they'd stepped into the shower, and massaged her scalp with his long, strong fingers. Now his caresses were slow and languorous as he smoothed the fragrant lather along her belly and between her thighs to wash away the sticky syrup, then down her long legs. His unhurried exploration was designed to relax and arouse, and he did both exceptionally well. She felt boneless, yet every one of her feminine nerve endings hummed in renewed awareness.

He turned her around and let the hot spray rinse the suds from the front of her body while he pushed her wet hair out of the way so he could lather up her backside. She braced her flattened palms on the tiled wall for support as he applied a skillful pressure to the taut tendons running along her shoulders, and she groaned in praise of his talented, sensual hands soothing her overworked and exhausted body.

"How did it go tonight at work?" he murmured, using his thumbs to loosen the tension along her nape.

Did he really expect her to think with a clear head while he bestowed such lavish attention upon her? Apparently so, and she did her best to switch mental gears from pleasure to business. "Actually, it went well. I was able to talk to Roxanne tonight, alone."

"And . . . ?" he prompted, his fingers working their magic down the muscles bisecting her spine, his firm touch spreading goose bumps along her flesh.

She closed her eyes, shivering as his palms slid over her hips and his big hands curved over her buttocks, squeezing and kneading her bottom. "Roxanne's been with The Ultimate Fantasy for about four months now, so she knows a bit about the fantasy parties."

"Does she go to them?" He easily nudged her feet farther apart and slipped his fingers along the crevice between her legs, grazing the swollen lips of her sex before retreating again.

She swallowed a moan at that teasing caress and managed a shake of her head. "No. Roxanne's not interested in being one of the 'party girls,' as they're called. She did remember Valerie when I mentioned her name, but admitted that she never hung out with her because she wasn't really her type," she said, trying desperately to keep her mind on the conversation she'd had with Roxanne and ignoring Steve's shameless attempts to distract her. "She gave me the name of another operator who Valerie was apparently friends with. Trixie Lane, but Roxanne didn't think that was her real name."

"Probably not." He readjusted the shower head so the water poured along her back in a fall of sensual heat, and he chased the soapy suds down her spine with his palms, leaving her skin satiny-soft and clean from head to toe. "Sounds like she's the next person we need to get into contact with."

She gasped as his parted lips skimmed the side of her throat and his tongue licked the moisture beading on her skin. His breath was hot, and her nipples puckered, tingled, aching to be caressed by his hands, his mouth. Again.

And still, she found the words to speak. Just barely. "Unfortunately, Trixie is now strictly one of the party girls and doesn't do the phone sex bit anymore, because of the money she's making on the parties. So, the only way we're going to be able to find her is to get invited to one of the parties and go from there."

"Then tomorrow night we turn up the heat on our phone calls," he said, nuzzling just below her ear, then nibbling on her lobe.

She automatically tilted her head to the side, giving him better access to her neck as the spray of water continued to drizzle over them. "Any more heat and I'm going to go up in flames."

He chuckled at her double meaning and stepped closer, aligning her back to his chest. A muscled arm slid around her waist, and he pulled her bottom to his groin so that his erection nestled cozily between her thighs. His free hand played with her breasts and lightly pinched her nipples, causing her to suck in a sharp breath and wriggle against him. His fingers strummed over her stomach, slid through her slick folds, opening her so that rivulets of water teased her clitoris, and his shaft glided along her tender, swollen flesh from behind.

Her entire body pulsed, and another orgasm beckoned. She wasn't at all opposed to letting him take her this way, but she grabbed his hand to stop his alluring assault. "I want to come with you inside me this time," she whispered. "And we don't have a condom here in the shower." Despite her curiosity about his being so adamant about using his own protection, she respected his request to use a condom at all times.

He eased his hold on her but didn't let her go. "Damn, you sidetracked me," he muttered against her neck.

She laughed, accepting his excuse, but knew they needed to finish their conversation about The Ultimate Fantasy before they moved on to more pleasant diversions. "You were talking about turning up the heat on our phone calls."

He exhaled, seemingly regathering his thoughts. "As I was saying, we need to take our conversations to the next level," he said, scattering soft kisses along her shoulder as if he couldn't help himself. "We're both going to express interest in wanting to meet one another in person, and let's hope that Antonio jumps on that and decides you're worthy of being a party girl, and I'm worthy of being invited to a party."

His plan was the next logical step in finding her cousin. "It's been almost a week since Valerie's been gone." The statement slipped past her lips, more somber than she'd intended.

He gently turned her around to face him, and the water cascaded over her shoulders and down her curves. She experienced a moment of vulnerability that had nothing to do with her naked body. Physically, she was all his in every way, but it was the raw emotions working their way up to the surface that made her feel so exposed to him. And as a man so in tune to her, he seemed to sense that change within her.

"Are you okay?" he asked, and gently brushed a wet strand of hair off her cheek with his fingers.

The warmth and compassion in his touch lingered, wrapping intimately around her heart, urging her to divulge her personal thoughts. "I'm just feeling frustrated and worried about Valerie." And more and more resentful that her cousin had put her in such a predicament. And then there was her own damnable guilt and sense of obligation that was nagging at her conscience and pushing her to such extremes.

The genuine caring reflecting in his striking blue eyes was nearly her undoing. "We'll find her."

She needed to believe him, and the evidence he'd uncovered and followed up on so far backed up his reassuring claim. "It's as simple as a phone call from Valerie if she's off somewhere having a good time with his Rob person, but Val isn't known for being courteous. The part of me that's frustrated just wants to say to hell with all this crap, but then I think of my aunt and uncle, and I just have to know that she's okay. They're the only family I have."

"I know," he said simply and with understanding. "As soon as we get Rob's last name, I can put a trace on him, and I'm sure, wherever he is, we'll find Valerie with him."

"I hope so." Her voice trembled, another show of emotion that slipped past her barriers.

He stared at her for a long moment, then cradled the back of her head in his hand and brought her mouth to his for a slow, soft kiss, as if that physical contact was the best way he knew how to comfort her.

His method worked like a charm, because he made her forget everything but the glorious, desirable way he made her feel. She opened to him, clung to him, and when his warm, damp tongue slid into her mouth, she greedily accepted it.

Her heart beat so erratically beneath her breast, she was certain he'd be able to feel the wild tempo against his chest. Thick, hot steam built around them, and the moisture from the shower made their skin slippery, erotically so. His breathing roughened, and the kisses deepened, grew more urgent and evocative. He backed her up against the warm tiled wall, ruthlessly pinning her there with his hard, muscled body. His palms slid down her sides, and he grasped her bottom in his hands and ground his hips against hers, his solid, unmistakable erection causing a wet, silken friction along the lips of her sex.

She shuddered and held on to his shoulders, her need for him becoming a tangible thing, strong and powerful and nearly overwhelming in its intensity. She wrenched her mouth from his, panting. "Steve . . . I need you inside me."

"I need to be there, too," he uttered in a low, gruff timbre, and his words thrilled her.

Shutting off the water, he grabbed her hand, pushed opened the stall door, and pulled her out with him. Water dripped from their bodies onto the floor mat, and he reached for the towel hanging over the brass rack. But instead of drying them off as she expected him to do, he laid the fluffy towel on the vanity and hefted her onto it, cushioning her bottom from the cold, hard surface.

He pushed her knees wide apart and moved in between, the hands splayed on her thighs branding her. His eyes were dark and hot as they took in her wanton position and her dewy, quivering breasts. He lowered his head, his lips parting for a nipple, and he sucked her deep inside, his mouth hungry, his teeth nipping, his tongue soothing.

She threaded her fingers through the soft, damp strands of his hair and groaned as his lips burned a path across her jaw, along her throat. "Steve, no more teasing."

He let her go just long enough to reach across the vanity for the condom he'd brought into the bathroom with them and quickly sheathed himself. "Lean back and brace your hands on the counter behind you," he ordered.

She did as he asked, and realized the position tilted her hips and gave him better leverage. He caught her knees in the crease of his elbows, spreading her legs wide for his possession. She was primed and ready for him, and the tip of his shaft unerringly found the entrance to her body, pressing in a teasing, tantalizing inch when she knew there was at least six more to go. Wrapping her legs around his waist, she urged him forward, and with a low, guttural growl he buried his face in the crook of her neck. Buried his cock into her tight warmth with one long, purposeful stroke that stole her breath.

He didn't give her much time to recover.

"God, you feel so damn good," he muttered, and began to move within her, withdrawing and plunging in hard, fast, rhythmic thrusts that had her instantly unraveling.

A wave of uncontrollable passion rolled over her, demanding her surrender to this man who was such an intimate part of her. Her thighs trembled, and her inner muscles clamped around him as her climax hit. Ecstasy, pure and sweet and so seductive, swept over her, through her, and in a sensual rush of sensation she came, shuddering and moaning his name.

"*Yes,*" he hissed, and tossed his head back, his jaw clenching. The muscles in his arms flexed, the ones in his abdomen rippled, and with one last deep surge his entire body shook as he gave himself over to his own scorching orgasm.

"I think Steve has a new girlfriend."

Steve had just taken a bite out of his meatball sandwich when his brother Eric decided to toss out that casual comment, making it fodder for discussion as they ate lunch at their favorite pub before heading off to the golf shop to pick out their father's birthday present. Since his mouth was full, all he could do was glare at Eric for bringing up Liz in Adrian's presence.

"A new girlfriend? Really?" Always interested when it came to the subject of women, Adrian, the youngest of the Wilde clan, jumped on the bit of gossip with the same enthusiasm that compelled him to skydive out of airplanes at fourteen thousand feet in the air. "Spill the details, Stevie."

He swallowed and washed down the bite with a drink of cold beer. He figured the best way to handle the situation was to give as little information as possible. "There's nothing to spill."

"Oh, come on, don't be so uptight," Adrian drawled, riling Steve the best way he knew how. "Is she hot?"

"Definitely hot," Eric said, looking much too smug as he shared his opinion with his brother.

Finished with his sandwich, Steve wiped spaghetti sauce from his fingers as he lifted a brow Eric's way. "What are you doing checking out Liz when you've got Jill?"

Eric shrugged unrepentantly. "It's hard not to notice that Liz has a great set of—"

"Don't say it," Steve said, cutting off his brother's remark with a deep, feral kind of growl.

Adrian snickered as he ate a forkful of potato salad, enjoying the exchange.

"Eyes!" Eric clarified, feigning such an appalled look that anyone would think he meant differently. "I was going to say she has a great set of eyes. They're a fascinating shade of green. Geez, what did you think I was going to say?"

Steve wasn't even going to go there, and he shot Adrian a look that told him not to share his own colorful answers to Eric's question, either, or he'd be dead meat.

"So, Eric's met this woman of yours," Adrian said, his tone thoughtful and curious. "Is it serious between the two of you?"

"Is it ever?" Steve snapped, feeling uncomfortable under his brother's scrutiny when he was beginning to recognize that his affair with Liz was turning into something more for him than a superficial fling to get her out of his system. And that realization came with a whole slew of emotional complications he wasn't sure how to deal with, since he truly wasn't looking for a long-term commitment with any woman. At least not the kind that led to marriage. And eventually, every woman wanted marriage.

"Hey, no need to get defensive about it." Adrian held his hands out in a placating gesture, his deep-blue eyes reflecting a hint of contrition for pushing what seemed to be a sensitive issue. "I'm just making sure that since Eric here has been bitten by the love bug, that it's not contagious."

Eric didn't deny being bitten, and the besotted grin on his face backed it up. "Be careful," he said to Adrian. "It might just sneak up on you and bite you in the ass when you least expect it."

Adrian shuddered dramatically. "Not likely. Been there, done that, and while I'll admit that you got lucky with Jill, I like my life the way it is, free of emotional commitments and demands. I come and go when I please and answer to no one but myself. It works for me." He dragged a french fry through the pool of ketchup on his plate and returned his attention back to Steve. "So, back to lover boy here and his girlfriend, Liz . . ."

"She's a client, and I'm working on a case for her," he said, hoping to dispel any further debate on his love life.

"Mixing business with pleasure, huh?" Adrian tipped his beer toward Steve in a masculine salute and waggled his brows.

Steve pushed his lunch plate aside and leaned back against the upholstered booth. "The last thing I want to do is discuss my relationship with Liz with the two of you." He felt very protective of her and wasn't about to taint what they'd shared so far. And he wasn't the type to kiss and tell. They weren't talking *forever*, but he respected Liz and wasn't about to let anyone think otherwise. Not even his womanizing brother Adrian, appropriately nicknamed the Wilde One.

"She's a nice woman," Eric said sincerely in a show of support. "She's the owner of The Daily Grind."

"I've heard of the place but haven't been there." Adrian reached across the table and filched the extra french fries Steve had left on his plate. "If the scenery is that good, I'll have to stop in there sometime."

"Stick to your sports groupies, Adrian," Steve said, knowing those wild, willing women were more his style. And he had a slew of them who were eager to please—in bed and out.

"You know I like a good challenge, and those women are too . . . well, easy—if you know what I mean."

Steve understood more than Adrian realized. His brother was finally becoming selective and discriminating, and gratuitous sex obviously no longer had an appeal for him. Steve was glad to see it happen, since Adrian had spent much too long using other nameless females to make up for the hurtful rejection of the one woman he'd fallen hard for.

The waitress came by, cleared their plates, and asked if they wanted a refill on their drinks, or dessert. They all declined, and Steve was slipped the bill. Lunch was on him, as he'd promised Eric the day before, though he'd foregone his threat of McDonald's in favor of their favorite pub. He pulled out his wallet to pay the bill so they could head on to the golf shop.

Eric cleared his throat and fiddled with the set of car keys he'd put on the table. "Hey, look, before we go, there's something I need to tell the two of you."

Steve was infinitely grateful that the spotlight was finally off him, and he welcomed the diversion, though his brother's suddenly somber mood concerned him. "Sounds important."

Eric glanced from one brother to the other. "It's one of the most important decisions I've ever made in my life."

Surprisingly, there was no wisecrack from Adrian, though Steve was plenty prepared to kick his younger brother's shin under the table if he demeaned Eric's need to tell them something so obviously significant. Eric had always been the easy-going, carefree bachelor of the three of them, and it wasn't often that he revealed such a serious side.

And that was enough to demand their attention.

"What is it?" Steve asked when the silence stretched out too long.

"I'm going to ask Jill to marry me."

"Are you crazy?" Adrian blurted, then tempered himself when Steve managed to follow through on his plan to give his brother a swift kick to knock some sense into him. "I mean, are you sure?"

"I love her," Eric said simply, unfazed by his brother's outburst. Reaching into the pocket of his trousers, he brought out a small velvet-lined box. "I picked this up this morning." He flipped open the lid, revealing an impressively sized diamond ring.

"Jesus, Eric!" Adrian turned his head, as if the glare from the stones were much too bright for him to take. "Blind us with that thing, why don't you?"

"Wow," Steve said profoundly, despite his own failed marriage. "You're serious."

"I wouldn't joke about something like this." He snapped the box closed again and tucked it back into his pocket for safekeeping. "I don't want anyone in my life but Jill. She's the one I want to be with for the rest of my life. I've even started thinking about kids lately and having them with Jill, and my biological clock is ticking," he joked.

Steve grinned. He'd never seen his brother so happy, and it warmed him deep inside that Eric had found someone he wanted to share his life with. "If you're looking for approval, you've got mine. Jill's perfect for you. And I know that Mom and Dad will be thrilled, too."

Adrian shook his head in awe. "You must be in love, because that ring had to have cost you a small fortune."

"She's worth it." Eric shrugged, as if money was inconsequential to what the ring symbolized. "I was thinking of proposing at Dad's party, in front of family and friends."

"Are you sure she'll say yes?" Adrian asked humorously.

"I wouldn't ask her if I didn't know with absolute certainty that she'll say yes," Eric replied confidently. "It's the next logical step in our relationship, and I think we're both ready for it."

Steve smiled. "I'm genuinely happy for you."

Adrian slapped Eric lightly on the back. "Me, too."

"Thanks. I'd propose to Jill regardless, but it means a lot to me that you guys are behind my decision." Eric sent both brothers a grateful glance, but his gaze remained on Steve. "You know, you might want to consider Jill's suggestion to bring Liz to Dad's party tomorrow. It's family and friends, so I'm sure she'd fit right in."

Inviting Liz was a big step into his personal life, and Steve wasn't sure he was ready to take that leap. So he opted to give his brother a noncommittal answer. "I'll definitely think about it."

Friday evening was a busy night for phone sex. After verbally satisfying over a dozen customers, Liz was certain every Tom, Dick, and Harry without a date had decided to call up The Ultimate Fantasy and make up for their lack of companionship and get lucky in the only way available. The switchboard operators were jammed with calls, and Liz was so busy, she worked through her break. As soon as she disconnected one call, another came in, giving her only enough time to catch her breath before greeting another client and starting all over again.

At ten after eleven, she was the unfortunate recipient of a call from a man named Stan, who'd just had his wife walk out on him for a young stud and needed a major confidence bolster from a woman. Any woman. And it wasn't sex or physical satisfaction he was after. He wanted to talk, and went on to tell her what he did for a living, how he'd met his wife, how long they'd been married, and how he'd found out about the affair. It didn't take her long to figure out that Stan was a lonely, insecure man who wanted to feel significant, and she did her best to fulfill his particular fantasy with compliments and reassurances.

It was the easiest and most undemanding call of her evening. Unfortunately, he kept her on the line for nearly thirty minutes, and while she was thrilled to earn the extra bonus money to help pay back Steve for his PI services, Liz prayed that she'd get a chance to talk to Steve before the night was over. They had a mission to accomplish.

As soon as she hung up with Stan at twenty to twelve, her line beeped again, and she connected the call anxiously. "Hi, lover, what's on your mind tonight?"

"You."

She smiled, the sexier-than-sin timbre of Steve's voice making her toes curl in her sandals. She leaned back in her chair as the night's tension drained from her limbs and was replaced with a welcoming buzz of awareness. "You've been on my mind, too." An understatement. The man was never far from her thoughts.

"I like that," he murmured. "Do you want to know what I've been thinking about all day long?"

She could only imagine. They'd spent the day apart, both of them busy with their day jobs, and she'd missed talking to him. Being with him. "Tell me."

His exhale rushed through the phone line. "I've been thinking about what it would be like to meet you."

Well, he certainly got straight to the point, she thought with a bit of amusement, but knew there would be more to tonight's conversation than just a request to meet each other.

"But you've already met me," she said, deliberately being coy and making it sound as though their acquaintance were all phone-related. "You know who I am, and you're with me every night."

"*Sindee,*" he said, using her call name. "I know your name; now I want to meet you. For real. In person. Face to face. Skin to skin."

Her stomach tumbled and her nipples tightened. Having had intimate knowledge of just how decadent "skin to skin" felt like with him, she wanted that just as much. "I'd like that, too."

"You've become more than a fantasy to me." His husky voice mesmerized her, as did his words. "I *crave* you."

A tiny thrill shot through her. "Even after last night, when you had me covered in caramel?" she teased, reminding him not only of their phone conversation but what had happened at her place afterward.

"Ummm." Another deep, rumbling growl from the back of his throat. "That only satisfied my craving for something sweet, and you were definitely that. What I want now is a hot physical contact. With you."

Her pulse quickened for the first time that evening, and she crossed her legs, knowing they were heading toward another provocative verbal exchange certain to make her ache and want. "If we met in person, what would you do to me?"

"I think you know." His tone resonated with dark sexual hunger. "And it's not hand-holding I have in mind."

She laughed softly, sensually. "I'd be very disappointed if it were."

"I think you and I would be like two strangers meeting for the first time, and there'd be an instant chemistry between us that neither one of us can deny," he said in a low, rich murmur. "It's powerful and irresistible, and we'd have to have each other, right then and there, at any cost."

She wanted him *now.* "Yes, I think it would be just like that between us. Urgent and sizzling hot," she agreed, and expanded on the fantasy. "The room is dark and shadowed, and our gazes connect and hold. We don't have to say a word, because we know what's going to happen, and we both want it."

"Our hands and mouths would convey everything we need." His breathing was ragged and beyond aroused. "And our clothes only make it half off before you're straddling my lap and I'm pushing deep inside you."

A low moan slipped past her lips before she could stop it.

"God, you're so hot and wet," he rasped, and groaned, too. "And every time you move on me, you squeeze my cock like a tight, hungry fist."

Her inner muscles clenched in reaction, and she closed her eyes with a shudder, which only served to conjure images of the two of them entwined so erotically. She could almost feel him within her, so smooth and full and hard.

"*I want you,*" he said fiercely, desperately, aggressively. "Meet me tonight."

"I . . . I can't." She resisted, only for the sake of the roles they were playing.

"Do you want to meet me?" he demanded.

She bit her bottom lip. "More than anything."

"Then let's be those two strangers who meet in the dark of the night."

"I don't know." She infused a believable amount of uncertainty in her tone. "I wouldn't want to break any rules here at work by fraternizing with a client without permission."

"You won't be breaking any rules if no one finds out," he countered, trying to sway her.

He was very persuasive, and while this was all an act between the two of them, she wondered if this was how her cousin had gotten involved with one of her clients. Had Rob been this convincing and Valerie hadn't been able to resist his allure? She could definitely see how that could happen.

"I want you," he went on, his possessive tone singeing straight to her soul, blurring the lines between fantasy and reality for her. "I want you bad, and I'll do whatever it takes to have you. No more phone fantasies. I want the real thing. I want to feel your skin against mine, smell your scent, and taste your desire."

Her head spun, her body caught fire, and her mind chanted, *Yes, yes, yes!*

"I want to take you every way you'll let me." His voice was raw and primal and sounded just as restless as she felt. "Do you want that, too?"

"Yes," she breathed. She was shamelessly turned on, her skin hot and prickly, her sex aching. She was his for the taking, any way he desired.

"Good." He sounded pleased, with an edge of arrogance thrown in for good measure. "Then see what you can do about making it happen."

"I will," she promised.

They'd put their plan into motion, both of them emphasizing their interest in each other. Now they just had to wait and see if Antonio took the bait.

Chapter

9

Unbridled excitement hummed in the air as their eyes locked and held from across the dimly lit room, direct and blatantly sexual. Focused and intent. Two strangers, instantly attracted to each other, on the brink of becoming intimate. There was no denying what they both desired—a sizzling, carnal encounter, with pleasure and satisfaction being the primary goal.

He was tall and leanly muscled, his hair dark and tousled around his head. His devastatingly blue eyes glittered with potent male heat as he offered up a silent challenge to play the game they'd instigated on the phone less than half an hour ago. From his chiseled jaw to his bedroom eyes to the day's stubble on his cheeks, he epitomized the kind of bad boy she was drawn to. Virile and seductive and a little bit on the dangerous side, his quiet, rock-solid confidence increased his appeal, making Liz excruciatingly aware of his prowess—and his wicked intent.

She welcomed the rush of adrenaline spiking through her veins. He moved closer, his gait slow and predatory as he closed the distance between them, and Liz's heart pumped hard in her chest in thrilling anticipation of the fantasy unfolding into reality.

They were in her small living room, which shared space with her equally small dinette set, but her vivid imagination put them in a more exotic locale, somewhere far away from her own responsible, sensible life.

He came to a stop directly in front of her, so close she could feel the heat of his body through his clothes, could inhale how deliciously male he smelled—a heady combination of heat and forbidden passion. His warm breath ruffled the wisps of hair along the side of her face, and pure, undisguised sexual energy crackled between them, a rare and irresistible chemistry that intensified with each moment that passed.

Her body softened, liquified, automatically readying itself for his possession. No words were spoken—none were needed—as she lifted a hand and curled her fingers around the nape of his neck. She pulled his lips to hers and kissed him deeply, avidly. His mouth was equally hot and eager, his tongue bold and greedy, consuming her with rich, unadulterated pleasure.

They pulled back, just long enough for him to quickly strip off his T-shirt and yank hers off, too. Their mouths met again, lips open, teeth nipping and nibbling, tongues touching, tangling. Her hands swept over the broad expanse of his chest, and she plied his nipples with her thumbs, then strummed her fingers downward to his taut belly. With a groan, he smoothed his palms along her shoulders and pushed her bra straps down her arms. They caught in the crooks of her elbows, and he left them there but didn't waste any time in pulling down the sheer, lacy cups so he could fill his hands with her breasts and roll her nipples back and forth between his fingertips.

She felt out of control, and she luxuriated in the untamed sensation along with the freedom to do things with and to this man that she'd never explored with another lover before. Like indulging in this stranger fantasy and luxuriating in mindless, unrestrained sex for the pure, intoxicating pleasure of it.

But ultimately Steve was a man she trusted with her body, and more. A man who made her feel amazingly feminine and lavishly seductive—as if she were made specifically for him, in every way. And for as long as their affair lasted, she was his, in every way.

Breathing hard and aching for that fast, frenzied joining the fantasy inspired, she blindly reached for his belt buckle and released the leather strap, then unfastened the top button and pulled the zipper down over his burgeoning erection. Grabbing the waistband of his jeans and briefs, she shoved both down to his thighs. His iron-hard shaft sprang free, and she encircled him with her fingers and stroked his length, used her thumb to smear the bead of pre-come that had gathered on the head of his penis.

His entire body jerked in response. He slanted his mouth across hers again with a rough growl, his tongue thrusting deep as he reached beneath the miniskirt she'd worn to work and pulled her panties down to her thighs. From there the scrap of fabric dropped to her ankles, and she kicked it aside and out of the way.

Hot, callused hands skimmed up her thighs, and long, seeking fingers delved into the crease between her legs. She was already wet, already excruciatingly aroused, drunk on passion and the excitement of the forbidden. He found her clit with his thumb and strummed across that knot of nerves in a sleek caress. All it took was that one electrifying touch, and she came in a fast, feverish climax that left her panting and gasping for breath.

He wrenched his mouth from hers and grabbed one of the dinette chairs from behind him. He sat down, quickly dug a condom from the pocket of his pants—still tangled around his knees—and sheathed himself. Then he was tugging her toward him, forcing her legs wide open on either side of his thighs. Grasping her waist, he guided her to sit astride his lap, and his cock slid along her slick flesh and unerringly found the entrance to her body.

He pulled her hips down at the same time he bucked upward, sinking into her tight heat and embedding himself to the hilt. She inhaled sharply at the abrupt invasion, and he groaned, long and low. He rocked her pelvis against his, his body tense and quivering. She grabbed on to his shoulders, easily picked up the rhythm he set, and rode him with utter abandon.

The material of her skirt floated around them, covering where they joined, which added to the eroticism of their tryst. His hand roamed up her spine, and his fingers fluttered along the nape of her neck, then wrapped the strands of her hair in his fist. He pulled her head back with that one hand and used the other to splay against the middle of her back, forcing her body to arch into him and her breasts to rub against his chest.

Their bodies were locked tight, and she continued to ride him as he scattered soft, damp, biting kisses along her throat and over the upper slopes of her straining breasts. He circled his tongue around one rigid nipple, blew a hot stream of breath across the peak, then did the same to the other. He lapped at her slowly, licked the taut tips teasingly, and nibbled until the madness was too much to bear. Grabbing a handful of hair from the back of his head, she pressed his parted lips to one aching, tingling crest in silent demand, and he obeyed, taking as much of her breast as he could inside the wet, velvety warmth of his mouth.

He sucked, and she felt that tugging, pulling sensation all the way down to her sex. She couldn't stop the whimper of need that slipped from her lips, couldn't hold back the convulsions that started deep inside where Steve filled her, full and throbbing. She moved on him, harder, faster, and came undone as a torrent of exquisite sensation flooded her limbs and sent her careening into an intense and fiery orgasm.

He released a harsh groan of surrender then and gripped her hips, rocking her in time to each frantic upward surge of his thick shaft within her. She wrapped her arms around him, holding him close as his own body shuddered in and around hers in long, deep, powerful spasms.

When it was over, they melted into each other, their arms and legs entwined, both of them too wiped out to move. Chest to chest, the wild beating of their hearts was all Liz could feel, and in that seemingly endless stretch of time, that profound connection between them was all that mattered to her.

Steve rummaged through Liz's kitchen cupboards for a late-night snack while she'd slipped down the hall to take a quick shower and change into something more comfortable. He'd promised her he'd stick around until she returned, and the truth of the matter was that he didn't want to leave. And because there was nothing left for them to discuss business-wise when they both knew the ball was now in Antonio's court, it made the issue of his staying beyond their midnight tryst a personal one.

He frowned at that realization as he snagged a peanut but-ter granola bar from the cupboard, but couldn't deny the truth. Beyond the incredible, mind-blowing sex they shared and the way they connected on a physical level, he enjoyed being with Liz as a woman who matched him intellectually, a person he enjoyed spending time with, and an intimate lover he couldn't get enough of. The three facets were intrinsically joined, in a way that fulfilled an emptiness within him he hadn't even known existed until she'd come along and filled that vast soli tude with her exuberant presence, her fortitude, and even her moments of vulnerability.

His heart thumped hard in his chest, and he immediately dismissed the notion that popped into his head. He was *not* falling for Liz. Yes, he enjoyed being with her. Yes, he cared for her. Yes, she was fun and sexy and turned him on like no other woman ever had, but there was no way in hell he was going to fall in love with her.

The mere thought made the granola in his mouth turn to dust, and his palms sweat. He liked his life the way it was, thank you very much, and being a bachelor suited him just fine. After one failed marriage and a sixteen-year-old daughter whom he adored, he'd already done the domestic thing and wasn't in the market for a wife, family, or long-term commitment with any woman.

Yet there was no denying that his feelings for Liz were shifting and changing, in a way that transcended wanting only a temporary fling with her.

"If you're hungry, I can make you a sandwich."

Liz's husky voice yanked him from his thoughts, and he turned his head as she padded barefoot into the small kitchen, a soft smile greeting him. She was wearing a well-worn thermal tank top with matching drawstring pants. Her hair was damp and ruffled around her head, her face scrubbed clean, and her skin pink from her shower. He caught a whiff of her shampoo, and his stomach knotted. He ached to nuzzle her neck, to immerse himself in her sweet, fragrant scent. He wanted to lie down with her on her bed and fall asleep with her cuddled in his arms.

Oh, yeah, he definitely had it bad for her.

"I was just passing time with a snack." He ate the last of the granola bar and washed down the bite with the bottled water he'd filched from the refrigerator. "By the way, I think you have a few messages on your recorder."

Her gaze went to the small machine on the counter next to her phone unit. A digital number flashed, indicating she had two messages waiting for her to pick up.

"Oh, crap." She crossed the kitchen, shaking her head. "I can't believe I didn't check the recorder first thing when I walked in."

"I think you were a little distracted," he teased.

"That's no excuse." Self-condemnation laced her voice,

and her eyes glimmered with unmistakable guilt. "What if it's Valerie?"

The vehemence in Liz's tone took Steve by surprise. He understood her desperation to locate her cousin, to be reassured that Valerie was okay. What he didn't understand was Liz's strong sense of responsibility for Valerie's disappearing act, when it was something she couldn't have prevented from happening.

Leaning a hip against the counter, he crossed his arms over his chest and opted for a practical approach. "If it's Valerie, then let's hope she tells you where she is, or at the very least lets you know that she's doing fine and is unharmed, and that'll be the end to your worries."

And this case, he thought. Would that then mean the end to them as well? Another startling realization, which came with an equally startling rise of emotion that made his chest tighten.

She turned away without replying and pressed the button on her recorder. The first call was a hang-up. The second one was Liz's aunt, leaving a message for Valerie, and Liz immediately stiffened when she heard Sally Clark's voice drifting through the speaker.

"Hi, Valerie, honey. It's Mom. I'm sure Liz gave you the message that I called earlier this week, but you've probably been busy. She told me that you were out of town for a few days with a friend, and I was hoping to get a hold of you just to see how you've been doing." Sally sighed, the sound rife with disappointment that she'd been unsuccessful in reaching her daughter. "Your father and I are heading down to San Diego for a four-day getaway, so I'll try and get in touch with you next week. We love you and miss you."

The line disconnected, the recorder beeped, and Liz hit the rewind button. With her hands braced on the counter, she hung her head, her shoulders slumped, and blew out a long stream of breath.

Judging by Sally Clark's message, Steve was fairly certain that Liz was keeping a pretty significant secret to herself. "You haven't told your aunt and uncle about Valerie, have you?"

"No." She lifted her gaze to his, the depths of her eyes brimming with a wealth of emotion, the most prominent of which was remorse. "I don't want to involve them unless I absolutely have to."

Not willing to let the discussion drop on such an intriguing note, he asked, "Why not?"

Her chin lifted. "Because my aunt and uncle have had enough disappointment to deal with in the past few years."

Retrieving a brass teakettle from the stove, she filled it with tap water from the sink. Her back was to him, her posture ramrod straight, giving him the distinct impression that she'd deliberately assumed that position to keep him from seeing and analyzing her expression. What she didn't realize, however, was that her tone, edged with self-recriminations, spoke volumes.

"Sounds personal," he said gently, trying to keep things light and easy so she didn't feel threatened by the conversation.

"It's very personal." She set the kettle on one of the burners, flicked on the gas flame, and turned to face him again. "My aunt and uncle have no idea that their daughter makes a living as a phone sex operator, and I'd like to spare them that bit of news if I can."

She spun back around and reached for a mug in the overhead cupboard, and her top skimmed upward, revealing a smooth expanse of soft skin he itched to stroke with his fingers, taste with his tongue. Better yet, he'd love to strip off her top and bury his face in those luscious breasts of hers and take her again, here in the kitchen.

He blocked those sensual thoughts from invading his body and mind and kept his focus on the discussion at hand. "Why do you feel the need to protect Valerie and hold yourself responsible for her actions?"

She frowned at him from over her shoulder as she ripped open a tea bag and dropped it into her mug. "I don't—"

"Yes, you do," he countered, cutting off her instantaneous denial. "For some reason, you're accepting part of the blame for Valerie running off with Rob, and I want to know why."

Her lips pursed in agitation, and her demeanor was defensive enough that he fully expected her to tell him to go to hell, that it was none of his business why she felt the way she did. But beyond her tough act, there was a hint of vulnerability in her gaze, a desperation that made his gut clench.

"Tell me, Liz," he cajoled, knowing he needed to hear what she had to say as much as she needed to get it out in the open.

She hesitated a few seconds before deciding to confide in him. "When my aunt and uncle moved to California almost a year ago, they asked if Valerie could move into my apartment with me so I could keep an eye on her. Considering this mess that she's in, I didn't do a very good job of that, now, did I?"

"Your cousin is twenty-four years old," he said reasonably. "She's legally an adult and plenty old enough to not need a keeper."

"What was I supposed to do, tell my aunt and uncle no, that I wouldn't let her live with me?" Her voice rose an octave in frustration and anger. "That I wouldn't keep an eye on her for them?"

"I'm sure Valerie would have found a place of her own if you told your aunt that you wanted your privacy."

The kettle whistled, and she picked up the wooden handle and poured a stream of hot water into her mug. A long sigh unraveled out of her. "Look, I don't expect you to understand my reasons. . . ."

"I *want* to understand, Liz." And he meant it, in a way that went beyond needing to know details for the case. This discussion *was* personal, for the both of them. There was no fighting the wave of emotion cresting within him that made him a part of her frustration, her pain, so he didn't bother to try. "I want to know why you feel so responsible for your cousin, and why you seem to be shouldering the blame for her disappearance when it was *her* doing, not yours."

She braced her hip against the counter and wrapped her fingers around the ceramic mug in her hand. "I just don't want to disappoint my aunt and uncle. Again."

He hated the space separating them but didn't dare close the distance when he was certain his advance would be rejected. "Again?"

She shook her head sharply, sending damp strands of her hair swirling about her shoulders. "It's complicated, and this is a discussion that you and I don't need to have since it's not relevant to the case." Moving past him, she headed into the living room, sat in the recliner chair, and sipped her herbal tea.

God, she was stubborn, which made him all the more determined to breach those barriers she'd erected around herself. Ignoring her dismissive tone and action, he followed her into the adjoining room and took a seat on the sofa catercorner from her. "Maybe this discussion is *very* important to the case."

Skepticism radiated off her. "How so?"

He shrugged, as if the answer was obvious. "You already told me that things have been strained between you and Valerie, and learning the reasons why would help me to get a better understanding of your relationship with your cousin."

She took another sip of her tea, her gaze narrowing on him over the rim. "And that would make a difference to the case, why?"

He catered to her reluctance gently, because he was coming to learn that this woman needed to be handled with special care when it came to emotional, familial issues. She was strong and diligent on the outside, and fragile and too susceptible on the inside, where she thought no one could see. But she'd given him plenty of glimpses, whether she realized it or not.

"By learning more about Valerie's personality, I can theorize a motivation for her actions." His explanation sounded logical, but his excuse was a deliberate ploy to get her to open up to him. To trust him with more than just her body.

Surprisingly, she did. "Valerie's actions are motivated by her need to get attention from whomever she can. And if it's her mother and father, all the better."

There was no bitterness in her voice, just an odd acceptance he ached to comprehend fully. "And what motivates Valerie's need for attention?"

"Me."

"You?" This time, *he* sounded skeptical. And confused.

"Yes, me," she confirmed more quietly, and stared into the depths of her mug. "When my parents died, I was twelve years old, and my Aunt Sally and Uncle Ben were my only living relatives. They took me into their home and raised me as if I were their own. At the time, Valerie was only six years old, and she was an only child. My aunt had an emergency hysterectomy after Val was born, and since she couldn't have any more children, Valerie was the center of my aunt and uncle's universe . . . until I came along."

Leaning forward, he braced his arms on his thighs and clasped his hands together. "I assume Valerie didn't take well to you becoming a part of the family?"

"No." She lifted pale green eyes to his, a sad smile curving her lips. "She resented any attention I received, though I didn't ask for much. She saw me as a rival, out to steal or take away half of everything that should have been completely hers." Her index finger idly traced the rim of her cup. "Everything became a competition with Valerie, but especially when it came to my aunt and uncle's attention. And since I no longer had my own mother and father, I craved my aunt and uncle's affection, which in turn infuriated Valerie."

"Sounds to me like she was spoiled rotten," he said roughly.

"She definitely wasn't used to sharing anything; that's for sure." Setting her mug on the coffee table, she curled her legs beneath her on the cushioned chair. "I dealt with the situation the best I could. I aimed to please my aunt and uncle. I was a good kid, I helped out around the house, I got good grades, and I stayed out of trouble. Valerie, on the other hand, turned into a wild child and an even more rebellious teenager."

He scrubbed a hand along his unshaven jaw, knowing good and well that his own daughter never would have gotten so out of hand, that out of control. Her strict but loving mother wouldn't allow it, and as Steffie's father, he wouldn't tolerate such incorrigible behavior, either. Even if he did live in a different state.

But every set of parents raised their children differently, he knew. "I take it Valerie got the attention she wanted?"

"Yes. My aunt and uncle gave her anything and everything she wanted, in an attempt to keep her happy." She ducked her head and swiped her fingers through the drying strands of her blond hair. "They made excuses for Valerie's defiant behavior, and of course, I knew all along that I was to blame for the drastic change in her."

"You were a child yourself," he refuted, hating that she'd held herself accountable, and at such a young age, too, when her biggest worry should have been what outfit to wear to school that day. "Any change in Valerie wasn't your fault."

He could tell that she disagreed but apparently decided it wasn't an issue worth arguing with him. "The only way I could make up for Valerie being so rebellious was by being a good kid. I wanted so badly for my aunt and uncle to be proud of me. I never wanted them to regret that they took me into their home and raised me. I always wanted them to know how grateful I was for the sacrifice they made for me, and how much I appreciated their love and support when I could have ended up in a cold foster home." A shudder shook her.

Yes, she'd been extremely lucky to end up with caring relatives, despite her own sense of misplaced guilt with Valerie. But there was still another point she'd brought up that wasn't clear in his mind. "Liz, you said you didn't want to disappoint your aunt and uncle again. What did you mean by that?"

"Like I said, I did everything I could to make them proud of me. I went to college, got my business degree, and when I made the decision to open up The Daily Grind, they believed in my ability to make the café a success and even gave me a loan to help start up the business." She absently twisted the gold band on her ring finger, the one that made her look taken by another man. "Everything was going so well, until I met Travis."

Ahh, he knew the story of her deceased husband, but there was obviously more to that tale than she'd originally told him. He waited patiently for her to continue, knowing he'd sit there for hours, days, weeks, to learn more about her. To know her inside and out. Dangerous stuff, that, but at the moment, he was beyond caring about anything else but her—insecurities, painful secrets, and all.

She closed her eyes for a brief moment, as if remembering; then her lashes lifted once again. Her gaze was distant, as though she were caught somewhere in the past. "I told you that my aunt and uncle were less than thrilled about my marrying Travis. That was the first time I'd really defied them. And after Travis died and I ended up on the verge of bankruptcy because of his debts, that was a very we-told-you-so kind of moment for me, though my aunt and uncle were gracious enough not to say anything to make me feel any worse than I already did."

She glanced back at him and managed a shaky half smile, but the gesture was forced over the emotional anguish flickering in her eyes. "I knew they were disappointed in me, and it hurt to think that I'd lost a bit of their respect for the rash and reckless decision I'd made. They're the only family I have left, and after everything they'd done for me, I'd let them down."

Her voice cracked, and she swallowed before speaking again. "So, here I am, just making a comeback after my disastrous marriage, and finally getting my business back to the point that it's solvent again, and I can't even handle a simple request to keep an eye on Valerie for them."

He refrained from grabbing her shoulders and shaking some sense into her. "Valerie is old enough to make her own decisions and suffer the consequences," he said one last time, but knew that was something Liz had to come to learn and accept on her own. Right now she was thinking with old childhood emotions clouding her judgment. Nothing he could say or do would make her realize the truth until she believed it for herself, as the adult she'd become. "Valerie is just damn lucky to have someone who cares so much about her, the way you do."

"I just want to find her and make sure she's safe." Liz worried at her bottom lip, the concern she harbored for her cousin weighing her down. "And hopefully, my aunt and uncle will never have to know about any of this."

Yes, this incident would pass, he agreed, but there would be more of her cousin's antics that Liz would take upon herself to bear. She'd go on feeling responsible and living her life to please her aunt and uncle instead of herself—because she believed that was what she needed to do to gain back their trust and respect. If she'd ever lost it. So far, Liz's description hadn't given him that impression. *She* was the one being so hard on herself.

Everyone made wrong or misguided decisions, along with mistakes they regretted. He had his own burdens to live with, as well—things he wished he could have done differently, like paying more attention to his marriage before it had started to deteriorate. But he'd learned that he couldn't allow those pitfalls to rule his life, that he had to deal with them and move on. But it appeared that Liz was still living in the past, for fear of failing the people she cared for the most.

At the moment, curled up in the chair all by herself, she seemed lost and all alone, even though he was sitting on the couch merely a few feet away. She was incredibly giving and selfless, to the very heart and soul of who she was. A woman who wanted nothing more than for everything around her to be good and right, yet all she could see in herself were imperfections and flaws.

Aching to bridge the distance between them, and wanting to offer her a semblance of comfort, he held his hand out to her. "Come here," he said softly.

She didn't hesitate to put her fingers into his palm, and the trusting gesture gave him an odd jolt of pleasure that warmed him from the inside out. Gently he pulled her from her chair and draped her across his thighs so that her bottom was nestled in his lap. She fit him perfectly, in ways that went beyond the physical.

"I'm here," she whispered sweetly, and gave him a tremulous smile that went straight to his heart and tugged hard.

Good Lord, what was happening to him? But deep inside, he knew what was happening, and he was beginning to realize he was helpless to fight the strong, undeniable feelings she evoked—no matter how much those emotions scared the hell out of him.

Placing one of her hands on his chest, she relaxed in his arms, snuggled closer, and sighed. "Tell me, did you and your brothers fight for attention with your parents, too?"

He stroked his hand up her back and lightly massaged the taut muscles at the nape of her neck, loving the silken texture of her hair threading through his fingers. Unlike her own unstable upbringing and the loss of her parents, his childhood had been very secure. "My brothers and I knew we were loved equally, and there was plenty of attention to go around, so there was no reason to fight for it."

She rested her head on his shoulder, her fingers absently fluttering over the pulse at the base of his throat. "You're very lucky," she said, her warm, moist breath drifting along his neck.

He heard the wistful note to her voice and brushed his lips across her temple. "Yeah, I am," he replied, and felt so damn stingy for possessing the kind of strong family ties and devotion she so obviously coveted for her own.

"Come with me to my father's party tomorrow afternoon," he said, expressing the thoughts that had been tumbling around in his mind before he could stop them.

Obviously startled, she lifted her head and searched his expression. Her eyes were wide, and she looked just as surprised as he felt, though he didn't regret issuing the invitation now that it was out in the open between them. He wanted to share something special with her, to make her forget for a little while about the anguish and uncertainties she'd been living with for the past week. There was no reason for her to be alone with her turbulent thoughts tomorrow while he was celebrating his father's birthday with his family. Not when he had the power to give her a sense of belonging and unconditional acceptance at a time when she doubted both.

She licked her lips nervously and shook her head. "Steve . . . I don't think that's such a good idea."

Cupping her cheek in his palm, he smoothed his thumb along her baby-soft skin, inhaled her shower-fresh scent. "Sweetheart, it's just a party."

"A *family* kind of party," she pointed out, making it clear that she wasn't related in any way.

"And what—I can't bring friend?" he countered wryly, and swiped a playful finger down the slope of her pert nose.

"Is that what I am to you?" she asked quietly, the question loaded with meaning. "A friend?"

She was his lover. A sexy siren who was tying him up in knots. A fascinating woman he couldn't seem to get enough of. "I'd like to think we're friends, yes. But you're also the woman I'm currently going out with." A woman he was falling hard and fast for.

So simple, yet so complicated.

She moved off his lap and sat on the cushion beside him, their warm and cozy moment over. "I don't want to give your family the wrong impression about us. I mean, we're not really *going out* going out."

An unexpected wave of frustration swept through him. "No?"

"We're not, well, dating." She waved a slender hand in the air between them, grasping for the right words. "We're just . . . having an affair."

The corner of his mouth twitched with exasperation. She made their relationship sound so brief and impersonal, and he was unjustifiably annoyed that she wanted to keep things so superficial, when that was what they'd agreed upon in the first place.

"Maybe we need to go on a date so that we're *officially* going out," he suggested quite seriously.

She laughed, but there was no real amusement in the sound. "I'm not asking for a date, Steve, or anything else from you. I accept our relationship for what it is, and I know where we stand with each other."

So she kept reassuring him, and she seemed fine with the arrangement. He was forced to admit that he was the one feeling restless, and wanting . . . more.

"I can promise you that my family will accept our relationship for what it is." He reached for her hand. Her fingers were cool against his palm, and he wrapped them in his heat. "Unlike my brother Adrian, who believes inviting a woman to meet Mom and Dad is the curse of his beloved bachelorhood, I have no problems bringing a lady friend to meet my parents."

He didn't bother to tell her that she was the only female

he'd wanted to bring home since his divorce. "My family understands that I'm not looking for anything serious, but I know they'll like you."

The lamplight in the living room softened her features and made her eyes appear luminous. He could tell she was wavering, and pressed his advantage.

"And it's not like you won't know anyone at the party." His thumb caressed her knuckles. "You've met my partner, Cameron, and my brother Eric, and you know Jill, so that's nearly half the family right there." Not counting the other fifty or so friends and relatives who would also be there. But there was no sense overwhelming her with that small detail.

"As for you," he went on purposefully, "I think the break will do you good and take your mind off of things for a few hours."

She opened her mouth to reply, and he instinctively knew what was coming, and thwarted her response. "And don't give me the excuse that you have to work at the café, when I know you have capable employees who can handle things for an afternoon."

A reluctant but humorous smile made an appearance. "What are you, a mind reader?"

"I'm just trying to head off every foreseeable argument you might come up with, because I'm not taking no for answer." He placed a kiss in her palm and enjoyed her reaction.

A matching spark of desire lit her gaze. "You're very bossy and persistent, you know that?"

"And you're very stubborn, so I think that makes us just about even, wouldn't you say?" He lifted a brow, daring her to still refuse him.

She rolled her eyes and conceded defeat. "All right, fine, I'll go."

"Good girl." Framing her face between his hands, he brought her mouth to his and kissed her, long and slow and deep.

With a sigh of acquiescence, she entwined her arms around

his neck, and he pushed her down onto the couch and stretched out beside her, so that he was half covering her body and one of his legs was insinuated between hers. With their lips still fused, he slid a hand beneath the hem of her pajama top and strummed his fingers along the underside of one plump breast in a featherlight caress, and felt the mound grow taut.

She sucked in a quick, aroused breath. His cock hardened in a rush.

Lifting his head, he flashed a wicked grin down at her. "I'm glad you changed your mind, or else I was going to have to resort to some very stimulating torture tactics."

She laughed huskily, clearly unthreatened. "Maybe you could torture me anyway?"

He tugged on the drawstring of her pants, loosened the ties, and skimmed his palm over her hip, dipped his hand between her thighs, and discovered that she wasn't wearing any panties. She was also hot and wet, and his fingers slipped inside her with ease, stroking deep. She moaned and arched into him, her eyes glazing over with passion.

"Oh, yeah," he rasped as he drew out the tension he was building within her, watching as she shuddered with need. "It would be my absolute pleasure to torture you."

And he did . . . a slow, sweet, delicious kind of torment that brought them both sensual enjoyment and immense satisfaction.

Chapter

10

Liz had been under the mistaken impression that Steve's father's birthday party was going to be a small family affair. Apparently, the man who'd coaxed her into coming to the celebration had failed to mention the fifty or so friends and relatives who'd been invited as well.

Sitting at a round table shaded by a large tree, Liz took a drink of her lemonade, completely overwhelmed by the sheer volume of guests milling about in the Wildes' large backyard, which had been festively decorated for the occasion in a country-western theme. A live band belted out all the latest country tunes as party-goers two-stepped on the patio. A catered barbecue buffet, the selections of which had been absolutely delicious, had been set up to feed everyone, and an open bar flowed with unlimited beer and drinks. Adding to the gaiety, the sun shone bright and warm, though a light breeze made the afternoon bearable.

The atmosphere was casual and fun, and while her appearance definitely drummed up interest and glances of speculation, especially with Steve insisting on holding her hand whenever he was by her side, his immediate family was just as accepting and genuine as he'd promised. She'd been introduced to his mother and father, whom she immediately liked. The only brother she'd yet to meet was Adrian, who, according to Steve's mother, Angela, was running late on a rock-climbing expedition he'd taken a client on earlier that morning. Adrian was expected to be there soon, and Liz was undeniably curious about the sibling both Steve and Eric referred to as the Wilde One.

A round of jovial laughter brought Liz's attention back to the occupants seated at the table. With herself, Jill, and Steve's good friend and partner, Cameron, as an audience, Eric and Steve were sharing humorous tales about years gone by, and their power of persuasion with the female gender at a very young age.

"Remember when you coaxed Tess Callen into our clubhouse and convinced her to play doctor with you, Eric?" Steve drawled, and took a drink from his cold bottle of beer. "The two of you were only seven, but even then she had a crush on you and willingly played as your patient."

Eric ducked his head and chuckled. "Yeah, I remember."

Jill slanted him a curious look, tempered with amusement, from her seat beside him, obviously wanting to hear more. "I can't wait to find out how you took advantage of that situation."

"Me?" Eric feigned innocence, though the naughty sparkle in his eyes gave him away. "I'd never do such a thing."

"Uh-huh, sure. I know better." Jill motioned for Steve to continue the story.

"Mom thought the kids might like some fresh-baked cookies, and when she peeked into the window of the clubhouse, she caught Tess with her pants down around her knees, and Eric giving her a pretend shot on her bare rump."

Laughter erupted around the table, and Liz joined in. She could easily imagine Eric as that precocious, mischievous little boy, flirting with girls to get his way.

Cameron saluted Eric with his beer and scooped up a handful of party mix out of the bowl on the table. "What a charmer you were."

"Still am," Eric replied with that trademark Wilde grin that had no doubt set plenty of pulses aflutter, but which now only belonged to one woman. "I've always been a sucker for a nice butt, even then. Lucky for me, Jill's is world-class."

Jill rolled her eyes, her cheeks flushing a becoming shade of pink. "Flattery will get you everywhere."

Eric nuzzled her neck, not bothering to hide his affection in front of friends and family. "God, I'm hoping," he growled playfully.

She jabbed him in the side with her elbow, a halfhearted attempt to make him stop. "You are so incorrigible. Try and behave yourself in public."

"Now, what's the fun in that?" He waggled his brows at her. "You know, if I remember correctly, I still have that doctor's kit packed away at the house—"

Jill pressed a hand over his mouth, cutting him off.

"Here's a bit of brotherly advice for you," Steve said as he reclined back in his padded folding chair. "You'd better stop while you're still ahead, or you're going to end up sleeping in the clubhouse tonight. Alone." He grinned.

"You're the one who started this," Eric groused good-naturedly. "In fact, you're not so innocent of wrongdoing, either, big brother."

"This I definitely want to hear." Jill perked up now that the spotlight was off her. "How about you, Liz?"

Liz warmed to the female comaraderie, though she was certain that Steve had been just as much of a rogue in the female department as his brother. "Oh, absolutely."

Eric smirked. "What about the time Dad took all three of us fishing at the lake for a weekend, and you spent the majority of the time ogling all the girls in their skimpy bathing suits."

Steve shrugged unrepentantly. "I was thirteen years old and my hormones were raging. Of course I was going to look."

"The problem was, you were also trying to impress them by looking like you knew how to handle your rod and reel."

Cameron snickered at Eric's play on words. "Oh, that was a good one."

Steve shot his friend a quelling look. "I knew exactly what I was doing with my rod and reel."

"Really?" Eric arched a brow, letting everyone know that there was much more to the story. "Then how do you explain the fact that when you tried to cast there was so much slack in your line that your hook got caught on the bikini top of the sixteen-year-old girl who was standing behind you?"

"That was an accident," Steve insisted, and draped an arm along the back of Liz's chair.

"One you took full advantage of." Eric munched on a few peanuts. "As soon as she squealed, you dropped your fishing pole and jumped right in to help her remove the hook from her itty-bitty bikini. Except from my vantage point, you ended up groping her breasts more than anything."

Steve grinned roguishly, his fingers absently grazing along Liz's arm. "She didn't seem to mind my attempts to unhook her."

"Until Dad stepped in to help your adolescent fumbling, and she found out you were only thirteen and still wet behind the ears."

"It was an easy mistake for her to make." Steve finished off his beer and set his bottle on the table. "I was *big* for my age."

"There you go again, exaggerating about size," Eric countered right back, his sibling banter filled with masculine innuendo.

The entertaining tales continued, with each brother trying to top the other with a more outrageous story. As the party went on around them amid loud music, great food, and hearty celebrating, Liz had to admit that she was enjoying herself. Immensely. For a few wonderful hours, and before she had to go to work tonight, she pretended that everything was right in her world.

Guests and relatives stopped by their table to say hello to Eric and Steve and introduce themselves to the faces they didn't recognize. There wasn't a person that Liz met that she didn't instantly like. A few had even been to her café and recognized her as the owner.

"Uh-oh, here comes trouble," Cameron muttered beneath his breath.

Liz followed his line of vision, along with everyone else's, to find a petite woman with silky black hair and silver eyes sauntering up to their table. She was wearing white jeans that rode low on her slender hips, and an off-the-shoulder top that bared her toned midriff and plenty of cleavage. Cameron, Liz noticed, was watching the other woman with a bland expression on his face that contradicted the hot look of interest in his eyes, while the other two men at the table welcomed her with a fond smile.

"I heard we had a new face in the crowd, and thought I'd come over and introduce myself," the pretty young woman said as she came up beside Liz and held out her hand in greeting. "I'm Mia Wilde, Steve's cousin."

Liz slipped her hand into Mia's for a warm and friendly shake. "It's nice to meet you."

"Mia, also known as the Wilde child," Cameron drawled, his tone deliberately taunting. "And the name certainly fits, now, doesn't it, sweetheart?"

Mia merely smiled at Cameron, taking no offense at his comment. "Being the only girl in a family of all boys does tend to spark a certain . . . wildness." She smiled, the gesture as seductive and daring as the awareness crackling between her and Cameron. "Care to try and tame me, sugar?"

"Not in this lifetime." Cameron tipped the beer bottle to his lips and took a long, thirsty drink.

"Aww, come on, Cam," Mia teased, and trailed her fingers along his shoulders as she came to stand by his side. "Many have tried; none have succeeded. You could be the first."

Cameron turned his head, and since his gaze was eye-level with her navel, he swept his glance upward, taking in everything between her belly and her face in a slow, lazy perusal. "What, have you run out of willing victims?"

"Not at all." She tipped her head, and her slightly wavy hair brushed along her jaw. "I just like a good challenge."

"Find yourself another plaything, Mia." His tone was dismissive, but there was no mistaking that his body was tense and she was the reason he was so on edge. "I'm not interested."

"What's the matter, sugar, afraid I'll bite?" She bared her straight white teeth for effect.

"Barracuda usually do," he replied dryly, though his gaze blazed with green fire and barely restrained control. "And I like my manhood intact, thank you very much."

"That shouldn't be a problem," she said huskily. "I like your manhood intact, too."

"Oh, boy," Steve murmured, so low that only Liz could hear over the music and din of conversation around them. But that simple statement was enough to let her know that the sexual attraction between Mia and Cameron was an ongoing battle that neither was willing to let the other win. But it sure was fun watching the two interact, Liz decided.

Cameron shook his head adamantly. "Thanks, but no thanks, sweetheart. That's not a chance I'm willing to take with such an important part of my anatomy."

She caressed her palm along Cameron's cheek. "I'd treat it with care. I promise."

Across the table, Eric choked on the drink of beer he was swallowing. "Jesus, Mia, can you be any more blatant?"

Her delicate shoulder lifted in a casual shrug. "Men usually find a woman who's up front about her intentions refreshing."

"That's where you're mistaken about me," Cameron said roughly. "I'm not like every other man you've wrapped around that little finger of yours."

"No, you're not. Maybe that's why I find you so fascinating." Her voice was soft and undeniably intrigued. "If you change your mind, you know how to find me." Before Cameron could issue a response, she waggled her fingers across the table at Liz and said, "It was nice meeting you."

Liz smiled. "Same here."

With that, the other woman moved on and blended into the crowd of guests, leaving Cameron staring after her.

Cameron jerked his gaze back to the witnesses at the table and scrubbed a hand along his jaw. "I swear, I've never met a woman so goddamn aggravating."

The corner of Steve's mouth quirked with amusement. "Funny, she's only like that with you."

"Because I'm not chasing after her like she's a dog in heat, like every other guy does?" Cameron downed the last of his beer and looked like he could use another one—or two.

"I'm sure that's part of your appeal to Mia, but don't let that vixen act of hers fool you," Steve said. "She's only twenty-five, but there's a whole lot of interesting layers beneath that tough facade of hers."

Cameron shifted in his seat, a bundle of pent up restlessness. "I don't want any part of her act."

But it was obvious that he did, and he was fighting her, and himself, for whatever reasons.

"One of these days, she's gonna make you snap like a dry twig," Eric said, expressing his own observations of Cam and Mia's love-hate relationship. "And then look out, for both of you, because the two of you together are going to be combustible."

Cameron snorted incredulously. "Not likely. Mia's a handful I don't want or need. I like my women soft and sweet, not infuriating me at every turn. She's like a rose with a shit-load of thorns attached, and I have no desire to be pricked over and over again."

"Maybe she just needs to be pruned," Eric suggested.

The two other men at the table groaned, and Jill smacked Eric on the arm. "Gawd, that was an awful analogy."

Cameron stood up and grabbed his empty beer bottle. "If you'll excuse me, I think I'm going to trade up to something much stronger." He stalked off toward the open bar, his agitation tangible.

Eric looked at Steve. "So, how long do you think it'll take before those two finally realize that they're perfect for each other?"

Steve laughed. "If you go by Cameron, it's not gonna happen in this lifetime."

"Hmmm, that's too bad," Eric said thoughtfully. "Because Cameron is exactly what Mia needs to ground her."

Jill arched a dubious brow at the man sitting next to her. "And when did you become such an expert on relationships?"

"Since you, of course." He gave her a quick kiss on her lips and abruptly stood, pulling Jill up with him. "Come on, they just cut the birthday cake. Let's go check out what's on the dessert table."

"Notice how quick he is to change the subject when it comes to discussing our relationship?" Jill's eyes sparkled with laughter, but she followed Eric, her affection and love for him open for anyone to see.

As soon as the other couple was out of earshot, Steve said, "That's because my baby brother is nervous as all hell."

"Nervous?" Steve's observation peaked Liz's curiosity. "He seemed perfectly fine to me. How can you tell?"

Steve reached out and smoothed wisps of hair off her cheek, his touch infinitely tender. "Because I know Eric and his moods, and I also know he's got every reason to be nervous tonight."

"Oh? Care to share those reasons?"

"Nope. I'm not at liberty to say, but you'll see what I mean in a little bit." He softened his refusal with a sexy grin that made her forget everything but him. "How about a refill on your lemonade?"

"Sure." Hand in hand, they headed toward the table holding the soft drinks. "So, what was that all about with Mia and Cam?" she asked, finding that whole scenario equally interesting.

"Cameron has been a friend of mine for years, and he's known Mia since she was a teenager. Mia has three older brothers, and she's always been a handful. She seems to like the thrill of the chase when it comes to men, and it drives her nuts that Cam is immune to her. But he's not, as you saw earlier."

"Which only makes her more determined to get his attention." That much was easy to figure out.

"Exactly." His tone was succinct as he filled a cup with ice and poured lemonade from a big barrel. "Honestly, she needs someone like Cameron, who isn't threatened by her aggressive, forward nature, but Cam is resisting big-time."

"Aggressive and forward, huh?" She grinned up at him as she took the cup from his fingers. "Sounds like a normal Wilde trait to me."

He cocked his head toward her. "Are you complaining?"

The man was entirely too confident, and she hid her smile around the rim of her cup as she took a quick drink. "No, just so long as you know where your real place is."

"In your bed?" he guessed wickedly.

In my heart. The thought jumped automatically into her mind, and her heart stuttered in her chest. "Yeah, you do real well for yourself in my bed."

He leaned close, slid an arm around her waist to pull her close to his side, and nuzzled near her ear, which sent a series of shivers skittering down her spine. "I do believe the pleasure is mutual."

And temporary, she reminded herself. As were her presence at this party, Steve's affection, and her place in his life. It could be no other way.

Steve's mother, Angela, appeared beside them and helped herself to a refill on her soda. She looked slightly frazzled but happy with the party's progress so far. "I've been so busy with all the other guests, I haven't had much time to talk to the two of you."

"We understand," Steve said, completely at ease with his arm around Liz, with his mother and fifty other people looking on.

Angela smiled at Liz, her eyes just as blue as her son's, and her sable hair cut into a trendy style. "Are you enjoying yourself?"

"I'm having a great time," Liz assured the other woman, and meant it. She was glad that Steve had convinced her to come along.

"Good." Angela sounded pleased. "Did you get enough to eat?"

"Plenty." Barbecue chicken, baked beans, and potato salad. "Everything was delicious."

"There's plenty more for seconds, so don't be shy about helping yourself to the buffet and desserts."

Steve's father, Paul, appeared next to his wife, a plate of birthday cake in his hand. "Be careful; she's raised three strapping boys—four if you count me—and she likes to make sure that everyone eats—*a lot.*" To back up his claim, he patted his stomach, which was still lean and trim despite his sixty years. "Even now that the boys are grown and gone, she cooks enough for a small army."

Angela drew herself up to her full five-foot-six height and gave Paul a very wifely look. "I like to cook, and I never know when one of the boys might stop by, and they enjoy my 'CARE' packages."

"Well, it appears that Jill is feeding Eric quite well, because his dinner visits are few and far between." Paul eyed his other son speculatively. "And I have to say that Steve hasn't been by as much the past month, either."

"I've been busy at work," Steve said as an excuse, though Liz wondered if his reasons for spending less time at his parents' for dinner was due to the increased amount of time he'd spent at her café the past month.

"Besides," Steve went on pragmatically, "you can always count on Adrian to help out with the leftovers. His stomach is like a bottomless pit."

"Hey, are you talking about me when I'm not here to defend myself?"

Liz turned toward the deep voice and found herself looking at another Wilde brother. There was no mistaking that pitch-black hair, blue eyes, chiseled good looks, and especially that bad boy demeanor he wore as easily as his tight black jeans and sage green knit shirt.

"Ahh, the daredevil son finally arrives," Paul said jovially. "Glad to see you survived another expedition and could join the celebration."

"I wouldn't miss your party for anything. Happy birthday, Dad." Adrian gave his father a warm hug, then kissed his mother on the cheek. "Hi, Mom."

"Have you eaten dinner yet?" Angela asked, and before he could reply, she added, "I'm sure you haven't eaten anything decent all day long, and the food's still warm over at the buffet."

"I'll head over there in a little bit," he promised, dazzling his mother with another flash of a smile.

She patted his arm. "Be sure that you do."

Steve's mom and dad moved on to mingle with their guests, and Adrian turned and trained those vivid blue eyes on Liz. A slow, appreciative grin lifted the corners of his mouth. "And who do we have here?"

"This is Liz," Steve said, his fingers tightening just the tiniest bit against her waist. "Liz, my other brother, Adrian."

She extended her hand. "It's a pleasure to meet you."

Instead of shaking her hand, he picked it up and brushed his lips across her knuckles, the gesture gallant and incredibly flirtatious. "No, believe me, the pleasure is all mine."

His gaze flickered down the length of her, then back up to her face before he glanced at his brother. "Wow, she really does have a great set of . . ." Liz felt Steve stiffen beside her before Adrian finished with "eyes."

Adrian winked at her, and Steve blew out a taut stream of breath, clearly annoyed at his brother for a reason Liz couldn't phantom. It appeared that Adrian's compliment was attached to some kind of private joke between brothers.

"I'm sure you could use a cold beer." Steve hitched his thumb toward the long line waiting to order a drink. "The bar's right over there."

"Actually, why don't you get me the beer, and I'll take Liz for a spin out on the dance floor." He took the cup of lemonade from her hand and gave it to Steve to hold, despite his brother's sudden frown. "I'm still working on an adrenaline high from the climb today. You don't mind, do you?"

Steve looked like he wanted to crush the cup that Adrian had just given him in his fist, and Liz was surprised by the undercurrents of sibling rivalry between the two—though she knew that Adrian was completely harmless. It was Steve's possessiveness she found so entertaining, as if he couldn't stand the thought of his brother's hands on her.

A muscle in Steve's jaw ticked, but he showed remarkable restraint and managed a gracious albeit tight smile. "Of course I don't mind."

"Great." Adrian tucked her hand in the crook of his arm and whisked her off to the patio, where the guests were enjoying the band's lively music.

In a smooth, fluid move, he had her in his arms, with his warm fingers resting lightly on the curve of her waist, her other hand held in his, and him leading her into a two-step along with the rest of the crowd. The man certainly knew how to dance, and judging by Steve's narrowed gaze from the sidelines as he watched the two of them together, Adrian knew how to provoke his brother, as well.

Green-eyed monster aside, Steve had nothing to worry about. Adrian might be drop-dead gorgeous and quite the ladies' man, but he didn't send her pulse soaring the way Steve did, and he did absolutely nothing for her hormones or her heart. All of the above belonged to his brother, it seemed.

But she did enjoy Adrian's easy-going personality, and she felt comfortable with him even when he was doing his best to charm her.

She smiled up at Adrian and called him on his incorrigible behavior. "Why do I get the feeling that you did that on purpose?"

He blinked at her, his not-so-guileless blue eyes sparkling with feigned innocence and mirth. "Did what on purpose?"

Oh, he was good, and she imagined that many women had fallen for that playful, sexy grin of his. "You deliberately riled your brother by insisting on dancing with me."

He chuckled as he smoothly maneuvered them around a couple dancing slower than they were. "Guilty as charged, though don't doubt for a second that my scheme is giving me double the pleasure." His hand casually slid from her hip to her lower back, bringing them another few inches closer. "I always enjoy having a beautiful woman in my arms, and it's not often that I can ruffle Steve's feathers. You're obviously a hot button for him, and I can't help but press it, because his reaction is just so damn comical."

She caught another glance of Steve, who was watching them intently from his line at the bar. He also looked as though he'd cheerfully strangle his brother for making their dance position more intimate, though her body wasn't even touching Adrian's. "You call that scowl of his comical?"

"Yeah." His tone was low and indulgent. "I can't remember the last time he was so possessive about a woman."

That was something that scared her to hear, no matter how much it thrilled her. "I think you're misreading his signals. Steve and I are just working on a case together, which should hopefully be wrapped up soon."

"Uh-huh." He twirled her in a quick circle and caught her around the waist again. "I know my brother, Liz, and I can assure you that his radar is tuned in on you and no one else. He'll never admit to being territorial, of course, but I'm enjoying the hell out of it. And you," he added with a quick wink. "Now that I've met you, I can see why Steve's so attracted to you. You seem very down-to-earth and genuine, yet open and fun, and that's exactly what Steve needs in a woman."

His sincere compliment warmed her, and since there was no sense arguing her temporary relationship with Steve to his brother, she accepted his flattering comments gracefully. "Thank you."

Adrian's gaze shifted to somewhere over her shoulder, and the gleeful grin that appeared on his face told her something was up. "Speaking of the devil, here he comes."

Seconds later, Steve was bringing their shuffling two-step to a halt and cutting in. "Here's your beer," he said, pressing the bottle into Adrian's hand. "Now it's my turn."

Without argument, Adrian disengaged his hold on Liz and relinquished her to Steve. "Don't worry, big brother, I promise she's unscathed, and her virtue is still intact."

"And not a moment too soon, I'm sure," he grumbled.

Adrian laughed and moved on, heading over to the buffet table and greeting people along the way. The band segued into a slow song, and Steve took advantage of the opportunity to pull her body flush against his and splayed his hand at the small of her back to keep their hips pressed close. She was wearing a sarong-style skirt and cotton top, and the heat of him managed to seep through the layers of her clothes, sending her hormones into a frenzy and accelerating the rapid beat of her pulse. It also made her wish they were alone, because she was aching to kiss him and let her hands wander. And have him do the same.

So instead of creating a public scandal, she let herself luxuriate in the delicious male scent of him and in being the sole focus of his attention.

Entwining her arms around his neck, which effectively crushed her sensitive breasts against his chest, she smiled up at him. "Your brother is quite the . . ."

"Pain in the ass?" he finished for her.

Seeing the glimmer of humor in his bright blue eyes, she laughed and shook her head. "I was going to say that your brother is quite the charmer."

"Hmmm." He gently tucked her head against his shoulder and stroked his fingers through her hair. "He has his moments, I suppose."

Content with just relaxing against Steve's solid strength, she closed her eyes and let him lead her around the patio to the slow beat of the music. It had been too long since she'd let a man take care of her, longer still since she felt so special. Much too soon the song ended, and instead of another one beginning, Eric's voice came over the speakers to address the party-goers.

"Everyone, I have an announcement to make," he said into the microphone, and all eyes went to where he stood up on the band's platform. "First of all, I want to wish my father a very happy birthday. Steve, Adrian, and I made sure we bought him a present he's sure to get a lot of use out of now that he's retired, but I have a special gift today that's for both of my parents. Where are you, Mom and Dad?" His gaze searched the crowd of people in the backyard until he found Angela and Paul waving from a group of guests they were visiting with.

"Pay attention," he said to his parents with a big grin, and then he crooked his finger toward the table where Liz and Steve had been sitting earlier. "Jill, can you come up here, honey?"

His girlfriend looked momentarily startled to be summoned up onstage, but she did as he asked, her expression reflecting confusion and the slightest bit of hesitation. She obviously had no idea what he intended. And neither did anyone else—except for maybe Steve, who was looking on with a bit of brotherly pride.

Once Jill was standing by Eric's side, and with everyone quiet and watching the couple avidly, he picked up her left hand, held her gaze steadily, and said, "I can't think of a better place to do this, since I'm surrounded by good friends, relatives, and family." Reaching into the front pocket of his khaki pants, he withdrew a small black velvet box and flipped open the lid, revealing a gorgeous, sparkling diamond engagement ring.

"Jill, will you marry me?" he asked, his voice smooth, clear, and confident.

Jill gasped and slapped a hand over her mouth, her eyes wide with shock and disbelief as she glanced from the ring to Eric's face.

The silence stretched on, and a crooked grin tugged at Eric's lips. "What, is the ring not big enough?"

"It's perfect." Her voice trembled, as did the hand she reached out to touch the velvet-lined box. "Oh, Eric, are you serious?"

He rolled his eyes at the ridiculous question. "Honey, I love you. Of course I'm serious."

Her eyes welled up with tears as she gazed at him with pure adoration. "I love you, too, Eric Wilde."

"Tell him yes and put him out of his misery!" Adrian yelled from across the yard, and everyone hooted and hollered their agreement.

Eric grinned at his sibling's show of support and returned his hopeful gaze to Jill. "Well?"

"Yes," she said in a whisper, then louder, *"Yes."*

He slipped the beautiful ring onto her finger, making the

engagement official. Clapping and cheers ensued, and Paul and Angela made their way up to the stage to congratulate their son and soon-to-be daughter-in-law.

Steve whistled, loud and shrill, adding to the merriment. "Way to go, baby brother!"

Angela hugged both Eric and Jill enthusiastically, obviously thrilled with the unexpected turn of events. Then she leaned close to the microphone, her blue eyes twinkling with delight. "One down, two to go!"

Steve groaned, and Adrian vehemently denied the possibility of such a fate, while everyone around them laughed at Angela Wilde's optimism.

The next few hours passed quickly, and the warm afternoon turned into a cool evening. Still the party continued, now with two reasons to celebrate and party, and the Wilde family did both quite well.

Liz was chatting with Jill and Mia and sharing in Jill's excitement while the men mingled elsewhere, when she realized it was nearly eight P.M. She excused herself and went to find Steve, who was talking to his cousins, Mia's brothers, Alex, Joel, and Scott, whom she'd met earlier. Three more gorgeous, single bad bays to round out the Wilde clan.

She touched Steve's arm to get his attention, and he glanced at her with one of those disarming smiles of his. "As much as I hate to leave, I have to go home and get ready for work tonight. There's no reason why you should have to leave, too, so I'll just call a cab."

"Absolutely not," he replied adamantly. "I'll take you home, then come back for a few hours. It's not a big deal."

. She appreciated his offer and didn't argue. She said her good-byes, thanked Angela and Paul for their hospitality, and walked with Steve out to his SUV. Once they were both seated in the vehicle, Steve threaded his fingers through her hair, cupped the back of her head, and pulled her forward so that she was meeting him halfway across the cab. Without preamble, he melded her mouth to his, and her lips parted of their own accord, inviting a deeper, intimate possession. His tongue swept inside, bold and ravenous, and she shivered at the heat and desire his kiss evoked.

He pulled back, much too soon for her liking, and rested his forehead against hers. The interior of the vehicle was dark, but the air around them fairly crackled with awareness and sexual tension.

"God, I needed that." His lips skimmed along her jaw, up to her ear. "I missed you today."

She tipped her head to the side, and he laved the sensitive spot right beneath her lobe. Her nipples pulled tight, aching for the caress of his hands, the tug of his mouth, the wet rasp of his tongue. "Correct me if I'm mistaken, but I believe I was by your side for most of the day."

"Umm, but it would have been tacky to make out with you in front of everyone like I wanted to do," he said huskily. "To touch you intimately and give you my undivided attention."

"Ahhh." Now she understood, and smiled. "In that case, I missed you, too."

His mouth took hers again in a lazy, mindless, tongue-tangling kiss that seemed to go on for long, slow minutes. By the time he let her up for air again, her skin felt flushed, and she was breathing much too fast.

Somehow, she managed to hold on to rational thought. "We really need to go so I'm not late for work."

His thumb dragged sensuously across her damp lower lip. "You can always tell them that you were with a client."

"Ha-ha." She wriggled her nose at him. "We still have to put on a convincing act on the phone first."

"That hasn't been a problem for us yet." He let her go, his reluctance to do so tangible. He started up the truck, and a minute later they were out on the main road, heading back to her apartment.

She rested her head against the back of the seat, wishing

she didn't have to go to work tonight. The last thing she wanted to do was field a bunch of sexual calls when she'd rather spend the rest of the evening alone with Steve. But she had a job to do, responsibilities to live up to, and a cousin to track down.

"Did you have a good time today?" Steve asked, gently rerouting her thoughts back to him.

"I had a wonderful time." With the lights from the dash illuminating his face, she took in his strong profile: the slope of his nose, his full lips, his strong jaw. "I like your family." And she envied him the closeness he and his siblings and cousins all shared, since that had always elluded her with Valerie.

Reaching across the console, he found the hand resting on her thigh and entwined their fingers together. "They like you, too."

Was he saying that just to be nice, to make her feel good? "And how do you know that?" she asked casually.

He came to a stop at a red light and glanced her way, the tenderness and caring in his gaze just as genuine as the tone of his voice. "Because they all told me so."

Little did he know, he'd just given her a perfect ending to an equally perfect day.

Chapter

11

Steve disconnected his evening call with Liz, ending another night of phone sex along with a second attempt to express his interest in meeting Liz in person.

Tonight, she'd delighted and aroused him with a personal fantasy of her own that had stirred his libido into a raging inferno of need. Even now, as he lay on his bed, his cock was granite-hard, full to bursting beneath his boxer shorts, and lust clawed at him as he replayed Liz's provocative fantasy in his mind while he waited another ten minutes for her to sign out and get to her car.

She wanted to be chased, captured, and forced to submit to a virile, lusty pirate, a man she secretly desired but would never admit to being attracted to, because it was so forbidden. In explicit, vivid detail, she'd pulled him into her enthralling tale, explaining the various methods by which the bold, dominant pirate would stake his claim on her, and how he'd possess her in wild, wicked, thrilling ways. But she wouldn't be his prisoner against her will, because despite all rules of propriety, she wanted the dark and dangerous pirate. And in the end, she'd surrender to him with abandon.

It was an erotic, exciting fantasy Steve wouldn't mind enacting for her. In fact, he was already considering the different ways to bring her private adventure to life.

For another few minutes he let his mind create various tantalizing scenarios; then he picked up the portable phone again and punched in her cell phone number. The line connected on the second ring.

"Hi there," she said, her voice soft with fatigue and not nearly so perky as she'd been with him just fifteen minutes ago. Her exhaustion wasn't surprising, considering the long day she'd had, and it was after midnight.

"Nice fantasy tonight," he complimented.

"You liked that, did you?" she murmured huskily, sounding pleased at her ability to seduce him.

"Oh, yeah, I liked. Very much." The hard-on that was still raging at full mast was testimony to her extraordinary talents to weave such sexy, tempting tales. "Would you like me to buy an eye patch?"

Her gentle laughter tickled his ear. "You look enough like a pirate without one."

He shifted on his bed, trying to find a cool spot on his sheets for his overheated body. "You sound tired."

"I am." She sighed, the slow exhale backing up her claim. "I think this week of working double shifts is finally catching up to me."

"You're probably right." He heard her stifle a yawn and smiled. "And today was busy, too."

"But well worth it." Honest appreciation laced her voice, making him glad he'd extended the invitation to his father's party, and that she'd accepted.

He'd only meant to share the day and his family with her, to distract her from everything else going on in her life. But she'd fit in so well, and having her meet his brothers, parents, and other relatives had evolved into something more significant for him. The emotions filling his chest definitely conflicted with the years he'd spent avoiding any kind of serious relationship with a woman, yet Liz wasn't like any other woman he'd dated since his divorce.

He had no idea what would happen between them once they located her cousin and the case was over, but he hoped Liz would be open to pursuing their relationship and seeing where it led them. A huge step for him, but one he was willing to take with her, because he just couldn't imagine letting her go.

"Tell you what," he said, making a split-second decision on both their behalf. "I'm kinda beat myself, so why don't we call it a night?"

"You don't mind?"

"Of course I don't mind." He ignored the throbbing in his groin that protested otherwise, telling himself a night of abstinence wouldn't kill him. "As much as I'd love to come over and be your pirate, I think you need a good night's rest more." And he needed time and distance to sort through his growing feelings for her.

"I can't argue with you there."

Steve couldn't tell if she was relieved or disappointed, but imagined she was a little of both.

"By the way," she went on, "I checked my schedule at The Ultimate Fantasy, and I have tomorrow night off, but I'll be spending the entire day at the café, getting caught up on paperwork and inventory for next week."

"I have things to do at the office, too." Sitting up on the edge of the mattress, he stared at his reflection in the mirrored closet doors across from him, which conjured up an idea or two in terms of her pirate fantasy. "I'm sure I'll talk to you at some point tomorrow."

"You know where to find me."

"That I do." He chuckled and regretted that he wouldn't be seeing her tonight, but knew it was for the best. "Drive home safely, and dream of me when you fall asleep tonight."

"Believe me, I already do."

* * *

Liz finished balancing her business checking account and was overjoyed to find that after all her expenses, she actually had a decent amount of money left over. According to her profit-and-loss statement, business was up by a good ten percent from the previous month, all great news since she'd spent the past three years struggling to claw her way out of debt. Gradually, she was getting there.

Now paying off her aunt and uncle was her main priority, and she was whittling away that financial obligation little by little, as well. She wrote them out a check, adding a couple of hundred dollars more to the monthly amount they'd agreed upon, because she could afford to do so this time around. She also earmarked another few hundred to add to the money she owed Steve for his PI services. Another debt she intended to pay off in full.

Satisfied with her day's work, she closed her accounting journal and slid it back into the office safe behind her desk. It was nearing seven-thirty in the evening, and while it had been a busy, productive Sunday, she felt more exhilarated than tired, because she'd gotten so much done.

She was surprised, however, that she hadn't heard from Steve. When she'd called her answering machine at home that afternoon to check her messages, there had been a call from Antonio, asking her to meet him at The Ultimate Fantasy Monday morning at eleven A.M., saying that there was an advancement opportunity within the company that he wanted to speak to her about. She'd been excited to have gotten the call both she and Steve had been waiting for, and had immediately dialed his cell phone number, only to get his voice mail. She'd left him a brief message but hadn't heard back from him yet—and that had been nearly three hours ago.

With a sigh that held too much disappointment, she picked up the stack of paid receipts and statements and began filing them in the old secondhand cabinet against the far wall. The task was a mindless one, allowing her thoughts too much freedom to stray and wonder about where Steve was, and what he was doing. One day apart and she missed him, more than was prudent, considering that such a wistful emotion had no business playing any part in their short-term relationship.

Her heart thumped hard in her chest, making her breath catch with deeper meaning, as was happening much too often lately. She shook herself hard. She couldn't afford to fall in love with Steve, knew she'd be setting herself up for heartbreak if she did so. Yes, he was wonderful and caring and a generous lover, but she didn't need another bad boy who rode a motorcycle and enjoyed adventure and spontaneity and said he didn't want a lifetime commitment.

He was fine for the moment as a fun fling, but not for the future. She'd already let one bad boy lead her astray, and she was still dealing with the fallout of that tumultuous relationship. Still trying to pay off debts and keep her business running smoothly and profitably while establishing her independence all over again—not to mention the responsibility she'd taken on to watch after her cousin.

"Hey, sexy," a low, deep voice said from behind her, jarring her out of her private thoughts. "Wanna get lucky tonight?"

Liz whirled around—startled, pleased, and thrilled to find Steve leaning lazily against the doorjamb of her small makeshift office. He was wearing tight black jeans and a long-sleeved black turtleneck, and his leather jacket was casually slung over his shoulder. He obviously hadn't shaved that day; dark stubble shaded his jaw and cheeks, and his thick, sable hair was rumpled around his head. A roguish grin curved his lips, and his bright blue eyes sparkled with shameless purpose.

He looked disreputable, gorgeous, and ready and willing to commit a whole lot of sin.

Okay, so he wasn't husband material, but the man was most definitely her every fantasy come to life. She'd already given herself permission to enjoy him for the time being, and that was exactly what she intended to do.

"Hi, yourself." She filed the last of the statements, closed the cabinet, and went back to her desk. "What are you doing here?"

He pushed off the doorjamb and strolled into the room, filling her sanctuary with his dominating masculine presence. "I was in the neighborhood and thought I'd stop by."

"I'm glad you did." She smiled as she secured a rubber band around the paid bills she needed to mail tomorrow morning. "Are you here for your caramel frappuccino?"

"No, I'm here for *you.*" Standing on the other side of her small desk, he cocked his hip and slid his fingers into the front pocket of his jeans. "Have you eaten dinner yet?"

She shook her head, realizing just how hungry she actually was. "No. I've been so busy that I haven't even thought about dinner."

"What are the chances of you getting out of here early and joining me for a bite to eat?" He winked at her.

She shivered at the naughty connotation to his words, no doubt deliberate on his part, judging by the wicked gleam in his eyes. "I'd say your chances are very good. I just finished up everything I needed to for the day. Let me go over a few things with my night manager; then I'm a free woman and all yours."

Fifteen minutes later, he was escorting her out the front door of the café and to his Harley-Davidson, parked at the curb. She stopped abruptly and glanced up at him. "Where's your truck?"

"At home." He unhooked one of the two black helmets from the motorcycle and held it loosely in his hand. "I thought it might be fun to take you for a ride on my bike. Are you okay with that?"

Surprisingly, she was, and knew it was only because she trusted him so much. He was offering her a bit of frivolous fun after a long day at work, an irresistible adventure that beckoned to her wilder side, along with the chance to indulge that bad girl inside her that only he had the ability to rouse.

She grinned, welcoming the rush of excitement infusing her veins. "I'm more than okay with that."

"You're gonna love it," he promised, and secured the helmet on her head, then held open his leather jacket for her to wear.

She slipped inside the fragrant warmth. He zipped her up and flipped the collar up around her neck, enveloping her in the delicious, heady scent of Steve, worn leather, and pure male heat. The jacket was two sizes too big for her, but it made her feel safe and protected, just as the man himself did.

While he put on his own helmet, her gaze drifted over the beast of a bike she was about to climb up on. The motorcycle was huge, all gleaming black enamel and shiny chrome, except for the words *Wilde Thing*, airbrushed in graduated shades of orange, yellow, and red on the gas tank situated between the handlebars and seat. The suggestive statement suited him and brought to mind the sexy lyrics to the song of the same name: "Wild thing, I think I love you."

She dismissed those thoughts as soon as they entered her head, fearing the truth inherent in those words. She inhaled the cool night air, knowing she'd never again be able to hear that song without thinking of Steve and her time with him.

He mounted the bike first, and with his instruction she straddled the leather seat and settled herself behind him, spreading her thighs to encompass the width of his hips. He started the engine, and the whole bike reverberated to life, as did her nerve endings. Her pulse leaped, the vibrations arousing her body and tickling her senses.

"Wrap your arms around my waist," he said to her over his shoulder.

He didn't have to ask twice. She leaned into the solid, muscular strength of his back, bringing them intimately close and

snug, and locked her fingers over his taut abdomen. He revved
the high-powered engine once more, and off they went.

He drove along Lake Shore Drive, taking her past North Avenue Beach and Lincoln Park. At night, the sights were incredible, a mesmerizing combination of colored lights and unob-
structed views. Sitting on the back of his motorcycle, with the
wide-open road ahead of them and the wind caressing her
face, Liz felt exhilarated, unrestrained, with a sense of freedom that had eluded her since before she'd married Travis.
She embraced the feeling, and Steve, and enjoyed the invigorating sensations rippling through her.

While she felt cocooned in warmth within Steve's leather
jacket, her fingers grew cold, and she grew bold, tugging up
the hem of his turtleneck a few inches so she could slip her
palms beneath his shirt and absorb some of his body heat.
Amazingly enough, his skin was blessedly hot, and she splayed
her chilled hands on his flat belly. He didn't so much as flinch
at the contact, and she groaned gratefully as she rubbed her
palms up along his ribs, and her fingers began to thaw and
warm.

Long after her hands had defrosted, she continued to stroke
him, to absently caress his chest, his sides, his stomach, just
because she liked touching him. Before long he was turning
down the street that led to the Navy Pier and the shops, attractions, and restaurants located along the popular board-
walk.

He parked the motorcycle and helped her off it. It took her
a moment to regain her footing since her legs were shaking
from the vibrations of the engine. He removed her helmet and
threaded his long fingers through her hair, restoring it to some
semblance of order, she guessed. The tender look in his eyes,
however, told her he'd combed through the silky strands for
the pure pleasure of it.

She glanced out at the pier as realization dawned. "Have
you just coerced me into a date?"

He chuckled and grabbed her hand, entwining their fingers intimately as they walked toward one of Chicago's largest landmarks and tourist attractions. "No coercing about it, sweetheart. You got onto the back of my bike willingly."

She couldn't argue with that—not that she wanted to. "That was fun," she admitted.

"What, feeling me up?"

She laughed, feeling more lighthearted and carefree than she had in the past three years. "That, and riding on your bike."

He gave her hand an affectionate squeeze. "I had a feeling you'd like it."

She tipped her head, regarding him speculatively. "Have you ever taken another woman on your motorcycle?" The question slipped out before she could stop it.

He didn't seem to mind her personal inquiry, though there was an intensity in his eyes that belied his casual demeanor. "You're the first woman I've ever asked."

His reply made her feel too giddy. "Lucky me," she said, uncaring how possessive she sounded.

He dropped a spontaneous kiss on her lips, which left her aching for a deeper, longer embrace. "More like lucky *me*," he murmured.

They ordered dinner at a casual seafood restaurant overlooking the harbor and shared a platter of fried clams, sauteed shrimp, steamed mussels, and crab legs. Messy finger foods that both of them fed to each other.

Liz took a drink of the frothy piña colada she'd ordered, and glanced at the man sitting next to her. "Did you get my voice mail message today?"

"Yeah, I did." He dipped a fried clam in cocktail sauce and brought it up to her mouth to eat, then licked the excess condiment from his own fingers. "I was out doing some surveillance work on a case and figured we could talk about things tonight, in person. What did Antonio have to say?"

"The message was brief but to the point, and exactly what we've been hoping for." She swirled the last shrimp in garlic-butter sauce and lifted it to his lips. He curled his tongue around the morsel of meat, slow and sensual, and her stomach fluttered with awareness. "I have an appointment to meet with Antonio tomorrow morning at eleven. He said he wanted to talk to me about an advancement opportunity within the company."

Steve wiped his mouth on a napkin, and since they'd pretty much cleared their platter, he motioned their waitress back to the table. "Which I'm sure translates to offering you a position as a party girl."

She waited while the young woman cleared their dishes, and Steve took the liberty of ordering a dessert for them to share—a slice of praline cheesecake drizzled with extra caramel sauce.

Once the waitress had moved on to fill their dessert order, she said, "I won't accept the offer if Antonio suggests I take any client other than you to The Ultimate Fantasy party."

A muscle in his jaw flexed, and his expression turned adamant. "You can bet I won't let you go to one of those parties by yourself, or without me on your arm. And there's no way in hell I'd allow another man to think you're his for the night."

The rough, territorial growl in his voice thrilled her. "What if we get to the party and don't get the information we need to track the guy Valerie was seeing?"

"There aren't any guarantees either way, so let's not jump ahead of things, okay?" He brushed his fingers gently along her cheek in a caring caress. "Let's take it one step at a time."

Once again she entrusted herself to him. "All right."

Their cheesecake was delivered with two forks, but Steve insisted on feeding her bites in between his. The dessert was smooth and delicious, the caramel just enough to tempt her palate and remind her of their erotic encounter a few nights ago.

He touched another creamy bite to her lips, coaxing her to open up and accept, which she did. "Are you trying to fatten me up?"

"Not at all," he drawled, and licked away a drop of caramel from the corner of his mouth. "I just want to make sure you've got plenty of energy for later."

"Later?" She lifted a brow, undeniably curious. "What have you got planned for tonight, Mr. Wilde?"

His dark, compelling gaze riveted her. "It's a surprise, *wench.*"

Desire began a slow burn inside her, and a hopeful grin spread across her face. "You're going to be my pirate?"

"Aye," he said in a decent imitation of a wicked, lascivious buccaneer. "You betcha, I am."

Oh, yes. She licked her lips, tasting caramel and praline and wishing it were Steve instead. "What are you waiting for? Take me home and ravish me."

Liz was learning to expect the unexpected when it came to Steve, which was part of what made him so breathtakingly appealing, so utterly irresistible. He didn't take her back to The Daily Grind for her to get her car, nor did he head toward her apartment. Instead, he drove them to a suburb just outside the city, where they wended their way though a residential area with large, well-kept homes that spoke of middle-class comfort.

No matter where Steve took her, Liz knew how the night was going to end—with a deliciously forbidden fantasy fulfilled, and her completely sated. The man didn't do anything halfway, including giving as much sexual pleasure as he received.

The vibrating rumble of the motorcycle's engine between

her thighs electrified her, building her anticipation for what was to come. Finally, the bike slowed and Steve turned into the driveway of a two-story structure. The metal garage door rolled up, and he pulled into a spot right next to his SUV and cut the motor.

In one smooth, fluid motion he moved off the bike, then held out his hand to help her do the same, though her legs weren't quite as steady as his. Their helmets came off, along with the leather jacket she wore, which he tossed across the seat of the Harley.

She rubbed her bare arms, feeling chilled straight through her blouse without his jacket, but knew he'd be warming her up again soon enough.

"Where are we?" she asked as she followed him to a door that led inside the house. Stupid question, but for some reason she needed him to confirm their destination.

He punched a quick code into the keypad on the wall, disengaging an alarm before he unlocked the door. "My place."

Yes, she was surprised, but didn't ask why he'd chosen to bring her to his home tonight. She refused to read anything deeper into the switch from her apartment to his bachelor pad, other than a change of scenery.

He opened the door, and she glanced from the dark, shadowed interior of his house to his equally dark, shadowed face. She stared up into his hot, hungry eyes and shivered, but not from the cold this time. With the dim light in the garage haloing his head, he looked like a fallen angel, a dangerous outlaw, and most definitely a plundering, pillaging pirate.

He inclined his head and murmured, "You have thirty seconds to hide from me, wench, before I come after you. And once I capture you, you're mine, to do with as I please, in any way I desire. Do you understand?"

She nodded jerkily, the intensity of her growing excitement making her feel light-headed, and damp between her thighs.

She was his prisoner, his captive, and he'd just established himself as her master. She might have begun the provocative game on the phone last night, but he would finish it now and stake a primitive claim on her. Without a doubt, she knew tonight's fantasy would be like nothing she'd ever experienced before.

"One . . ." he began, counting down the seconds he'd given her as a head start. "Two . . ."

Adrenaline pumped through her, heating her blood and making her heart beat wildly in her chest. She bolted into the house, and it was like plunging into an unknown maze of obscure doorways and furniture, shadowy corridors, and darkened rooms. Gradually, her eyes adjusted to the dimness. Steve had the benefit of knowing the layout of the house, but she wasn't at all daunted by her disadvantage, because she eventually wanted to be seized and ravished. But first she intended to enjoy the very adult game of hide-and-seek, and that meant evading her master's capture.

At his count of twenty, she turned to the left and found herself in what appeared to be a living room with suede couches and a big-screen TV. She had no idea where to go from there, and her pulse rioted within her as he neared the thirty-second mark; then the house filled with an ominous silence.

Experiencing a burst of animated panic, she turned down a hallway and saw Steve's silhouette approaching from the other end. Startled, she gasped and sprinted in the opposite direction, running into the kitchen with a large, wooden butcher block dominating the middle of the room. She spun around just as Steve entered, giving her no choice but to rush to the far end of the kitchen and use the big block of wood as a barrier between them.

He peeled off his turtleneck and tossed the garment onto a nearby table. Slowly he circled around one side of the slab of wood and toward her. The slice of moonlight streaming through the kitchen window illuminated the breadth of his chest and made his eyes gleam like quicksilver. "Take off your blouse, or I'll rip it off when I catch you."

"*If* you catch me," she taunted bravely.

He continued to stalk her, a predatory smile curving his full lips. "Don't doubt that I will, so consider yourself fore-warned."

With him having cleared one side of the counter, she dashed out of the room and down another hallway. Seemingly out of nowhere, he appeared in front of her, from another doorway. She yelped and turned to run back into the kitchen. Just as she entered, he caught her around the waist and pulled her backside hard against his chest.

His parted lips grazed the side of her neck. "You can run, but you can't hide," he breathed into her ear.

She shuddered, a delightful, eager sensation. Playing the stubborn, rebellious captive, she tugged at the arm banded around her middle, and struggled to find a way out of his grasp, but she was no match for his superior strength, and they both knew it. He maneuvered her up against the butcher block, trapping her hips between the edge of the solid counter-top and himself, behind her. Her bottom was tucked tightly against his groin, the thick erection confined behind denim searing her even through her own jeans.

With the pressure of his hips keeping her immobile, he raised his hands to the first button on her blouse and dipped his fingers into her cleavage. He stroked over the mounds of her breasts, and her nipples hardened into aching points. True to his word, he tugged on the fabric, hard, and sent the first button skittering across the kitchen. Another fierce yank of material, and her top split wide open with a resounding rip. She sucked in a stunned breath, and moaned when he roughly pushed the cups of her bra down and his big hands closed over her breasts. He squeezed and kneaded her flesh and deli-cately pinched her nipples between his fingers.

She bit her lower lip to keep from crying out in pleasure. As his prisoner, she wouldn't give him that satisfaction. He pulled off the shredded fabric that was now her blouse and dropped it to the floor. Seconds later, her bra followed. He turned her in his arms, keeping her spine locked against the counter, and clamped his hot, wet mouth over one rigid nipple and sucked while his other hand continued to fondle her other breast.

Swallowing a whimper, she closed her eyes and gripped the edge of the wooden block at her sides. His velvet-soft tongue licked and swirled, and his teeth nibbled, sending waves of heat rolling through her. Long, questing fingers grazed her belly, and he took a step back to give him more room to release the snap on her jeans.

Refusing to give in to him so easily, she made a quick decision and darted to the side, managing to evade his grasp since he hadn't expected her to bolt. She hightailed it down the dark hallway and took the stairs double-time to the second level of the house. She instinctively headed left and slipped through the second doorway on the right. A bathroom, she realized, that adjoined another room, from what she could tell in the darkness.

She heard the creak of a stair, knew he was coming to find her, and moved behind the bathroom door. She flattened her back against the wall, excruciatingly aroused, dizzy with desire and the thrill of the forbidden.

The man was incredibly light-footed; the only thing giving away his presence was his shadow as he moved past the bathroom, then stopped. She held her breath when he pushed the door open wide and stepped inside but didn't switch on the light. The cool wooden door touched her bare nipples, and the anticipation of getting caught made her stomach flutter and her mind spin. God, she hoped she didn't pass out from lack of oxygen. A few seconds later he backed out and continued down the hallway to the next room, and she gulped air back into her lungs.

"Come out, come out, wherever you are," he cajoled, his voice low and mesmerizingly sensual as he hunted for her.

With him in another section of the upper level, she silently moved into the adjoining bedroom, which turned out to be a home gym. Making her way to the threshold that led back out into the hallway, she waited there, listening for any sounds or movement from Steve. Unfortunately, all she could hear was the thudding of her heart in her chest and the roar of blood in her own ears.

Taking a chance, she rushed out of the room, made a sharp left down the corridor, and ran headlong into a solid wall of virile male muscle. Steve grabbed her upper arms, steadying her. Before she could regain her equilibrium, he pinned her up against the wall. His hands framed the sides of her face, holding her still as his mouth took hers, open and hot. His silky tongue thrust deep and tangled with hers, and he crushed his hair-roughened chest to her breasts, the heat of his flesh branding her. Widening his stance so that his knees bracketed hers, he rolled his hips, grinding his rock-hard sex against the notch between her thighs.

She moaned into his mouth and flattened her hands on the wall behind her, trying to remember that she was his hostage and he was the one in control. That this fantasy was all about her resisting, and Steve forcing her to submit. It was the resisting part she was having a difficult time with.

This time when he reached between them and wrenched open the button on her jeans, she let him. His hands pushed into the waistband of her pants and underwear, slid over her hips and around to her buttocks. Ruthlessly he shoved the material down her legs and left it bunched around her knees, effectively restraining her.

Then he was kneeling in front of her, his mouth open, hot, and wet on her belly, his tongue stroking over her hip, his teeth nipping her mound. Her sex pulsed, ached, and throbbed for the touch of his tongue, the caress of his fingers, the long, heated thrust of his cock filling her. He splayed his hands on her bare legs, widening them as much as the tangled denim allowed, and bit the sensitive inner flesh of her thighs, making her gasp and tremble. The stubble on his cheeks abraded her soft skin, adding to her heightening need.

His palms slid upward, and he delved his thumbs between the slick folds of her sex, separating her nether lips and forcing her swollen, glistening clit up and out, all his for the taking. She waited, her breath suspended in her lungs as he leaned forward and buried his tongue deep. He licked and circled her labia, pressing hard, retreating slowly, teasing her to the brink of her climax, only to let her orgasm ebb.

Her hands clenched in tight fists in her attempt to resist the frantic impulse to grab the back of his head and increase the pressure of his mouth, the friction of his tongue. "Steve," she said, and heard the desperation in her voice.

He looked up at her, his eyes dark and glittering with lust. "I want you to beg me for what you want."

She shook her head defiantly, and he proceeded to torment her further, laving her, suckling her, but keeping her release just out of reach. The pleasure grew with every hot pass of his tongue, heat and tension building higher and stronger. Her head rolled against the wall, and her body arched against his ravenous mouth of its own accord, striving for the peak that was so, so close . . .

He withdrew, and she whimpered at the loss of contact. "Beg, wench," he ordered roughly, and licked her again. And again, his tongue dancing wickedly over her flesh, so skilled, warm, and sleek.

Her frustration was so overwhelming, she sobbed and finally gave her pirate what he demanded from her.

"*Please,*" she panted, barely able to speak, but knew the one word would not gain her what she yearned for. "Please . . . let . . . me . . . come."

A long, thick finger thrust inside her at the same time he

closed his mouth over her clitoris and used the suctioning swirl of his tongue to draw her into a toe-curling, mind-bending orgasm. A hoarse, ragged cry ripped from her throat as her climax crested and her entire body spasmed with the force of her release.

As soon as those internal ripples subsided, Steve yanked at the pants and underwear around her knees. Still crouched in front of her, he anxiously shoved them down her legs and helped her step out of them, stripping her completely bare. Refusing to let him retain the upper hand as her captor, even after he'd so generously pleasured her, Liz pushed at his broad shoulders before he could stand back up and take her against the wall. The unexpected move caused him to lose his balance and fall back on his ass.

She sprinted to the side and out of his reach, and he cursed around a bout of deep, masculine chuckles that belied the dark, intimidating persona he'd assumed for the sake of their fantasy. Taking advantage of the handful of seconds she'd bought herself, she ran down the hallway . . . and straight into the master bedroom. Realizing her mistake, she whirled around to head down the stairs and came to an abrupt halt when she found Steve silhouetted in the doorway, blocking her only means of escape.

Her pulse fluttered at the sight of what a formidable opponent he made, so utterly sexual, so impressively virile, with his muscular arms and washboard stomach that spoke of his superior strength. The long, hard length of his erection was a blatant outline inside his black jeans, and somewhere along the way he'd taken off his shoes and socks.

"You're gonna pay for that little stunt, you ungrateful wench," he murmured, and though she knew this was all fun and games, that he would never do anything she objected to, she couldn't help but shiver at the sexy threat in his tone.

He played his part exceptionally well.

Pushing the bedroom door shut, he locked it with a resounding click, then flipped a switch on the wall that turned on a bedside light. She swallowed hard as his gaze raked down the length of her naked body.

"Now I have you right where I want you." He crooked a finger at her. "Come here," he ordered.

She jutted her chin out mutinously. "No."

Seemingly taking her refusal as a direct challenge, a seductive smile curved the corners of his mouth, and he strolled deeper into the room. For every confident step he took toward her, she took one back, the excitement and awareness between them building as they played a provocative game of cat-and-mouse. He continued to stalk her until he'd managed to maneuver her into the far corner of the bedroom, though there was still plenty of space separating them.

"Come here," he said again, this time more firmly. "Surrender, and I'll be gentle with you. Disobey, and suffer the consequences."

She didn't want *gentle*. She was excruciatingly aroused again, eager for a hot, aggressive kind of joining. And she wanted to see what kind of punishment he had in mind. She attempted to skirt around him, but he lunged toward her. His fingers caught in her hair and brought her up short with a yelp.

Startled, he hesitated for a moment, his eyes gentling as he searched her expression to make sure he hadn't gone too far with her. When she didn't issue a protest to his rough handling, he continued with the fantasy.

"Since it seems you need to learn your place, get on your knees," he said in a voice so low it was almost a growl.

The downward tugging on her scalp gave her no choice but to comply, and she knelt in front of him, her face level with that huge bulge in his pants. With his free hand, he managed to unbuckle his belt, open the fly of his jeans, and reach inside to release his stiff shaft and balls.

He stroked the length of his cock with his fingers, and she watched, fascinated, as he thickened even more. Bringing her head closer, he rubbed the broad, swollen head of his penis against her closed lips. His flesh was as hard as granite, textured like heated velvet, and seemed to quiver with need.

"Open up, wench, and take me in your mouth."

The hand fisted in her hair tightened to keep her from pulling away, but she wasn't going anywhere. She submitted to his domination because she wanted to pleasure him, too.

Looking up the length of his body and holding his hot gaze, she parted her lips and took him as deep as she could, surrounding him in wet heat and the silken caress of her tongue along the underside of his shaft. She relaxed her throat, practically swallowing him as his hand cupped the back of her head, holding her, guiding her, while his hips rocked rhythmically and his cock slid in and out of her mouth.

"Yessss," he hissed, and a muscle in his jaw clenched in restraint.

She knew he was close to coming; she could taste the change in him, hot and salty, could feel the steady throb of the vein running along the underside of his cock, and his testicles were drawn up close to his body. A shudder rocked him, and she swirled her tongue over the engorged, sensitive tip, then closed her lips tightly over the crown and sucked, hard, pushing him higher, increasing his pleasure with each stroke of her mouth on his sex. He groaned, closed his eyes, and made the mistake of loosening his hold on her hair.

She'd gained control, a heady sensation she couldn't help but exploit as his prisoner. Emboldened, she took him deep one last time, felt his body jerk, and knew he was on the verge of exploding. She drew back, released him from her mouth, and scrambled away and to her feet before he knew she was gone.

His brilliant blue eyes narrowed, fierce and hungry, contradicting the way the corner of his mouth twitched with a grin at her cunning. "Expect no mercy when I catch you."

Dismissing her for a moment, he walked to the nighstand beside the bed, withdrew a foil packet from a box, and sheathed his erection with a condom. He didn't bother taking off his jeans; the front placket remained wide open, framing his jutting sex, giving him the decadent appearance of a hedonistic bad boy intent on debauchery. And she was the object of his lust.

Lucky, lucky her. Heat and passion swept through her limbs, and her heartbeat accelerated with anticipation.

He turned toward her, once again stalking her. There was nowhere to hide, no way to avoid him, and they both knew it. But it was obvious that he reveled in the hunt, chase, and final capture. Before long, he trapped her between him and the bed, giving her no choice but to try to breach that barrier without getting caught. She made a run for it and scrambled across the mattress but only made it halfway across before a large hand clamped around her ankle and ruthlessly tugged her back.

She gave a shriek of startled surprise and thrashed, her legs flailing. She accidently kicked him in the hip, and he grunted, then muttered a curse, but continued to drag her back to where he stood at the other end of the bed. Her feet touched the floor, but the hand he flattened on her back kept her bent at the waist, with her breasts mashed against the soft comforter. She squirmed to free herself, and he pinned her to the edge of the mattress with his hips. She felt the hot, heavy pressure of his erection along the crease of her bottom, and an illicit thrill shot through her.

She heard the hiss of leather sliding through his belt loops and experienced a jolt of shock when he reached down and quickly secured the strap just above her knees, binding her legs together so that she couldn't move, couldn't run or escape again.

He leaned over her from behind, aligning their bodies intimately, the heavy weight of him pressing her deeper into the mattress. "Would you like your hands restrained behind your back, as well?" he whispered roughly in her ear.

She shook her head, though the image of herself helplessly bound for his pleasure did excite her. "No," she said breathlessly, and instead curled her fingers into the covers, suspecting she was going to need that anchor. "I'll be good. I promise."

His legs widened on either side of her thighs, the coarse denim of his jeans scratching her skin in an arousing way. He smoothed a palm down her spine, glided his hand over her buttocks, and dipped his fingers into the firm crevice between. He delved lower, found her positively drenched with desire for him, and stroked her wet folds, spreading her moisture, preparing her for his entry.

She moaned, lifting her hips and straining toward him as much as her position would allow, eager to be filled by him. He fitted the head of his shaft against her slick opening and pressed into her an inch, just enough to tease her. She sucked in a breath, wished she could open her legs wider, yet the clench of her thighs made for a tighter fit, a more erotic possession.

He leaned over her again and braced his arms on the mattress at her sides. His mouth skimmed her cheek, his breath hot, heavy, and moist on her skin. "Is this what you want, wench?" he rasped.

"Yes," she begged shamelessly. "Oh, yes."

He thrust the rest of the way into her, lifting her feet off the floor as he drove her hips up onto the bed, the size and hot, silken length of him stretching her as he impaled her to the hilt. She bit back a sharp cry, and he groaned and withdrew before plunging forward yet again, and again, moving against her, over her.

No mercy, he'd said, and he granted her none. He scraped his teeth along her shoulder, nipped at the side of her neck, and she whimpered as fiery, exquisite sensations spiraled down to her sex. His fingers tangled in her hair, and he turned her head, forcing her to look at the mirrored closet doors across from them.

"Watch me fuck you," he demanded huskily.

She couldn't have looked away from their reflection even if she wanted to. The sight of them together, playing out such a carnal fantasy, mesmerized her. As did the sight of him mounting her from behind, half dressed, his body pinning hers down, making her a slave to anything and everything he desired.

His face was taut with restraint, his unshaven jaw clenched, his expression a little savage. His hips pumped against hers, the muscles in his arms and down his back shifting and bunching each time he thrust deep. Digging her palms into the mattress, she lifted her bottom and pushed back, giving as good as he gave. A growl rolled up from his throat, and the length of him shuddered. Fisting her hair tighter in his hand, he locked an arm around her waist, holding her still, in ultimate control of her body, their movements, and her pleasure.

His hand glided lower as he continued to drive into her, slipping over her mons and working his fingers between her tethered thighs, where she was wet with wanting and aching for a more explicit touch. The first illicit stroke along her clitoris made her tremble and melt. The second skillful caress tore a low, ragged moan from her throat. His mouth opened on her neck, his tongue laved her skin, and then he sank his teeth into the tender flesh where the curve of her shoulder began. The triple sensual assault of his mouth, his cock, and his fingers manipulating her body shattered her defenses, and she came on a long, shockingly intense orgasm.

Her inner muscles clamped around him, milked him, and he panted, sucking air into his lungs as he pushed into her higher, harder, deeper. Relentlessly. With a low, primitive growl he finally surrendered to his own climax. He tossed his head back, thrust into her one last time, hard and fast, then stiffened. Her name tumbled reverently from his lips as his scalding release sent him over the sharp edge of pleasure and straight into the realm of mindless physical sensation.

Chapter

12

Liz rolled onto her back and stretched languidly, feeling amazingly rested, considering that Steve had physically exhausted her last night. A dreamy smile touched her lips, and she buried her face into the soft pillow, inhaling the musky scent of sex and the familiar, manly smell that was Steve's alone. A combination of heat and leather, with a faint overlay of the citrus aftershave he wore.

She opened her eyes with a sigh and was disappointed to find that she was alone in Steve's bed, then remembered him waking her at dawn with the slow caress of his hands on her breasts, his mouth on her throat, and his body easing over hers. She'd stirred beneath him, automatically spreading her legs to accommodate his hips as he sank into her and began to move.

Unlike last night's fast and frenzied joining, he'd taken her slowly and lazily, nuzzling her neck, threading his fingers gently through her hair, and arching into her so that his pubic bone rubbed her just the right way. He'd lifted his head, their gazes locking as he watched her expression as he stoked the fire between them. The buildup of her orgasm had been gradual, a tingling, sublime sensation that crested through her in undulating waves of bliss. He came with her on a long, low groan that rumbled his chest against hers.

It had been a lovely way to wake up.

She remembered stroking her fingers down his back and over the muscled slope of his firm butt and recalled the sleepy, instinctive words she'd spoken: "I should go."

"It's already five in the morning. Go back to sleep for a while." His lips drifted affectionately across her cheek, and he withdrew from her soft, satiated body. "I'll take you back to your apartment later."

She'd been unable to resist his sweet, caring suggestion to rest a bit longer, and snuggled back beneath the warm blanket and comforter. She heard him get up and take a shower, but she was too tired and replete to wake up fully and join him, despite how much the thought tempted her. Instead, she'd fallen into a deep, peaceful sleep. And now, as she glanced at the digital clock on the nightstand, she realized it was a quarter past eight, when she was normally up by six A.M. to start her day.

She wasn't worried about The Daily Grind. Her morning shift could handle the early Monday rush without her. But she did have an appointment with Antonio today, a meeting she wasn't about to be late for or to miss, considering all that was at stake.

Tossing off the covers, she reluctantly sat up on the edge of the mattress and shivered as the cool morning air hit her bare skin. She found a men's long-sleeved shirt draped over the end of the bed and assumed that it was for her to wear, since Steve had shredded her blouse last night. She slipped into the soft cotton and cuffed up the sleeves a few times since they hung past her fingertips. She had no idea where her panties were, so she went sans underwear, grateful that the hem reached mid-thigh.

She padded into the bathroom, finally seeing his bedroom in the light of day, and took care of business. Catching a glimpse of herself in the mirror, she grimaced. Her hair was a tousled mess, and her eye makeup was smudged—a morning-after look she'd been able to spare Steve until today. She used his brush to untangle her hair and restore some semblance of order to the unruly strands, then scrubbed her face clean.

She spotted a packaged, unused toothbrush on the vanity and studied it for a moment, her mind conjuring up all the reasons why Steve might have an extra stash of toiletries on hand. She chastised herself for making a big deal out of the fact that he was prepared for overnight guests, and tried to ignore the stab of jealousy that hit her squarely in the chest, before snatching up the toothbrush, ripping off the wrapper, and using it to scrub her teeth.

But that persistent ache remained, right in the vicinity of her heart—a tenderness and yearning that seemed to grow with each encounter with Steve. It was as if she gave a little part of herself to him each time they were together, each time they had sex.

Last night they'd definitely had hot, uninhibited sex. But this morning . . . dear God, this morning it had felt like they'd made love in its purest, most intimate sense. Stunned and shaken by the realization, and feeling overwhelmingly vulnerable, she pressed a hand over her rapidly beating heart, struggling to contain the emotions rioting within her. Emotions she was helpless to deny.

But how she felt about Steve didn't change anything—not their arrangement, their business deal, or their temporary relationship.

With that reminder fresh in her mind, she gathered her composure and headed downstairs to face Steve.

Sitting at the kitchen table, Steve flipped through the Monday morning paper, reading the features and articles but not really processing them. His thoughts were on other things . . . like the woman he'd left sleeping in his bed upstairs. The first woman he'd wanted to wake up to in the morning since his divorce.

He knew he could have easily taken her back to her apartment after their tryst last night, but he'd been completely satisfied to keep her snuggled so trustingly in his arms, her warm, silky body entwined with his. And when the gray shades of dawn had roused him from slumber and he'd opened his eyes to find Liz sleeping beside him, he hadn't panicked or freaked out. Instead, he'd reached out and gently caressed a hand over her hip, and her automatic response to his touch had fired his blood all over again.

Having her in his bed all night long had felt amazingly, perfectly right.

Standing, he went to the counter and poured himself a cup of coffee from the pot he'd just percolated. He'd been content to live the life of a carefree bachelor the past six years, dating when the urge struck him, without commitments or promises. Keeping his emotions out of the equation had been easy, but this morning he was struck with the realization that it was a matter of finding the right woman who evoked those needs. There was something to be said for a monogamous relationship and having one special woman in his life.

And for him, that woman was Liz.

Their short time together was no longer just about great sex and how compatible they were in bed. Yes, she was his perfect match sexually, open for anything that gave them pleasure, just like last night's erotic fantasy. But it was becoming increasingly obvious to him, with each day that passed, that being her temporary lover wasn't going to do it for him. He wanted—*needed*—more than a short-term affair with her.

He'd already broken one of his own personal rules by bringing her home with him and letting her stay the entire night in his bed. That had been a huge, unspoken gesture for him, one he hoped would show Liz that he wanted her in his life beyond the brief affair they'd originally agreed upon, and longer than it took to locate her wayward cousin.

"Umm, do I smell coffee?"

Steve turned at the sound of Liz's sleep-husky voice, and his body stirred at the sexy way she filled out his shirt, along with the adorable blush on her cheeks. Oh, yeah, he could get used to having her at his place on a regular basis.

"I just brewed a fresh pot," he said, smiling. "Would you like some?"

"I'd love a cup." She came up to the counter beside him and pushed her fingers through her softly disheveled hair, appearing self-conscious and wary. "I'm sorry. I didn't mean to spend the night."

Her tone was reserved, as was her expression, which Steve found too ironic since that should have been *his* reaction to their intimate morning-after situation.

Bringing down a mug from the cupboard, he filled it with steaming coffee and tried to put her at ease. "I wanted you to stay, and I liked waking up to you. No harm, no foul," he teased.

And just in case she didn't believe him, he slipped his arm around her waist, lowered his mouth to hers, and kissed her with heat and a passion that seemed to grow stronger every time he touched her. Her hands came to rest on his naked chest, and his mouth seduced hers until she finally gave him what he wanted from her—a soft, surrendering sigh, and the tension in her limbs replaced with the lush, feminine press of her curves against his.

Before he gave in to the urge to find out what, if anything at all, she was wearing beneath his shirt, he pulled back and skimmed his thumb along her damp lower lip. "Mmm, you taste minty fresh."

She laughed lightly and moved smoothly out of his embrace, seemingly a bit skittish with all this morning-after intimacy. "Thanks to you." She spooned sugar into her coffee and slanted him a speculative look. "Do you always keep a stash of toothbrushes on hand for overnight guests?"

He'd hoped to ease her misgivings about staying the night, but the glimpse of insecurity he detected in her tone spoke volumes. It also gave him a deeper clue that she was feeling more uncertain about the change in their relationship, and about him.

She was also under the mistaken assumption that he entertained many female guests. He sought to reassure her, to ease the fears and apprehension her deceased husband had no doubt instilled in her.

"I hate shopping, as you'll see by the sorry state of my kitchen cupboards and nearly empty refrigerator, so I tend to buy things in bulk when I can," he told her. "The toothbrushes came five in a pack, and I can show you the other three that are still left if it would make you feel better."

She blushed a furious shade of pink and shook her head. "I apologize. That was uncalled for on my part." She ducked her head and took a quick sip of her sweetened coffee, apparently unable to look him in the eyes now. "You have every right to have women spend the night, and I have no business interrogating you."

With any other woman, he would have agreed, but Liz wasn't just any woman. Not any longer. He recognized and accepted that fact. And he supposed it was time he offered up a little proof to her of that realization.

Leaning a hip against the counter, he touched his fingers beneath her chin and raised her gaze to his. Her wide eyes flickered with another bout of uncertainty, a vulnerability that wreaked havoc with his insides. A vulnerability he took very seriously.

He drew a deep breath and catered to those shadowed emotions. "Since my divorce, you're the first woman who has slept the entire night in my bed."

She blinked at him, obviously shocked by his confession. Then the significance of his comment sank in, and a quick flash of alarm shimmered in her eyes. Damn, was he going too fast for her? At this point, he decided he had no choice, because he suspected he only had a handful of days left with her, in which to sway her to his way of thinking. She was more than a temporary lover to him, and he wanted her in his life. Permanently.

Because he loved her.

His heart pounded hard and fast, an adrenaline rush that swept through him as he finally put words to the emotions tumbling around in his chest. He didn't fight the sentiment, didn't deny its existence. Instead, he allowed it to flow through him, and let himself get used to the feeling of knowing that this one special woman complemented him so perfectly, in ways that made him feel whole and complete, physically and emotionally.

He kept his revelation to himself for the time being, because he suspected that if she knew the depth of his feelings for her, she'd panic and withdraw from him more than she already had this morning. And that wasn't a chance he was willing to take with her and their relationship just yet.

"You don't ever have to hesitate to ask me something," he said, filling the silence that had stretched too far and long between them. "If it's a question I can answer, I will."

With that, he crossed the kitchen to the pantry, determined to resume a casual morning routine with her, even though nothing would ever be the same for him as far as Liz was concerned.

He rummaged through the meager contents lining his cupboards and was able to scrounge up a few things to eat. "Looks like you have a choice of Captain Crunch cereal or strawberry Pop-Tarts."

"Breakfasts of champions, huh?" She grinned, her features relaxing once again, which relieved him as well. "Are the Pop-Tarts the frosted kind?"

He heard the hopeful note to her voice and chuckled. It appeared she was a woman after his own heart, in more ways than one. "Yep, sugar-coated for an extra morning kick to go with your caffeine."

She sat down and placed both of their mugs of coffee on the table. "Perfect. I'll take one."

"Good choice, especially since I'm out of milk and you'd have to eat the cereal dry," he added wryly, and set the box within her reach.

She laughed, the sound genuinely lighthearted. Snagging a cellophane wrapper sealing a pair of Pop-Tarts, she ripped it open. "You weren't kidding about hating to shop, were you?"

"Nope." He took the chair next to her and grabbed a pack for himself. "I don't like to cook, either."

She broke off a bite of the strawberry-injected pastry and popped it into her mouth. "Ahh, a true bachelor."

He shrugged. "Fast food works for me just fine, a carryover from my days as a cop, when I worked the swing shift and wasn't home for dinner. And my dad wasn't kidding the other night when he said that my mom is always making up CARE packages of food for us boys. All in all, I eat pretty well." He took a big bite of his Pop-Tart, swallowed, and said, "If you'd like something more nutritious, I've got leftover ribs and chicken from my father's party if you'd like to have that for breakfast."

She wrinkled her nose at him. "No, thanks. I'll stick with the Pop-Tart."

They continued to eat their breakfast, and she cast him a sidelong glance that lingered on the tattoo encircling his arm. It was obvious to him that something was on her mind, and he waited patiently for her to decide whether she wanted to ask the question glimmering in her eyes.

She picked at her second Pop-Tart, and when he met her gaze, she drew a deep breath. "So, I can ask you anything I want, huh?" she asked, taking him up on his earlier comment.

Her tone held a teasing lilt, but his instincts told him her attempt at levity was a cover-up for something far more significant. "Sure. What's on your mind?"

"There's something I've been curious about." She reached out and traced the tribal band encircling his arm. "There's the name Steffie inscripted into your tattoo. Is it your ex-wife's?"

Like many other women who'd asked before her, he almost instinctively evaded the too personal question. But he'd promised Liz that she could ask him anything, and more important, he was ready to let her into that private part of his life—knew it was a huge step in their developing relationship. She knew little about his past, his marriage, and his daughter, and he wanted her to understand who he was really was, beyond the PI she'd hired and the man she shared her fantasies with.

Besides, whatever was happening between them demanded total honesty and complete openness, and he was willing to do his share. "Steffie is my sixteen-year-old daughter, Stephanie."

Liz's soft green eyes widened with astonishment. "Wow, you don't look old enough to have a sixteen-year-old child. I mean, you'd briefly mentioned that you had a daughter, but I thought maybe she was ten years old, tops."

"Thanks for the compliment, but I'm thirty-six, and some days I feel twice as old," he joked.

He watched her mentally do the math in her head as she ate another bite of her breakfast. "Which means you were nineteen when she was born."

He nodded and finished off his coffee. "That's right."

She brushed the pastry crumbs from her fingers, apparently speculating upon that revelation. "So, did you go out and get the tattoo when she was born?"

"No. I decided to get the tribal band after my divorce was finalized. It was one of those spontaneous, rebellious acts I've surprisingly never regretted. As for Steffie's name, at the time I figured she'd be the only woman to forever hold my heart, and I'd never have to worry about having her name erased from the design."

Liz's eyes danced with laughter and something more sentimental. "That's incredibly sweet. She's lucky to have a father like you."

"She's a joy, and I love her very much." Leaning back in his chair, he absently ran his finger around the rim of his empty coffee mug. "Unfortunately, I don't get to see her as often as I'd like, since she lives in Texas with her mother, Janet, and stepfather, Hugh."

She tipped her head and tucked the honey-blond strands of hair that brushed across her cheek behind her ear. "That has to be difficult for you."

"It is. And my parents miss her, too, since she's their only grandchild. But I take whatever I can get with her, whether it's a month in the summer, a week here or there, or even a card in the mail." He smiled, as he always did when it came to his daughter. "She loves to E-mail, so I'm always getting chatty letters from her that keep me fairly up to date on what's going on in her life."

He recalled the latest E-mail he'd received from her, and the pictures he'd printed out on photo paper to add to his collection. He stood, took both of their cups to the sink, and took their sharing one step further.

"Come with me. I want to show you something." He gestured for Liz to follow him out of the kitchen.

He led the way into the living room, to the open oak bookcase against the wall, filled with music CDs, movie tapes, and a slew of photographs. He picked up a framed print of Steffie wearing a softball uniform, at the age of eight, with a gaptoothed smile, and showed it to Liz. "This is my little girl, who isn't so little anymore. When this picture was taken, she was going through a tomboy stage."

"She's adorable," Liz said, and glanced up at him, her gaze

traveling over his features. "She has your deep-blue eyes and smile."

"Yeah, she does," he said proudly.

He showed her the rest of the photographs, which ranged from toddler to teenager and the varying stages in between. There were snapshots with him, his parents, and Janet with her new husband, Hugh, at Steffie's eighth-grade graduation ceremony. And then there were the most recent prom pictures his daughter had sent to him.

He showed that one to Liz, as well. "She just E-mailed me this photo, and it nearly killed me to see her all grown up like that."

"She's grown into a beautiful young woman, and her date seems very taken by her."

He frowned. "Yeah, don't think I didn't notice that."

Liz raised a brow, a humorous smile quirking the corner of her mouth. "Are you worried about what's going on in that boy's head where your daughter is concerned?"

"Hell, I *know* what's going on in his head," he said with a low, fatherly growl of disapproval. "Janet and I started going out when we were sixteen, and it didn't take us long to move past the hand-holding and kissing stage."

She studied another picture, with Janet and Steffie together. "High school sweethearts?" she guessed.

"Yeah. And two years later, fresh out of high school, she got pregnant, and we got married." He grinned wryly. "And yes, before you ask, we were using birth control. Would you believe we were one of the statistical one percent the Pill failed with?"

She cringed, then seemed to recall the comment he'd made a few nights ago when she'd told him that she was on the Pill. "There's no such a thing as too much protection," she said, repeating his words.

"In my experience, anyway. Steffie's proof of that, but I can't imagine my life without her in it."

She was quiet for a moment, then tentatively asked, "Do you mind me asking what happened to your marriage?"

He couldn't deny the curiosity gleaming in her eyes. Didn't want to. "Not at all. Come sit with me." He grabbed her hand and led her toward the brown suede sofa.

Once they were settled next to each other, he stretched out his long legs, crossed them at the ankles, and laced his hands behind his head. "Let's see, where do I begin?"

"At the beginning," she suggested helpfully.

If she was interested enough to listen about his past, then he was more than willing to lay it all out on the line for her. "Janet and I obviously got hitched because she was pregnant, which isn't a great way to start a marriage, but we did love each other, and we were determined to make things work for the baby's sake. For the first two years, I worked back-to-back jobs to make enough money to keep Janet at home with Steffie; then I decided to pursue my interest in being a cop, which didn't thrill Janet, but it was a decent-paying job with great benefits—and every day was a new adventure, which I enjoyed."

Turning toward him, she drew her legs up beside her and pulled the hem of his shirt down over her bare thighs. "Now, why doesn't that surprise me?"

Because she was beginning to know him well. He kept the remark to himself, certain that was more than she was prepared to handle at the moment. "What can I say. I like the thrill of the chase," he drawled, and winked at her.

She rolled her eyes in amusement. "Go on with the story."

"Anyway, my job as a cop put a lot of stress on my marriage to Janet—along with raising a kid at such a young age. I worked a lot of graveyard and swing shifts, and I took the overtime when it was offered, so we'd be able to put away extra money. Unfortunately, the long hours and the danger of the job started wearing on Janet and, eventually, our marriage. Then I got shot in the line of duty, and that didn't help matters any."

She sucked in a quick, startled breath. "You were shot?"

"Yeah, right here." He lifted his right arm and pointed to a puckered scar hidden within the intricate design of his tattoo. "The tattoo makes for a nice camouflage, don't you think?"

"That it does." She lifted her gaze back to his, and the concern he detected in her expression warmed him. "Did the bullet cause any permanent damage?"

"There was nerve damage, just enough to affect my reflexes when it's cold outside, or when I overuse my right hand or arm. I know my limitations, but my lieutenant wasn't willing to take the chance of having me out in the field and not being able to properly fire my weapon." Looking back, he knew his lieutenant's decision had been the right one to make, no matter how angry Steve had been at the time.

"So, that was a turning point for me, since I wasn't about to accept a mundane desk job," he went on. "That's just not me. I need to interact with people, and I like solving cases. So, becoming a PI was a natural transition."

"And your marriage?" she prompted.

"Pretty much fell apart after I got shot." He scrubbed a hand over his unshaven jaw. "It was more than Janet could take, and we both knew that after ten years it just wasn't working out between us, that we were mainly staying together because of Steffie. But neither one of us was truly happy. So, we opted for an amicable divorce."

"It's nice that the two of you remained friends," she said softly.

Steve couldn't imagine their split being any other way, and he wondered if Liz was thinking of the way things had ended for her and her husband, which hadn't been pleasant at all, but strained and bitter because of his deceit and cheating.

He slipped his hand beneath the hem of the shirt she wore, and flattened his palm on her thigh, just to keep some kind of physical connection between them. "Janet and I have a daughter together, and her mental well-being is the most important

thing to both of us. She's an amazingly well adjusted kid, despite the divorce, and she gets along great with Janet's new
husband, too."

Desire darkened her eyes as he stroked her smooth skin
with his thumb, but his caress didn't distract her from their
conversation. "Would you have married Janet if she hadn't
gotten pregnant?"

The question wasn't an easy one to answer, and it wasn't
something he'd really thought about. At the age of nineteen,
he'd owned up to his responsibilities and never questioned
what he knew he had to do. "I think Janet and I would have
stayed together for a while, but I don't know if our relationship would have ended in marriage. Before she got pregnant,
she had plans to go to college back East, and I always wanted
to be a cop, which she never liked, so and I think we would
have eventually gone our separate ways. But there's no use
speculating on what-if's, and I've never regretted or resented
the way things turned out."

"You're amazingly well adjusted," she joked, a small smile
etching her lips.

"Everything in life happens for a reason, and sometimes
you just have to roll with the punches." Just like his feelings
for her. Unexpected, yes, but not unwanted.

He watched her twist that ring of hers around her finger and
knew he'd given her a lot to think about this morning—from
his confession that she was the first woman to spend the night,
to his past and marriage. Now it was time for her to get into
the mind-set of meeting with Antonio.

"Why don't you go get ready, and I'll take you back to The
Daily Grind for your car so you're not late to your appointment this morning," he suggested.

She nodded and stood, then glanced back at him. "Do you
mind if I take a quick shower here and get that out of the
way?"

"The bathroom is all yours," he said, and felt an odd, tangible loss when she moved off the couch and stood. "Use whatever you need."

She fingered the collar of his shirt she was wearing. "Since my blouse is shredded, I'll definitely be borrowing your shirt until I get home, if you don't mind."

"Of course I don't mind." *As long as you bring it back smelling of you.*

She turned and headed out of the living room, and he watched her make her way up the stairs. He ached to follow her, to tell her how he really felt about her, to make her admit that her feelings for him had changed, as well. But Steve knew it was more important right now to give her space to process everything that had happened between them the past twenty-four hours, to bring her around slowly instead of forcing something she wasn't quite ready to face just yet.

Her heart might be there, but her head hadn't yet accepted the truth, and he refused to crowd her, or make her any more wary than she ready was. And ultimately, it was unfair of him to put any kind of emotional burden on her right now, when her focus needed to be on resolving her issues with her cousin.

And Lord knew her issues ran deep. He just hoped that when this mess with Valerie was over, Liz would come to realize that she no longer needed to live her life for others—that it was time she lived her life for herself.

Liz sat as calmly as she could manage, in the chair situated in front of Antonio's desk. Her hands were clenched in her lap, and her stomach rolled nervously as he met her gaze and smiled at her in a way that was easy-going and friendly.

Despite the fact that Antonio pedaled sex for a living, he was, surprisingly, very likable. He was also a good-looking businessman who dressed in high-dollar clothes and jewelry, drove a top-of-the-line Mercedes, and ran what Liz suspected was a multimillion-dollar company. He treated his employees decently and fairly, and from what she'd heard from other operators, that was unusual in this particular business. He also knew how to flatter and bolster a woman's confidence to get what he wanted, and right now that charm was focused on her.

"I'm extremely impressed with your transcripts so far, particularly with your nightly eleven-fifteen P.M. caller," he said, getting right to the crux of his reason for meeting with her. "It appears you've ensnared yourself a steady client who's very interested in meeting you."

"Yes, so it seems," she said, playing along, the warm, sweeping blush on her cheeks very real when she thought about Antonio being privy to the explicit conversations she'd had with Steve. "He's very persistent, too."

"And very loyal to just you, according to the calling pattern he's established." He leaned back in his high-backed, leather chair and regarded her thoughtfully over the fingers he'd steepled together. "How do you feel about that?"

"I'm flattered, obviously, and he seems like a nice enough guy," she said, smiling. "And the extra bonus money coming in from his calls is especially nice."

"Would you like to make more money?" he asked, homing in on that part of her reply, just as she'd intended.

Because of her conversation with Roxanne, Liz knew exactly what he was insinuating, but played it low-key. "Of course I'd love to make more money, but I'm not sure what you're getting at."

"When I hired you on, I mentioned advancement within the company if you performed well, which you have—beyond what most operators accomplish in a month's time." His tone was very complimentary. "A lot of the operators I've employed have advanced on to becoming party girls, which entails attending private parties and catering to a client's requests and desires on a more intimate level. And because I think you're ready to take that next step, I'm going to offer you one of those opportunities, if you're interested."

She feigned a nonchalant shrug. "If there's more money involved, of course I'd be interested."

He seemed immensely pleased by her response. "How do you feel about meeting your client in person and establishing a physical relationship with him?"

If it were with anyone other than Steve, and if it weren't for the sake of needing to make contact with Trixie Lane, Liz would have flatly refused the offer. Hell, she wouldn't even be here right now if it hadn't been for Valerie's disappearing act.

"What's in it for me?" she asked boldly.

He grinned, apparently appreciating her straightforward manner. "Money, of course. A sixty-forty split of a thousand dollars, which is what it costs the client to attend a party."

A thousand dollars. Liz's head spun at the amount he so casually tossed out there. She was stunned and amazed that anyone would pay such an exorbitant fee to attend a fantasy party. Unless . . . "What do I have to do for that kind of money?"

"Entertain your client for the night, in any capacity he wishes." Antonio shrugged, his expression all business. "Make the fantasies you share with him on the phone a reality."

She'd already accomplished that with Steve, and then some. And now she would be taking their affair into a more public arena, she thought with a shudder, uncertain of what she'd gotten herself into, but determined to see it through.

Antonio went on. "There are many amenities that the two of you can take advantage of and enjoy, along with private fantasy playrooms and sexual stimulants that can be accessed for an extra fee on the client's part."

She couldn't imagine that they'd stick around long enough to indulge in stimulants, or what those playrooms had to offer. Once they had the information they needed on Rob, *if* they were able to uncover anything substantial at all, she wanted out of there. For good.

She swallowed the hard knot that had gathered in her

throat, and pretended enthusiasm. "What do I have to do to set this up with my client?"

"He's already established his interest in meeting you, so tonight when he calls you, extend the invitation for him to accompany you to an Ultimate Fantasy party tomorrow night. If he agrees, then you transfer him over to Doreen, who will handle the monetary details, along with transportation to The Ultimate Fantasy mansion. You'll both be taken there by a private company limousine."

Liz sat quietly, absorbing the details, so very grateful that Steve would be by her side the entire night.

"If you find you enjoy being a party girl, you can make the choice of remaining strictly a party girl, or you can go back to being an operator, or do both. The choice is yours, but the more men you invite to the parties, the more money you make in a night's time."

Liz inwardly cringed, knowing that being a "party girl" was equivalent to working as a high-dollar escort. Was that what Valerie was involved in, of her own choice? The thought made Liz feel physically ill. Then again, she was learning a whole lot of things about Valerie's personality that went beyond the rebellious cousin she'd grown up with and the young girl who'd grown into a woman who needed attention focused on her in any way she could get it. What Valerie was doing was flat-out dangerous, stupid, and selfish to those who cared about her.

And Liz was beginning to wonder if she cared too much.

She immediately shoved that thought to the back of her mind, because it went against everything she believed in when it came to family—even her cousin who'd never wanted to share her mother and father with an orphaned girl who only wanted to be loved and accepted. She'd made a promise to her aunt and uncle to look after Valerie, and it was a responsibility she took seriously.

And disappointing her aunt and uncle again wasn't an option.

They wrapped up the meeting, with Liz agreeing to make the leap to party girl and invite Steve as her first client, for a fee of one thousand dollars. But as she left Antonio's office, it wasn't attending the party she was worried about; it was the money issue that weighed heavily on her mind. Another thousand dollars out of Steve's pocket, and another thousand dollars to add to what she'd have to repay him for his PI services.

She'd planned on signing over her paycheck to him with whatever she earned as an operator, and he'd get back the forty percent of the money she earned after escorting him to The Ultimate Fantasy party, but that didn't cover all his charges to date.

Now this—still more she owed him, and another debt to repay. Another obligation to pile on top of the others.

Chapter

13

Steve watched as Liz paced restlessly in front of his desk while she explained the details of her meeting with Antonio less than an hour ago. She'd come straight to his office after her appointment, and while it appeared that everything had gone smoothly and as planned with Antonio, there was something else that had Liz on edge.

"If everything went so well, what's bothering you?" he asked, concerned.

She stopped and met his gaze, her lips pursed, and he knew whatever had her so agitated was finally about to be brought out into the open. "It's going to cost an extra thousand dollars for you to get into the party."

He certainly didn't expect that they'd get in for free, but it was obvious by the disconcerted look on Liz's face that she was devastated by yet another expense in her search for her self-centered cousin.

"That's not a problem," he said evenly. "I'll cover the expense."

Her chin lifted adamantly, and she crossed her arms over her chest. "You know I'll pay you back. Every last penny."

Oh, he believed her, not that he was concerned about when

or how she would pay him back. That was the furthest thing from his mind when it came to her. "I'm not worried about payment, Liz."

The case might have started out with expenses for her to gradually reimburse, but he was fronting the fees for the party out of his own personal pocket because he cared for Liz and this was important to her. Which made it equally important to him, regardless of how he felt about the situation with Valerie, and Liz's involvement.

He stood, rounded his desk, and gathered Liz into his arms. She was stiff and tense at first, and he caressed a hand down her back, soothing her with his touch. He smiled when she uncrossed her arms and slipped them around his waist and leaned into him, finally accepting his physical and emotional support.

He wondered when the last time was that someone had taken care of Liz, or simply comforted her as he was doing. He'd bet it had been years, considering Liz's penchant for worrying about everyone else, and her misplaced need in trying to please her aunt and uncle and make up for her rocky, rebellious marriage to Travis. She was so afraid of losing the people who loved her that she went to the extreme to compensate, and that ingrained habit of hers wouldn't change until she accepted that she only had to answer to herself in life.

"Listen, the most important thing is that you were able to get us into the party," he said, and brushed his lips tenderly against her temple, inhaling her soft, feminine scent. "And when I call tonight, everything will go as we've planned. I'll agree to escort you to the party, you connect me over to Doreen to handle the details, and hopefully, by tomorrow night we'll get what we need from Trixie, so I can trace Rob and his whereabouts."

As if realizing how much she was leaning on him, Liz stepped out of his embrace. "I swear, it never seems to end when it comes to Valerie." Frustration vibrated through her tone. "I'm just getting my business back on its feet and Travis's debts paid off, and now this."

While Steve would cheerfully strangle her cousin for putting Liz through such hell, Liz herself needed to realize that Valerie was a grown woman, that the choices she made—right, wrong, or dangerous—were her own to make. And any resulting consequences were Valerie's to bear. No one else's. Just as Liz's choices were her own.

She'd let herself feel guilt where none was warranted, thereby feeding into Valerie's need for attention. So long as Liz did that, her cousin would continue to manipulate her emotions. And all Steve could do was show Liz that he'd be there for her, to make sure she knew how much he cared. He'd protect her to the best of his ability and do his damnedest to locate her cousin and end Liz's worry.

After that, any future they might have together was up to her.

"I have a special delivery for Liz Adams."

Liz looked up from the Irish cream latte she was making for a customer, and glanced at the young man standing on the other side of the counter. He was wearing a navy work shirt with a courier service embroidered on the pocket, verifying his claim as a delivery man. A clipboard was tucked beneath his arm, and he held a flat white box in one hand, secured with ribbon and topped with a huge red velvet bow, and a plastic garment bag in the other.

Startled and a whole lot confused, she handed her customer the drink and met the other man's gaze. "I'm Liz Adams."

"Great." He grinned, and shuffling the items in his hands, he managed to set the clipboard on the counter and produce a pen for her signature. "Sign on the bottom line, and these items are all yours."

She dried her damp hands on a terry towel and shook her

head. "But I didn't order anything." At least not from Sensual Pleasures, the name of the boutique imprinted on the garment bag.

"Hey, I just deliver the stuff," the guy said with a shrug. "And if you're Liz Adams, then this delivery is yours, no matter *who* ordered it."

Feeling self-conscious with her employees and patrons looking on, Liz signed off on the packages and took them from the courier. She told Katie to finish up with the few customers still waiting in line, and that she'd be in her office if she needed extra help.

Once she was in the back room, she hung the vinyl garment bag from a peg on a metal storage shelf and set the lavishly decorated box on her desk. Catching sight of the small white envelope attached to the garment bag with her name on it, she plucked it off, withdrew the card inside, and read the note written in a bold, masculine print.

See you tonight. Love, Steve.

Liz's hand trembled, and her heart beat hard and fast in her chest as she stared at the valediction Steve had used. Not *sincerely*, not *warmly*, but *love* Steve.

The single word tugged on her emotions, made her yearn to embrace all the subtle changes in Steve she'd noticed the past few days, which were becoming increasingly difficult to ignore or dismiss with a pat excuse. There was no denying the tenderness and genuine affection in his gaze when he looked at her, and then there was the way he touched her that had nothing to do with sex, and everything to do with a gentleness and understanding she'd been without for too long.

Love. An emotion that was so wonderful yet so complicated and scary for all it implied.

She exhaled a shaky breath and refocused on the gifts that Steve had sent her, instead of the insistent ache in her chest. She hadn't opened anything yet, but she was fairly certain that her bad boy had gone shopping and purchased an outfit for her to wear tonight, to the Ultimate Fantasy party.

Last night, their phone conversation had gone without a hitch, as had inviting Steve to the exclusive party. According to Steve, the transaction had gone smoothly with Doreen, and Liz was set up for his escort and date. A company limousine would arrive to pick her up first at six tonight, then Steve, and take them both to the Ultimate Fantasy mansion together.

She hadn't seen or spoken to Steve since last night, when he'd gently told her to go home and get a good night's rest. She'd been disappointed that he wasn't going to come by her apartment, but knew it was for the best. At least for her. At the rate that things were progressing for the case, another day or two and her affair with Steve would be over, and she needed to get used to the lonely nights ahead. Again.

A knock on her open office door made her jump and jarred her out of her troubling thoughts. She turned around to find Mona sauntering into the room, her eyes alight with curiosity as she glanced from the box on her desk to the still unopened garment bag behind Liz.

"Hey, what's with the special delivery?" Mona asked unabashedly.

It figured that Mona had witnessed the courier's arrival and had shamelessly come over to snoop, Liz thought with amusement. "It's from Steve." Tucking the card back into the envelope, she slipped the private, intimate note into the top drawer of her desk. "Tonight's the big night."

Mona's gaze widened in understanding. "The two of you are going to one of the fantasy parties?"

"Yes." Liz gave her friend a brief rundown of the events of the past few days in terms of the case, and her finally inviting Steve to the private party. "I'm pretty sure Steve sent me over an outfit to wear for tonight."

"Well, what are you waiting for?" Mona said with an encouraging grin. "Let's see what kind of taste Steve has when it comes to dressing a woman."

"Yes, let's," Liz agreed, just as anxious to see what the garment bag hid.

Unzipping the front closure, she pushed the sides apart. She and Mona gasped in unison as she revealed a beautiful, dazzling red dress unlike anything she had ever owned before.

"Oh, wow," Liz murmured, and grinned, recalling Steve's preference to the color red on a woman, over classic black.

" 'Wow' is right. You have to try this on so I can see it on you," Mona insisted.

And Liz supposed she ought to make sure that the dress actually fit. "I'll be right back," she said, and took the outfit to the employee restroom located in the back of the storage area.

Minutes later, she was staring at her transformed reflection in the small mirror above the sink, which only allowed her to see to where the hemline of the dress ended, just above the knee. But it was enough to confirm that the little red dress did indeed fit, from the deep, V-halter neckline that shaped her breasts and left her entire back bare, to the flattering empire waist that hinted at her curves but didn't blatantly display them. The hemline was flared, and swirled around her hips and thighs when she walked or turned.

She'd planned to wear something from Valerie's closet but was secretly thrilled at what Steve had chosen for her. She'd never worn anything so decadent and sensual, never had any reason to, and couldn't remember the last time she'd felt so sexy and confident in an outfit. It was a novel sensation, one she couldn't help but like and enjoy despite the circumstances.

With one last look in the mirror, she headed back to her office, where Mona was anxiously awaiting her return.

A huge grin lit up her face when she saw Liz. "You look amazing, and I'm so impressed. Steve Wilde certainly has great taste."

Liz twirled around so Mona could see the outfit from all angles. "And apparently, a good eye for my size," she added with a light laugh, though it helped that the dress wasn't a form-fitting sheath but loose and flirty from the waist down. The only thing that was snug was the halter-top-style bodice, which displayed a fair amount of cleavage.

"He's obviously seen enough of you in the buff to make a fairly close judgment call on what would fit your shape." Mona waggled her brows teasingly. "Shall we take a look at what's in box number two?"

Liz slipped off the ribbon and bow, feeling giddy, like a young girl who was being spoiled with such lavish birthday presents. Except it wasn't her birthday, and that made this unexpected surprise, and Steve's attention, so much more special and memorable.

Tossing the box top aside, Liz parted the pale pink tissue paper and felt her body flash hot at the all-red, provocative ensemble she discovered. She fingered the edge of a satin-and-lace garter belt that came with nude silk stockings, and felt her body stir with desire when she caught sight of the sheer, barely there panties with convenient side ties—the only thing that held the scrap of fabric together. There was no bra, but the dress he'd bought for her didn't require one.

"Oh, my," Mona said, and lifted her gaze from the sexy lingerie to Liz. "Steve certainly went all out, didn't he?"

Liz could only nod, overwhelmed by Steve's generosity. "He even included a matching purse. The only thing missing to complete the outfit is a pair of red strappy shoes."

"Which screams for the two of us to go shopping this afternoon." Mona grinned. "I've got an extra employee at the bookstore who can handle things for a couple of hours; how about you?"

She owned an old pair of red leather pumps, but she refused to ruin the effect of the striking outfit Steve had sent her with a staid pair of shoes. "Yeah, I can wing it." Besides, she'd rather be out shopping than sitting here in her office worrying and growing increasingly nervous about tonight's party.

"And while we're out, let's get your hair and nails done, too," Mona suggested, her eyes bright with anticipation. "I'm guessing Steve spent a small fortune on everything, and you can't wear a head-turning dress like this and not look the part of a sexy siren."

Mona's comment was made innocently and out of pure excitement, but Liz felt a moment's hesitation at the realization of how much Steve had spent on her. For once, she ignored that sensible little voice in her head and refused to think about the cost of Steve's gift. This was one present she'd accept from him guilt-free, because she wanted so badly to look and be the part of a seductive, sophisticated woman who'd captured his interest.

Tomorrow the fairy tale would be over, but for tonight, she'd be his every fantasy.

Steve couldn't take his gaze off of the gorgeous, breathtaking woman sitting next to him in the backseat of the limousine as their chauffeur drove them to the Ultimate Fantasy mansion, located in an exclusive area of Lincoln Park.

She quite literally took his breath away.

When he'd chosen the red dress for Liz to wear, he'd imagined she would look stunning, but he was unprepared for the full effect of the dress, combined with artfully applied makeup that enhanced her green eyes yet didn't overwhelm her pretty features, along with the way she'd worn her hair. Her blond tresses were swept up into a soft, sensual style that showed off her neck and the line of her jaw and gave him access to plenty of bare flesh—from her shoulders all the way down to the base of her spine. Then there were those red, sexy strappy heels she was wearing that made her stocking-clad legs look impossibly long and slender.

But for as centerfold-seductive as she looked, it was the

sweet, wholesome, down-to-earth woman beneath all the outer trappings who drew him the most, and always would. And as her gaze met his in the dimly lit interior in the backseat of the limo, he could tell she was nervous about what the night would bring.

He picked up her hand, those red, polished nails of hers turning him on, and sought to distract her with other things, like how taken he was with her. "You look absolutely amazing."

A blush swept across her cheeks, matching the glossy shade of red she was wearing on her lips. "Thank you . . . for the compliment and everything else."

Grinning, he stroked his thumb along the pulse in her wrist. "You're welcome, for the compliment and everything else."

He winked at her, telling her without words that he knew exactly what "everything else" applied to: the outfit and lingerie he'd sent to her. Although the partition between them and the driver was raised, there was no telling if anyone was listening in on their conversation; therefore, they still needed to keep things low-key.

He splayed his palm on her knee and playfully fingered the hem of her dress. "Mind if I take a peek at everything else?" he asked shamelessly.

"Be my guest," she invited boldly.

He slowly, gradually pushed up the bright-red material, taking in the way the nude stockings made her legs shimmer and the lacy band at the top hugged her thighs. Lifting his gaze back to hers, he used his imagination as he traced the garter strap with his fingers, smiled as he touched her panties, and her breath quickened. He found the ties at the sides of her hips, and his groin tightened at the thought of how easy it would be to tug on those ties and remove that flimsy barrier between his fingers and her soft feminine flesh.

"Very, very nice," he murmured, and withdrew his hand from beneath her dress.

"Thank you." Her sultry voice was laced with the same desire shining in her eyes.

He stroked his fingers along her throat and down the deep, plunging V neck of her dress, watching with pleasure as her breasts quivered at the illicit caress, and her nipples peaked against the fabric. "For as incredible as you look, the dress is missing something, though."

She frowned at him. "I can't imagine what."

"Let me show you." Reaching into his coat pocket, he withdrew a flat, velvet-lined box and flipped open the top, revealing a delicate choker of sparkling diamonds shaped into connecting hearts, along with matching earrings.

She gasped in shock, and her wide eyes shot to his. She shook her head, the gesture as firm as her tone when she spoke. "Steve, *no.*"

He'd anticipated her reaction, but he wasn't taking no for an answer. "I'm sorry, sweetheart, but I insist." Very casually he removed the necklace from the velvet lining and released the clasp. "If you're going to be mine tonight, I want you to look the part of a pampered escort."

Considering the charade they were playing, his request was simple enough, and it would be in bad taste for her to argue, and she knew it, too. But he could tell she wasn't happy about accepting yet another gift from him, even as she turned in her seat and allowed him to put the choker on for her.

It had been a spur-of-the-moment decision to buy her the extra accessories. When the woman at the boutique had suggested one of their inexpensive rhinestone necklace sets to compliment the dress, Steve decided that he wanted her to wear the real thing. She deserved the real thing. And he could easily afford it.

Once the necklace was secured, he let his fingers linger at the sensitive nape of her neck and kissed her warm, smooth shoulder. He felt her shiver, and she glanced over her shoulder at him, searching his face, his expression, which he hoped revealed exactly how he felt about her.

"This is too much," she protested in an aching whisper.

It wasn't nearly enough, not when he wanted to give her everything she desired, if only she'd let him into her heart. "Let me be the judge of that, okay?"

She swallowed hard and touched the necklace reverently, tracing the line of connecting diamond hearts with her fingers, her gaze never leaving his. He saw the love shimmering in the depths of her eyes, knew it was there even if she wasn't ready to admit to the emotion.

And for now, for tonight, that knowledge would have to be enough.

Liz kept her arm linked through Steve's and remained close to his side as they mingled in the casual, cocktail-party atmosphere, using him as an anchor as well as making sure that the other party girls knew that he was taken, *by her*. Many interested gazes connected with both her and Steve—silent, sexual inquiries that made it clear that swapping couples during the course of the night was more than welcome, as was enjoying multiple partners.

Liz shuddered at the thought, took another swallow of her wine to subdue the jitters in her stomach, and tightened her hold on Steve's arm. She wouldn't be sharing her guy with anyone, and they would be out of there just as soon as they gleaned the information they were after.

She'd also made up her mind that if this party produced no results as far as Valerie was concerned, then she was going to call her aunt and uncle and let them handle the situation, no matter how much it pained her to do so. She'd done all she could on her end, and she refused to drag out her cousin's absence any longer than the week she'd been gone.

"Are you doing okay?" Steve asked, apparently sensing her

discomfort. "Because if you're feeling uneasy about any of this, we can leave."

She appreciated his concern and protective, sensitive nature, but she had to see this through. She drew a deep, fortifying breath and flashed him the kind of sensual smile an escort would bestow upon her client. "We've come this far; I'm not about to turn back now."

"Good girl. I'll get you out of here as soon as possible," he promised, and kissed her, long and slow and deep, staking his claim on her for anyone who cared to watch. When he finally let her up for air, he murmured huskily, "What do you say we go check out the rest of this swanky place?"

She managed a nod, set her empty wine glass on a passing tray, and followed Steve into the "fantasy" section of the stately residence, where other party girls and clients were viewing playrooms and signing up for the ones that appealed to them—for an extra fee. While Steve appeared intrigued at all the extras that were offered, and Liz was undeniably curious about the props, decorations, and different playrooms she caught sight of, she had no intentions of venturing into that forbidden side of The Ultimate Fantasy.

The mansion was huge and lavishly decorated, with five upper levels of rooms and two other levels that were below the main floor. Each playroom they passed or entered was a complete den of iniquity, decorated in themes that catered to carnal desires and sinful fantasies and touched on every fetish or kink imaginable. Voyeurism, domination, the dungeon, group sex, and the classic ménage à trois were among the most favored playrooms. There were floor-to-ceiling mirrors in most of the lounges, large, plush couches for lovers to enjoy, a free-for-all edible body painting event, and a sex-toy shop complete with all the latest sexual gadgets. In keeping with safe sex, there were bowls of condoms everywhere, and guests weren't shy about plucking up a handful as they passed.

She recognized a few of the operators she worked with,

scantily clad in some of the most risqué outfits Liz had ever seen, making her feel overdressed in comparison. Some of those women were bold enough to flirt blatantly with Steve in front of her and let him know they were game for *anything*. More than a few times, Liz experienced a flash of jealousy and had to force herself to tamp down that green-eyed monster while Steve played along with their charade, flashing a charming smile and using their attention to his advantage to ask casually where they could find Trixie Lane.

They quickly learned that Trixie was a popular party girl, and very elusive.

As the evening progressed, the playrooms rapidly filled up with eager participants, and the atmosphere throughout the mansion changed from casual to hedonistic pleasure being the main objective, and there were many who didn't care where the sex took place. She and Steve remained in the bar area, with a large dance floor that was filled to capacity. The heavy, sensual beat of the music inspired a lot of bumping and grinding, and embraces that were as intimate as the dance of sex itself.

Drinks flowed freely, loosening inhibitions, and more than once Liz felt the pass of a hand over her bottom and along her thighs as the guests grew more aggressive despite the fact that she was clearly with Steve. The crush of bodies on the dance floor grew overwhelming, and when she told Steve that she needed fresh air, he didn't hesitate to take her out onto the adjoining balcony. Unfortunately, they weren't alone as Liz had hoped; other lovers apparently had exactly the same idea.

Steve leaned against the wrought-iron railing and pulled her to him so she stood between his thighs, their bellies and thighs aligned. He stroked his hands down her bare back, let his palms gently caress her bottom, and nuzzled her neck.

"You're completely wound up," he said, obviously feeling the tension thrumming through her. "Are you ready to go?"

Liz bit back a moan as Steve's warm, soft mouth opened on

her throat. She didn't want to give up so soon, but they'd been at The Ultimate Fantasy for over two hours, and she was beginning to think their search for Trixie was going to end up being fruitless. She also felt extremely out of place among the couples who were growing increasingly more physical with one another. Just mere feet away on a lounge chair, two women and a man were going at it hot and heavy, clothes were being shed, and there was no doubt in Liz's mind how that threesome was going to end up.

"Lucky guy," Steve said, his tone warm with amusement as he, too, watched the erotic scene unfolding next to them.

One woman straddled the man's bare torso and leaned into him, offering her breast to his mouth, while the other party girl lowered the zipper on his pants, released his burgeoning shaft, and gave him a blow job.

Mutual moans of pleasure echoed out on the balcony, and Liz's breathing deepened and her skin felt flushed. Steve rolled his hips against hers, fitting his erection in the notch between her thighs, and Liz was shocked to realize that she was wet and highly aroused. It was like watching an X-rated movie, but live and in person.

She tried to look away, but Steve wouldn't let her.

"If they're doing it out here in front of everyone, there's nothing wrong with watching and letting it turn you on," he said, his hot breath teasing her ear just as his fingers teased the backs of her thighs, opening them wider so he could exert a more illicit pressure against her aching sex.

The trio was switching positions, with the man lying flat on his back. One woman sank down on his cock and rode him with abandon, while the other rode his mouth, which allowed the two party girls to pleasure each other as well.

Liz decided she'd seen more than enough, and just as she opened her mouth to tell Steve that she wanted to leave and finish their own *twosome* somewhere private and alone, they were interrupted.

"I hate to break the mood, lovers," a husky feminine voice purred from behind Liz, "but I heard you were asking for Trixie Lane."

Steve's entire demeanor changed instinctively, shifting from amorous to aware in a heartbeat. He straightened and moved Liz so she was standing by his side instead of in front of him, though he still held her hand in his.

The gorgeous, voluptuous redhead wearing a nearly see-through black dress touched a hand to the swell of her breasts and smiled at Steve—a very practiced come-hither smile that no man, or woman, could mistake.

Whoever this woman was, she wanted Steve.

"And you are . . . ?" Steve drawled pleasantly.

"The woman you're apparently looking for." Trixie ignored Liz and gave Steve an appreciative once-over, her eyes alight with interest. Apparently liking what she saw, she extended a more intimate invitation. "Why don't you come with me, alone, and we'll talk about what I can do for you."

A blatant solicitation if Liz ever heard one, from the one woman who could give them the information they so desperately needed.

With an artful, seductive toss of her cascading tresses, Trixie turned and walked back through the balcony's French doors, slender hips swaying, confident in knowing the effect she had on the opposite sex, since most were ogling her as she strolled away. She glanced one last time over her shoulder and crooked her finger at Steve, beckoning him to follow.

His jaw clenched, and the frustrated look he shot Liz told her that he was torn between staying and going. This was the lead they'd come here for, and while Liz couldn't bring herself to give him the verbal okay he seemed to be waiting for, they both knew what he had to do.

"Shit," he said, clearly unhappy about the turn of events. "I'll be right back." He strode after Trixie, pursuing her through the throng of people gathered inside the bar and dance area.

Liz followed at a discreet distance, watching from afar as Trixie headed up to the second floor, where the playrooms were located. She stopped at the top of the stairs and waited for Steve to join her. A sinful smile curved the other woman's lips when he arrived. Trixie leaned toward Steve, much too close for Liz's liking, said something in his ear, then sashayed down a hallway.

Liz's stomach knotted when Steve hesitated only a few seconds before following. Liz definitely did not want to know how Steve planned to extract the information he needed from Trixie Lane—or what the other woman might expect from him in return.

God, she needed a drink.

"You look like you could use a drink."

Startled by the comment that echoed her exact thoughts, Liz glanced up at the blond-haired, good-looking guy who'd issued the statement, and wondered if she looked as desperate and devastated as she felt.

Seeing no harm in accepting his offer, she summoned a smile and said, loud enough for him to hear over the music, "I'd love a glass of Chardonnay."

He returned with her drink minutes later, and she took a huge gulp of the liquid, then another.

"Thank you," she said, immediately feeling the warm, calming effects of the wine.

"You're welcome. The name's John. Care to dance?" He hooked a finger toward the crowded dance floor.

She was beginning to feel relaxed and tingly, and decided there was no harm in enjoying a fast song with John. It would certainly keep her mind off of whatever Steve and Trixie were doing upstairs. And it wasn't Steve she was worried about; it was Trixie Lane and her feminine wiles and how she chose to wield them that concerned her the most.

"Sure, why not?" She finished off her Chardonnay and let him pull her into the crush of gyrating bodies.

As she moved to the beat of the music, her body grew hot, her skin much too tight and sensitive. Her nipples tingled, and an insistent throbbing gathered low in her belly, between her thighs, the pressure gradually building with every second that passed. She felt sexually charged, feverish, needy in a way she couldn't seem to control.

John smiled knowingly, and he was suddenly reaching for her, pulling her to him, his eyes heavy-lidded with lust as his hands began to roam over her curves. Lost in a sea of bodies, with her mind spinning and her nerves prickling with too many stimuli, she seemed helpless to resist him. Helpless to stop the urgent hunger building, building, building within her.

Confusion and a strong sense of foreboding mingled, making her heart beat fast in her chest. God, what was happening to her? Then the answer came to her in small degrees . . . her drink, she realized. Someone must have put something in her wine.

Another person aligned himself behind her, and it took her fog-induced mind longer than normal to register that she was deliberately sandwiched between two hard, undeniably aroused male bodies. The two men rubbed against her, grasping her hips, stroking up her thighs. A tongue touched her shoulder, and she shuddered in revulsion. She felt frantic and out of her element, her inhibitions slowly being stripped away by whatever she'd consumed.

"Let's take her up to one of the playrooms," she heard John say to the other man, and she shook her head and uttered the word, "No," but her small voice was lost in the loud music.

Then she was being tugged through the crowd of dancers. Apprehension and fear welled up in her when she realized what these two men intended. She tried to pull out of their grasp but knew she was no match for their strength, not with her mind and body feeling so hot, so lethargic, so hypersensitive.

They cleared the bar area and were brought up short by Steve, who was coming down the stairs from the upper level. Liz could have wept with relief . . . until she caught sight of the red-haired beauty who was standing by his side, an extremely smug and satisfied expression on her face. Vaguely Liz wondered what was worse—seeing Steve and Trixie together and imagining all the things they'd done together upstairs, or being groped by two strangers intent on slaking their own lust with her.

Steve's gaze narrowed on the two men flanking her, each of whom was holding one of her arms. "Where are you going with her?" he demanded.

"It's none of your business," John said, and started past him.

Steve planted a hand in the center of the man's chest, stopping him midstride. His smile was positively feral. "I'm making it my business, buddy," he said in a low, dangerous tone of voice that immediately loosened the man's grip on her arm. "I paid for the night with her, and unless she's consented to accompany the two of you, she's mine." His gaze shifted to Liz, and beyond the protective, possessive emotion, she detected his contrition for leaving her alone and so vulnerable to someone else's advance.

Liz shook her head wildly, which only made her dizzier. "No. No, I didn't consent to anything," she croaked, her mouth feeling as dry as dust.

"Find yourselves another playmate, boys," Steve said, and both John and the other man let her go.

The two men backed away, not happy with the turn of events but obviously unwilling to test Steve, either. Seconds later, they disappeared back into the bar area, most likely to find themselves another woman to enjoy.

Steve's gaze searched hers, silently asking if she was okay, but before he could verbally express his concern, Trixie stole away his attention.

"You were the easiest money I've made in a long time, sugar," Trixie murmured seductively, and caressed a hand down Steve's chest, all the way to the waistband of his slacks. "It was a pleasure doing business with you."

Liz glared at her, tamping down the impulse to claw the other woman's eyes out with her bright-red nails. Unfortunately, her furious mood was lost on Trixie, whose gaze remained on Steve.

The smile Trixie bestowed upon Steve was just as intimate as her touch. "If you and your date are interested in a threesome, come to me first and I'll show you both a good time," she said, then sauntered away and mingled her way back into the party atmosphere.

The emotions rippling through Liz ranged from indignation and jealousy to the more prominent sexual sensations still vibrating along her nerve endings. She tried to ignore the latter, even though her blood felt on fire, her sex aching for release, her nipples hard and peaked.

Despite her physical condition, she managed to say to him, "If that's what you're into, count me out."

"I'm a one-woman kind of man," he said, and shrugged. "I'm old-fashioned that way."

Swallowing hard, she took a step back, out of his reach, feeling raw and insecure and provoked. "Oh, really? So old-fashioned that you'd slip off with the redhead *upstairs* and leave your date behind?"

He lifted a brow at her cutting tone and uncalled-for remark, but she turned and walked away before he could reply. With her body buzzing and her head in no better shape, she had no idea where she was headed, but that didn't seem to matter when Steve curled his fingers around her upper arm and guided her into a lounge area next to the bar and dance floor.

The music from the bar drifted into the room, and the lighting from the fringed Tiffany lamps made the room dim and sensually shadowed. Everything was decorated in velvet: the heavy drapes, couches, chairs, pillows, and even the artwork on the wall.

"The Velvet Room," it was appropriately named. The couples around them, and what they were doing, ended up being a blur as Steve led her to a secluded corner of the room, turned her around, and pressed her up against the wall, which was textured with velvet wallpaper, too.

He flattened his hands on either side of her head, leaned close so she could see the heat in his eyes—and the frustration, as if he couldn't understand her reaction and was hurt that she'd doubt him. She opened her mouth to apologize, to tell him that whatever kind of drug she'd been slipped was making her irrational, as well as making her feel incredibly aroused and needy, but he cut her off before she could explain.

"What I just did upstairs with Trixie was all business," he said gruffly. Skimming his lips along her jaw, he pinned her hips to the wall with the slow grind of his and said into her ear, "I haven't so much as thought of another woman since I laid eyes on you. You give me everything I need sexually, and then some."

She closed her eyes and moaned, his words escalating her desire. The hard, long length of his shaft pressing against her mound increased her hunger to have him filling her full, stroking her, giving her the orgasm her body was beginning to scream for.

"Do you want to know what Trixie and I did in that room upstairs?"

She shook her head and slipped her hands to the waistband of his pants, her breath quickening at the thought of releasing him from the confines of his slacks and taking him in her hand, her mouth. "No, I don't want to know." She trusted him. She really, truly did. It was her state of mind that was playing tricks on her, making her imagine the worst. She felt as though she were on an emotional and physical roller coaster ride with no end in sight.

"I'm going to tell you anyway," he said, and lifted his head to stare into her eyes. The room was dark, but their gazes had no problem connecting. "I gave Trixie two hundred bucks, and all she gave me was Rob's last name and a bunch of other information that'll go a long way in tracking him and your cousin. Trixie was Rob's last lover, and she apparently knows him well."

Okay, she was eternally grateful for that assurance, and now that Steve had eased her insecurities, there was something more pressing she needed to attend to, no matter that there were other couples in the room with them. Most were too busy with their own pleasure to pay attention to anything else going on around them.

Reaching between their bodies, Liz unbuckled his belt, but before she could pull the tab of his zipper down, he stopped her.

He sucked in a startled breath. "Damn it, Liz, what are you doing?" he growled huskily.

She nipped at his jaw and cupped him in her palm through the fabric of his slacks, massaging the impressive length of him with her fingers. "Someone put something in my drink, and I'm burning up. I need you inside me. Here. *Now.*"

He swore beneath his breath, his body tensing protectively, possessively, and she knew he was thinking about hunting down those two men and beating the shit out of them.

Right now, Liz had something else in mind for those wonderful hands of his. Catching his wrist, she slid his palm beneath the hem of her dress and determinedly guided his fingers upward, past the lacy band of her stockings. "Steve . . . touch me."

She groaned and trembled when he slipped two fingers beneath the edge of her panties and into the hot, wet folds of her pulsing sex and stroked her engorged flesh. She came immediately, biting her bottom lip as her release slammed through her in a pounding rush of sensation that nearly overwhelmed her with the pleasure of it.

But that one orgasm wasn't enough. Not when she could already feel a second one waiting in the wings, another wave of heat building, slowly cresting to a peak of desire.

"Steve, *please,*" she begged.

He lifted his dark head and stared deep into her eyes as his fingers, wet from her, skimmed up to her hip and tugged on the side ties of her panties. "Please what?" he asked, his tone low and rough.

This particular fantasy had turned dark and forbidden, a naughty, shameless tryst that surprisingly turned her on, beyond the stimulant she'd been given. There was no reason to couch what she wanted and needed in a flowery request. Right now, she needed a hard, fast coupling for the pure sake of satisfaction.

"*Fuck me,*" she whispered. A plea. A dare.

His restraint shattered, and instead of releasing the second tie on her panties, he ripped them off her hips, then shoved the scrap of fabric into his coat pocket. In a heartbeat, he released his shaft, plucked a foil packet from the bowl on the table next to them, and rolled the condom on.

Then he was back, curling his fingers under her bare bottom, pulling her forward, spreading her legs, and lifting her all in one smooth motion. Her thighs clamped against his hips, and he shoved forward, entering her in a long, hard thrust that impaled her to the hilt. The cry that escaped her throat was lost in the pulsating beat of the music drifting into the velvet room from the bar area.

With Steve standing in front of her, and with the dim lighting, all anyone could see was a couple in an erotic embrace, if they could see anything at all in the dark corner Steve had chosen. Anyone could imagine exactly what they were doing, but they were completely and decently covered—by her dress and the jacket he wore.

Which made the encounter that much more exciting.

She anchored her arms around his neck, locked her ankles against the small of his back, and felt the powerful muscles in his arms, along his shoulders, and in his buttocks flex as he pumped into her. She welcomed this primal side to Steve, the way he could so easily lose control with her.

Burying her face in the curve of his neck, she inhaled his hot male scent. She bit his earlobe, dipped her tongue into his ear, and felt the clench of her inner muscles around his shaft as another orgasm beckoned.

"Oh, God," she rasped into his ear, poised on the brink of tumbling over yet another exquisite peak. "I'm going to come again."

"*Yes.*" His breathing was hot and moist against her throat, labored; and with a hard, convulsive shudder, he let go and went over himself.

When the tempest was over, she sagged against him, felt him shift with her still in his arms, then gently lowered her feet back to the floor.

He met her gaze and tenderly brushed tendrils of hair off her cheek. "We got the information we came for, so let's get the hell out of here."

She couldn't agree with him more.

Chapter

14

They took a cab home instead of using the company limousine, and as soon as they were inside Steve's place and made their way up to his bedroom, Liz was worked up all over again. She couldn't seem to get enough of him—a fantasy in and of itself, despite how furious Steve was at whoever had given her a sexual stimulant. But now all he could do was give her more of what she needed, and in the private haven of his bedroom, without an audience, he could do just that.

Heat against heat.

Flesh against flesh.

Heartbeat to heartbeat.

But she was going too fast, her movements anxious and aggressive as she pushed his coat from his shoulders, then began unfastening the buttons on his dress shirt. That came off in a frenzy, too, and then she was attacking the front closure on his slacks, trying to get those off him as well.

This was not how he'd imagined that their night together would end. Oh, he'd anticipated that they'd end up in his bedroom, but she was taking charge and aiming for mindless physical pleasure, and he meant to make this night one she'd remember emotionally. Because now that he had the information he needed to trace Rob, he instinctively knew this was his last night with Liz. Tomorrow would bring answers and possibly a firm lead on Valerie's whereabouts, and once Steve gave Liz the assurances she was searching for, she'd most likely end their affair, because she believed she wasn't ready for a relationship, that other responsibilities and obligations were more important than her own happiness.

And if tonight was all he had left, he damn well intended to make it a memorable one, in every way that mattered.

Gently grasping her wrists, he pulled her hands away from the front placket of his slacks. "Liz, slow down."

"I want you," she said urgently, and kissed his chest, ran her tongue up to one rigid nipple, and grazed the tip with her teeth.

He drew in a shuddering breath, tried to keep his thoughts from straying to her shameless attempts to distract him. "I want you, too." But his longing for her went deeper than surface sensations. He wanted her heart, her body, and her soul.

She looked up at him with eyes bright with desire, her skin flushed and feverish. "Steve, I need—"

He pressed his fingers over her warm, soft lips, cutting off her demand. "Shhh. I know what you need, and I gave you what you wanted back at the mansion." A hot, fast, wild coupling. "Now it's my turn to be in charge, and I'm going to make love to you. Slowly, leisurely, thoroughly."

Wrapping an arm around her waist, he brought her body up against his, holding her securely in his embrace. He caressed her cheek with his palm, felt her tremble with a renewed urgency, and lowered his mouth to hers. He calmed her jitters with a lush, deep kiss, tamed her frenzied passion with the slow, lazy stroke of his tongue against hers. Despite her attempts to quicken the pace, to devour him, he controlled her response until she softened against him.

When he finally felt that she was more relaxed, he loosened his hold and unfastened the top part of her halter dress. Letting the two panels of bright-red material fall open, he bared her from the waist up, except for the glittering diamond heart choker around her neck and the matching earrings winking in the room's lamplight.

"You're so, so beautiful," he whispered reverently.

He glided his lips along her jaw, and her hands landed on his chest, her nails lightly grazing his taut flesh. He swirled his tongue down the side of her neck and filled his palms with her generous breasts, and she released a long, blissful sigh. Dipping his head, he laved her nipples with his tongue, drew them into his mouth, sucking first one, then the other stiffened crest.

She cried out hoarsely and moved restlessly against him in a silent plea for more. Her fingers threaded through his hair, holding him in place, encouraging a deeper pressure of his mouth on her breast. He gave her everything she wanted, but at his own leisurely pace, which increased her excitement, her need for him, just as he intended.

Slipping his hands into the waistline of her dress, he pushed the outfit over her hips and let the silky fabric fall to the floor at her feet. His large palms passed over her bottom, smooth and naked since he'd ripped off her panties earlier, and traced one of the straps of her garter belt down to the stocking hugging her thigh.

He pushed her back toward the mattress, made her lie down in the center of the bed and watch as he took off his shoes and socks, and stripped out of his slacks and briefs. Her gaze took in his erect, jutting cock, and she licked her lips and touched her fingers to her belly, teasing him, testing his restraint. Her green eyes were hungry, eager, and her body moved restlessly against the covers, as if her skin was too prickly to bear.

With a seductive smile, he crawled up onto the mattress from the foot of the bed and took off one of her strappy red shoes, then the other, and tossed both to the floor. He rubbed her feet and arches until she moaned with gratitude; then he unclasped her garter belt and slowly, leisurely rolled her stockings down her legs and off. Wanting to pamper her, he stroked her supple skin and caressed and massaged her thighs, her calves, and felt the tension drain from her limbs. Finally, her body grew pliant, her breathing deep and even.

He looked up the length of her, taking in her sweet, feminine curves, the sparkling entwined hearts she still wore around her neck and which claimed her as his, and the way she trusted him so implicitly with her body and her pleasure. If only she'd grant him that much trust with her heart and emotions.

He'd managed to mellow her for the moment, to decrease that rush of sexual adrenaline she'd been riding on, and when she opened her legs in invitation and whispered his name like a prayer, he felt something fierce and tender clench inside his chest and knew without question what that emotion was. *Love.*

He moved over her, fitting his hips between her spread thighs, crushing her breasts against his chest, and braced his arms on either side of her head so that they were face-to-face. Refusing to let her look away, he stared into her eyes, watched her expression as he slowly pushed inside her. Without the barrier of a condom, she enveloped him in a tight, slick heat that made him suck in a quick breath at the exquisite sensation of being one with her, without anything to separate flesh from flesh.

She gasped, startled, and with her palms braced against his shoulders, she struggled beneath him. "Steve . . . wait . . . stop." Panic laced her voice. "You didn't wear a condom."

He caught her pushing hands, stretched her arms above her head, and entwined their fingers so she was pinned beneath him. "You're on the Pill," he reminded her huskily, but knew that wasn't her main concern. She knew the significance of this joining, understood the sacrifice he'd made to forgo any protection on his part. "You feel so good with nothing be-tween us. So hot, so silky soft and tight."

She closed her eyes and moaned as he thrust into her—long, slow strokes that increased the building pressure, the in-credible, delicious friction. He kissed her lips, chased her tongue with his, and arched his hips high and hard, forcing her to wrap her legs around his waist as he rocked against her sex. Then he stopped, lifted his head, and captured her gaze with his.

"Can you feel that?" he murmured, keeping his chest pressed to hers.

He watched the pulse at the base of her throat flutter, and knew she'd try to evade the answer. "Feel . . . *what?*"

"The beat of our hearts. Yours and mine. Together." He waited, letting her absorb their mingling heartbeats before laying his emotions for her out in the open. "And the love. Can you feel that, Liz?"

He expected her to deny her feelings for him, but the tears gathering in her eyes stunned him as much as her reply did. "Yes," she said in an aching, wistful voice, as vulnerable as he'd ever seen her before. "I can feel it."

It was time he offered her the ultimate commitment, and the declaration came much easier than he'd ever expected, and felt incredibly, perfectly right. "I love you."

He didn't wait for a response, because none was needed. He knew how she felt about him even if she didn't verbalize those emotions, and he'd left no doubts in her mind how much he cared about her.

He continued making slow, sweet love to her, letting his body worship hers, and gave her every reason to stay with him. For the night. Forever.

But by morning, Liz was gone, leaving behind the diamond heart earrings and necklace on his nightstand—one of many gifts she refused to accept from him.

Steve rubbed a hand over his unshaven jaw, more disappointed than surprised that she'd left sometime in the middle of the night without waking him or saying good-bye. It was a clean break, with no messy emotional issues or any argument for her to deal with—just as she'd spent years avoiding that same kind of confrontation with her cousin. And now she was living a solitary, one-dimensional life as a result.

The case was over. By one o'clock that afternoon, after speaking briefly with Liz on the phone and giving her his final report on her cousin, Steve closed the file he'd started on Valerie Clark and Rob Easton, satisfied with the knowledge that Liz's cousin hadn't been kidnapped or taken against her will. She was off enjoying a week-and-a-half-long holiday in Paris with a client she'd met through The Ultimate Fantasy.

With the personal information that Trixie had shared with him the previous night at the party, tracing Rob had been ridiculously easy. The tidbits the other woman had offered had been invaluable. Steve now knew that Easton was the CEO of a software company based here in Chicago, and that he lived in a very exclusive area of Lake Shore Drive. According to Trixie, Rob had a penchant for pretty women, indulging in phone sex and attending the fantasy parties to satisfy his numerous fetishes. Rob also enjoyed vacationing in exotic locales with the ladies he met through The Ultimate Fantasy. Valerie wasn't the first woman he'd taken abroad, and she most likely wouldn't be the last.

According to the itinerary he'd been able to outline from the bits and pieces of information he'd discovered this morning, he'd learned that today was Rob and Valerie's last night at a high-dollar Paris hotel, and they were due to check out and fly back to the states tomorrow. Their international flight was due to arrive at O'Hare in the early evening.

There was nothing to indicate foul play, or that Valerie was in any kind of danger, and that had relieved Liz the most when Steve had spoken to her. Yet he couldn't help but wish that Liz would embrace a bit of anger when it came to Valerie and the way she continually manipulated her emotions and, on some level, her life. But that was the heart of the problem with Liz—she was too caught up in doing the responsible thing, too intent on pleasing her aunt and uncle causing her to sacrifice her own happiness in the process and give up any chance at a future: with him. That had been abundantly clear when she'd sneaked out of his bed last night.

Her withdrawal had also been evident in her tone when he'd talked to her on the phone a while ago. She'd been all business, as if they'd never been intimate. She never strayed beyond their conversation about Valerie, never acknowledged the fact that he was in love with her and had told her as much the night before. He supposed it was easier for Liz to ignore that fact, to pretend it didn't exist, than to deal with all the emotional repercussions that came with such a deep, heartfelt revelation.

Releasing a long exhale, he pulled another case file to follow up on, determined to move on to the best of his ability. He spent the next couple of hours making calls on another missing-persons case, tracing leads, and searching Internet files for information he needed in another state.

The speaker on his phone buzzed, followed by his secretary's efficient voice. "Steve, Liz Adams is here to see you."

An odd sense of déjà vu washed over him. It had been a week ago that she'd come to his office seeking his services, which had been the beginning of an affair that had turned into so much more for him. While her visit this afternoon was unexpected, from all the signals she'd sent out thus far, he doubted she was here to continue their relationship or profess her love in return. But he was curious to know what had brought her by his office when they'd pretty much wrapped everything up with Valerie and the case over the phone.

"Go ahead and send her back to my office." Standing, he rounded his desk just as Liz entered the room.

He smiled at her, and she smiled in return, though the gesture didn't completely erase that damnable wariness that was back in her eyes, shining like a beacon and warning him to keep his distance. So he did, no matter how much he ached to reach out and touch her, to pull her into his arms and hold her.

They were beyond polite pleasantries, and there was no sense skirting around the reason why she was there, so he jumped straight to the heart of the matter. "What brings you by?"

She absently adjusted her purse strap over her shoulder and straightened, her demeanor much too formal considering how informal they'd been with each other the past week. "I just wanted to thank you for everything you've done for me, and for finding Valerie. It's a huge relief to know that she's okay."

And what about the fact that your self-centered cousin doesn't give a damn that you've been overwhelmed with worry and concern for her welfare? He bit back the sarcastic remark, knowing he'd only get a defensive explanation from Liz in return. One that would undoubtedly involve that never-ending promise she'd made to her aunt and uncle, feeling guilt over her past actions, and trying to make up for her disappointing marriage to Travis.

"If I remember correctly, finding Valerie was a joint effort," he pointed out instead, doing his best to keep a tight rein on his frustration. "I couldn't have gotten the information on Rob as quickly as I did without you getting invited to one of The Ultimate Fantasy parties."

"Regardless, I appreciate your advice and guidance along the way. I can't imagine going to that party last night without you being there."

She shuddered, and he knew she was thinking about the two men who'd nearly taken advantage of her, and would have if he hadn't shown up after his meeting with Trixie.

She tucked a strand of hair behind her ear and shifted on her feet. "After I talked to you on the phone, I went to The Ultimate Fantasy and quit, and I wanted to say good-bye to

Roxanne, who is the only woman who really befriended me. I'm glad to be out of there, but I feel so bad for her and her situation."

Steve realized she was babbling, talking faster than normal, and suddenly seemed nervous. She was here for another reason, he knew, and when she opened up her purse and withdrew an envelope, he steeled himself for what was to come.

She held the unmarked envelope out to him but wouldn't look him in the eye. "I also wanted to stop by to give you this."

He thrust his hands into the front pockets of his jeans, refusing to take what she was offering. "What is it?" he asked, even though he knew what was inside that sealed envelope.

Her shoulders lifted in a casual shrug. "It's my paycheck from The Ultimate Fantasy, signed over to you. It's a good amount for a week's worth of work, including my cut from the party last night. I also had some extra money at the end of the month from the café, so I took a draw and included a check for that in here, too. Between both, it's a decent amount, and should help to pay off what I owe you."

His entire body flashed hot with irritation, and his jaw clenched so tight, he was certain he'd grind his teeth to dust. He'd had more than he could take of her obligation to him, and resented the fact that she believed she could wrap up their relationship all neat and tidy with a check to pay for his services.

"I don't want your money, Liz. Or your gratitude, either." He curled his hands into fists in his pockets, looking from that envelope that stood between them to her face. So beautiful. So vulnerable. So fearful of taking a chance on *them*. "What I did for you, I did because I wanted to. Our agreement might have started out with a loan, but what I want and need from you now isn't money or your appreciation."

He wanted, needed, her love.

Her eyes widened with surprise at his frank, straightforward approach, along with deeper insecurities that controlled too much of her life. But she remained silent.

"I'm disappointed that you think this is all about owing me anything," he went on, figuring he had nothing left to lose. "Then again, you measure everything in your life based on responsibility, guilt, and obligations to everyone but yourself, so why should this be any different?"

She stiffened defensively. "You have no idea what my life is like."

"That's insulting, considering how intimate we've been and all that we've shared. I understand your life, and you, better than you think," he said, unable to hold back the roughness in his tone. "When are you going to stop hiding behind the guilt and obligation to your aunt and uncle for them taking you in after your parents died? Not to mention a responsibility to a cousin that doesn't deserve it?"

"I have no idea what you're talking about," she said, her denial coming much too quickly.

"I believe you do." He leaned back against the edge of his desk, hating that he was causing her pain, but knew it was necessary in order for her to get past all the emotional issues she'd carried with her since she was orphaned as a child. "It's easier and safer for you to be the responsible one and strive to please everyone else than risk getting hurt. I don't want to hurt you, Liz; I want to love you. But you have to let me in."

She shook her head jerkily. "I can't give you what you need," she said, her voice raspy and loaded with burdens. "I'm just getting the café back to where it should be, I've got Valerie to look after, and after everything with Travis—"

He held up a hand, bringing her excuses to a halt. "We all have issues to deal with, sweetheart, and it's all in the way we handle and resolve them." And she obviously hadn't resolved hers, and possibly wasn't willing to. "You need to live your life for yourself, not everyone else. And that means taking chances and making choices that make *you* happy."

Not touching her was killing him, and he finally reached out and ran his knuckles down her warm, soft cheek. "You're so busy taking care of everyone else, but who takes care of you, Liz? Who is there for you when you need a shoulder to lean on, a smile to get you through the day, or a hug to soothe your fears and make you feel like you're not alone?"

She had no answer, and that saddened him. "Let me be that person for you," he whispered. "Trust me, and trust your feelings."

She swallowed convulsively but made no reply.

Picking up her hand, he placed a kiss in her palm, felt the tremble of her fingers against his jaw, and knew he'd said everything he could. The rest was up to her. "When you're ready to take a chance on me, on us, you know where to find me."

She set the envelope on his desk and glanced at him one last time before she turned and left. It gave him no satisfaction to see the well of tears in her eyes, or to watch her walk out of his office and his life.

Liz had never felt so alone and miserable in her entire life, even while being surrounded with her employees and customers at The Daily Grind. She'd kept her mind and hands busy the entire day in an attempt to work off the restless, anxious, edgy feeling that had settled within her since she'd walked out of Steve's office the previous afternoon. But now, curled up on the couch in her apartment and drinking a cup of hot tea while she waited for her cousin to finally walk through the front door, she had too much time to think. Too much time to replay her conversation with Steve in her mind. Too much time to question herself, her actions, her life, and her future.

Too much time to wonder if all the emotional sacrifices she'd made over the years had been worth it—the biggest sacrifice of which was letting Steve go and believing that was for the best.

He loved her. The mere thought made her chest tighten and her pulse race. The last night he'd made love to her had been magical, a joining of not only their bodies but their hearts as well. She might not have been able to speak the words aloud, but there was no denying that she'd fallen in love with him, too.

She just didn't know what to do about it, because her fear of letting Steve into her heart was stronger than her desire to let him so completely into her life.

Sighing discontently, she dragged her fingers through her hair and took another drink of her tea, letting the warmth seep inside her and take away the chill that went bone deep. Unfortunately, there was no antidote for the ache in her chest or the tight squeeze of her heart.

The rattling of a key being inserted into the front door lock pulled Liz out of her troubling thoughts and had her bolting anxiously across the living room to wrench open the door.

Valerie, standing on the other side of the threshold, surrounded by shopping bags and luggage, gasped in startled surprise, then glared at Liz. "Jesus, give me a heart attack, why don't you?" Her gaze traveled the length of Liz in one single sweep, and then she smirked. "You certainly look like hell."

Liz shook her head in disbelief at her cousin's greeting. No "Hello, how are you doing?" Or "Gee, I suppose I should have let you know that I was going to be out of the country for a week and a half."

Instead, Valerie was more concerned with Liz's appearance. Amazing.

"I guess compared to you, I do look like hell." Liz certainly felt like it. Her hair was a mess from repeated finger-combs, she had no makeup on, and she was dressed in her rattiest jammies. Her cousin, on the other hand, looked incredibly chic with a new hairstyle, an impeccably made-up face, and a cute little outfit that showed way too much skin.

Valerie picked up a brand-new designer suitcase and sauntered into the apartment. "Grab a few bags, would you? I nearly killed myself trying to get all this stuff up to the apartment."

Gritting her teeth, Liz dragged two of the bigger pieces of luggage into the living room, just to help speed up the process, while Valerie handled the shopping bags. Though Liz did wonder why Rob hadn't been gentleman enough to see her to the door. Probably because Rob was no gentleman and was undoubtedly just as selfish as her cousin. Which made them a perfect pair, Liz realized.

Valerie flopped down on the couch and released a dramatic sigh. "I'm absolutely exhausted."

"And I've been half out of my mind worrying about you," Liz replied, no longer able to keep a rein on the frustration that had been stewing for the past twenty-four hours. "Where have you been?" She knew the answer but needed to hear it from her cousin.

"In Paris, having the time of my life," Valerie said with a satisfied smile, apparently oblivious to Liz's concern. "And the best part of the trip was that it was all-expenses-paid."

In exchange for sleeping with Rob, no doubt, Liz thought, but kept the rude comment to herself. Instead, she crossed her arms over her chest and pinned her cousin with a direct look. "Did it ever occur to you that you could have let me know where you were?"

Valerie's shoulder lifted in an uncaring shrug. "I left you a note."

"A very vague note that said you were going to a weekend work party with some guy named Rob, not that you were going to be out of the country for a week and a half." Liz's voice rose with exasperation.

Valerie studied her French-manicured nails and picked at a cuticle. "My plans changed. So sue me."

Irritation welled inside Liz as she stared at her self-centered cousin, her upset so strong it nearly overwhelmed her. "Since you bought luggage and applied for a passport before this trip, you obviously knew you were going to be gone longer than a weekend, so don't give me any crap about your plans changing. You knew about this trip in plenty of time to let me know, and considering you're living with me, it would be basic common courtesy to let me in on where you're going and when you're coming back."

"You want to know why I didn't tell you about my trip? Well, here's the truth," Valerie said, bitterness vibrating in her tone. "If I told you where I was going, and with whom, I'd get a lecture, just like you're starting to do right now. And I didn't want to listen to it. You've never approved of what I do anyway, so what's the point of telling you ahead of time?"

"Because I care about you."

There was no reply from her cousin, no warmth or reciprocal words of affection. And knowing that Valerie resented her so much hurt Liz to the very core of who she was—a woman who ached for acceptance, even from a cousin who so openly harbored ill feelings against her for stealing away half of her parents' attention and love.

"Damn it, Valerie, at the very least you could have called me from Paris or left some kind of message to let me know you were okay and safe. I was worried sick about you, whether you want to acknowledge that or not." Her cousin continued to stare at her from the couch, cold and unresponsive. "Your mother has called more than a few times since you've been gone, and I've already had to lie to her once. I wasn't about to do it again."

"Did I ask you to?" Valerie snapped.

"No, you never asked me to, but what did you expect me to tell your parents?" Liz began to pace restlessly—anything to burn off the extra energy building within her. "That you're a phone sex operator who dates her clients, attends sex parties with them, and flies abroad with a virtual stranger? Do you really want your mother and father to know what kind of job you have and everything it entails?"

Valerie stiffened defensively. "You have no idea what my job entails."

"Yes, unfortunately, I do," Liz said, her distaste for her cousin's choice of occupation clear. "I worked for a week at The Ultimate Fantasy in order to find you, and I went to a fantasy party in order to track down Trixie Lane to get information on Rob, who seems to have quite a reputation with most of the party girls there. So I know exactly what your job is all about, and most of it isn't pleasant."

"Wow, Ms. Goody-Goody I'm-the-Responsible-One actually sullied herself for me?" Valerie drawled insolently. "It's nice to know that you have a bit of daring and adventure left in you after all."

Liz dismissed her cousin's sarcasm. "I did it for you, Valerie. Because you're my flesh and blood and I wanted to make sure you were safe and okay. And I also did it for your parents."

Valerie stood and closed the distance separating them, until she was only a few feet away and Liz could see the condemnation in her cousin's green eyes. "Whoever asked you to do anything for me?" Valerie asked. "I certainly never have, yet you always seem to take it upon yourself to try and control my life, to make sure I stay on the straight-and-narrow. Here's a news flash for you, cousin: I have no desire to be a good girl like you, so why don't *you* get a life instead?"

Liz opened her mouth, then snapped it shut, feeling as though she'd been slapped upside the head with Valerie's verbal assault. She blinked, clearly seeing the selfish woman Valerie had become. It suddenly became apparent to Liz that she'd always striven to be the opposite of her cousin to compensate for Valerie's frivolous, reckless behavior, and when her marriage to Travis had ended so disastrously, Liz had subconsciously compared her own shortcomings to Valerie's. She'd compounded her disappointment and sense of guilt because she'd wanted her aunt and uncle's approval so badly and felt compelled to please them in any way she could. It had been her way of repaying them for giving her a home and a family when her parents had died.

She'd always be eternally grateful for their raising her, but she no longer had to make choices that they approved of. She was an adult, and while she'd made a mistake with Travis, her cousin had made even bigger ones, and through it all her aunt and uncle loved them both the same.

Valerie's words stung, but boy, did they have a ring of truth to them.

Yes, it was past time that she got a life of her own, just as Valerie had so sarcastically suggested. And that new life was about to begin, right here and now. No excuses, no burdens, no guilt.

She couldn't change Valerie—not who she was or how her cousin felt about her. It was obvious that Valerie would always cling to past resentments, but that was Valerie's problem, not Liz's. She didn't have to put up with her cousin's self-indulgent personality or her contemptuous attitude. They were both grown women, and Liz no longer needed to be responsible for anyone but herself.

It was time that Valerie did the same.

She met Valerie's gaze and pleased herself for a change. "I think it's time you found your own place to live," she stated calmly but very seriously.

Valerie looked completely appalled at the suggestion. "I'm not going anywhere," she protested.

"Fine. Then consider the apartment all yours, and I'll find somewhere else to live." Liz knew she'd have to explain things to her aunt and uncle, but she'd deal with them in the same firm, straightforward manner in which she'd just handled Valerie. "I can't deal with this situation anymore. I *won't* deal with this, and you, because I don't have to."

Her cousin's expression filled with absolute shock and disbelief, mainly because Liz had never been so assertive before. But Liz's confidence felt damn good, and so liberating.

She was tired of the guilt and burdens she'd put upon herself. Tired of being alone and so fearful of taking a risk on a man who was everything she'd ever dreamed of and so much more. A bad boy who gave her the kind of adventure and excitement she craved, yet kept her grounded and would never, ever deliberately hurt her. A tender, generous man who wasn't afraid to wear his heart on his sleeve.

A gorgeous, sexy man who loved her and was waiting for her to come to her senses.

Passing her cousin, Liz went to her bedroom and changed into a pair of jeans, T-shirt, and tennis shoes. After putting her hair into a quick ponytail, she grabbed her purse and keys and left the apartment and Valerie behind so she could begin her new life.

The street lamp illuminated the interior of her vehicle and glimmered off the ring encircling her left ring finger. Swallowing hard, she removed the band of gold that gave the impression that she was taken, and put it on her right hand, leaving her openly single and available, with a heart that yearned to belong to the bad boy who owned her soul.

Steve was waiting for her, and there was only one thing left to do—go and stake a claim on her man.

Steve picked up the portable phone next to the living room couch on the second ring, and with his mind on other matters instead of the game show playing on TV, he answered with an absent and automatic, "Hello?"

"Hi, Wilde Thing," a familiar feminine voice whispered, grabbing Steve's full attention. "How are you doing tonight?"

It was Liz, speaking to him in the same husky tone she'd used for their nightly phone sex calls. His body responded to that provocative voice, even while he wondered what she was up to.

What had changed, and why? He intended to find out.

Ever since she'd walked out of his office two days ago, he'd been distracted, his mind constantly thinking of Liz and wondering if he'd pushed her too hard and fast for a commitment. Wondering if he'd lost her for good because he wanted and needed her love like he needed nothing else in his life.

And now here she was, taking the first step to contact him when he'd believed it was over between the two of them. He was hopeful but still cautious.

Lowering the volume on the television with his remote, he answered her question honestly. "I could be better."

"Me, too." A believable amount of regret infused her soft voice. "I'm sitting here all by myself, feeling so alone, and I knew you'd keep me company. I'm thinking maybe we could make each other feel better."

He settled into the corner of the couch, all too willing to follow her suggestion and see where it led. "What do you have in mind?"

"I want to tell you a fantasy of mine."

Knowing just how potent their fantasies could be, awareness stirred within him—a physical reaction that was backed up with a wealth of emotion. "I'm listening."

He heard her draw a deep breath for fortitude before speaking. "I work in a coffee shop, and there's this man that comes in a few times a week. He wears a leather jacket and drives a Harley that's inscripted with the appropriate name *Wilde Thing,* and he's so incredibly sexy that my heart pounds whenever our eyes meet across the room. I often wondered what it would be like to be with him, to just let loose of responsibilities, obligations, and inhibitions, and take a walk on the wild side with this man."

A slow smile curved the corner of Steve's mouth, and he stood, wandering restlessly around the living room. "And did you follow through on that desire?"

"Oh, yes," she breathed, and he imagined she was smiling,

too. "Circumstances brought us together, and we began a hot, erotic affair that exceeded anything I've ever imagined. He's exciting and adventurous, and also a wonderful, generous lover. But he's also incredibly sensitive and tender when it counts. And when I'm with him, I feel like I've finally found my other half."

Steve's hand tightened on the receiver, matching the sudden pull across his chest. "So what's holding you back?"

"I was afraid to trust in my feelings for him," she said, a vulnerable catch to her voice. *"For you."*

His doorbell rang, twice, and Steve ignored the interruption, because at the moment nothing mattered but Liz and this conversation with her—and how it would all end. "And now?"

"I'm ready to take a chance on you. On us."

Yes. Adrenaline and elation pumped through Steve, though it was quickly shattered by a knock on the front door. Not expecting any visitors, Steve again dismissed the intrusion. "What changed your mind, Liz?"

"Valerie came home tonight, and confronting her forced me to confront my own fears. I realized that you were right, that I had to stop living my life for everyone else. I'm taking chances and making choices that make me happy."

That revelation pleased him, because she deserved to be happy in any way she chose. Even if that meant choosing a life without him in it. "Good for you, sweetheart," he murmured.

"There's something I need to tell you," she went on, an anxious note to her voice. "Something I should have told you days ago."

Another knock, this one more insistent, demanding that Steve find out who was at the door. "Damn it," he growled in pure frustration, suspecting that Liz was on the verge of saying something profound. "Hold on to that thought a second."

Steve stalked into the foyer and yanked open the door, prepared to tell whoever was standing on the other side of the threshold to get lost. But it was Liz, haloed in the buttery glow of the porch light, her green eyes shining with hope and affection and confidence.

She disconnected her cellular unit. "What I have to say needs to be said in person and not over the phone. This is the best part of the fantasy, because it's become my reality." She held his gaze, her expression glowing with the kind of promises he longed for with this woman. "I trust you, Steve Wilde. With my heart and soul, and I'm ready to give you both, completely and unconditionally. I need you in my life, and most importantly, I love you."

Fearful that she'd change her mind, that all this was a figment of his imagination, he pulled her inside his house and kicked the door closed. In seconds they were in his bedroom, right where she belonged.

Framing her face in his hands, he kissed her, a long, deep, soulful joining that expressed his own feelings for her. When he finally lifted his head, they were both breathing hard, and he couldn't wait to get inside her, be a part of her. He removed his shirt, then stripped off hers as well. She wasn't wearing a bra, and he cupped her breasts in his hands, caressed her nipples with the brush of his fingers over the hard tips.

Closing her eyes, Liz sighed blissfully and arched into his touch. "I know you're not looking for marriage, but for as long as this lasts between us, I want to be with you."

He'd forgotten about his vow never to marry again, but he'd changed over the course of their affair, just as Liz had, too, and he needed to rectify that original impression. "I love you, Liz, and I intend for it to last forever."

Liz's lashes snapped back open, and she stared at him in confusion.

He smiled and explained. "I'll admit that I didn't go into this relationship looking for more than an affair, but it happened, and what I feel for you is so much richer and more mature than anything I've ever felt before. But you have to want it, too, not just physically but emotionally. I've discovered that I'm a very greedy man, and I want it all."

"What does 'all' encompass?" Her eyes were wide and brimming with anticipation as she waited for his reply.

"I never thought that a woman could make me want to get married again, or start a new family, but I want that with you," he said, his own heart beating rapidly in his chest. "Marry me, Liz."

"Yes, I'll marry you." Tears of joy shone in her eyes. "I want you to be that shoulder for me to lean on, and it's your smile I want to see every morning, to get me through the day. And I need your hugs to soothe my fears and let me know that I'm not alone."

He remembered asking Liz who would be that person for her, and he was so glad it was him. "I'll be there for you. I promise."

"I want to be all those things for you in return." She wrapped her arms around his neck and brought his mouth to hers in a silent, heartfelt affirmation of their feelings for each other. He laid her back on the bed, and their kisses grew more amorous, more aggressive and eager as they fumbled with their clothing, until they were both naked and excruciatingly aroused.

He moved over her, fitting himself between her spread thighs, feeling her hot and wet against his shaft. So ready for him. But he didn't enter her, not just yet. For the moment, it was enough just to have her beneath him, the tip of his erection sliding against her lush sex.

She pressed a hand to his jaw and smiled tenderly at him. "I have to tell you, your proposal couldn't have come at a better time, considering I'm homeless."

"Excuse me?" He frowned, certain he'd misheard her.

"I told Valerie to find another place to live, and when she refused, I told her she could have my apartment, and I left."

He chuckled, amazed at how far this woman had come. And

thrilled that she'd made the decision to come to him. "I'm so proud of you."

Her chin tipped upward, a feisty show of the wild spirit Steve had always known she possessed. "I was pretty proud of myself, actually."

Growing serious, he finally slid into her, a perfect fit, and gave her yet another promise to believe in. "This is your home now. Here. With me."

Please turn the page for a preview of
STANDING IN THE SHADOWS
by Shannon McKenna.
Available soon from Brava.

The silver cell phone that lay on the passenger seat of the beige Cadillac buzzed and vibrated, like a dying fly on a dusty windowsill.

Connor slouched lower in the driver's seat and contemplated it. Normal people were wired to grab the thing, check the number and respond. In him, those wires were cut, that programming deleted. He stared at it, amazed at his own indifference. Or maybe amazed was too strong a word. Stupefied would be closer. *Let it die.* Five rings. Six. Seven. Eight. The cell phone persisted, buzzing angrily.

It got up to fourteen, and gave up in disgust.

He went back to staring at Tiff's current love-nest through the rain that trickled over the windshield. It was a big, ugly town house that squatted across the street. The world outside the car was an infinite array of clammy shades of gray and green. Lights still on in the second-floor bedroom. Tiff was taking her time. He checked his watch. She was usually a slam-bam twenty-minutes-at-the-most sort of girl, but she'd gone up those stairs almost forty minutes ago. A record, for her.

Maybe it was true love.

Connor snorted to himself, hefting the heavy camera into place and training the telephoto lens on the doorway. He wished she'd hurry. Once he'd snapped the photos her husband had paid McCloud Investigative Services to procure, his duty would be done, and he could crawl back under his rock. A dark bar and a shot of single malt, someplace where the pale gray daylight could not sting his eyes. Where he could bear down and concentrate on not thinking about Erin.

He let the camera drop with a sigh, and pulled out his tobacco and rolling papers. After he'd woken up from the coma, during the agonizing tedium of rehab, he'd gotten the bright idea of switching to hand-rolled, reasoning that if he let himself roll them only with his fucked-up hand, he'd slow down and consequently smoke less. Problem was, he'd gotten good at it real fast. By now he could roll a tight cigarette in seconds flat with either hand, without looking. So much for that pathetic attempt at self-mastery.

He rolled the cigarette on autopilot, eyes trained on the town house, and wondered idly who had called. Only three people had the number: his friend Seth, and his two brothers, Sean and Davy. Seth, for sure, had better things to do on a Saturday afternoon than call him. The guy was neck-deep in honeymoon bliss, besotted with his new wife. Probably writhing in bed right now, engaged in sex acts that were still against the law somewhere in the South. *Lucky bastard.*

Connor's mouth twisted in self-disgust. God knew Seth had suffered too, from all the shit that had come down in the past few months. He was a good guy, and a true friend, if a difficult one. He deserved every bit of the happiness he'd found with Raine. It was unworthy of Connor to be envious, but Jesus. Watching those two, glowing like neon, joined at the hip, sucking on each others faces, well . . . it didn't help.

Connor wrenched his mind away from that dead-end track and stared at the cell phone. Couldn't be Seth. That left Sean or Davy.

Boredom tricked him into picking up the cell phone to check the number, and as if the goddamn thing had been lying in wait for him, it buzzed right in his hand, making him jump and curse. *Telepathic bastard.* Davy's instincts and timing were legendary.

He gave in and pushed "talk" with a grunt of disgust. "What?"

"Nick called." Davy's deep voice was brusque and business-like.

"So?"

"What do you mean, so? The guy's your friend. You need your friends, Con. You worked with him for years, and he—"

"I'm not working with him now," Connor said flatly. "I'm not working with any of them now."

Davy made an inarticulate, frustrated sound. "You made me swear not to give out this number, and I'm already regretting it. Call him up, or I'll break my oath."

"Don't do it," Connor warned.

"Don't make me," Davy said.

"So I'll throw the phone into the nearest dumpster," Connor said, his voice casual. "I don't give a flying fuck."

He could almost hear his older brother's teeth grinding. "You know, your attitude sucks," Davy said.

"If you stopped trying to shove me around, my sucky attitude wouldn't be in your face so much," Connor pointed out.

Davy treated him to one of his famous, eloquent long pauses, calculated to make Connor feel guilty and flustered. It didn't work. The wires were cut, the programming deleted. He just waited right back.

"He wants to talk to you," Davy finally said, his voice carefully neutral. "Says it's important."

The light in the town house bedroom went off. Connor lifted the camera to the ready. "I don't even want to know," he said. "You cannot imagine the profound depths of my indifference."

"Wise-ass," Davy growled. "Got Tiff's latest adventure on film yet?"

"Any minute now. She's just finishing up."

"Got plans after?" '

Connor hesitated. "Uh . . ."

"I've got steaks in the fridge," Davy wheedled. "And a case of Anchor Steam."

"I'm not really hungry," Connor hedged.

"l know. You haven't been hungry for the past year and a half. That's why you've lost twenty-five goddamn pounds. Get the pictures, and then get your ass over here. You need to eat."

Connor sighed. His brother knew exactly how useless his blustering orders were, but he refused to get a clue. Typical Davy. His stubborn skull was harder than concrete. "Uh, look, Davy. It's not that I don't like your cooking—"

"Nick said to tell you that if you're tired of pouting yet, he's got some news that might interest you about Novak."

Connor shot bolt upright in his seat, the heavy camera bouncing painfully off his scarred leg. "Novak? What about Novak?"

"That's it. That's all he said."

"That fuckhead is rotting in a maximum security prison cell! What news could there possibly be about him?"

"Guess you better call and find out, huh? Then hightail it over here. I'll mix up the marinade. Later, bro."

Connor stared at the phone in his hand, too rattled to be annoyed at Davy's casual bullying. His hand was shaking. *Whoa.* He wouldn't have thought there was still that much adrenaline left in the tank.

Kurt Novak, who had set in motion a chain of events that had effectively ruined Connor's life. Or so he saw it on days when he was particularly prey to self-pity, which was getting to be way too often lately. Kurt Novak, who had murdered Connor's partner, Jesse. Who was responsible for the coma, the scars, the limp. Who had blackmailed and corrupted Connor's colleague Ed Riggs.

Novak, who had almost gotten his vicious, filthy claws into Erin, Ed's daughter. Her incredibly narrow escape had given him nightmares for months. Oh, yeah. If there was one magic word on earth that could jolt him awake and make him give a shit, it was Novak.

Erin. Oh, God. He rubbed his face and tried not to think of the last time he'd seen Erin's beautiful face, but the image was brutally vivid, wrapped across his mind in wide-screen Technicolor. She'd been bundled into the patrol car, wrapped in a blanket. Dazed with shock. Her liquid brown eyes, staring through the car window at him, huge with horror and betrayal.

He was the one who had put that look in her eyes.

He gritted his teeth against the twisting ache of helpless anger that went along with that memory, and the explosion of sensual images. They made him feel guilty and sick, but they just wouldn't leave him alone. Every detail his brain had recorded about Erin was erotically charged, right down to the way her dark hair swirled into an elvish, downward-pointing whorl at the nape of her neck when she pulled it up. The way she had of looking at the world with those big, thoughtful eyes. Self-possessed and quiet, drawing her own mysterious conclusions. Making him ache and burn to know what she was thinking.

And then bam, her shy, sweet smile flashing out unexpectedly. Melting his brain down into steaming mush like a bolt of lightning.

All his crystal-clear memories of Erin just kept on endlessly transforming themselves into hot, explicit fantasies of all the things he could never have. Not the way things were now. Involuntary self-torture.

A flash of movement caught his eye, and he yanked the camera up to the ready with a curse. His concentration was shot to hell. Tiff had already scuttled halfway down the steps before he got in a series of rapid-fire shots. She shot a furtive glance to the right, then to the left, her long dark hair swishing over her beige raincoat. The guy followed her down the steps. Tall, fortyish, balding. Neither of them looked particularly relaxed or fulfilled. The guy tried to kiss her. Tiff turned away so the kiss landed on her ear. He got it all on film.

Tiff got into her car. It roared to life, and she pulled away, faster than she needed to on the rainy, deserted street. The guy stared after her, looking bewildered. *Clueless bastard.* He had no idea what a snake pit he was sliding into. Nobody ever did, until it was too late.

Connor let the camera drop. The guy climbed his steps and went back inside, shoulders slumped. Those pictures ought to be enough for Phil Kurtz, Tiff's scheming dickhead of a husband. Ironically, Phil was cheating on Tiff, too. He just wanted to make sure that Tiff wouldn't be able to screw him over in the inevitable acrimonious divorce.

It made Connor nauseous. Not that he cared who Tiff Kurtz was sleeping with. She could boff a whole platoon of balding suits if she wanted, and Phil was such a whiny, vindictive prick, he almost didn't blame her. And yet, he did. He couldn't help it. She should leave Phil. Make it clean, honest. Start a new life. A real life.

Hah. Like he had any right to judge. Like he was the expert on getting a real life. He tried to laugh at himself, but the laugh petered out with no breath to bear it up. He just couldn't stomach the betrayal. The lying and sneaking and slinking around in the shadows like a bad dog. It pressed down on his chest, suffocating him. Or maybe that was just the effect of all those unfiltered cigarettes he was sucking on.

It was his own damn fault for agreeing to help Davy out with his detective agency. He couldn't face going back to his job after what happened last fall, but he should've known better. After putting a colleague behind bars for setting you up to die, well, following cheating spouses around was not exactly therapeutic. And Davy must figure that Tiff was just the kind of stultifying no-brainer that even his washed-up little brother would have a hard time fucking up.

Oh, man. This was ugly. He was wallowing in self-pity like a pig in shit. He clenched his teeth, breathed deep and tried to adjust his attitude by sheer brute force. Davy unloaded Tiff and her ilk onto him because Davy was bored with them, and who could blame him. And if Connor couldn't take it, he should shut the fuck up and get another job. Security guard, maybe. Night shift, so he wouldn't have to interact with anybody. Maybe he could be a janitor in some cavernous industrial facility. Shove a push-broom down miles of deserted corridors night after night. Oh yeah. That ought to cheer him right up.

Connor fished the unsmoked cigarette out of his coat pocket and stared at the tobacco stain on the ends of his thumb and index finger, disgusted. Everything got dirty and stained, everything broke down, everything had a price. It was time to accept reality and stop sulking. He had to get his life back. Some kind of life. Any kind.

He'd liked his life, once. He'd been an excellent undercover agent. Brilliant at feeling his way into the parts he played. He'd seen his share of ugly stuff, and yeah, he'd been haunted by some of it, but he'd also known the bone-deep satisfaction that came from doing what he was born to do. He'd been deep inside the game, wired to a taut web of interconnected threads: touch one, and the whole fabric rippled and hummed. Senses buzzing, brain working overtime, churning out connections, deductions, conclusions. He'd loved it.

But now the threads were ripped. He was numb and isolated, alone in free-fall. What good would it do for him to hear about Novak? He couldn't help. His web was cut. He had nothing to offer. What would be the point?

He lit the cigarette and groped around in his mind for Nick's number. It popped up instantly, blinking on the screen inside his mind. Photographic memory was a McCloud family trait. Sometimes it was useful, sometimes it was just a dumb parlor trick. Sometimes it was a curse. Like that white eyelet lace halter top that Erin had worn at the Riggs family Fourth of July picnic. Six goddamn years ago, and the memory was as sharp as if it were yesterday. She'd been braless that day, so it was by far the best view he'd ever gotten of her beautiful tits. High and soft and tenderly pointed, bouncing and quivering every time she moved. Dark, taut nipples pressed hard against the thin fabric. He'd been amazed that Barbara, her mother, had allowed it. Particularly after Barbara had caught him staring. Her eyes had turned to ice.

Barbara hadn't wanted her innocent twenty-one-year-old daughter hooking up with another cop. Look how it turned out for her.

He knew better than to try to shove memories away. It just made them stronger, until they were huge and muscular, taking over his whole mind. Blotting out everything else. Like the image of Erin's dark, haunted eyes behind the patrol car window. Full of the terrible knowledge of betrayal.

He sucked smoke into his lungs and stared at the cell phone with unfriendly eyes. He'd thrown away the old one after what happened last fall. If he used this one to call Nick, then Nick would have the new number. Not good. He liked being unreachable. It suited his mood.

He closed his eyes, recalling the Christmas morning that Davy and Sean had forced him to accept the damn thing. He'd leafed through the manual, putting on a show of interest so as not to hurt their feelings. He vaguely remembered a function that blocked the incoming number from the display. He flipped through the pages in his mind, found the sequence. Keyed it in, dialed.

His stomach knotted up painfully as it rang.

"Nick Ward," his ex-colleague answered.

"It's Connor."

"No shit." Nick's voice was stone cold. "Had a good sulk, Con?"

He'd known this was going to be bad. "Can we skip this part, Nick? I'm not in the mood."

"I don't care about your fucking mood. I'm not the one who sold you out. I don't appreciate being punished for what Ed Riggs did to you."

"I'm not punishing you," Connor muttered defensively.

"No? So what have you been doing for the last six months, asshole?"

Connor slumped down in his seat. "I've been out of it lately. You'd be stupid if you took it personally."

Nick let out an unsatisfied grunt.

Connor waited. "So?"

"So what?"

Nick's truculent tone set Connor's teeth on edge. "Davy said you had some news for me," he said tightly. "About Novak."

"Oh. That." Nick was enjoying himself now. "I thought that might get your attention. Novak's out of prison. Free as a bird."

Adrenaline slammed through Connor like the bolt of a cross-bow. "What the fuck? When? How?"

"Night before last, at one in the morning. Him, and two of his goons. Very slick, very well planned, very well financed. Help from the outside and probably the inside as well. No body got killed, amazingly enough, so it's being kept quiet for now. Daddy Novak must've been behind it. You can do a lot of damage with billions of dollars."

Nick paused, waiting for a reaction, but Connor was speechless. The muscles in his bum leg cramped up, sending fiery bolts of pain through his thigh. He gripped it hard with his fingers and tried to breathe through the red haze of pain and fury.

"One of the guys who left with him was Georg Luksch. Remember him?" Nick went on, his voice still elaborately light. "He has a personal bone to pick with you. Ever since that day last November when you smashed all the bones in his face—"

"He was under orders to hurt Erin. I did what I had to do." Connor's voice vibrated with tension. "And it was less than he deserved."

"He never touched her, Con," Nick said coldly. "We have only Ed's word that he was planning to. And you, above all people, should know that Ed's credibility is worth shit. He was trying to save his own skin, but did you think of that before you went racing off to the rescue? Oh no. You just had to be the big hero. For the love of Christ, Con. It's lucky you weren't on active duty. You would have been crucified."

"Georg Luksch is a known assassin," Connor said, through clenched teeth. "He was willing to hurt her. He's lucky he's not dead."

"Yeah. Sure. Whatever you say," Nick said. "Anyhow, your white knight complex aside, I just wanted to tell you to watch your back. Not that you give a shit, or need anybody's help, of course. And I know you've got better things to do than talk to me, so I won't waste any more of your valuable time—"

"Hey, Nick. Please. Don't."

Something in Connor's voice made Nick pause. "Oh, what the hell," he said wearily. "If things get weird, call me, OK?"

"Yeah, thanks," Connor said. "But, uh . . . what about Erin?"

"What about her?" Nick said slowly.

"Novak hasn't forgotten about her," Connor said. "No way has he forgotten. Somebody should be assigned to guard her. Immediately."

Nick was silent for an agonizingly long time. "You are seriously hung up on that chick, aren't you, Con?"

Connor barely controlled a savage burst of frustration. "No," he spat out. "It's just obvious to anybody with half a brain that she's going to be on his hit list."

Nick sighed. "You haven't been listening at all, have you? You're still lost in your own fantasy world. Wake up, Con.

Novak's back in Europe. He was seen in Lyon last night. They got him on a bank surveillance video. A positive ID. He's a monster, but he's not an idiot. He doesn't give a shit about Erin. And don't make me regret keeping you in the loop, because you don't deserve to be there."

"Fuck," Connor muttered. "I cannot believe this."

"Let it go. Move the fuck on with your life. And watch your back."

Nick hung up abruptly. Connor stared down at the phone in his shaking hand, ashamed of having blocked the number. He disabled the function and hit redial. Quick, before he could change his mind.

"Nick Ward," his friend said tersely.

"Memorize this number," Connor said.

Nick let out a startled laugh. "Whoa. I'm *so* honored."

"Yeah, right. See you, Nick."

"I hope so," Nick said plaintively.

Connor broke the connection and let the phone drop onto the seat, his mind racing. Novak was filthy rich. He had the resources and the cunning to do the smart thing: to buy a new face, a new identity, a whole new life. But Connor had been studying the guy for years. Novak wouldn't do the smart thing. He would do whatever the fuck he pleased. He thought he was a god. It was that very fact that had flushed him out before. And it was that same fact that made him so deadly dangerous when his pride was stung.

Particularly to Erin. Christ, why was he the only one who could see it? Jesse would have understood, but he was long gone. Erin had slipped through Novak's fingers. He would never tolerate that. He would never let it go just for the sake of expediency. Never.

The thought made his leg muscles cramp up again. He and his brothers had each other for protection, but Erin was wide open. Practically laid out on the sacrificial altar already. And Connor was personally responsible for putting her there. His testimony had sent her dad to prison, and she had to hate his guts for it.

He covered his hot face with his hands and stifled a groan. Erin would be at the very forefront of Novak's twisted thoughts.

Just like she was always at the forefront of his own.

He tried to think it through logically, but logic had never had much to do with these impulses. He had to feel his way through it.

If the Feds wouldn't protect her, then he had to step into that empty space and protect her himself. He was so fucking predictable, even to himself, that he almost started to laugh. Erin was luscious and innocent and clueless: calculated to push all his lamebrain, would-be-hero buttons. And all those years of hot, explicit sexual fantasies about her didn't help much either, when it came to thinking clearly.

But what the hell. The thought of having a real job to do, a job that might actually mean something to somebody, jerked his mind into focus that was so laser-sharp it was almost painful. It rolled back the choking fog that had shrouded him for months. His whole body was buzzing with wild energy, tense and jittery.

He had to do this for her, no matter how much she hated him. And the thought of seeing her again made his face get hot, and his dick get hard, and his heart thud heavily against his ribs.

Christ, she scared him worse than Novak did.

And we don't think you will want to miss
UNEXPECTED by Lori Foster,
coming in early fall from Brava.
Here's a sneak peek.

She'd already signed the contract.

Backing out now would blow her reputation with the agency, and besides, this mission was a piece of cake, so there was no reason for dragging her feet. She needed the money, she was free at the moment and it'd be a routine run, nothing more, nothing less. If anything, it'd be easier now than it had been in the past. Everything had changed . . .

Unfortunately, herself included.

She shook her head at that thought. True, she was older now, wiser, more settled. But at the core, she was the same. Her skills, as much a part of her as her hair and eye color, were still finely honed. She knew what she could do—and damn it, she'd do it. Hell, she'd *missed* doing it.

So why, when she pushed the door open and stared into the dim, smoky room of the bar, was her heart heavy in her chest? It wasn't the depressing gray cloud that hung thick in the air, not only from cigarettes, but from disgust and ambivalence and antagonism. This was not a happy place, but then, she'd known it wouldn't be. By necessity, it was an obscure hole in the Chicago slums where meetings like this one, with people like her, could be handled with discretion.

But it wasn't like her to borrow trouble or dwell in indecision. Doing so undermined her credibility, so she was done with it. Instead, she'd concentrate on getting this over with fast and easy, with no complications.

She had everything planned out.

Flipping her bangs off her forehead, she strode into the room, ready to get things started.

She knew several heads turned her way, scrutinizing her, making note of her appearance. Calculating. For much of her life, she'd gotten undue attention for one reason or another, most of the reasons uncomplimentary. She'd long since gotten used to the stares and the whispers. She ignored them all and with luck, they'd show her the same courtesy.

Peering through the obscuring smoke, she scanned the tables and booths, searching out each darkened corner. Country music blasted through tinny speakers, vying with the boasting and bragging of drunken men. It was the typical atmosphere of a seedy bar. Without thinking, she rubbed her stomach, feeling slightly sick with a rush of vivid memories.

Then her gaze locked onto his. Wow. The past faded away under the impact of the present—*his* impact. She felt . . . invaded.

Bright hazel eyes, radiant in the otherwise dismal interior, held her captive. She stared at him; he stared back.

Never before had she seen such intense emotion in a man's expression. For a moment, it knocked her off guard. Without moving, he appeared turbulent, frustrated, filled with determination and impatience.

Because of his situation, or because she'd arrived late?

Ha. She watched him a moment more, taking his measure. He was bigger than most of the men she knew or had worked with. And he had a more self-assured air. That he'd be trouble, she didn't doubt—he fairly screamed it with a capital T. But how much trouble, that's what she needed to know.

Lounged back in his chair, he allowed her perusal, and even took the time to look her over too. Slowly. But then, amazingly enough, he dismissed her by giving his attention back to the entrance of the bar.

Cynical amusement nudged away the lingering nervousness. So, he hadn't realized her identity? She wasn't what he'd been expecting? Typical. And here, for only a brief moment, she'd thought he might be more astute than the others.

Anticipating his reaction when she introduced herself, she started toward him. He sat at a solitary table at the far end of the room, his back to the wall so he could face the bar, a rear exit to his right. It was a guarded position she would have chosen, but probably mere coincidence for him.

She wove her way around tables, drunks and proffered drinks without once taking her eyes off him.

As was her usual habit at such meetings, she'd dressed all in black, her clothes plain and unadorned. It made it easier to disappear if necessary, and didn't draw added attention that more complimentary clothes might have.

Her long-sleeved tunic hung to mid thigh, loosely fitted so it wouldn't impede her movements should she need to take physical control of the surroundings. Her jeans were slim, her low-heeled boots only ankle high. She never wore jewelry—in fact, she didn't own any to wear—but she did carry a black briefcase. The case was an annoyance, but it usually proved necessary to have it handy.

When she stopped in front of him, his gaze came to her face, arrested for only a moment. Then slowly, very slowly, he looked her over again, his attention lingering in certain places like her chest, below her waist, her thighs. His look was so intimate, so personal that it brought on a mélange of sensations—outrage, disgust and strangely enough, heat. Surely not embarrassment, she told herself. She was too old and far too jaded to be disconcerted by the likes of him.

His visual inspection was appreciative and felt like a tactile touch. Damn it, she didn't like being touched, not without permission.

Her eyes narrowed, prompting him to a softly uttered, reluctant rejection. "Sorry, honey. It's unfortunate, but I'm already busy tonight."

The nerve. Despite her exceptional control, antagonism bristled to the surface. Her every movement rigid, Ray hooked a chair and drew it out. She seated herself, placing the briefcase at her feet for safekeeping.

He cocked one dark brow upward and braced his forearms on the rough, scarred table. The new position emphasized the width of his shoulders, the brawn of his arms. She'd expected another wimpy, slim GQ look-alike, but this man could be a bouncer. He wasn't bulky, just big and hard and solid.

Added to the fine physique were the eyes of a predator, now filled with annoyance. He leaned toward her with a scowl.

"I'm Ray Vereker," she drawled, refusing to back down from that concentrated stare. She didn't say anything more, didn't offer her hand in polite greeting. She just waited for the usual signs of disbelief and disparagement.

They were slow in coming.

Rather than gape, he leaned back and studied her anew. If she'd thought the earlier perusal was intimate, it was nothing compared to how he looked at her now. For a lesser person, for someone without her skills and background, it might have been an unnerving process. His eyes were such an unusual shade of mellow hazel, cat eyes, bright with intelligence, almost menacing. They went from heated notice to cool regard.

Deciding to do her own up-close and personal inspection, Ray draped one elbow over the back of the chair and slouched down in the seat to get comfortable. Wearing an air of unconcern, she took in his appearance from his dark brown hair cut in precise lines to his straight, masculine nose and high cheekbones to his mouth, now flattened with irritation at her boldness. He had a stubborn jaw, she noted, proving he'd be plenty of trouble, indeed.

The black Tee he wore looked softer than heaven, fitted over that broad chest. Even his jacket bespoke wealth, made of fine leather and deliberately scuffed to appear fashionably worn. The watch on his thick wrist probably cost as much as her truck. Maybe more. And his nails were impeccably clean.

Thanks to the table, she couldn't see below his waist, but she'd be willing to bet the rest of him was as sturdy and strong as what she could see. Maybe it was a good thing half of him was hidden. Half was about all she could take at one time. The man made her heart race.

Though she doubted he'd ever been in such a ramshackle bar in his life, *he* didn't look the least bit ill at ease. Even her presence, which had to be a shocker, hadn't really rattled him.

To be honest with herself, she admitted he was very fine to look at. She appreciated strength and self-control. Apparently, he had both in spades.

Not that it mattered. He was still rich, and given what she'd seen so far, not arrogant for his own good. What fool came into such a place and advertised himself as an easy mark? And that was exactly what he'd done by wearing the watch and the jacket.

He was a fool, all right. And for the next few days, she owed him her service.

As the silence stretched on, Ray sighed and crossed her legs. She knew his tactic. He hoped to remain silent so long that she'd begin to babble nervously, giving herself away as a fool also. He underestimated her. He could sit in strained silence as long as he wanted. Time was money, *his* money, and she didn't mind wasting it if he didn't.

He looked at her mouth, rubbed his own, then pinned her in place with a laser-sharp gaze. In a flat tone devoid of any telltale emotion, he said, "I requested the meanest son-of-a-bitch they had."

She gave a slow smile. "I know what you requested. I have your papers with me."

"And?"

She lifted one shoulder, held up her hands to indicate her presence. "And they complied."

Eyes closed, he pinched the bridge of his nose, muttering under his breath. Ray noticed that his hands were large, sprinkled with brown hair. They looked like capable hands, not the pampered, smooth hands of a rich boy.

Catching herself, she jerked her attention back to his face. He scrutinized her, then asked with some disbelief, "Do you have any idea what it is I want from you?"

"Sure."

With a touch of disbelief, his gaze slid all over her again, appraising, before both brows lifted. Ray never moved a muscle. He could look a dozen times if it helped. She wouldn't be changing.

"I assumed 'Ray' would be a man."

"Assumptions are nasty things. They can get you into trouble."

He waved that away. "What's your whole name?"

"Why does it matter?"

Ray could feel his growing tension deep inside herself. It was an odd sensation, one she'd never experienced before. She half expected an explosion at any minute and braced for it, making herself tense too.

"I'm wondering," he said slowly, his unnerving attention on her mouth again, "if there's some feminine nuance I'm missing."

She smirked. "In me, or my name?"

His gaze snapped back to hers and he barked a laugh. "Honey, despite the hard attitude, your appearance is most definitely *un*manly."

He said that with . . . interest? No, no way. She was lousy at judging men and their various moods in regard to the whole man-woman thing, but she understood reality very well, thank you. No man in his right mind would be thinking of anything but the mission. Not with her. Not now.

And most definitely not after the mission ended, when her special skills had been revealed.

During her ruminations, the silence grew and finally, because she had no reason not to, she said, "Ray Jean Vereker. But I go by Ray and only Ray. You're given fair warning right now not to use my middle name, ever."

Oddly enough, her warning evoked amusement. Oh, he didn't laugh, didn't even smile. But she saw the lightness that entered those mysterious eyes. "Yeah? Or what?"

Done with the small talk, with the nonsense, Ray said, "Or I'll walk out and you'll be left to settle for the second meanest son-of-a-bitch there is."